For testimonials from law enforcement,
visit Carolyn Arnold's website.

ALSO BY CAROLYN ARNOLD

Brandon Fisher FBI Series
Eleven
Silent Graves
The Defenseless
Blue Baby
Violated
Remnants
On the Count of Three

Detective Madison Knight Series
Ties That Bind
Justified
Sacrifice
Found Innocent
Just Cause
Deadly Impulse
In the Line of Duty
Power Struggle
Life Sentence

McKinley Mysteries
The Day Job is Murder
Vacation is Murder
Money is Murder
Politics is Murder
Family is Murder
Shopping is Murder
Christmas is Murder
Valentine's Day is Murder
Coffee is Murder
Skiing is Murder
Halloween is Murder

Matthew Connor Adventure Series
City of Gold
The Secret of the Lost Pharaoh

Assassination of a Dignitary

CAROLYN ARNOLD

SHADES OF JUSTICE

HIBBERT & STILES
PUBLISHING INC.

Hibbert & Stiles Publishing Inc.
www.hspubinc.com

This is a work of fiction. Names, characters, places, and
incidents are the products of the author's imagination or are
used fictitiously. Any resemblance to actual events, locales, or
persons, living or dead, is entirely coincidental.

Publisher's Cataloging-In-Publication Data
(Prepared by The Donohue Group, Inc.)

Names: Arnold, Carolyn, author.
Title: Shades of justice / Carolyn Arnold.
Description: [London, Ontario] : Hibbert & Stiles Publishing
    Inc., [2019] | Series: A Detective Madison Knight mystery
    ; [book 9]
Identifiers: ISBN 9781988353784 (paperback) | ISBN
    9781988353807 (hardcover) | ISBN 9781988353777
    (ebook)
Subjects: LCSH: Women detectives--Fiction. | Murder--
    Investigation--Fiction. | Justice, Administration of--
    Fiction. | Family secrets--Fiction. | LCGFT: Detective
    and mystery fiction.
Classification: LCC PS3601.R66 S53 2019 (print) | LCC
    PS3601.R66 (ebook) | DDC 813/.6--dc23

Additional format:
ISBN: 978-1-988353-79-1 (paperback 5 x 8)

SHADES OF JUSTICE

Carolyn Arnold

One

Madison should turn around and forget all about the meeting she'd arranged. Only she couldn't. Her feet were frozen to the sidewalk, her body facing the hole-in-the-wall diner where her contact would be waiting inside.

Her breath fogged in the chilly morning air and tiny snowflakes clung to her lashes. The weathermen were calling for heavy snow squalls today, and given the threatening gray February sky, they might be right.

She burrowed deeper into her coat and tucked her hands into its pockets as a gust of cold air whipped around her—yet she still hesitated to go inside the warm diner. Once she did, once she laid out her plan to her contact, there'd be no turning back. She had to be crazy to even consider setting into motion what she intended. After all, it had only been a couple of months since Madison's poking around where she shouldn't have resulted in her and her sister being targeted by a Russian Mafia hit man. Her sister had been kidnapped, and when Madison went to save her, they'd barely escaped with their lives, but here she was again, putting herself and loved ones at risk. She should just walk away, focus instead on the upcoming Saturday—four days away and counting. It would be Valentine's Day, but more importantly, her friend Cynthia's wedding, and Madison looked forward to being her maid of honor.

Madison pulled her phone from a coat pocket and turned it to silent. She didn't want any distractions or for her partner, Terry Grant, to call about some case. Whatever it was, it could wait until she was finished here.

She looked over a shoulder to the parking lot and her Mazda 3. A mere thirty steps and she'd be in her car and able to drive the hell away from here, but she found herself moving toward the diner.

A bell rang when she opened the door, and heat embraced her, making her face and hands tingle.

A waitress behind the counter smiled at her and said, "Sit where you like, honey."

Madison nodded. Patrons filled the window booths, and some sat on stools at the counter. She let her gaze travel over all of them, until she found the person she was looking for.

Leland King was tucked into an interior corner booth. He looked up, and their eyes met, but he never made any move toward a friendly gesture. No smile, no waving hand. It would only draw attention to them.

Madison slipped onto the bench opposite Leland. He was nursing a coffee, while a closed menu rested on the table. There was also one in front of her, which she pushed aside. Her stomach wouldn't accept food right now. It was clenched tighter than a fist.

"I was starting to wonder if you were coming," Leland said.

"I was too," she admitted.

"It's not too late to call this off."

While she hadn't provided him much information about today's meeting, she had told him that it could have grave consequences. She'd selected him based on his knack for investigating and for his connections.

The waitress who had greeted her came up to the table with a notepad and a pencil poised over the page ready to record her order. "What can I get ya, honey?"

Madison glanced at Leland's coffee.

"It's good stuff." Leland smiled, plastering on the charm for the waitress, who flushed. Leland may have been in his fifties, average in most ways—except for his distinct wide, flat nose—but he had a way with the ladies.

"Sure, I'll take one," Madison said. Even if she never took a sip, she'd have something to hold on to, to use as a slight distraction.

The waitress pointed with her pencil to the closed menus. "Anything to eat?"

Leland glanced at Madison and answered on her behalf. "Nothing right now, darling." With that, the waitress left. "She's quick," Leland told her. "We'll wait for your coffee before we start talking."

Madison took a deep breath and nodded. She still had time to forget all about this, to cut and run. She was bouncing her legs under the table and wringing her hands in her lap.

The waitress returned and set a brown porcelain mug in front of Madison, then filled it from a coffee carafe.

"Cream, milk, sugar, and sweetener are on the table." The waitress bobbed her head toward the holder that also housed napkins and condiments. "Just holler when you're ready to order food. Keep in mind we serve the best Western sandwich in ten counties." She winked at Leland before walking away.

Leland met Madison's eyes and pulled out his phone. "I'd like to record—"

"No." Madison reached her arm across the table and bumped her mug. Coffee sloshed over the rim, and she snatched a wad of napkins to clean up the mess. "No recording," she said firmly.

"I got that." He watched her wad up the used napkins and set them aside. "But it's something I normally do."

"Not this time." She stared at him until he slipped his phone back into a coat pocket. "You promise me that it's not recording?"

"I promise you."

Madison cradled her mug and looked around. No one was to their left or right, or even in the booths behind or in front of them. Leland had chosen a good spot.

"Madison, you don't have to—"

"There are corrupt cops in the Stiles PD," she blurted out, keeping her voice low.

Leland's eyes snapped to hers. "Why not just go to IA?"

Internal Affairs.

"That's a loaded question," she said, not feeling much like elaborating. At the root of it, she didn't know whom she could trust, even among the upper echelons at the Stiles PD—or within IA, for that matter. She wanted to obtain intel and discover all the players before making her move. She also wanted to make sure she had enough to make a solid case. She didn't just want to flush out corrupt cops, she wanted them to pay.

"I see."

Leland's response was something people said when they didn't understand, but Madison would simply accept his words at face value.

Leland took a sip of his coffee. "Does this have something to do with…" He left the rest unsaid, but his gaze told her he was thinking about the Russian Mafia. It wasn't a leap on her part to make this assumption. Leland knew her history with them, and how it went back as far as her grandfather's murder before Madison was born.

"If I'm reading your mind correctly, it does," she stated sourly, still not verbalizing the Mafia.

"Maybe you're just seeing ghosts? I'd heard they'd left Stiles."

That was the word within the Stiles PD, and Madison would love to believe it, but she felt the streets had a different story to tell. Really, all the PD knew for sure was that some high-ranking associates had left town, but if you cut off the head of one serpent, more always rose in its place. She also couldn't ignore that the don, Dimitre Petrov, was still serving a sentence in a Stiles prison. There was no way he'd be left without a support system of some kind—if history were a teacher. Dimitre had proved repeatedly he had a reach from behind bars, and she was more apt to believe the Mafia was simply running operations on the down-low.

"They're still here." A cool sweat prickled her skin. It was as if she could feel their eyes on her now, waiting to exact revenge for her incessant interference in their operations. Madison went on. "And these cops I'm about to give you need to get off the street yesterday, but this isn't going to be a fast over-and-done-with-it job."

"So the long haul?"

She nodded. "Months, maybe years."

"I can handle that."

She trusted that he could, or she'd never have come to him. She questioned whether she'd have enough courage and patience to see it all through. "I'm aware of evidence that has gone missing while in the care of certain officers, but I know there's more to it than that." A piece of that evidence factored into a Mafia-related hit, but she wasn't telling Leland that just yet. She continued. "If they're no longer working for the Mafia, I'd bet money they're available at a price, and it won't be long before they find themselves another payday." She had no doubt in her words. Once a corrupt cop, always a corrupt cop. It was a sweep of a brush, but evil had a way of slithering out of the cracks of darkness into the light and seeking out others of similar persuasion.

"And what do you need from me?" Leland asked.

"I need you to do some digging on my behalf."

Leland lifted his cup and took a slow draw on his coffee. "So I'd be doing *you* a favor?"

"We'll be doing each other one," she countered. "I can't go poking around without being found out by the brass. I can't infiltrate the lives of these officers because they know who I am. You have anonymity, some leeway. You know, without my saying so much in words, what's in it for you."

Leland's skill set came from being an award-winning investigative journalist for the *Stiles Times*, and she was promising him the exclusive story at the end of all this.

Leland said nothing, just scanned her eyes. Eventually, he nodded.

"Before I give you names, I need to lay out the rules. There can't be any recording of our conversations. No paper or electronic trail. There can't be *anything* connecting us. Whatever notes you make or things you uncover, keep them under lock and key. Now you know who could potentially be behind the scenes, you can appreciate how, if any of this gets out—"

"We could be killed." Leland didn't so much as blink.

"Uh-huh."

"How do we communicate?"

Madison pulled a burner phone from her coat pocket and handed it to him. "I've got one, too. I programmed my number into yours. This is the only way we can communicate from here on out."

Leland checked the phone over and then tucked it away into the inner pocket of his coat. Silence settled into the space between them.

The waitress came over. "Have you decided?"

Leland scooped the menus off the table and handed them to the waitress. "We'll just stick with coffee."

The waitress grimaced briefly, appearing

insulted, but recovered with a pressed-lip smile before leaving again.

"Hopefully, she's gone for a while this time," Leland said, turning back to Madison. "Basically, you need me to dig up the dirt and be your eyes and ears."

"Yeah, and see how far this corruption goes. When I go to IA, I want solid evidence to back up my claims against them. I want them to pay for their crimes."

Leland squared eye contact with her. "Is there anything I can say to talk you out of this?"

"No." The answer left her lips without thought, and she sat up taller, feeling confidence run through her. There was no way she could ignore what was going on. When she'd donned the badge, she'd vowed to protect and serve, and that's exactly what she intended to do. No matter the personal stakes, no matter the cost. Serving in law enforcement was a post of self-sacrifice. The people of this city put their lives in her hands—in those of the Stiles PD—and she'd root out any cops who violated the very oath she held dear.

"Okay. How many are we talking about?" Leland leaned across the table.

"A couple I'm quite sure about. There's probably more we'll uncover as we go along. I'll only be giving you one name today." Withholding from Leland would ensure he didn't just run off with the information he'd gathered. It would keep him tethered to her. It wasn't a matter of trust, but rather minimizing the possibly he'd be tempted to pursue matters on his own.

"And that name would be?" Leland asked.

Madison pinched her eyes shut for a second. Once the name was out, the ball was in motion. "Dustin Phelps."

Leland tapped a finger to his left temple. "It's in the vault. Do you have anything you want to start me off with besides the name?"

"Well, he's a few years younger than me and holds the rank of officer."

Leland smiled subtly. "A few years younger. I should know what that is, but—"

Madison narrowed her eyes. "He's thirty-two," she said. "He's married, has two young kids. Both of them in private school."

"Private school on a cop's salary?"

"Uh-huh, my feelings on the matter," she said, thinking Phelps's money source was where she'd be looking first. "I can't exactly go pull his financials and see what's going on there."

"Leave that with me."

"You could always speak with the people at the school and find out how much it costs. Again, I'd have done it, but I just can't have it getting back to him somehow." She hated giving something so relatively simple to someone else to take care of.

"Don't you worry. I have my ways of getting

everything I need."

Madison smiled. "Why I came to you."

Leland dipped his head.

"I also know that he has an aging mother who's in a nursing home," Madison continued. "A really nice one. Think Club Med of retirement communities."

"Must be nice," Leland said. "My mom's in a home, and she gets excited when she gets Jell-O for dessert."

"With your salary, I'd think you could afford someplace nice."

"Oh, I've offered, but Mom's stubborn." Leland smiled with pride. "I can dig around the nursing home angle. You mentioned he's married. Does his wife work?"

Madison shook her head. "She's a stay-at-home mom. Oh, and they live in Deer Glen," she tagged on. Deer Glen was located in the north end of the city, and one of the most prestigious neighborhoods in Stiles.

Leland's mouth formed an *O*. "I'd say this guy's certainly overextended, unless he won the lottery, or they came into a sizable inheritance."

"Exactly. Something stinks." Now that her suspicions were out, it felt good to share the burden with someone else, and to know that Leland saw validity in her concerns felt even better. She hadn't told anyone else, not even Troy, and he was the man she loved and lived with and was "raising" a fur baby with. She'd especially kept Troy out of this loop. He was safer that way—so was Hershey, the chocolate lab—and she didn't need Troy talking her out of doing this, reminding her of the dangers involved with poking around.

Her eyes went to a clock on the diner's wall. Just before nine in the morning. She had to get to the station. She got up to leave and remembered the coffee. She reached into a pocket for some cash, but Leland stayed her hand.

"It's on me," he said, his brow furrowing. "Just watch your back."

"You too."

She left the diner. On one hand, it felt like a weight had been lifted. On the other, it felt like another had been added.

Two

Chocolate was the only thing that could help Madison's nerves. She drove to the station, a woman on a mission, and the second she got there, she made a beeline for the top right-hand drawer of her desk where she kept a stash of Hershey's bars. Good news: there was no sign of her partner, so she'd be saved the need to defend her chocolate munching first thing in the day. Bad news: she wasn't seeing any chocolate.

"Shit. Don't tell me..." She pulled the drawer all the way out and rummaged through business cards, pens, clips, elastics. "Son of a..." She slammed the drawer shut.

She must have eaten the last bar yesterday. She patted her pockets for change, holding out hope the vending machine in the cafeteria would come through for her, but she came up empty-handed. Now she wished Terry was around to mooch money from, even if it came with a lecture on healthy eating.

"Hey there, beautiful."

She turned to see Troy approaching her. Talk about impeccable timing. He'd just saved the world and didn't even know it. She smiled brightly at him. "You wouldn't happen to have a buck, would you?"

He closed the distance between them and looked around. With the coast clear, he tapped a kiss on her lips.

They'd been together for almost a year, and her heart still sped up when they came into contact. What woman could blame her? Troy had blond hair and piercing green eyes, was six-foot-three, and had six-pack abs. When he held her, she felt safe enough to weather any storm.

She licked her lips and held out a hand. "A buck?"

Troy looked at her hand and up to her eyes, no smile. He didn't part with them easily, but his eyes sparkled with amusement. "Let me guess. Time for a chocolate bar, and your inventory's out?"

"Now, who's the detective?" she jested. Troy headed up a SWAT team, but when those services weren't needed, he performed officer duties as necessary.

"No need to get hostile." He reached into a pocket and came out with change. "You know the stuff is going to kill you."

She snatched the coins from him. "If it does, I'd die with a smile on my face." So maybe she was a little transparent when it came to her cacao-bean addiction and how she craved it like a smoker did cigarettes. Surely, chocolate was healthier than nicotine. She took off toward the vending machine, Troy following her.

"I take it your Tuesday's gone downhill since I saw you last?" The devil danced in his eyes. The day had started off with them in a heap of sweat, tangled in sheets. Heat flushed through her at the memory, but she wasn't letting it derail her current mission.

She popped the coins into the vending machine and made her selection. The curly metal started to turn—then it stopped! The Hershey's bar was suspended.

"This can't be happening." She kicked the machine and writhed in pain. The bar stayed put, taunting her. "Stupid, fucking mach—"

"Hey." Troy shuffled up beside her and nudged her out of the way. "It's okay. I'll get it."

"I don't need a man to—"

He'd already grabbed both sides of the machine and was in the processing of shaking it. The candy bar fell loose. He retrieved it from the bin and extended it toward her. She reached for it, and he pulled it back.

She cocked her head. "Someone's living dangerously."

He leaned in and whispered in her ear. "That's what you love about me."

Her damned heart fluttered—again. She

grabbed the bar, stepped back from him, tore the wrapper, and bit off a mouthful. She closed her eyes and let out a moan.

"You two should get a room," Troy said, a slight smile lifting the corners of his mouth.

"Hmm, not a bad idea." She took another bite and leaned against the machine, allowing herself a few minutes' bliss.

"You never did answer my question." He tilted his head, that morning's escapades reflected in his eyes.

"You couldn't have expected it to get better." She narrowed her eyes seductively and planted a deep kiss on him, savoring the taste of him— *maybe* even more than the chocolate. Or was it the combination of him *and* chocolate? She'd have to remember that for the bedroom and was surprised they hadn't already tried the combination.

Troy pulled back. "I did say something about getting a room—"

"Cut it out," she teased.

"Hey, you're the one who kissed me. I wish I could ignore the fact that you did so to distract me from the serious implication of my question. Is something wrong?" His gaze bored through her.

He knew her far too well. "Nope, everything's fine." She hated keeping secrets from him— even this one and knowing that she did so for his own good. If that fact ever changed, which she doubted it would, she'd reassess, but for now, the less he knew about her side investigation, the better. She didn't want to think too hard about the fact she might be withholding from him for a while to come.

He studied her. "You know you can talk to me about anything."

"I know." Her heart swelled. Troy would willingly be her knight in shining armor, but she didn't need him fighting her battles.

"Well, whatever it is, I'm sure you've got it licked, Bulldog."

She shoved his shoulder, and he laughed. He knew she didn't love the pet name he had for her, but he'd likely pulled it out to lighten her mood—and it worked. "I love you," she said, the sentiment profoundly sincere.

"And I—"

"There you are. I've been looking for you." Terry blew into the room and gestured with a tri-folded piece of paper he was holding toward the bar in her hand. "For some people, it's breakfast time."

She rolled her eyes. "Chocolate comes from a bean, so it's technically a vegetable. We've been through this before." She bobbed her head side to side. "The way I see it, I'm eating healthy." She stuffed the last of the Hershey's bar into her mouth.

"Uh-huh," Terry said, not convinced.

Troy stepped back from her and passed a

glance to Terry. "Well, you two have fun." He gave one final look at Madison and, when he was behind Terry, blew her a kiss.

"What's up?" Madison asked her partner as she bunched up the empty wrapper and tossed it into a garbage bin. It bounced off the edge and then went in. Score: three points.

"Where have you been?" Terry's face was flushed, his nostrils slightly flared, his eyes wide, his chest heaving. Even for looking unhinged, every one of his blond hairs lay perfectly in place. She, on the other hand, resembled a blond cockatoo most of the time.

"I'm waiting," Terry pressed. He was certainly in a mood this morning, and he was coming across as if he were the senior detective. He was three years her junior. "I tried calling you five times, left two messages. Why weren't you answering your phone?"

Crap. She'd been so focused on chocolate she'd forgotten to turn her phone's ringer back on. She rectified that and saw the missed calls. "I had an appointment."

Terry pointed to her phone. "You had your ringer off?"

"I had an appointment," she repeated while shifting her weight to her right hip and jutting out her chin.

"While you've been off doing whatever, we had a double homicide land in our lap." Terry tapped the paper he was holding, and it sank in that it was likely a search warrant. "Quite a high-profile case at that," he added.

He already had her attention with "double homicide." As a city of about half a million, Stiles saw its share of murders, but rarely were two bodies found together at the same time. "I'm listening."

"A man and a woman. Don't have an ID for him, but she's Lorene Malone."

"*The* Lorene Malone?" The Malones were a wealthy family that founded Malone's, a chain of furniture stores that catered to middle-income families. They had three locations—one in Stiles and two in surrounding communities.

"The one and only," Terry said briskly. "Both were shot in the head and found naked at the bottom of the Malones' indoor swimming pool."

"*Naked?* And we don't know who the man is? Was Mrs. Malone having an affair?"

"Too early to say."

"Who found them?"

"The Malones' eldest, Kimberly Olson-Malone."

"Does she live in the house?"

"Nope. She's forty-two, divorced, and has two young kids."

"What was her reason for being at her parents' house this morning?"

"Says she was there to pick her mother up for a seven-thirty yoga class."

"Early for yoga," she said. "What time did she

show up at the house?"

"Around seven ten."

"Does the daughter know who the man is?"

Terry shook his head. "Claims not to."

The picture forming in Madison's mind wasn't a pretty one. If Lorene Malone was having an affair and that was what had driven the murders, one person would have more motive than anyone. "What was Mr. Malone's reaction to the murders?"

"Don't know."

The skin tightened on the back of her neck. "How can you not—"

"I can't reach him," Terry cut in. "Kimberly doesn't know where he is but told me that her parents just celebrated their forty-seventh wedding anniversary."

"That hardly excludes him as a suspect. We've got to find him *and* fast," she said. "I assume that's the signed search warrant you're holding?" They'd need one before the house could be processed, as Lorene Malone wasn't the sole occupant.

Terry lifted the paper in his left hand. "Yep. It just came through. I'm headed back to the Malones' now, but thought I'd look for you first."

A moody partner, a high-profile double homicide—oh, this week would be getting a whole lot worse before it got better. "Let's go," she said.

Three

They say someone's always having a worse day than you are. Who the heck are "they," and how would *they* know, anyway? Madison was pretty sure days couldn't get much worse than the one Kimberly Olson-Malone was having. Madison couldn't imagine finding her own mother dead—and naked with another man, no less. As much as she felt for Kimberly, she couldn't let it cloud her judgment. Kimberly had been the one to find them and that alone made her the first suspect.

Terry pointed to the next street as they drove. "Turn right there."

Even though Terry knew where they were going, Madison was the one driving.

She took the corner, and he pointed at a two-story, gray-brick mansion. With the exception of the forensics van and a police cruiser parked in the three-car driveway, the house had terrific curb appeal with its large front windows and double-door entry.

Madison parked out front on the street.

"Before we go in, I'm going to give you a warning," Terry said.

She glanced over at him, her hand letting go of the door handle. Was he going to tell her it was a messy scene? There wasn't much else that turned her stomach as did the sight and stench of a lot of blood. She gulped. The victims had been shot.

"Okay," she said with trepidation.

"Cynthia's on the warpath," Terry said. "She makes your bad moods look like—"

"Be careful of your next words."

"Or what?" He wriggled his fingers as if to say, *Bring it on.*

Terry really was the brother she never had. "Why's she in a bad mood?" Madison asked but could think of at least one off the top of her head: her wedding was mere days away, and a case like this would take a lot of time for evidence collection and processing. That thought led to another. "Oh, no."

"What?"

"We had plans for a final dress fitting tonight. We might have to push that off."

Terry arched his brows. "I'm not a wedding planner, but shouldn't dress fittings have been done ages ago?"

It wasn't for the lack of trying, but it turned out that when dresses were ordered from different shops, they could be made from different dye lots. With Cynthia's sister and bridesmaid, Tammy, living in Alabama, she'd gotten hers there while Madison ordered hers in Stiles. With take two, they returned their initial dresses and arranged to get new ones from the same bridal shop in Stiles. "It's a long story," was all she said.

"Okay." Terry dragged out the word, but quickly moved on. "Well, she's pissed because the firemen who responded to the nine-one-one call pulled the bodies out of the pool."

"Oh," Madison said slowly, appreciating that her friend would be livid about contamination of the crime scene. Cynthia wouldn't care that the firemen were wired to save lives until—or unless—they could confirm death.

The two of them got out of the car, and at the front door, Madison looked up. The place had looked big from the curb, but standing next to it only impressed just how successful the Malones were.

Officer Tendum was stationed at door. He was younger, a little wet behind the ears, and he and Madison had butted heads more than once. Then again, it was his stupidity that had resulted in her former training officer, Reggie Higgins, being shot during a murder investigation about a year ago. At least Higgins had been fortunate enough to recover and return to work.

Tendum stepped to the side to allow Madison and Terry to enter the house.

Inside, they were greeted by a grand entry with two sweeping staircases that hugged the curves of two walls. A large, teardrop-crystal chandelier punctuated the center of the space. Abstract paintings adorned the walls with lighting mounted over them. Madison didn't know much about art, but flea-market finds didn't typically wind up in fine frames with specialty lighting.

The smell of chlorine hung in the air, and she started following her nose—and Terry—toward the back of the home.

They passed an expansive living space that could have served as a lobby for a fine hotel. A bottle of red wine sat on a coffee table as did two wineglasses, each with some wine in them. The kitchen off to the right gleamed with high-end stainless steel appliances, and a breakfast bar lined the wall.

"All this for two people," Madison said, thinking about the imbalances of wealth distribution.

"Yep, all eight thousand square feet," Terry responded.

He opened the door to an atrium with a million-dollar view of the Bradshaw River that ran through Stiles. The rectangular pool, surrounded by a tiled patio dotted with lounge chairs and tables, took center stage. A hot tub, large enough for six, was to the right end of the pool, and in the corner of the room, there was a sauna. Blood spatter was to the immediate edge of the pool, to the left of the pool ladder, along with the two bodies.

Matching bullet holes marked both their foreheads, but the water had cleaned the wounds. For a shooting, there was minimal mess.

Cynthia was next to the bodies, along with Mark Adams, one of her employees from the Stiles PD forensics lab she headed up. Sam, short for Samantha, and Jennifer—never Jenn or Jenny—were also in the room photographing and marking potential evidence.

Cynthia got up and approached Madison and Terry. "I keep thinking I'm being punked." She was scowling and shaking her head. "They tromped in here without any regard for the crime scene. Did they really think they'd find the vics alive? They were at the bottom of the pool, and they took ten minutes to get here." She swept out her arms. "*And* as if I don't have enough going on."

Any other time, Madison might have laid a reassuring hand on her friend's shoulder, but to do so now would be at her own risk.

Cynthia set her gaze on Terry. "You have the warrant?"

"I do." He tapped it in his hands.

"Great." Cynthia's tone deflated the meaning of the word. "We're legal now," she called out to her team and then turned to Madison. "Of all the days, too, eh? It's going to take us hours to work through all this. We'll probably have to put off our plans for tonight. We might need to pull an all-nighter."

"I was thinking the same thing. I'll call Tiffany's Bridal, reschedule for tomorrow night."

"Thanks." Cynthia put her hands on her hips. "I hate that it's all coming together so last minute. Everything has to be perfect."

"I'm sure it will be." It was strange seeing Cynthia worked up like this. Normally, she had such a cavalier, go-with-the-flow, laidback approach to life—but everything about Cynthia settling down was shocking. She had long, dark hair, a slender frame, and legs that didn't end, not to mention a metabolism Madison would kill for, and men loved her. She'd dated *a lot*. Then again, play with fire for long enough and you'll get burned. She'd started seeing Lou Sanford, a major crimes detective with Stiles PD, and her black book got tossed out the window.

"I sure hope you're right." Cynthia's face softened, but it didn't last long. Her brow took on sharp concentration, and she jutted her chin toward her team. "We're doing what we can to protect the evidence, but I'm sure some of it's been washed away or trampled on." She pointed toward a lounge chair about six feet away. Next to it were two piles of clothing. "It seems likely they belong to the victims, but this will still need to be verified. No wallet in the pockets, and I couldn't find either one of their phones."

"I put in a request to trace Lorene Malone's phone and am waiting for the result," Terry added. "Should have it soon, I'd imagine."

"You probably saw the wine on your way back here?" Cynthia asked.

Madison nodded, trying to keep up with Cynthia's updates, which seemed to be all over the place.

"We'll be bagging and tagging it, of course, and now that the paperwork's out of the way, we can really dig in," Cynthia said. "At quick inspection, there aren't any signs of forced entry."

"So, the killer could have been someone either Mrs. Malone or our John Doe knew and let in," Madison suggested. "We're sure that robbery didn't factor in at all?"

"Nothing indicates that so far," Cynthia started. "I mean his wallet's missing and both cell phones, but as you can see, he's wearing a watch. It's not a Rolex, but it's still not cheap, and she's wearing one, too, as well as her wedding rings."

"They got undressed but didn't take their watches off?" Madison mused aloud and let her gaze go to the bodies. "They weren't planning to take a dip."

"I wouldn't say so," Cynthia agreed.

"But they are naked. Was this an affair gone wrong?" Madison turned to look at the clothes.

They were on the floor as if the victims had just stepped out of them. Was there some sort of clue in that? Surely in the throes of passion, the clothes would have been discarded haphazardly, strewn about everywhere, possibly more in a trail than in a couple of piles. An affair would present strong motive for Lorene's husband or Doe's wife—assuming he was married—if they'd found out about their mate's infidelity. The lack of a wedding band on Doe's hand wasn't proof he was single; a lot of married men didn't wear them.

One flaw in the theory that one of the spouses killed them was the missing wallet and phones. Still, they needed to talk to Mr. Malone and get a feel for their marriage. By extension, they'd ask anyone close to the family about the Malones' relationship. It just as well might have been John Doe who'd attracted the killer, but without an identity, they'd start by focusing on Lorene's life.

"We need to talk to the daughter and find out what she can tell us about her parents' marriage," Madison said. "Do you know where she is, Cyn? I didn't see her as we came back here."

Cynthia slid a glance to Terry.

"What is it?" Madison asked, turning to her partner. She didn't care for the way Cynthia and Terry were looking at each other, as if the two of them shared a secret.

Eventually, Cynthia said, "Sergeant Winston

took her home."

"He what?" Madison spat.

Cynthia held up her hands. "I'm just the messenger."

A responding officer should have taken Kimberly's statement, and she should still be here for Madison and Terry to question. At the very least, she should have been taken to the station and set up in a soft interview room, nestled on a sofa.

"Tell me you at least swabbed her hands for GSR," Madison said.

"I did," Cynthia replied, "but it will take a bit before we'll be able to process it and get the results."

Madison had a feeling Cynthia would tell her that, yet the sergeant still let Kimberly go home. Not that testing negative for gunshot residue should have been enough to excuse her, either. GSR findings were fickle and didn't rule out guilt.

"What about bullet casings? Did you find any?" Terry asked.

Leave it to Terry to carry on like nothing's wrong.

"None." Cynthia shook her head. "No sign of the murder weapon, either."

She shook aside her fury at the sergeant and redirected her thoughts to the case. If Lorene had been cheating, Madison could somewhat understand where Mr. Malone was coming from if he'd been the one to kill his wife and her lover. After all, she was familiar with the pain of being cheated on, all because of Toby Sovereign. He had been her fiancé at the time she'd found him in bed with another woman. That image and resulting heartbreak took her over a decade to purge. Toby wasn't her favorite person on the planet, but they'd at least made peace. It still didn't mean she was looking forward to walking down the aisle with him at Cynthia's wedding. He was Lou's best man. Lucky her.

But if Malone was behind the murders, it's likely he would have acted in the heat of the moment, so he would have lacked the necessary wherewithal to clean up after himself. Then again, a person of means didn't need to dirty their own hands. He could have hired someone for the murders, the removal of the wallet and phones a ploy to mislead the investigation.

"Does the husband own any guns?" Madison asked.

"One of the first things I looked up. He has several registered to him," Terry replied.

Madison's gaze went to the bodies, to the wound on their foreheads, and it was hard to tell exactly what caliber was used. Once Cole Richards, the medical examiner, arrived, he'd have that answer.

Mark set down a marker by a drop of blood to the side of Mrs. Malone and took a photo. He then proceeded to pull out a swab, mark the case number and assign an evidence number, put it beside his find, and take another photo. Next, he swabbed the blood and sealed the sample.

"Where are they?" It was Sergeant Winston's voice, and with each word, he sounded as if he was getting closer. If that wasn't enough to give it away, she felt a cold front moving in.

She and her boss rarely saw eye to eye, but sometimes, when the moons aligned, they could tolerate each other. The greatest fissure between them was the fact Winston was old-school, and to him, law enforcement would always be—and should have always remained—a boys' club.

The atrium's door swung open, and Winston entered. He pointed immediately to the bodies but put his eyes on her. "We need this solved yesterday, Knight."

"I agree."

"Don't be smart with me."

"I'm not, I swear." *Cross my heart and hope to die.*

"You do know who she is, don't you?" Winston was panting, practically grunting.

"I do." To Madison, *who* Lorene was didn't matter as much as finding her—and John Doe—justice.

"Then give me some answers." Winston puffed out his chest. His slightly rotund belly expanded, and he placed his hands on his hips.

She took a deep breath. It was like the man had forgotten his days in the field and that answers didn't come immediately. They took time. Summing up her first impressions for the man was always a case of "damned if you do, damned if you don't." He wanted *something*, but then he'd hold it against her if her initial assumption turned out to be wrong. Sometimes, it was best to swerve and avoid. "I'm just arriving, but once I have more to go on, I'll let you know."

"They were shot," Terry put out there, drawing Winston's gaze. "It's not looking like a murder-suicide. No gun and no casings."

"A professional hit?" Winston speculated.

The location of the gunshot wounds would support that. Meat of the forehead, between the eyes, instant death. "It's possible." Madison's stomach tossed with the admission. Verbalizing the prospect touched far too close to her near-death encounters with the Russian Mafia.

"But?" Winston drilled his gaze in on her. "I'm sensing there's a 'but.'"

He had a way of teeing things up for a smart remark, and she had to bite down the urge to counter with one. "It's too soon to conclude anything."

"You've given me your initial impressions before."

And they bite me in the ass—every time.

"Even if this was a run-of-the-mill hit, we don't have motive," she began. "We don't even know the true target or whether both of them were."

"The victims' phones are missing, as well as Doe's wallet," Terry chimed in.

"At least one of you is talking to me."

Ever the drama queen. "Fine, you want to know my first thoughts?"

Winston stared at her blankly.

Here goes.

"It's possible they were having an affair. Mr. Malone found and put an end to—"

Winston's expression hardened. "Must I remind you that the Malones are highly respected in the community."

As if that made an ounce of difference where infidelities were concerned. Affairs found themselves within the walls of the White House.

Winston went on. "The Malones are also one of the largest contributors to the Stiles PD, and we owe it to Steven to find his wife's killer immediately."

One of the largest contributors to the Stiles PD? Steven? Now it was also abundantly clear why the sergeant was so concerned about the murders being solved quickly: it was to impress a benefactor. She hated that Winston had cast John Doe aside as if his life had meant nothing.

Winston rambled on. "If you're going to point a finger at Steven Malone, you'd better have something solid to back it up."

She hitched her shoulders. The impulse to be sassy was too overwhelming to ignore. "Well, no one seems to know where he is at the moment.

That's a little interesting, in my opinion."

Winston scowled. "Not solid."

She looked away to hide her amusement. She'd gotten under his skin.

"Before you got here," Terry started, "we were discussing Kimberly Olson-Malone."

Madison faced Winston again. "We'll need to ask her about her parents' marriage."

"I'm warning you, Knight. Handle the situation with discretion."

"I'll do my job." That was all she could promise. Justice rarely came without a struggle, without ruffling feathers and making enemies.

"I'm not sure if that's supposed to comfort me, but I guess it's where I'm at. Just keep me posted every step of the way."

"Sure," she said.

"I want to hear you tell me that you'll communicate with this case."

"I'll communicate with this case," she parroted in the tone of a rebellious teenager who says whatever necessary to appease a parent.

"Good." Winston left the atrium.

She leaned in toward Terry. "That man bugs the hell out of me."

"I'd say the feeling's mutual."

She shrugged that off as a victory. At least she wasn't the only one suffering in their imposed relationship. Regardless of their feelings toward each other, she wasn't going to let the sergeant tie her hands with political bullshit. She'd do whatever it took to find the killer and get justice for *two* people—even if it meant getting on Winston's bad side. She'd been there, done that, and she'd be there again. She might even live there. Conflict with the male brass was the circle of life.

Four

The entry wounds are consistent with a .357-caliber bullet," Richards concluded as he worked over the deceased. He was crouched next to John Doe.

Madison and Terry were getting ready to leave and pay Kimberly Olson-Malone a visit when the ME arrived.

"It's likely we're looking at a revolver then," Madison said, applying her knowledge of firearms. "If that's the case, there'd be no casings, no need for the killer to clean up behind him- or herself." It would also be the ideal weapon for someone emotionally despondent. "Does Mr. Malone own any revolvers?"

"I'll look it up." Terry pulled a small tablet from a back pants pocket. It was one of the department's latest gadgets and promised information at their fingertips.

Madison addressed Richards. "What are you ruling as cause of death?" It seemed apparent, but it wasn't necessarily the bullets that had done them in.

Richards looked up at her, his dark skin pinching around his eyes. "I'd say it's quite likely the gunshot to their heads, but I'd prefer to get them back to the morgue, run some tests, find out for sure."

"What about time of death?" Terry piped up, pausing from his search efforts.

"I'd put the TOD window somewhere between seven and ten last night."

Terry nodded and returned his focus to the tablet.

Richards added, "I'll conduct their autopsies first thing tomorrow."

"This afternoon," Winston overruled as he walked into the room again.

Richards's jaw clenched. "Unfortunately, with my schedule, that won't be possible."

"Make it possible or get someone who can make it happen, or I will."

"I'll get it taken care of," Richards said with resignation and turned to Madison. "I'll keep you posted on the time."

Madison didn't look at Winston but heard him *hmph* as if Richards had slighted him by addressing Madison instead of him.

"Okay, sooo…" Terry pulled his eyes from the tablet. "It turns out Mr. Malone has a .357 Smith & Wesson registered to him."

"Discretion." Winston wagged a pointed finger at her, and she had flashbacks to the former police chief who'd had a bad habit of doing the same thing.

"We'll do our best," Madison told him and turned to leave.

"Where are you going?"

If he was planned on micromanaging the investigation, there might be more bodies before it was all over. "We're off to speak with Kimberly Olson-Malone."

"Okay," Winston stamped his approval. "Know that she has my cell number and that I told her to call me if she has any concerns about the way her mother's case is being handled."

Stated again as if Lorene Malone had been the only victim. Madison huffed it to the front door, wanting to put as much distance between her and Winston—as fast as possible. She could only hope the crisp winter air would cool her temper. She stepped out, prepared to take a deep inhale, and found Officer Tendum struggling with a gray-haired man of over six feet in a suit and trench coat. Behind them, a black luxury sedan was pulling away from the curb.

"This is my house. Let me in there," the man said loudly.

"Release him," Winston barked, and Tendum did as he was told. "My apologies for Officer Tendum here, Mr. Malone."

Malone ran his hands down the sleeves of his coat. He was breathing deeply, nostrils slightly flaring, and a vein was bulging in his forehead.

It was hard to align the man before her with the grinning grandfather figure presented in the ads for his furniture stores.

"What's going on?" He looked squarely at her.

Madison disliked notifications under ideal circumstances, if there were such a thing. But there in the man's driveway, in the cold, with curious neighbors peeking out their windows— potential suspect or not—she wasn't going to deliver the news like this.

"I'm Detective Madison Knight, and this is my partner, Detective Terry Grant. Unfortunately, we can't let you into your home right now, and it would be best if you came with us down to the station."

"What's going on?" Malone repeated and let his shoulder bag fall to the ground. He blinked slowly and made a move toward the door. Madison and Terry restrained him. Malone bucked against their hold. "I demand to be let into my house immediately!"

"Let him be, detectives," Winston directed them.

Hairs rose on the back of Madison's neck, but she released her hold on Malone.

"There's been an incident involving your wife," Winston started to explain.

"Just tell me what's happened."

"Why don't you come with me down to the station?" Winston reached for Malone's elbow, but the man moved out of reach.

"Please, I can imagine it's next to impossible to walk away, but go with the sergeant, Mr. Malone," Terry pleaded.

Malone remained immobile and silent for what felt like a minute, then conceded. "Fine. I'll go—" he jerked his head toward Winston "—with you."

As the two of them walked to the sergeant's SUV, Madison turned her attention to Tendum. "Did Mr. Malone say anything to you? Where he'd just come from?"

"Nope. Just that he wanted to know what was going on. As you could see, he didn't take too kindly to my blocking access."

In a way, Madison understood Malone's aggravation. In another, had he planned the timing of his arrival to help cast the shadow of suspicion away from himself? She couldn't afford to let her guard down.

She and Terry got into the department car, she behind the wheel again and Terry in the passenger seat. She started the vehicle, and cold air blasted from the vents. A feeling of foreshadowing ran down her spine and knotted her stomach. Winston had been so quick to intervene on Malone's behalf, it was nauseating. So was all his admonition to use discretion. She turned to her partner. "If that man killed his wife, is the sergeant going to turn the other way because of who he is? *One of the PD's largest contributors, highly respected in the community,*" she mimicked the sergeant.

Terry cocked his head to the side. "Play nice."

"Oh, this is how I play nice. I play *fair*. Steven Malone needs to be treated like any other suspect. He acted like he had no clue—"

"He might not."

She shook her head, her mind starting to lock in on a theory: jealous husband exacts revenge. It seemed the more the sergeant wanted to push her focus away from Malone, the more inclined she was to look at him. "I don't think I'm buying that, Terry. His wife was inside with another man, *naked* with said man. By all accounts, it would seem she was having an affair. Jealousy is a motive as old as time."

Terry's brow drew downward. "What's it like living in your black-and-white world?"

She held eye contact with her partner, admitting to herself that personal experience could be tainting her perspective. "I'm just looking at what's in front of me," she defended and put the car into drive.

"We still headed to speak with the daughter? See what she has to say about her parents' marriage?"

"Nope."

"Oh, crap, and it begins." Terry snapped his belt into place.

She stared at her partner. He was more combative than normal. His normal she could handle. It bordered more on sarcasm and lent itself to a sister/brother relationship. This attitude was something else entirely. First, the blow about her living in a black-and-white world, now his sharp remark. "What do you mean by 'it begins'?" Heat licked her tone.

"Just that. You tend to latch on to one scenario so tightly that you become blind to any other possibilities." No preamble or tact, straight for the gut.

"And I'm a damn good detective. My close record—"

"*Our* close—"

"Attests to that. We rule out things as we go."

"Mr. Malone, though? You always lean toward the cheated-on spouse. Actually, correction, it's usually men you lean toward."

"That's not true." The claim made her feel hypocritical. She did tend to look at men first. "The husband could be good for this," she added.

"So could the daughter," he served back. "We don't even know that Mrs. Malone and John Doe were having an affair."

"Why were they naked, then?" Her voice rose in pitch with each word.

"The killer could have had them strip for some reason," Terry countered matter-of-factly.

"Very well," Madison conceded. "Does the daughter have any guns registered to her that fire .357-caliber bullets?"

Terry pulled out his tablet. "Let me find out."

Madison shook her head and headed in the direction of the station. The daughter may have found the bodies, but the husband needed to account for his whereabouts.

Five

Madison saw Sergeant Winston talking with Malone in the soft room as she and Terry were approaching. Malone was hugging the arm of the couch, legs crossed. Winston excused himself to Malone, who looked up and caught Madison's eye. Something in his gaze told her that he knew his wife was dead.

Winston joined them in the hall.

"You told him," Madison accused.

"Of course, I did." Stated as if that was a no-brainer, but Madison stiffened. She'd been robbed of gauging Malone's initial reaction.

"How did he react?" She tried to press down her temper.

Winston glanced in at Malone and proceeded to usher Madison and Terry down the hall outside of Malone's view. "How do you think?" Winston spat. "His wife is dead. He's angry. He's in shock."

"Did you tell him that she was found naked

with another man?"

Winston's face hardened, and his cheeks went red with fury. "Yes, he's aware, but you're going to have to leave your assumptions at the door, Knight. We can't treat Mr. Malone like other suspects. We've been through this. It's a sensitive situation that demands discretion."

If Madison heard the word *discretion* one more time, she might explode.

"You can't go in there with your guns loaded, tossing out accusations," he continued.

Truth was she'd manipulate the situation any way necessary to uncover the truth. Sometimes, the gentle approach worked—the application of honey—but she specialized in harsh extraction. Attacking situations and suspects rather than dancing around them brought results and caught killers, but she held up a hand as if making a pledge. "I'll behave."

"Don't play smart with me." Winston's face turned a deeper shade of red. "I know what the scene lends itself to, but he needs to see that we're on his side, on his family's side."

"And John Doe's?" Madison countered. "We owe justice to *both* of them." Terry might have called her black-and-white, but Winston was guilty of the same thing, affording liberties to the rich.

Winston went quiet and studied her. "As I said at the house, keep me updated on the investigation. If it helps, pretend you're a puppet and that I'm holding your strings." He leaned forward and locked eyes with her. "The image clear enough?"

Too clear. "Crystal," she said.

"What's going to be your approach in there?"

"Your wife was sleeping with another man and—"

Winston clenched his jaw. Terry let out a jagged breath.

"Gee, no sense of humor." Madison paused. "I'll be approaching him like I would the spouse of any other murder victim." She held up her hand, hoping it was enough to keep Winston quiet. "I'll ask the questions we need answers to, including where he was and for how long. We also need to put our hands on his registered .357 S&W as it might be the murder weapon, but we'll need to clear it if it's not. Pretty straightforward."

"And the entire time, you'll be going at things from the angle of assuming his innocence," Winston stressed.

"Innocent until proven guilty. That's the law."

"You make sure she sticks to that philosophy, Grant." Winston looked at Terry.

"Will do," Terry said without much conviction.

"Best I'm gonna get, I suppose." Winston sighed. "If one word gets back to me about you bullying the man, I will take you off this case. Am I understood?"

"You are," she replied.

"You have fifteen minutes and—"

"I what?" she rushed out.

"You have fifteen minutes to say what you need to say. Then let the man alone. He's grieving."

"He's also a murder suspect!" The words flew from her. First, she was supposed to handle Malone with kid gloves, and now she had a time limit? Winston was taking playing favorites too far.

Winston scowled. "Lose that mindset, Knight."

She clenched her teeth, too mad to talk, her entire body quaking.

"As a heads up, he's also called in his lawyer." Spoken as if Winston had just done them a huge favor by letting them know.

"Why would an innocent man need a lawyer?" she countered.

Winston scowled. "Steven Malone is a businessman. He must protect himself. He's not refusing to talk with you until the lawyer gets here. Just know one's coming."

Malone having lawyers on retainer for business matters, Madison could understand, but why would the man have a criminal defense attorney in his back pocket? It made Madison curious about something. "Was his mention of a lawyer before or after you mentioned the man with his wife?"

"Urgh." Winston ran a hand over his balding head. To Terry, he said, "Make sure she stays in line," and left in the direction of his office.

Madison snarled at Terry, "I don't need a babysitter."

"Good, because I don't want the job."

MADISON PACED IN A CIRCLE, shaking from the interaction with the sergeant, and took a few deep breaths. *Fifteen minutes.* The sergeant had lost his mind.

She entered the room with Terry following. "Would you like a tea or coffee? Water?" she asked Steven Malone, feeling some sympathy for him and his loss, but not letting that emotion trip her up. After all, she'd seen killers put on a show with their crocodile tears and staged sorrow before. Malone might not be crying, but grief was a tangible entity in the room.

Malone shook his head. "I'd like to know how this happened," he stated it as if he were demanding updates in a business meeting. It made Madison question the way he was portrayed in the media. Sure, she was catching him on his worst day, but there was a coolness about him that made her think he was typically more aloof.

Madison sat in a chair while Terry remained standing. He started to jingle the change in his pocket—something he often did to throw suspects off in the interrogation room.

Malone glanced at him then back to Madison. "I'm waiting," he said impatiently.

"We're sorry for your loss, Mr. Malone," Madison offered and meant every word. "Please know that we intend to find out who is behind the murders."

"Start by telling me who the man was."

"At this time, we don't—"

"You don't know? Is that what you're going to tell me? My wife is *dead*."

"Currently, we have no way of identifying the man," she admitted.

Malone held out a hand, palm out, and wriggled his fingers. "Show me his picture."

Madison threw a quick glance at Terry. "Given the graphic nature of the crime scene, we—"

"Show me a goddamn picture!" Malone roared.

Madison didn't flinch but simply squared her shoulders and stared him down. "I can appreciate that you want to see him. We will be getting a sketch together that—"

"Oh, dear God." Malone slapped his hands on his thighs. Revelation dawned in his eyes as if it were just sinking in that they were violent murders.

Terry stopped jingling his change.

Madison let the man sit with his grief, though she glanced at the clock. Four minutes of her fifteen were chewed up already.

"Sergeant Winston told me they were naked," Malone broke the silence, his voice cracking on the last word.

Madison nodded.

"You're probably thinking she was having an affair."

Madison remained still and quiet, afraid that if she said a word or twitched, he'd stop talking.

Malone went on. "I know my wife, and Lorene would never do that to me—never."

Madison felt for him and his possible naivete, but if he were guilty, he'd want them to believe he didn't hold suspicions of an affair. "A lot of times, the spouse doesn't know."

"I'd know." Malone pressed a hand to his chest. "I know my wife."

There'd be getting nowhere if they stayed fixated on the wife's loyalty. Madison pointed at Malone's luggage bag on the floor. "You were away."

He nodded. "Arkansas on a business trip, since last Thursday. The flight just got in at nine thirty this morning."

The guilty had been known to orchestrate alibis, but having one gave her and Terry a place to start. "You won't mind if we check up on where you stayed? Confirm your flight?" Madison asked.

Malone provided the hotel and flight details.

"I'm not completely blind or unsympathetic as to how this must look to you." Malone took a not-too-subtle U-turn with the conversation. "You think I killed her for cheating on me, but I'm telling you, my wife would never cheat on me, and I would never kill her."

Was he repeating himself to convince *them* or *himself* of his wife's faithfulness? There was nothing Madison could say that would placate him. She decided to move on. "Tell me more about your business trip. What was it all about?"

"One of our largest suppliers was hosting a home show where they introduce new furniture collections. I see what I like, buy what I think will sell, and it gives us an edge." Malone's pitch of the event fell flat partway through.

"Do you go to a lot of these shows?" Terry piped up.

"About three to five a year. Ah, I see what you're trying to do. You think that I don't know what goes on in my own house because I'm on the road." Malone scowled. "Sure, she had opportunity to cheat. Is that what you want me to say? Where does that get me?"

On my suspect list, Madison thought without hesitation.

"Instead of trying to dig up dirt on my family, put your focus on solving my wife's murder." Fire sparked in Malone's eyes.

Madison straightened her back and tilted up her chin. "Help us help you."

"I'm trying to do that, but what more do you need from me? Verify my trip—"

Madison glanced at the clock. Five minutes left, on the generous side. Time to get a little more direct. "You can be sure that we will. Your wife was shot with what looks to be .357-caliber bullet."

"You know that I have a .357 Smith & Wesson?" he interrupted.

Madison nodded.

Malone angled his head and studied her. "You do think that I killed my wife."

No one could say the man was dense. "We're just trying to find out who did." She retreated to playing nice, but she still had fangs. "It's easy enough to clear you. Just tell us where your gun is, and we can test it."

"My gun locker is in the den. Have at it." Malone was passive, compliant. Maybe he truly wasn't involved. He tacked on, "You'll need the passcode," and he proceeded to provide it to her.

"And we should find your .357 Smith & Wesson in there?" Madison asked.

"As far as I— Oh." Malone's face fell.

Madison leaned forward. "*Oh*?"

"You actually won't find it there." He ran a hand over his mouth.

She prepared herself for story time. "And why's that?"

"I lent it to Craig. Years ago, before you ask."

"Your son, Craig?" She wanted clarification.

"That's right."

Terry stopped jingling his change. "Why

would Craig borrow your gun?"

"He loves shooting. It's his de-stressor, like smoking, drinking, or eating is for other people."

"He doesn't have his own guns?" Madison asked incredulously. For someone who apparently has such a passion for shooting, it would seem logical he'd have his own.

"He does, but he wanted to borrow my .357 Smith & Wesson." Something flickered across Malone's eyes. "He wouldn't have done this."

A hopeful thought but an empty claim. "Just leave the matter with us, Mr. Malone."

"You think he did this now?" he lashed out. "Me a suspect, I understand—but Craig? That's ludicrous." His voice rose in volume the more he spoke. "What motive would he have?"

Madison opened her mouth to speak, but Malone wasn't finished. He went on. "You probably think that Kim is somehow behind the murders, too? She did find them."

To admit that everyone was a suspect until they were ruled out might antagonize him. To say nothing felt like she relinquished her power. Madison felt stuck.

"Have you fired a gun recently?" Terry inquired, saving her from needing to decide.

"Not in over a week."

"Then, let us swab you for gunshot residue. It could help rule you out," he said, stretching the truth.

"Do whatever you have to in order to speed

this along." Malone held out his hands toward Terry.

Terry took out some testing swabs and ran them over Malone's hands. "When the test comes back clean, it will protect you," Terry began. "You are certain that you haven't fired any guns recently, though?"

"Owning firearms is my American right," Malone said haughtily.

"Oh, I wholeheartedly agree," Terry replied, "and it's possible that the killer knew that."

Madison stared at her partner. Where the hell was he going with this?

Malone's shoulders stiffened. "You're suggesting that one of my guns could have been used to frame me?"

"Could be." Terry sealed the swabs in an envelope for the lab.

What the hell was her partner doing feeding the man a possible defense?

"It's much too early to make any conclusions," Madison said, hoping to squelch all talk of Malone being framed before it gained momentum. "Let's focus on why someone would want to kill your wife. Do you have anyone in mind that might have disliked her, held a grudge against her?" The question implied Lorene was the prime target, but it was a place to start.

"No, everyone loved Lorene." Malone shifted his gaze to Terry. "If one of my guns did kill

Lorene, someone is definitely wanting to frame me."

So much for a diversion. Madison was seeing red when she looked at Terry. Her partner had a subtle smile on his face as if he were pleased.

She glanced at the clock. Three minutes remained.

"There's something else you could do for us and yourself," Madison said. "Give us access to Lorene's phone records and financials." They would be subpoenaed, but asking could provide her with some insight into the man.

"Why on earth would you need to look at my financials?" Malone spat. "How's that going to help you find her killer?"

Now she was more curious than ever to see those records. "Do you have any debts? Owe the wrong people?" she asked. A well-known adage in a murder investigation was to follow the money—and for good reason.

Malone tugged on his suit jacket. "No."

"It is a murder investigation, and things have a way of coming out," Madison warned him.

"Well, you're not going to find anything that speaks to a motive for someone killing Lorene," he spat, and his wall only heightened Madison's curiosity.

The door opened, and Blake Golden walked into the room. Madison wilted into her chair. Of all the defense attorneys in Stiles, why one of her exes? His presence emitted warning signals.

He lined his pocketbook with profits made from the wealthy and corrupt, including the Russian Mafia. Why that had taken her so much time to see remained a mystery.

"Mr. Malone, not another word," Blake said, then turned to her, "Detective Knight."

She didn't respond with a greeting. She didn't even nod.

Winston entered behind Blake. "Mr. Malone, the department would like to put you up at the Marriott for as long as you need. It's the least we can do."

Madison got up and left the room. Her legs didn't want to move as fast as she wanted to go, but she needed to put as much space between her, the sarge, Malone, Blake—and Terry, for that matter—immediately. Everything was upside down. Since when did the police department spring for accommodations while a crime scene was being processed?

Six

Madison wound through the station's hallways toward her desk.

"Madison?" Terry called out from behind her. "Wait up."

She took a few more steps, stopped, and spun around.

"What's your problem?" Terry raised his brows.

"You really have to ask?" She flailed her arm in the direction of the soft interview room. "You fed him a defense."

"Hey…" Terry retreated a few feet and held up his hands. "You might be having a bad day, but don't take it out on me."

"Oooh." Eggs would fry on her earlobes. And where was a Hershey's bar when you needed one? "Just explain your thinking to me." Lord knows she couldn't figure it out on her own.

"Well, you look at things one way, and I look at them in another." His calm demeanor only aggravated her more.

"What other possible angle are you seeing? You—"

"The thought that someone might be framing him came out quickly." Terry paused, letting that sit, but she was failing to understand. "That means—"

"I must be missing something. The idea of being framed only entered his mind *after* you suggested it."

"He latched on to it quickly, though, didn't he?"

Awareness dawned. "He has someone in mind."

Terry pointed a finger at her. "Precisimo."

My partner and his made-up words.

"But he didn't volunteer who," she said slowly.

"No, and I didn't get a chance to ask if he had someone in mind before Blake came in." The lawyer's name might as well have been a swear word the way it had come off Terry's tongue. "I saw the way you were looking at me, by the way, like I'd lost my mind."

"Well…" She winced.

"But…" Terry rolled his head and started to take a bow.

"Not bad." There was no sense going overboard and swelling his head.

"That's it? Just give me something to hold on to."

She rolled her eyes and smiled. "You're so much smarter than I give you credit for."

"Ouch, Knight." He plastered on a pout and pounded a fist to his heart. "I'm so abused."

"Oh, knock it off." She snickered.

Terry's face became serious. "We figure out who hates Mr. Malone, and we might have our killer."

"Well, it's past time that we talk to Kimberly. Maybe she'll know. Lord knows there's a barricade around Malone right now."

"We got some good information from him, though."

"Sure we did," she conceded, "but there's more we didn't get out of him. We've got a place to start with Craig Malone. We need to talk to him and get ahold of Malone's .357 S&W. We also need to check on Malone's alibi." She flicked a finger toward Terry's pocket where he kept his phone.

Terry whistled, mocking her recap statement of the obvious. "You're on top of things. That's why you're the senior detective. It's not just because you're older." He laughed and juked out of her reach.

"Watch it, mister."

"Or what?"

He had her. There was nothing she could do, at least right now, but payback was a bitch. "Come on, we have a job to do." She resumed walking to her desk, her back to him, and smiling. He truly was the brother she'd never had. One minute, she loved him; the next, she was ready to beat him. But she wouldn't have it any other way. Everyone should have a Terry in their lives.

"By the way," Terry started, "after you stormed off, I got word back on Lorene's phone. It was last active at the Malone residence."

"Why am I not surprised?" One step forward, one back.

Seven

Madison and Terry had checked off several items from the to-do list before leaving the station for Kimberly Olson-Malone's. Terry had called the hotel Malone had given them, and Madison had texted Cynthia the passcode for Malone's gun locker and called Craig Malone. She had to leave a message. She wasn't sure how Terry had made out yet. He'd become rather quiet and sullen and had an energetic barrier that made Madison want to recoil, and that was saying a lot. She wasn't normally easily dismayed.

Madison looked over at Terry in the passenger seat. "You want to tell me how you made out with Malone's alibi?"

"It checked out," Terry started. "The hotel in Arkansas puts him there from last Thursday until this morning at four thirty."

"Guy has money. He can pay people to say anything. He could have had someone check in under his name."

Terry turned to her. "Wow, you really don't like the guy."

"Guilty."

"You sure it's not just the sarge getting under your skin? You know, like a parent who tells their kid, 'Don't do that' and the kid does it just because it will piss off the parent?"

"Can the hotel send a pic of Steven Malone in their lobby?" She wasn't about to get head-shrinked by her partner. Her actual shrink, who she'd been seeing for about a year, did enough of that.

"I doubt they'd have something like that," he said. "Customer privacy and all."

"Well, they'd have security cameras somewhere on their premises."

"Sure. Go ahead and make that call."

She looked over at him, surprised by the attitude he was dishing out. She was the senior detective, and if anyone was giving directions, it was her. "Let me know how you make out," she said coolly.

"Hmph."

It wasn't like Terry to be this closed-minded. They often had their disagreements, which only added some color to life, but he'd often bend to her will. Something had changed between the time they'd had their meeting with Malone and now. Then again, he'd been in a mood earlier this morning. She knew better than to push him when he was like this and decided she'd stay focused on the case. "Were you able to confirm Steven Malone went to the home show he'd mentioned?"

"I confirmed he was registered," Terry said. "The organizers have no way of verifying his actual attendance. Wow, you're really suspicious of the guy."

"I really believe that Malone's hiding something. You saw his strong reaction to parting with his financials."

"What is it with you and rich people?" Terry countered. "And men, for that matter."

"Okay, what's your problem?"

"I don't have one."

"Pfft. You certainly do." She took a righthand turn into another high-end neighborhood similar to the one in which the Malones lived.

"I just—" His phone rang, he consulted the caller ID and put his phone away without answering.

"Who was it?" she asked.

"No one."

"We're in the middle of—"

"It had nothing to do with the case," he stated firmly.

His tone reminded her of the last time he was this moody. Back then, he and his wife, Annabelle, had been having problems. Now the two of them had a daughter, Danielle— Danni for short. She was seven months old. "Everything all right at home?" she ventured.

He continued to stare straight ahead. "Just hunky-dory."

"Why am I not believing that?"

"I don't care if you do. Can we please just discuss the case?" He looked over at her.

She held up her hands in surrender.

"Hands on the wheel!" he squealed.

"What? This scares you?" She lifted her hands from the wheel again. "Look, no hands." The expression catapulted her back to childhood and riding a bicycle.

"Stop it." Terry's eyes widened with panic.

She giggled. "Lighten up, Terry. Your day could be a lot worse." Her statement sank in. They could be in the morgue like Lorene Malone and John Doe. Terry didn't say anything, and she felt foolish for assuming Terry's problem wasn't weighty.

Her phone pinged a message, and she picked it up, splitting her attention between the road and her phone.

"You do realize how many accidents are caused from texting and driving?"

"Good thing I'm not texting." She had her nose buried in her phone.

"Same diff."

Madison laughed.

"And now you're going to pick on my speech," Terry moaned.

"Never." If she was going to pick on him, it would have been over "precisimo."

Terry flipped a hand toward her phone. "What's the message?"

"Cynthia got into Malone's gun locker and the .357 S&W wasn't there."

"Malone told us he gave it to Craig," Terry said matter-of-factly.

"Yeah, we'll see." She was skeptical, sure, but this job made that necessary. People lied more than they told the truth.

She turned into Kimberly Olson-Malone's driveway, her thoughts not far from what was affecting Terry and who his caller might have been.

Higgins answered Kimberly's door.

"Hey, Sarge," Madison greeted him with her nickname for him. Technically, she outranked him, but that was only because Higgins had no aspirations to climb the ladder within the Stiles PD. If he'd put his mind to it, he'd already be at the top. After all, he had been Madison's training officer.

"They're in here." Higgins led them to a parlor.

The room was immaculate with mahogany walls and wainscoting reminiscent of the Victorian era, a time when men and women separated after dinners, the men to their cigars and brandy, and the women to their wine and gossip. The room itself was furnished chic modern with a neutral palette of white and shades of gray.

A man and woman were on the couch, rocks glasses on tables next to each of them, amber liquid in both.

"A couple questions," Madison started, speaking softly and turning to Higgins as they stood in the doorway. "Who's the man? And you let them drink?"

"Nope, the booze wasn't my idea, but I let it alone. Sergeant Winston stressed that he wanted Kimberly to be as comfortable as possible."

She should have known Winston was behind "the comfort." "And who's the man?"

"Kurt, the youngest Malone," Higgins answered.

Madison nodded. It would have been too easy if it had been Craig Malone.

"Ms. Olson-Malone," Higgins said, speaking a little louder to net her attention.

Kimberly turned in their direction but didn't move to get up. Kurt jumped off the couch.

"These are detectives Madison Knight and Terry Grant." Higgins made the introductions.

"We're sorry for your loss," Madison offered.

"Thank you," Kurt said. His eyes were bloodshot, and intense grief exuded from him, stabbing Madison in the heart. No matter how much the job requested that she detach from her cases, it was easier said than done.

Kimberly got up and slunk across the room like a panther in a black, skin-tight pantsuit. She squared her gaze on Terry. "Terry Grant?

Like that movie star *Cary* Grant?"

How much alcohol had she drunk? She was acting like she was meeting Terry for the first time, but they would have talked briefly at her parents' house.

"My mother was a fan, my father not as much," Terry said, easing into the role of good cop.

"Ah, so you got a slight variation." Kimberly touched Terry's forearm. "Your mother has good taste."

Terry smiled at Kimberly. "She likes to think so."

"Most people know him for his role as Nickie Ferrante in *An Affair to Remember*, so suave and debonair. Hard for women to resist," Kimberly purred.

"Why don't we all sit down?" Madison gestured toward the couch, beyond ready to move past *An Affair to Remember*. It might be her go-to chick flick, but that was irrelevant right now, and there was no way she wanted that secret coming out. She'd rather get a bullet to the head.

Kimberly looked thoughtfully at Madison, blinking slowly. "Do you know who that man was with my mother?"

Kurt squeezed his sister's hand.

"Unfortunately, not yet," Madison replied, leading the way into the parlor, hoping the Malones would follow. She sat on a chair that faced the couch Kim and Kurt had just vacated, and Terry sat in one next to Madison.

"There was no identification left behind," Madison added.

"None?" Kimberly's voice sounded strained. "You're sure?" She dropped back onto the couch, her brother beside her.

"We are. Have you ever seen him before?" She was running with the assumption that Kimberly had seen the bodies after they were pulled from the pool.

"No." She licked her lips and bit softly on the bottom one.

"Do you have a picture of him? Maybe I'll know who he is," Kurt said with hope in his voice.

"We will," Madison said. "A sketch will be done so you'll be able to look at him—" she slid her gaze to Kimberly "—and you can have a better look."

"We haven't been able to reach Dad," Kurt offered out of the seeming blue, "or Craig."

"Your father showed up at the house," Terry said. "He's fine."

"We tried reaching your brother but had to leave a message. Do you know where he might be?" It wasn't as if hours or days had passed, or even multiple messages had been left, but he was a person of interest in the case, and tracking him down sooner than later was the goal.

Kimberly crossed her legs, picked at

something on the fabric of her pants, and sank into the couch. "His assistant at the store told me he's on a getaway."

"Where?" Madison asked, striving to keep skepticism from her voice. Most of God's green earth had cell service, not that it meant Craig was tethered to his phone.

Kurt glanced at his sister, his eyes seeking answers. Kimberly met Madison's gaze.

"I don't know," she confessed in a huff. "Neither did Emily."

"And Emily is…" Madison prompted.

"My brother's assistant."

"Are you and your brother close?" Madison asked.

"We are."

"But you don't know where he went?" Madison countered, though it was conceivable that the siblings didn't keep each other apprised of their every move.

"I don't. All I know is Emily said he took off last minute for a few days."

"Does he do that often?"

Kurt shifted on the couch, putting a leg under him. "He used to, but he hasn't in a long time."

"I wouldn't think too much of it, Detective," Kimberly interjected.

Madison didn't care much for Kimberly telling her what to make of things. "If you hear from him, you'll let us know," Madison said, more as a directive than a question.

"I will."

Madison leaned forward and Kimberly leaned back. "Why were you at your parents' house this morning?"

"I was there to take Mom to yoga class, just like every Tuesday and Thursday morning." Kimberly crossed her arms and rubbed one as if she were fending off a chill. "I told all this to Officer Higgins and him." She flicked a hand toward Terry.

"You normally pick her up?" Madison disregarded Kimberly's dismissive behavior.

"Yeah."

"What time?"

"Anywhere from seven ten to seven fifteen."

"That was when you were there today?"

Kimberly nodded.

"Where do you go for yoga?" Madison kept the questions going.

"Wellbeing Yoga on Main Street."

Madison nodded. "Just a few more questions, and some may be hard to answer. Kimberly, just for the record, did you touch anything when you were at your parents' house this morning?"

Kimberly shook her head. "Well, just the doorknob to let myself in. Come to think of it, the door wasn't locked, and the security system wasn't armed."

"And that's unusual?" Madison assumed so for her to specifically mention those things but wanted confirmation.

Kimberly nodded. "Usually, I need my key and bypass code."

Kimberly brought light to another angle they needed to pursue. There'd been no signs of breaking and entering. Did that mean Lorene let her killer in, or did the killer have access with a key and bypass code of his or her own? They needed to find out who had keys to the Malone kingdom and eliminate them one by one. She'd get to the list of people, but first she wanted to go down another path.

"What can you tell us about your parents' marriage?" she asked. "Were they—"

"*Not* having problems, and Mother's not an adulterer." A shot of red bloomed in Kimberly's cheeks.

Madison suspected Kimberly had personal experience with being cheated on, given that her reaction was a blend of disgust and embarrassment.

Kurt put a hand on his sister's arm. "We know how it must look, Mom being found with that man…naked." Kurt's Adam's apple bobbed as he swallowed roughly. "It's just Mom and Dad were always a united front, impenetrable and untouchable."

Kimberly reached for her drink, her hand shaking the entire way.

"You agree?" Madison cornered Kimberly.

Kimberly tipped her glass back and gulped a large mouthful.

Something about the topic of her parents clearly made Kimberly uncomfortable, but was that all or was there also fear?

"So your parents got along well? No issues that you know of? No affairs?" Terry pierced the silence.

"They were good parents, sweet and kind people," Kimberly said, and pressed her lips to her glass again.

"Sadly, it's possible someone out there might not feel that way," Madison started. "They were successful, and that alone can make enemies." She paused, allowing the Malones time to jump in, but neither of them did. She went on. "I imagine it would be hard to think of anyone wanting your mother dead—" She stopped talking when Kimberly polished off the rest of her drink and set the glass back on the table.

"It's a nightmare is what it is," Kurt burst out, got to his feet, and paced. "God, I can't believe this is really happening." He ran a hand through his hair and stared at the carpet.

Kimberly stood and hugged her brother, then cupped his face and put her forehead to his. "We will get through this," she told him softly.

"Yeah." Kurt blinked tears and ran his index finger under his nose, sniffling. He put his hands in his jeans pockets, pulled them out, put them back in, as if he wasn't sure what to do with his hands.

The two returned to the couch, Kimberly's

arm around her younger brother.

"Everyone loves our parents," she said with a bitter edge.

Was she insulted Madison had questioned otherwise, or was she being defensive and hiding something?

"Sometimes the killer is the person you'd never expect," Terry offered gingerly.

Kimberly patted her brother's knee. Was the movement to shelter him from the possibility Terry had suggested or an aversion to the subject matter?

"It could even be someone who is close to your family," Madison opined, going one step further.

"How do we even know Mom was the real target when you don't even know who that man is?" Kimberly delivered her question as if tossing a grenade.

"We are on the same side here. We want to know what happened to your mother, and until we know who that man was, we must work with what we have. It can't be ignored that the murders were in your parents' home."

"That's why you're zoning in on people who hated our parents." Kimberly took her arm from her brother and clasped her hands in her lap.

"It's part of the process," Madison defended.

"I suppose some people envied Mom and Dad," Kimberly conceded as if it had been forced out of her. Surely, Kimberly didn't live in a fairy-tale bubble where everyone got along. After all, she and her husband were divorced.

Madison leaned forward. "Do you have any names that come to mind?"

"Bert Rowe," Kurt rushed out and lifted his gaze from his lap to Madison.

"And who's Mr. Rowe?" she asked.

"Dad's former accountant," Kurt replied. "Dad fired him."

Kimberly turned to face her brother. "Then why kill Mom?"

"Could have been to hurt your father," Terry interjected.

Kimberly bit her bottom lip, and Madison swore she trembled.

"When was Mr. Rowe fired?" Madison asked.

"Last week," Kurt deadpanned.

It was possible Rowe had sought revenge, even if it might seem indirect. John Doe could have been collateral. While killing over the loss of a client might seem extreme, Malone taking his business from Rowe could have had harsh consequences for the man. He could have been let go from his job if he worked for someone else, or if Rowe ran his own firm, it could have greatly impacted the company's finances.

"Does Mr. Rowe run his own firm or work somewhere?" Madison asked.

"He owns Rowe's Accounting," Kurt said.

"Is it a big firm?" Terry asked, getting into the questioning loop.

Kurt shook his head.

Madison felt the back of her neck tightening. Rowe could figure in, but would the accountant have access to the Malone house? Depending on the full nature and length of the business relationship, it was possible that Lorene would have known Rowe enough to open the door to him. "Did Mr. Rowe take care of the books for a long time?"

"Since I was old enough to be aware of it," Kurt replied, and Madison glanced at Kimberly, who nodded.

"He became a family friend, then," Terry surmised.

"I wouldn't go that far," Kimberly countered.

"Although—" Kurt looked at his sister "—I think Mom had lunch with him sometimes."

Now the question became why Lorene was lunching with the accountant. "Was your mother involved with the accounting side of the business?"

Kurt consulted his sister, and both shook their heads.

Kurt's face fell. "Come to think of it, I don't know why she'd be having lunches with him."

Madison felt a pang of doubt emanating from Kurt, as if he might be questioning his mother's loyalty to his father. Kurt's reaction opened Madison's eyes to the fact that if Lorene had been having an affair with their John Doe, what's to say she hadn't also been sleeping with someone else? Forget a jealous spouse, a jealous *lover* could be behind the murders. Madison put a cap on her imagination—for now—and went back on point. "Do you know why your father fired him?"

"I'm not sure," Kurt replied with a shrug.

"Do you work for your father at Malone's?" Terry inquired.

Kimberly answered on his behalf. "Kurt's only twenty-six, and he's still in school."

Terry turned to Kimberly. "What about you?"

"I never had the passion for it," she said.

Madison took in the house again. It was pretty swanky, and the mortgage wouldn't be cheap. "What do you do for work?"

"My ex, Joe, is a computer programmer," she said it as if that explained the high-end neighborhood and luxury SUV Madison saw in the drive.

"He must get paid well," Madison countered, letting the fact go that Kimberly never really answered her question. At least for now.

"They love him over there." Kimberly gave a tight smile.

"What do you do, though?" Madison repeated, not about to move on without the answer.

Kimberly's cool eyes met Madison's. "I'm a mother to two children, Brad and Brianna. They both take a lot of my time." She turned to Kurt. "Thank God it's Joe's week with the kids.

I don't know how I'm supposed to tell them..." Her voice petered out and disappeared.

"I'm sure you'll figure out the right things to say," Madison assured her. "Were you close with your mother, Kimberly?"

Kimberly held Madison's gaze, but Kurt looked away and sniffled. He'd shown more grief than Kimberly since they'd walked in the door. She was calm, if not steely.

"We went to yoga every week," Kimberly told them.

It sounded like a desperate reach to claim a closeness with her mother, but Madison let that go. Madison placed her attention on Kurt. "And you?"

"We got along all right."

Kimberly nudged his elbow. "Better than all right. You're the youngest, and they've always spoiled you, especially Mom."

"When did the two of you last see your mother alive?" Terry asked.

"Last Thursday, but we spoke briefly on the phone yesterday," Kimberly said and looked at her brother.

Tears fell down Kurt's face. "I'm not exactly the golden child. It's been a while for me."

Kimberly wrapped an arm around her brother. "Nonsense. You're amazing." To Madison and Terry, she said, "He keeps himself busy, but he should be having the time of his life right now."

"But it's been a while?" Madison prompted.

"Yeah," was all Kurt offered, and he avoided eye contact, seemingly caught up in a world of self-flagellation.

"What about your father?" Terry inserted. "When was the last time you saw or spoke with him?"

Kimberly's eyes drifted across the room, and she rubbed her throat. "It's been a while," she mumbled.

Madison jumped on Kimberly's response. "You're not close, then."

Kimberly looked at her brother who was watching her expectantly. She took his hand. "Our father and I have a complicated relationship." The confession seemed to cause her a great deal of discomfort, and given Kurt's sorrowful eyes, it was a surprise to him.

Kimberly went on. "He devoted his entire life to making Malone's a household name. He sacrificed hours away from his family when he was building it from scratch. That's the way, though. That's normal for entrepreneurs, especially in the beginning. Anyway, that's Dad. Mom's a different story."

Madison noted how Kimberly had made excuses for her father and downplayed his absence from her childhood by speaking about the situation from a detached perspective. "So your mom was always there for you?"

"Yeah."

"You said you spoke to your mother yesterday?" Madison asked.

"That's right." Kimberly tilted up her jaw just slightly.

"What did you talk about?"

"Just about the kids. Not for long, a few minutes max."

Madison nodded. "And what was her mood like?"

"She seemed happy to me. She was laughing."

"Mom had a way of walking into a room and making people smile," Kurt added. "You mentioned enemies or people who would hate her, but I don't understand. She did so much for the community. She was a member of many social clubs and involved with a lot of charities, but you probably know that."

She knew about the Malones' contributions to the Stiles PD, but nothing about philanthropy work outside of that. "We're going to need the names of those organizations."

"Can I email them to you?" Kimberly cut in on her brother's behalf and looked at Terry.

Terry handed her one of his cards. "My email's on there."

"Just give me some time."

"When you have it, send it over."

"Thank you for your understanding." Kimberly palmed her cheeks again, though tears had yet to fall or even make any sort of appearance. Her eyes were dry.

"Would you two be able to provide us with a list of people who had keys and security codes for your parents' home?" Terry inquired.

"Their cook Marie Rauch and housekeeper Patty Beaulieu, for starters," Kimberly said. "Not that I can see either one of them doing this or having reason to."

"What about anyone else? Did your mother have any close friends she might have given a key or code to?"

"Sabrina Darbonne," Kurt said, "but she'd never—"

Kimberly patted the back of her brother's hand. "We'll get you everyone's information." The offering wasn't backed up by any movement.

"We'll wait," Madison replied.

The Malone siblings pulled out their phones and fed them the numbers for the cook, the housekeeper, the former accountant, and the best friend. The charities were promised as forthcoming.

"Now, is that all?" Kimberly asked as if they'd been an intrusion on her day, rather than playing necessary roles in finding her mother's killer.

"Actually, before we go," Madison started, "we need to ask you both where you were last night between the hours of seven and ten o'clock."

Kimberly's eyes snapped to Madison's. "You really think one of us killed our own mother?"

Madison remained quiet, although she was

tempted to say *I've seen it before.*

Kimberly got to her feet. "You want to know, you go through our lawyer."

Madison said, "If you feel like you have something to hide—"

"No, I'm not getting caught up in a guilt trip." Kimberly gestured to the doorway. "Now, if you'll see yourselves out."

Eight

Rrom what I overheard, you played nicer than usual in there." Higgins motioned toward Kimberly's house with a twist of his body.

Madison, Terry, and Higgins were gathered in the driveway, despite the chilly air and the snowflakes falling in rapid succession.

Madison sighed. "Don't even get me started."

"Yeah, please don't," Terry said drily.

She tossed her partner a mild glare.

"Huh, as I suspected," Higgins said. "Winston's got you on a leash, given who the Malones are."

Madison nodded. "And what they have." Money afforded the wealthy luxury and a status in society that gave them advantages, but offering them special treatment during a murder investigation was sickening.

"Do you think one of the family's good for the murders?" Higgins asked.

"Too early to say." She looked at Terry. "I think Kimberly's hiding something. What, I don't know."

Terry didn't say anything, but Higgins jumped in. "I heard the husband showed up at the house. He was away?"

"His alibi confirms as much," Terry interjected.

"The hotel confirmed that someone by his name stayed with them during the time of the murders," Madison specified, and Terry shook his head. The sooner he got his personal matter sorted, the more pleasant it would be to work with him. She added, "I'd be more confident it was Steven Malone himself if I saw his face on camera."

"You think you have enough for a warrant?" Higgins asked.

"I doubt it," Terry answered on her behalf, then looked down the street as if something interesting had caught his attention, but nothing was there.

Madison burrowed into her coat. The damp chill was sinking into her bones. "We could get a warrant for the airport video and review the footage around the time of Mr. Malone's flights."

"Probably even harder," Higgins pointed out. "Besides you'd need to watch the video from the time Mr. Malone left Stiles until he returned, every minute. He could have come back, done the murders, and flown back out again." Higgins put a hand on her shoulder. "Didn't mean to ruin your day. And I better get back in there."

With that, he returned to the house.

Madison and Terry got into the department car, and she started the engine. Cold air blasted from the vents, and she regretted that she hadn't had the vehicle warming while they'd been talking. She directed the vents away from her and cranked the heat.

Terry clicked his seat belt and turned to her. "There's got to be another way to verify Malone's alibi to your satisfaction."

To my *satisfaction?*

Why did it feel like she was the only one wanting to solve this case sometimes? She held her hands in front of the vents that were beginning to blow warm air. "I never said we were going to look at the airport video."

"I know you. You'll want to."

"You know me, yet you're failing to realize you're pissing me off." Any empathy she had felt for what might be going on in his life was squashed under the weight of her temper. "What's going on with you, anyway?"

Terry looked at his phone in his lap.

"You don't want to tell me? Fine." Though it was far from fine. It was causing contention and a rift between them. More importantly, it was detracting her full attention from the case.

Terry met her gaze and shook his head. He didn't spew off some snide remark or tell her to mind her business. Her rage started to dissipate.

The wipers squeaked in the silence between

them and the sky darkened as if a cosmic switch had been dimmed.

"Promise you'll tell me if there's anything I can do to help," she offered.

"There's nothing anyone can do." He sounded defeated, and it tugged at her heart.

"Okay, now you really have me worried." She angled her body toward him.

"Let's just talk about the case," he said.

"Okay."

"You said you think the daughter's hiding something?"

"I do." Madison couldn't shake the fact that Kimberly hadn't shed a single tear.

"Normally, I'd counter with, 'You think that about everyone.'"

"But not this time?"

"Nope. This time, I'm with you."

Yet he hadn't bothered to say as much in front of Higgins. "So, no bets?" she said lightheartedly and smiled at him gingerly. Sometimes, they made wagers on certain aspects of investigations.

"No need unless you want to put bets on Mr. Malone's innocence," he countered.

"You mean guilt." She'd said it to carry on in jest, but the statement came out in all seriousness. She hadn't released the husband as a suspect, despite the verified alibi.

"Our regular amount, then. You think he's guilty; I think he's innocent." Terry extended a hand to shake on the deal, and she put her hand to his.

"Twenty bucks is twenty bucks and better in my pocket." She smiled.

"Someone's presumptuous."

"I prefer confident."

"You bet against the husband, even though you think the daughter's hiding something? I might be collecting the money yet." The start of a smile tugged at his lips.

"I never said I'm taking the leap to her being the killer, although she did react quite strongly when we asked for her and Kurt's alibis."

"That only tells me the siblings are close and maybe she did so to protect her brother," Terry countered.

"From what? She thinks Kurt killed their mother?"

"I didn't say that."

"I don't think Kimberly's as close to her mother as she tried to convince us," Madison began. "Did you notice how put together she was? Not even a single tear."

"Might not mean anything. People grieve differently."

She looked at Kimberly's house. Kimberly and her brother stood at the front window, peering out. "Time for us to move." Madison backed out of the driveway, not sure where to go next and just ended up parking down the street. She resumed the conversation. "Kimberly builds up her parents, about what great people they are, but I'm not sure she'd buy what she's trying to sell. Maybe the scene was exactly what it looked like."

"Meaning?"

"An affair. They were naked. They'd been sharing a bottle of wine."

"You're assuming they did. Prints from the wineglasses haven't been processed yet."

"You're giving me a rough time on the wine?"

"Well…"

"Fine, but the likelihood of the wineglasses tracing back to someone else is small in my opinion." Her mind walked through the scene again. An opened bottle of wine, two glasses, and discarded clothing pointed toward an affair, but the missing ID and phones, not so much. If the killer had wanted to expose the lovers, one would think he or she would have left behind both.

"Maybe the killer set things up to make it look like an affair," Terry suggested.

"Why?"

"Or let's say whoever killed them believed they were having an affair," he said without missing a beat, as if he had been prepared to say this before her interjected question.

"That doesn't explain the missing ID and phones, but go ahead."

"I'm just talking possibilities out loud. Maybe whoever killed them *thought* they were having an affair. Then set it up to look like that, or mostly. I can't explain the missing phones or ID either," he added.

Madison's mind cut right to Kimberly and Kurt's relationship, and she got goose bumps. "Maybe Kurt and Kimberly were involved in the murders. Maybe they worked together. I'm just totally spitballing. They could have taken off with the phones and Doe's ID to delay the identification process, maybe even a sign of regret for what they'd done."

"Why not dress them, then?" Terry shook his head. "I still think it's quite the reach. Even if they thought their mother was having an affair, how would that really affect them? They're both grown and out of the house."

"The family's dominant in the community. They have a reputation to uphold. Then again, it could be as simple as the affair possibly hurting the family's bottom line financially." As she put out the idea, she thought of the former accountant. Had his lunch meetings with Lorene been strictly business or something more?

"You're thinking they just wanted John Doe out of the way? Then why not kill just him? They could have gotten to him when their mother wasn't around," Terry kept the brainstorming going. "And where does Craig Malone fit in all of this?"

"Good question," Madison replied. "He's taken off on a last-minute getaway. They don't know where he is. He's not returning his own sister's messages. Steven said Craig has his .357 S&W. Is it the murder weapon?"

"Again, you're diving right in," he accused.

"I'm either all for something or against it. You should know that by now." It was just how she worked. She cleared people as suspects as she worked along. Unfortunately, right now the suspects were piling up.

"It's innocent until proven guilty, not the other way around." His snide comment catapulted her right back to Winston's words from a few hours ago.

"If you have a problem with the way I work—"

"Sometimes I do."

His confession stole her breath. "Listen, if you're taking out your problems at home on me, cut it out now."

Terry let out a jagged exhale and faced forward.

She instantly felt regret for lashing out, even if he'd deserved it. His mood was a delicate pendulum. "I didn't mean to—"

"No, you're right. Where to next?"

"Terry—"

"I mean it. Let's stick to the case. The Malone children: Kimberly and Kurt didn't provide alibis, and Craig Malone is unreachable, supposedly with a .357 S&W in his possession, which could be the murder weapon, as you said."

"Yeah. I'd suggest we track his phone, but—"

"There's no way the sarge is going to allow that," he finished. "We haven't even been trying to reach him for long."

"I just hate feeling like my hands are tied."

"I don't like it either, but it's the way it's going to be with these people." Terry seemed to be coming back to her, having shuffled his personal issues aside again.

"He could have the murder weapon," she seethed. "And what? We can't do anything about it?"

"Not yet."

"We could stop by the store Craig manages and see if any employees can tell us where he went."

"According to Kimberly, Craig's own assistant didn't know."

"Doesn't mean he didn't talk to someone else there."

"It doesn't, but we also have another potential suspect we could visit."

"The former accountant," they said in unison.

If Terry thought she was going to back down from looking at the Malone family for the murders of Lorene and John Doe, he and the sergeant were sorely mistaken. After all, justice and truth trumped any special treatment.

"Maybe we'll find out he killed them," Terry added. "That'd take the pressure off."

"You never know."

She put the car into gear, not looking forward to driving with the worsening conditions. The snowflakes were now the size of large gumballs, and the wipers barely kept up at full speed. If the change in weather was any indication, a storm was coming.

Nine

Madison flashed her badge to the woman at the front desk of Rowe's Accounting. "We're detectives with the Stiles PD. We'd like to speak with Bert Rowe."

The receptionist's assessing eyes looked at Madison and Terry over glasses that were perched on the tip of her nose. "Do you have an appointment?" Her dry and authoritative response paired with the gray dusting to her hair attested to many years of experience manning a front desk.

Madison lifted her badge a bit higher. "This says we don't need one."

"Throwing your weight around might work on other people, but it doesn't on me."

Madison could play nice and empathize with the fact the woman was just doing her job as a gatekeeper or really stamp down her authority. She let go of her badge, and it fell along with its chain back against her chest. She then leaned on the counter. "We have questions for Bert Rowe in regard to a murder investigation," she said firmly.

The woman's jaw slackened, if only minutely. "Why would he know anything about—" She stopped there, her words failing her.

"It's just some routine questions. That's all," Terry assured her kindly. He passed a sideways glance at Madison, suggesting she cool it.

"Well, he's…" The woman rubbed her throat where red blotches were blossoming. "I'll see if I can get him, but he's working on a client's file right now. It is tax season."

"We appreciate that he might be busy, but we think he could help us with a case we're working on." Again, Terry was the one to speak, and he was certainly playing the role of good cop.

"I'll see what I can do. He just hates being interrupted." She reached for the phone slowly as if she were reaching out to pet a venomous snake. "Mr. Rowe, there are a couple of detectives here who want to speak with you… Yes, I told them that." She added in a whisper, "They say it's regarding a murder investigation."

"You know what?" Terry waved a hand. "We can let ourselves in." He pointed toward a hallway to the receptionist's right. "Is his office down there?"

The woman nodded in slow motion, and Terry was off.

So much for good cop.

Madison followed him. The receptionist

started speaking more loudly into her phone. "Yes, I know, Mr. Rowe, but they—"

"They'll have to make an appointment," a man said from an office on the right.

Terry had his badge held up as he rounded the doorframe and entered the room. "Detective Grant." He gestured to Madison. "And Detective Knight."

Bert Rowe hung up his phone and stared at them, his mouth partially agape. "You can't just let yourselves in." He adjusted his thick-framed glasses and fanned a hand over the mountain of paperwork on his desk. The disease had spread to his office floor, too, making Winston's office look organized and tidy by comparison.

"We just did, though." Terry dropped into an empty chair. "We tried things the nice way, but it wasn't working."

"I don't have anything to say…about a murder." Rowe squinted, wrinkles fanning out from his eyes.

Until then, he'd looked younger, but now Madison would place him in his sixties. He was still a handsome man with bulging biceps beneath his collared shirt. Mr. Number Cruncher worked out. Besides the glasses, he didn't fit the image for the stereotypical accountant: a Supercuts haircut, a cheap polyester suit, and a belly that tugged at the buttons of a dress shirt. She didn't imagine that he had a boring personality or owned a cat, either. If anything, he looked more like a dog person. Her gaze then fell on a framed photograph of a chocolate lab on a filing cabinet, and she walked over to it.

Rowe swiveled in his chair, watching as she crossed the room. "What are you—"

She picked up the picture and smiled. His fur baby made her think of Hershey. "Nice dog. What's his name?"

Rowe clasped his hands in his lap. "*Her*. Chelsea."

My sister's name.

She might have fallen prey to Hershey's chocolate eyes and soft fur, letting him weasel his way into her heart and sometimes into her bed. She might have taken the plunge into "motherhood," but she still wasn't on board with giving animals people's names.

"I have a lab, too," she told him.

Rowe's shoulders relaxed, and he smiled. She bristled at the shift in his demeanor. They had a bond as dog lovers, but she had to remember that he was a potential murder suspect. By extension, he should be anything but comfortable around her.

Having a dog was making her soft. She put the frame down and walked back to the front of his desk.

She cleared her throat and said, "Lorene Malone was murdered, and we understand—"

"Lorene's—" Rowe's face contorted into shock "—dead?"

"She was found murdered in her home along with a man," She put it out there as gingerly as possible.

"Her husband?" Rowe's eyes pooled with tears, and he blinked quickly.

Madison shook her head and closed her eyes briefly. "No."

Rowe sat back, his brows furrowed. "I don't understand. Who was the man if it wasn't Mr. Malone?"

"We're hoping you could tell us," she replied.

"Me? How could I possibly know?" His face blanched. "Oh, do you think I killed them?"

"We just have some questions for you. We understand that you worked for the Malone family for many years," she said.

Rowe frowned. "I did."

"Did you work for the Malones on their personal finances, business, or both?" Madison asked.

"Both."

"Well, what happened?" Madison preferred to hear the reason from Rowe himself.

"He fired the firm last week." Bitterness clung to his tone of voice, but there wasn't enough there that Madison was sniffing blood in the water just yet.

"Looks to me like you *are* the firm," Terry said, and it had her turning to look at him. She wasn't used to him being overbearing with a potential suspect.

"We might be small in size, but we pull in good money." Rowe leaned back in his chair.

"Even without the Malones?" Terry pressed.

"I'm not going to lie and say their leaving didn't ding the bottom line, but it's not like we'll be filing for bankruptcy anytime soon."

"So you weren't upset when Mr. Malone took his business elsewhere?" Terry seemed to have grabbed hold of the interview.

"Yes and no."

"Why no?" Madison cut in.

Rowe met her gaze. "Let's just say we weren't seeing eye to eye anymore and leave it at that."

Madison didn't want to leave it at that, but she didn't want to push too hard and risk Rowe's clamming up. She had a feeling he might be helpful to the case even if he wasn't the killer.

Rowe let out a jagged exhale, and a tear snaked down his cheek. "Lorene's why I was their accountant in the first place," he offered out of the blue.

"How so?" Madison rushed out before Terry could harass the poor man. He gave her a mild glare as if she'd interrupted him.

"Long story."

Madison sat down in another chair next to Terry. She crossed her legs and splayed her palms open. "We have the time."

"Well, Lorene and I met in college and hit it off right away."

"You were romantically involved?" Terry

butted in.

"Oh, no, it was never like that for us. She always had eyes for Steven."

"Go on," Madison prompted, wondering if and when that had changed for Lorene.

"Well, I'd fallen into hard times about ten years after college. Lorene heard and helped me out."

"You kept in touch over the years?" Madison asked hopefully. If Rowe had a long-lasting relationship with Lorene, he could provide a solid testimony about her character. He might even know if she'd be the type to be unfaithful or if she had been happy in her marriage.

"Off and on," he said.

Her high hopes sank.

Rowe continued. "I'm not exaggerating to say that I was going through hell back then. My marriage dissolved, and things weren't amicable at all. My ex got all my money in the divorce, and it made me bitter."

"That would make anyone bitter," Terry empathized, but she detected an underlying judgment that again cast Rowe as the bad guy.

"My attitude only made things worse," Rowe continued. "They say you attract what you think about. As I said, I was bitter, and I wallowed in my misery. I turned to the bottle, and it cost me the high-paying job at an accounting firm, a job I'd had from the moment I graduated college. It was Lorene who helped me turn my life around again."

Madison sat up straighter, feeling they were finally reaching the heart of it. "How did she do that exactly?"

"She got me into AA, even went with me to the first few meetings. She also put the bug in my ear to start my own company. I admit I was terrified to do that at first. Going out on my own, being an entrepreneur? All this on top of being single again? But Lorene made it sound like everything would be just fine. 'Better than fine,' she'd tell me. She got Steven to give me their business." There was a pocket of silence. Rowe sniffled. "I came to realize the truth of the statement, 'If you're going through hell, keep going.' If it hadn't been for all the crap I went through, I probably wouldn't have ever opened my own company, and it sure beats punching a clock for someone else's profit." In the next breath, he added, "I can't believe she's dead."

"Do you know of anyone who hated either Lorene or Steven enough to do this?"

Rowe's mouth opened, then shut.

"If you know of someone," Terry said, "talk to us."

"I probably don't have to tell you this, but anyone in the public eye is going to have enemies. The Malones are an influential couple. *Were*, now, I guess. Someone might have taken their dislike too far."

Madison deflated. She'd been certain he

was going to give them at least one name, but maybe if she poked at the fabric of the Malone family, moths would fly out. She'd start from the affair angle but play it diplomatically. "You said Lorene only had eyes for Steven?"

"Oh, yeah, from the time she'd first met him, she was smitten. There's no better word for it." Rowe's gaze fell to the desk, then up to meet Madison's eyes. "He got into a lot of trouble in college, and Lorene would always take the heat for it."

"What sort of trouble?" Terry asked.

"He crashed his parents' car, and she said she was driving. He got ahold of her parents' credit card and maxed it out. She took the blame for that. He almost got kicked out of school, and she jumped in to defend him."

Did Lorene tire of covering for her husband, and was it a factor in her murder?

"Do you know if they had a solid marriage?" Madison inquired.

"Hmm." Rowe looked like he was being yanked from someplace else, his mind obviously on another journey.

"Mr. Rowe?" she prompted.

"Lorene always put on a happy front, but I'm not sure how genuine or deep it was."

"It sounds like you were good friends. Did you ever ask what was bothering her or if she was all right?"

"Sure, I'd ask, but she'd detour. We might have

been good friends, but once she got married to Steven, she put a wall up around herself. I can understand it to a degree, as Mr. Malone has always placed high importance on appearance. In hindsight, I should have pushed her more, but I respected her privacy too much to do so."

"When was the last time you saw her?" Madison asked.

"We had lunch a few months ago. She refused to let me pick up the bill." Rowe chuckled softly, pulled into the memory. "She could be so stubborn."

"How was she that day?" Madison started running with the questions, but it didn't seem Terry minded.

"Oh, something was on her mind, but she wasn't sharing it with me."

Madison leaned forward. "And that made her seem sad or…"

"Definitely sad."

Madison nodded. "Do you think it had anything to do with her marriage?"

"I'd rather not say," Rowe admitted.

"So that's a yes?" She studied Rowe, but he was closed off.

"That's a 'I'd rather not say.'"

Okay, so the Malones' marriage was now off the table. Madison would move on. "What do you think about their children?"

Rowe's mouth opened, then closed. Eventually, he said, "I've never been a fan of their son Craig."

Her throat constricted thinking about Craig's last-minute getaway and that he could have the murder weapon in his possession. "Why is that?"

"The kid's head was never screwed on right, if you ask me. He's always had a fascination with guns and explosives."

"He loves shooting. It's his de-stressor, like smoking, drinking or eating is for other people." That's what Steven had said. The hairs stood on the back of Madison's neck, and she glanced at Terry.

"Did he ever show signs of hating his parents, his mother specifically?" she asked.

"Not sure about that, but he was quite rebellious as a teenager. More than his father had been in college." Shadows crept across Rowe's face. "He drove drunk at sixteen—with no license, to boot. He assaulted his high school shop teacher when he'd insulted his project. If that's not enough, he was accused of raping a girl in college. If it wasn't for his father's clout, I have no doubt he would have been locked up in juvie."

All of this was truly enlightening, and it emphasized the need to pull some backgrounds. They also had to find Craig—sooner than later.

Ten

Before leaving Bert Rowe, they'd obtained his alibi, which they were able to verify with the receptionist on the way out. He'd been in the office with her during the time window of the murders.

Madison and Terry stepped out to a wall of white. Snow was falling so heavily, it was hard to see ten feet ahead. It could have been night except for the glow in the sky that hinted at the existence of a sun behind the precipitation. It took them a bit of time to dig out the department car, but it was all warmed up by the time they'd finished.

"I'm curious what the 'we didn't see eye to eye' was about. Did it factor into the murders?" Madison tossed out. "It makes me want to see the Malones' financials more than ever."

Terry remained silent.

"I say our next stop is Malone's, the location where Craig manages," Madison suggested, looking over to see if her partner was even breathing. "Did you hear me?"

"I heard you," he mumbled. "If we're going to start poking around, though, we should update Winston."

"I'm not going to update him every step of the way."

"You told him you would."

"I always say that."

"I'll text him, then."

"Do what you have to do," she pushed out. "We need to find out where Craig went—*if* he went anywhere. We shouldn't just take Kimberly's word on the matter, and she did tell us she can't reach her brother. He still hasn't returned my call, either."

"If we're going to Malone's, we have to approach it with *discretion*." Terry put finger quotes around the last word and smiled.

She reached out and batted the air near him. "I thought you were seriously giving me a hard time about this."

"I thought I'd play it up." He was still smiling.

"Is that what you did in there?" She nudged her head toward the Rowe's Accounting building in front of them.

"Not really. Sometimes even I get tired of tiptoeing around."

"I'm starting to see that."

Terry did up his seat belt. "Just keep in mind, going into Malone's, that Craig might have been screwed up as a kid, but that doesn't mean the *man* is, and very few of us like our parents as teenagers. Craig's tune could have changed."

"It could have," she admitted. "Rowe said his father helped him to avoid juvie. That should have endeared his father to him."

"Yeah, I'm not seeing a motive yet. What's your plan of approach at the store?"

"We just tell them we need to tell Craig something. No need to go in guns blazing, even if that could be fun." She smiled diabolically.

"That could work, but I stand behind what I said a bit ago. We should update Winston."

"I thought you were 'playing it up.'"

"Yes and no. But he did say he wanted to be updated on every step of the investigation."

"Good for the man to want and not always get." She shrugged. "Something my mother used to say."

"Well, I'm not a fan."

"Of my mother?"

"The saying. It's usually always better to get."

She agreed, and she'd always hated it when her mother would say the phrase, but when it came to dishing it out in Winston's direction, it felt right.

"Here's the thing…" Terry shifted and sat up straighter. "We go to Malone's, and it's quite likely going to get back to Winston anyway. We know that Craig liked going to the gun range. Let's just visit the ones in the area—"

"And what? Hope we strike it lucky that they

know where Craig is?" She gestured out the windshield. "Do you see the weather? We can't afford to be spending our time driving around aimlessly. How do you think Winston would handle that update?" Then a thought struck. "You're concerned about keeping him up-to-date, but we didn't tell him we were visiting Rowe."

Terry winced. "I texted Winston."

"Ooh, Terry."

"Hey, I don't want to get the spray when crap hits the fan. I have too much going on to worry about job security. I have a family to provide for and—"

She looked out her window, trying to calm her temper. She hated it when he pulled out his family as an excuse for playing within the lines, but that was her partner, never wanting to cause waves. It was why Winston had told Terry to keep an eye on her.

"I'll take the heat if it comes to that," she assured him. "You have nothing to worry about."

She navigated the slippery streets cautiously, taking them in the direction of Malone's.

It took thirty minutes to reach the store, which in good weather would have taken less than fifteen. The parking lot had less than a dozen vehicles in it, and this location served as the company's main warehouse. The building had a large footprint and was easily fifty thousand square feet.

Inside, Madison was blinded by fluorescent lights and overwhelmed by the sales floor. There was furniture as far as the eye could see: living room sets, dining sets, bedroom sets, electronics. Oversized yellow tags hung from the ceiling advertising that specially tagged items were reduced by forty percent for three days only.

A white-haired man approached her and Terry as they made their way toward the customer counter that was wisely placed in the rear of the store. The trek presented temptation and encouraged impulse purchases. Even those coming in to pay against their credit account with Malone's risked becoming prey—again.

The salesman smiled at them, the expression lighting his eyes. "Good afternoon."

Afternoon? She glanced at her phone. *1:31 PM*. Wow, time did fly!

"Would Craig Malone be in?" She'd been thinking about the initial approach on the way over and figured it might be best to start from scratch, as if they knew nothing. Really, it wasn't far from the truth.

The salesman's face fell, no doubt seeing his commission taking a nosedive. "He's not—" He stopped talking when Madison flashed her badge. "Is something wrong?" The man looked at Terry, concern creeping into his voice.

"We just need to speak with him," Terry told

the man.

"Well, as I started to tell you, he's not in."

"Oh?" Madison packed the one syllable with as much surprise and disappointment as she could. "As my partner said, we just need to speak with him about something. Does he have an assistant we could talk to? Maybe they'd know how we could reach him?"

"Did you try his cell phone?" The salesman was leaning slightly forward, an indication he wanted to help as much as he could.

"We have," Madison admitted.

"Okay." The man turned and looked toward the customer service counter. "Follow me."

He took them to a blond twentysomething who was smacking gum. It seemed to disappear once the salesman told her who Madison and Terry were and that they were looking for Craig.

"Come with me." The blonde, Emily, as she'd introduced herself, led them to one of the offices positioned behind the counter. "Thanks, Frank." She closed her office door in the salesman's face and proceeded to sit behind her desk. "Please, sit." She pointed to two chairs facing her, and Madison and Terry both did as Emily had asked.

"What can I help you with exactly?" Emily ran the tip of a long, manicured fingernail across her bottom teeth, then dropped her hand. "Is Craig okay?"

"We don't know," Madison said.

Emily sat straighter and flung her long, straight hair over her shoulders. "Whatever I can do to help."

"We understand he went away," Madison began. "Do you know where?"

She shook her head. "He didn't tell me, not that I didn't ask." Emily blushed, and Madison had a gut feeling.

"Are you two…"

Emily met her gaze and nodded. "For a few months, but it's nothing serious."

Her words said one thing, her eyes another. They revealed she was hurt that Craig hadn't let her know where he was going. With the observation, Madison was stung with guilt. She was harboring a secret from Troy about Leland King and the investigation into corrupt cops. Did the fact she did so for his own safety make any difference?

Madison shook her personal thoughts aside and asked, "Did he have the trip planned a while in advance?"

"No, it was *sooo* last minute. All he told me was that he had to get away to clear his mind."

"When did he decide he was going away?" Terry inquired.

"This morning," Emily said. "He just called in and told me he was taking off for a week."

"He told you he wanted to clear his mind. Was he under a lot of stress?" Terry asked, holding Emily's attention.

"He was, but I'm not sure why." Her voice sounded strained. "There's nothing particularly stressful going on here these days. Everything is pretty much the same every day," she stated with a tinge of boredom.

"Any idea why he'd said he needed to clear his mind, then?" Madison pressed.

"None."

"Does he normally open up to you?" Terry asked.

She tucked a strand of hair behind an ear. "Our relationship is mostly sexual. We don't talk much."

"But your relationship is also professional," Madison began, "and you are his assistant."

"I am."

Terry leaned forward, shifted a desk calendar, and glanced at Madison. The logo at the top was for Bradshaw Gun & Country Club.

"How long is Craig gone for?" he asked.

"Just this week. He'll be back on Monday."

Emily pursed her lips.

Madison read the body language. "You're angry with him?"

"Heck yes." She crossed her arms, the motion tugging the buttons of her fitted blouse, but then she let her arms fall loose. "When I saw you two, and you wanted to talk to him, I was afraid that you...that you found a body or something and thought it was his." She paled. "Especially with his sister Kimberly calling and looking for him, too."

"We're just trying to reach him with news," Madison said.

Emily scooped a pen from her desk and leaned forward, poised over a notepad. "I can pass on a message to him, have him call you."

Madison stiffened. "You're able to reach him?"

"I haven't tried to since he left, but I assume…" Emily's gaze drifted between the two of them. "You tried reaching him on his phone?"

"We did." Madison pulled out her phone and opened her call history. "Can you just tell me what the number is again, and I'll double check I have the right one?"

"Sure." Emily rattled off the number.

"Yeah, that's the one I have, and I've already left a message for him."

"I can leave one, too, if you'd like."

"You can. If you reach him, have him call Detective Madison Knight." She gave Emily her card. Then she and Terry thanked Emily for her help and left the store.

"Guess we know where our next step takes us," Madison said.

"Bradshaw Gun & Country Club?"

"Direct hit."

Eleven

It was nearing two thirty when Madison pulled the department car into the lot for Craig's gun range—or at least they assumed it was the one he frequented, given the desk calendar. Regardless, it was a potential lead to Craig's whereabouts they couldn't ignore.

"Steven Malone says Craig destresses at the firing range, so what had him so stressed out that he had to get away?" Madison parked, cut the ignition, and looked at Terry.

"Your guess is as good as mine. Maybe shooting wasn't enough to calm him this time?"

"Was it knowledge of his mother's affair eating away at him?"

He gave her a warning look. "Let's keep an open mind."

"Or maybe it was the planning and carrying out of the murders," she persisted.

Terry got out of the car and slammed his door. She followed him, with a smile, into Bradshaw Gun & Country Club.

Guns in glass cases and racks of T-shirts, camouflage clothing, bulletproof vests, and ball caps filled the storefront. There was even a display of bumper stickers and magnets.

A man with a straggly beard, the color of crème brûlée and resembling a frayed scouring pad, stood behind a long counter that had been heavily varnished. Adding to the ZZ Top look he had going on, he wore a patterned handkerchief under a cowboy hat. He was stocking a shelf with boxes of ammunition.

"Can I help you?" He touched the tip of his hat in a friendly gesture, but his arm dropped at the sight of their badges. He turned his attention back to stocking the shelves. "What are you here for?" ZZ Top mumbled.

Madison would have expected a better reception than this. After all, many police officers held memberships at gun clubs to keep up their firing skills, but if this level of service was the norm here, no wonder the officers she knew of went to Stiles Gun Club.

"We have some questions about Craig Malone." Madison grounded her stance, legs shoulder width apart, hands lightly clasped in front.

The man put down a box he'd been holding and faced them. "What's to say he's even a member?"

"You obviously know who he is," Madison concluded from his response.

"So what if I do?"

"We need to find him."

"Well, good for you." Spoken as if it wasn't his problem, but little did he know that she wouldn't be going anywhere until she got some information.

"We know that he's a customer of yours." She might have been stretching the truth by a skosh.

"Why do you want to find him?" ZZ Top asked, leery.

"That's between us and him, but maybe he has some friends around here," Madison laid out in a casual manner.

ZZ Top bent over and leaned on the counter with both arms. "You're looking at one of them, but why should I talk to you about him?"

"We need to reach him with some news. The sooner we can do that, the better."

"Something happen?"

Madison and Terry remained silent. Eventually ZZ Top would learn they were there to ask questions, not answer any.

"Fine." ZZ Top straightened up. "I can pass on a message."

"We're not at liberty to leave a message with you for him," Madison said.

"Too bad then." ZZ Top lifted the box of ammunition and started to turn, but a door in the back of the store opened.

A man in his late thirties came through, wearing goggles and orange soundproof earmuffs. The sign on the wall next to the door read MUST WEAR GOGGLES AND SOUND PROTECTION FROM THIS POINT. This was no doubt the entrance for the indoor firing range.

The man looked at Madison and Terry and removed his muffs and goggles. "Chuck, I need some more ammo."

"You got it." ZZ Top, a.k.a. Chuck, snatched a box of .22-caliber bullets and handed it over to the man. "You're burning through the bullets today, man."

The customer laughed. "Add it to my tab? I'll pay before I leave."

"Consider it done."

The man put his goggles in place and lifted his earmuffs.

"You sure there's nothing you can do to help us find Craig?" Madison rushed out, her question intended to get the customer's attention.

"Sorry?" The customer lowered his earmuffs around his neck and put his goggles in a pocket. "Did you just say 'Craig'?"

"I did." Madison feigned innocence and glanced at ZZ Top, who glared at her. She fought off a smirk and addressed the customer. "You know him?"

"If you're talking about Craig Malone, yeah, I know him." The guy walked toward Madison and Terry. "Quite well, in fact."

"We're looking for him. I'm Madison Knight, and this is Terry Grant," she said, presenting herself and Terry as friends, not as cops on a mission.

He held out his hand to Terry, then Madison. "Joel Phelps."

Any relation to Dustin Phelps, the man I have Leland investigating?

"You're both cops." The man smiled knowingly.

"Detectives," Terry corrected. "What gave us away?"

The man angled his head. "The biggest tipoff is the holstered standard-issue Glocks, but I also have family in the department."

"Stiles PD?" Madison asked, her throat tightening.

"Yeah. My dad's retired now, but my younger brother's still in. He's mostly patrol, but he's worked in evidence lockup, too. You might know him. Dustin Phelps?"

"I know him," Terry spoke up, and both he and Joel looked at her.

"Me too." She tried to smile but wasn't sure it fully formed. She cleared her throat and asked, "Are you and Craig close friends?"

ZZ Top eyed her before returning to his stocking of shelves.

"We go back to public school." Joel ran a hand through his hair. "Why are you trying to reach him?"

"We're not at liberty to tell you that, but do you know where he might be?" she asked.

"Sure do, and there's no way you're getting through to him on his cell. I assume you've tried that."

Madison nodded.

"He's up north at a buddy's cabin. No cell towers there, no power, and no running water. It's peaceful as hell."

It sounded like *hell.* Room service and a massage—that was peaceful.

Joel was grinning. "He's a lucky bastard. I wish I could have gone with him."

"Where's the cabin?" she asked.

"Alaska."

"Alaska?" Madison croaked. Why would anyone choose to go to Alaska in the dead of winter? Sure, it was said that being in nature brought people closer to themselves and God, but there had to be easier, more civilized options.

"Yeah. Some remote village." Joel laughed. "I take it that doesn't sound like your sort of vacation."

"Not at all," she confessed. "And backwoods in Alaska isn't somewhere you think of as being a last-minute destination." Or one a person would actually choose.

"So you came here knowing he was away."

Busted.

"Yes, we knew that much," she admitted.

"Well, Craig's not your typical guy, and he's prone to making rash decisions, but that's what you get when you're untethered, I suppose." Joel twisted the wedding band on his finger and noticed Madison watching. He held up his hand and wriggled his fingers. "The wife's part of the reason I couldn't go with him."

She bit back her temper. "How's it her fault?"

Joel tucked his left hand into a pocket. "It's always about money, and I had to work."

Yet here he was at a gun range on a Tuesday afternoon. "You don't hold typical office hours."

"I don't work in an office. I'm a freelance writer."

"You could write in Alaska."

"No power for charging a laptop," Joel stressed. "Besides, I've got an important interview coming up this week, and I'd prefer to make that one in person."

"You said he went to a buddy's cabin," Terry redirected the conversation. "Did this buddy go up there with Craig?"

"Yes. Usually a group of us go, but this time it's just Craig and David Reade, who owns the cabin. I can get you Molly's number...that's David's wife."

"That would be good," Madison said. "Does David have a sat phone?"

Joel gave her Molly's number, then said, "To answer your question, David's got a sat phone, but it's not going to do you any good. It doesn't take messages, and David doesn't leave it on. He just turns it on to call Molly. That's why if you reach Molly, tell her what you need, she can pass it along to David when he calls."

"Molly doesn't go to the cabin?" Madison asked.

"Heck no. She's got zero interest."

The woman has good taste.

"Besides, they might be each other's soulmates, but they still need time apart," Joel added.

"Whose idea was it to go this time around— David's or Craig's?" Madison wanted to get a handle on the reason for the last-minute urge to vacate Stiles.

"Oh, David's been planning it for a few weeks now, and the invite was out there to us guys, but Craig just decided to go this morning."

"All right, thanks for your help." Madison took a step toward the door, as did Terry.

"Don't mention it. Anything for a friend." Joel pulled his goggles from his pocket and pulled up his earmuffs.

Madison left the gun range walking tall. They had a fresh lead for tracking down Craig.

Twelve

Madison and Terry returned to the station, knowing they had some phone calls to make and background reports to pull. Terry was starting on the latter while Madison reached out to Molly Reade. She'd had to leave a message and was now on the phone with Marnie Simpleton from Wellness Yoga.

"Does Kimberly Olson-Malone and her mother take yoga classes at your studio?" Madison asked.

"They do." Marnie's answer was succinct and soft-spoken, just like the rest of her responses thus far. At this rate, it might take the rest of the afternoon for Madison to draw out what she needed.

"Do they attend any specific ones with regularity?"

"Tuesdays and Thursdays at seven thirty."

"And they've been in a habit of doing these for a while now?"

"Years."

"You're sure?" Madison wanted to see if she could stir up some life in the yoga lady. Surely, she wasn't this zen all the time.

"I pride myself on knowing my clients." Still no indication of excitement.

"So you know them well?"

There was a brief silence on the other end of the line, followed by, "You could say that."

"Personally, or strictly in a professional manner?" If Marnie and the Malones were friends, it could affect the validity of her testimony.

"We are all connected."

Oy vey. "Do you know if they carpooled to the classes?"

"I don't, sorry." The apology felt obligatory. Finally, there was a little crack in her calm energy. "Will that be all?"

"For now." With that and a rather insincere thanks, Madison hung up. She placed the handset on the cradle. As she made some handwritten notes in a file, it occurred to her that Marnie hadn't asked once what had prompted the call or given her some speech about customer privacy. It could have just been Marnie was more forthcoming than most people, but it was possible she had been tipped off by Kimberly that someone from the Stiles PD would be calling. If that were the case, Madison wasn't feeling too warm toward the eldest Malone child.

She finished her notes and looked over at Terry. "How are you coming with the backgrounds?"

"I've pulled and printed ones for the Malone family."

"I'll get started on the Malones' help. You want to get one for the best friend?"

"Sure."

Madison went about getting her share of the reports and thought about pulling one on Joel Phelps while she was at it. But without real cause, she wasn't going to risk drawing any attention to herself.

She finished printing the reports and updated Terry on her call. "So I spoke to Marnie Simpleton at the yoga studio, and she confirmed what Kimberly had said about her and her mother going on Tuesdays and Thursdays. She wasn't able to say if they carpooled."

"I can understand a Simpleton not knowing," Terry deadpanned, then his mouth twitched and blossomed into a smile. "You get it?"

"Yes, Terry." She shook her head at her partner's somewhat skewed sense of humor.

He snickered, still amused at his own joke.

"I had to leave a message with David Reade's wife to call me back." Her stomach growled loudly.

"Next stop lunch?"

She dismissed the idea—and her gnawing

hunger—with a wave. "I was thinking Lorene's best friend. She might be able to tell us who John Doe is."

"If we're going there, may I suggest we don't run with the assumption Lorene was having an affair?"

Madison understood Terry's concern. Attack the reputation of the woman's dead friend, and she might not be too open to talking, but Darbonne might know John Doe's identity. That was assuming Lorene had confided in her. "We'll see how things unfold."

"Why doesn't that reassure me?"

She narrowed her eyes. "I'm not dismissing the possibility of an affair, but I'm keeping an open mind."

"Impressive."

She tossed out one of his lines, "Hardy-har."

"Hey, you two look real busy." Troy was walking toward them, and Madison felt herself coming alive at the sight of him. She wanted to get up and greet him the proper way—with a huge hug and a hungry kiss.

"More than I can say for you," she teased, somehow managing to keep her butt in the chair.

"I'm allowed some breaks."

"Uh-huh. It seems to me you're just wandering around today." There were many days their paths didn't cross at work at all. She would consider this a good day, from that perspective at least.

"You get breaks?" Terry asked incredulously. "We must be doing something wrong, Knight."

Troy positioned himself next to Madison's desk, and the faint smell of his cologne hit her nose in the most pleasing way. She inhaled deeply.

"What do you have on the go?" Troy asked her.

"A double homicide," Madison answered.

"Wow. Really?"

"I kid you not," she said, "and it's a high-profile case, too."

Terry left with his mug in hand, headed toward the coffee machine in the bullpen.

"Guess that answers my next question," Troy said.

"Which was?"

"If you'd be interested in seeing a house tonight. Estelle called, and she was ready to arrange a showing."

Estelle Robins was their real estate agent.

"Yeah, tonight's not going to work."

"I can appreciate that. A double homicide? Who were they?"

"Well, have you heard of Malone's, the chain of furniture stores?"

Troy put his hands in his pockets. "I have."

"Lorene Malone and—"

Troy stepped back, almost stumbling, and stared through her. "Steven?"

"No, a John Doe." She cocked her head, studying him. "Do you know the Malones personally?"

He cleared his throat. "I'm...uh, I should probably go."

He turned to leave, and she jumped to her feet and hooked his elbow.

"Troy, what's going on?"

The way he looked at her chilled her to the core.

"It's nothing." His eyes glazed over. "We'll talk later." He set off, waving an arm over his head.

What the—?

"All good in lovers' paradise?" Terry's voice cut abruptly through her thoughts as he returned and held his filled mug toward Troy's retreating form.

"I don't know." She watched Troy until he was out of view. What did the Malone family mean to him, and why had he refused to let her know? Lorene's death was obviously personal to him, and she'd wanted to push him, but when Troy put up his walls, it was best to let him be for a while—not that she had to be happy about it. She snatched her coat off her chair and turned to Terry. "You ready?"

"I—" Terry's gaze dropped to his coffee.

She raised her brows.

"Okay," he said. "Where to?"

"Sabrina Darbonne's."

Terry put his mug down and slipped into his

coat. "Can we grab a bite first?"

"Maybe, if it's something quick." The interaction with Troy had made her appetite disappear. The last time Troy had lost someone he'd cared about, he'd shut her out, and it seemed he was doing the same thing again.

"I DON'T THINK THERE'S ONE thing on this menu that isn't deep-fried or slathered in grease." Madison set the menu down, frustrated. It's not like she was a health nut. She loved her chocolate, and dieting was the devil, but she tried to make wise food choices when she could. She liked to tell herself it had to do with being more fit for the job, but she didn't think sleeping with a hot guy from SWAT hurt her motivation.

She and Terry had requested a table in the corner of the restaurant so they'd have some privacy to discuss the case.

"Is that a complaint or a compliment? It's hard to tell." Terry laughed. His hands were clasped on top of his closed menu.

"A complaint."

"Coming from a woman who eats chocolate for breakfast."

"Very funny." It was predictable that he would call her out on the chocolate.

The waitress stood at the end of their table, a pen poised over her order pad, and looked at Terry. "Have you decided?"

"I'll take the Greek salad with a grilled

chicken breast." Terry handed the waitress his menu.

How had she missed that option? Was she wired to only see comfort food?

"And you?" the waitress asked Madison.

"The same, with a soda."

"Water for me," Terry said.

"I'll put your orders in and grab your drinks." She smiled and off she went.

"You just had to show me up with the water," Madison jabbed.

"I didn't realize this was a competition of some sort, but do you realize how much sugar is in a soda?"

"I have a feeling you're about to tell me." She sank into the booth. Unlike her, Terry *was* a bit of a health nut. He actually *chose* to run—an activity she detested—and he did so every morning before shift.

"Thirty-three grams. That's thirteen grams more than women should have in a day and almost the limit of what a man should have." Terry served these facts with the pride of a walking Wikipedia.

"Fascinating." She rolled her eyes.

"It's never too late to start taking care of yourself."

"Hey," she said, ready to go down his throat and out his ass, but he was smiling, "it's a good thing I like you." She turned her gaze out the window. The snow was still falling heavily, but she put her attention on the passing traffic and pedestrians. People on the sidewalks were hustling, no doubt in a hurry to arrive at their destinations and find warmth inside. One man reminded her of John Doe, and she faced her partner. "When I said we could stop for a quick lunch, I figured it would be something that came in a paper bag through a window. Not sure how you talked me into actually stopping."

"It gives us some time to actually chew our food, you know—a novel concept." There was the hint of burnout to his voice and a flicker in his eyes. Madison suspected the cause was whatever was going on in his personal life.

She was about to ask him what was going on, but he continued. "I know we've really been considering the affair angle, and that could still be a factor, but maybe Doe was the true target. Taking his ID would hold up the investigation. We can't look into the life of a man we don't know."

The waitress returned with their drinks and a pleasant smile, then sauntered off to help other customers.

Madison leaned across the table. "If John Doe was the true target, why strike at the Malones' house? Lorene Malone had to be a target, too. I think we need to bench motive for now and focus on who had means and opportunity."

Terry pulled out his notepad and pen. "We know that Kimberly had access to her parents' house, and it's likely the other two Malone children did as well: opportunity." He scribbled their names down, but Madison could barely make them out, given his cryptic handwriting.

"The maid and the cook," she added, refusing to be the one who said Steven Malone. "Oh, and what about the best friend? She could have a key."

Terry wrote down Sabrina Darbonne's name along with the helps'. "We also need to keep in mind that the killer might not have a key and a security code. They just need to be someone that Lorene would have opened the door for."

"That, or she was coerced to let them in," Madison said. "We know the killer was obviously armed." The feeling of defeat and being overwhelmed rolled over her, the way it often did at the onset of an investigation. Usually there were so many suspects to wade through and so little time. "Let's start with a focus on people who have keys and a passcode to the Malones' house."

"Then it would seem Lorene was the true target."

Madison nodded. "We stick with that for now."

"Then Steven's going on the list." Terry added the husband's name to his notes.

She was satisfied he hadn't made her say his name. "Now, who had the means?"

"We don't have the make and model of the

gun yet. We do know .357-caliber bullets inflicted the damage."

"We know that Craig should have a gun in his possession that fires that type of bullet."

"A .357 S&W that is technically Mr. Malone's." Terry wrote *Means?* beside Craig's and Steven's names.

"What I would give to get our hands on that gun, even if it's to rule it out," she lamented. She pulled out her phone and glanced at a screen free of call and message notifications. It felt like she'd fallen into the twilight zone.

"Here you go," the waitress said. She set salads in front of each of them. "Is there anything else I can get you?"

Madison looked over her meal and inhaled. The aromas coming from the dish were heavenly, and there certainly wasn't a shortage of toppings: freshly cut onions, tomatoes, peppers, feta, and black olives. A sliced chicken breast sat on top, sprinkled with seasonings. The dressing was in a ramekin on the side of the plate. "I'm good," she told the waitress—*and salivating.*

"Me too," Terry said.

"All right, then. I'll leave you to it."

Terry sprinkled pepper on his salad and poured his dressing methodically to make sure he distributed it evenly. She dumped the dressing on hers and stabbed her first forkful.

Chewing, she looked out the window, at

the falling snow and the crawling traffic. She watched as a woman stepped off the sidewalk onto the road, a cell phone to an ear.

Madison chomped on another mouthful of salad, not taking her eyes off the woman.

Traffic to her right side was three lanes wide. Two straight-through and one for left turns only. A van was at a standstill in the left-turn lane, and there was an SUV in the middle.

Madison's blood cooled when she saw a car steadily approaching the intersection. It didn't look like it was going to stop.

She bolted to her feet. "He's moving way too fast."

Thirteen

Real life is far more horrific than television, but as Madison watched the car strike the woman, and her body roll up the hood before it was tossed like a ragdoll a few feet into the intersection, it all played out as fiction in slow motion.

Madison ran toward the woman, who was more girl than woman and couldn't have been more than twenty-five.

The girl said, "I've just been hit by a car," into her phone that was still pressed to her ear.

Madison glanced over her shoulder, blinking snowflakes from her eyelashes, and saw Terry on his phone, likely calling in the accident.

She hunched beside the girl. "Don't move, okay?" Madison was calm, adrenaline blanketing her with a sense of serenity. "Help is coming."

"Who? What?" The girl's eyes rolled back in her head, her eyelids fluttering. Her hand fell limp, and the phone fell free of her grasp and settled on the snow-covered asphalt.

"Just stay with me," Madison told her. "What's your name?"

"Bec—" Her eyes closed, and her head lolled to the side.

Madison took the girl's wrist and felt for a pulse. It was weak at best.

The wails of ambulance sirens grew louder.

"Come on, stay with me," Madison encouraged, her gaze drifting to the phone. What was wrong with society when people were so glued to their phones and electronic devices that they were oblivious to their surroundings? Texting while driving was dangerous, but apparently so was talking on the phone while walking.

Madison could faintly hear someone's voice coming through the phone. She took a deep breath and picked it up.

"Becca?" The woman on the other end was frantic.

"This is Detective Knight of Stiles PD."

"Where's Becca? Is she," she gasped, "all right?"

"There's been an accident," Madison told her.

"She said she was...hit by a car? Is she okay? Tell me what happened. Please."

Madison could only imagine how traumatic this situation would be for Becca's friend, but Madison told her someone would be in touch with an update and ended the call.

An ambulance parked in the middle of the intersection near Madison and the victim. People were gathering in clusters, and their numbers were growing. Civilian vehicles were at a standstill, some at odd angles, possibly having slid on the slick roads when the drivers had applied their brakes. The vehicle that struck the girl had come to stop just past the crosswalk lines.

Terry was talking to the driver, but Madison couldn't make out the face from her vantage point between the heavily falling snow and shadows cast across the windshield. She got up to join Terry, prepared to give the driver a piece of her mind. He'd been driving far too fast for the conditions. And hadn't he seen the girl crossing the street?

Madison was almost to the vehicle when a couple of cruisers pulled up. A few officers got out to control the crowds, but one was coming straight toward her. Dustin Phelps. She went cold.

"Detective Knight," Phelps said, "surprised to see you here."

Her body stiffened. "I was in the area."

"Let me guess. You were eating lunch and ran straight out here?"

"How did—"

"No coat helped. You leave it in the diner?" He butted his head toward the restaurant.

She looked down at herself and rubbed her

arms, suddenly aware of the crisp winter air.

"Did you see the whole thing go down?" Phelps stared through her—or at least it felt like he did. There was something threatening in his gaze, though it was possible that was all in her head. He'd have no way of knowing she had someone looking into him, would he? "I'd like to take your statement after I speak with the driver," he added.

"Sure, but I—"

"Thanks," Phelps cut her off before she could tell him she hadn't seen everything and left to speak with the driver.

She stood paralyzed and insulted that he'd interrupted her.

"Madison," a man cried out.

Chills snaked down her back at recognition of the voice.

Jim? She looked around for her brother-in-law until she finally caught sight of him behind the wheel of the vehicle that had struck the girl.

Strength drained from Madison's legs. This was a bad dream, not real life. Surely if it was Jim, she'd have recognized the car right off. Then again, it wasn't the only one on the roads. She ran toward Jim.

"Thank God you're here," Jim exclaimed, panic crackling in his voice.

Phelps and Terry stepped back to give Madison room to approach the driver's window.

"I'll do whatever I can to help." She felt like

a hypocrite when just a second ago she was going to lay all the blame for the accident on the driver's shoulders, but with Jim being the driver, that changed things. Maybe she hadn't seen the accident go down the way she thought she had. There had to be an explanation.

She glanced at the girl, who was now sitting up and being tended to by paramedics. When Madison turned around, her eyes met Phelps's briefly. She couldn't dare ask her brother-in-law what had happened with him standing around. Phelps had assumed she'd seen everything, and she hadn't denied it—not that she was given the chance.

"I tried to stop," Jim rushed out. "I stood on the damn brakes." His eyes were full of tears. "She came out of nowhere." His chest heaved for breath. "I had a green light. I swear to you. I know I did."

Madison reached inside the window and squeezed his shoulder. "We'll get this sorted out," she assured with more confidence than she felt, given Phelps's presence. If he was the corrupt cop she suspected he was and had something against her, he might try to manipulate the situation to really hurt Jim.

"Detective, if you could step back," Phelps said, though it was more a directive than a question. "I need to take his statement."

She turned to face him but didn't move out of the way. Phelps's gaze carried the clear message that he indeed had a beef against her.

"Madison," Terry prompted, "let Phelps in there."

She looked from her partner back to Phelps, then glanced at Jim. She should have pretended not to know him.

Terry pulled back on her shoulder, urging her to hand the situation over to Phelps, but there was no way she could do that. Terry didn't know that Phelps was for sale to the highest bidder.

"The girl was crossing against the light," Jim pleaded. "I saw her on her phone, distracted."

"So you're blaming her for getting hit?" Phelps asked incredulously.

Madison spun and squared her posture. As much as she wanted to punch Phelps in the face, she didn't dare lay one hand on him. She had to keep her mind on the bigger picture: ridding the Stiles PD of corrupt cops—and her plan would fall apart if she became emotionally unhinged.

"Officer, a word?" Madison hissed.

"I'll be with you in a minute, sir," Phelps told Jim.

Madison and Phelps stepped away from the window and out of earshot of Jim. They both peacocked their postures.

"You have an issue with me. Fine," Madison seethed. "But don't take it out on him."

"Really? Who says I have an issue with you?" He smiled, but the glint in his eyes had her stomach clenching.

He walked back to Jim, and guilt moved in on her like a summer thunderstorm—quickly and damaging.

"Sir, I'm going to need you to get out of the car," Phelps directed Jim.

Madison took a few steps forward, ready to intervene. Terry pulled her back and stared her down.

"Is there something going on with you two?" Terry asked.

Bile shot up into her mouth, and she swallowed, unwilling to say a word. Terry was watching her, attempting to draw her out, but she thought it best not to say a thing. The less people she caught up in that web, the better.

She looked on as Phelps essentially interrogated Jim and peppered him with questions.

"Have you been drinking?"

"Were you on your phone at the time of the accident?"

"Were you speeding?"

Watching this play out was making her sick, and she turned and scanned the ever-growing crowd. A person was intelligent and rational, but a crowd wasn't. Even if Jim was right and he'd had the green light, what if Phelps managed to twist an eyewitness's testimony and effectively destroy her brother-in-law's life, and by extension, her sister's and her nieces' lives?

There could be one saving grace, and Madison

looked around fervently for any sign of a traffic cam. She came up empty.

Phelps was having Jim breathe into a breathalyzer.

God, she hoped her brother-in-law hadn't had a thing to drink. She looked down at her bare hands. They were shaking.

Phelps consulted the device and tucked it away in a pocket. "You're sure you weren't on your phone at the time of the accident?"

Madison felt herself go cold. Phelps had just asked that a few minutes ago. It would seem he'd latched onto something.

"I wasn't." Jim shook his head.

"Then why is your phone on the passenger seat?" Phelps pointed inside the car.

"I—" Jim followed the direction of Phelps's finger. "I always set it there. It's too bulky in the pocket of my pants."

"Huh. Why not put it in a coat pocket?"

Madison lunged toward Phelps. "He answered your question," she said through clenched teeth.

They were within inches of each other, and Phelps didn't pull back. His height made it so she had to look up at him. "I'm going to have to bring him in for further questioning," he said.

"You're being unreasonable." Madison hated the sound of desperation that seeped into her voice.

"The law is the law." Phelps let his statement hang there for a few seconds, then added, "Until we've gathered eyewitness testimony and know for sure what exactly transpired here—"

"You know where he lives if you need to talk to him later."

"I am well within my rights to take him downtown."

Behind Phelps, Jim was beseeching her with his eyes.

"They were all stopped," she rushed out. "The other vehicles on the road."

"I'm not sure how that helps your brother-in-law's case."

"The light had just changed," she said, grasping, lying. Her heart was beating in her ears, her mind blank except for the stopped van and SUV, the girl crossing the road, and the approaching car.

"Did you see that he had a green light?"

Her insides were jelly, and she glanced at Jim. What if Jim hadn't had the green light? Why couldn't she have been watching the lights instead of being spellbound by the imminent accident?

"I'll take your silence as a no." There was a subtle, resting smirk on Phelps's lips, and Jim was shaking his head.

"You'll be fine, Jim," Madison said. "I'll make sure of it."

"Come on, let's go." Phelps directed Jim to his cruiser.

Jim glanced over a shoulder at her, fear

etched on his face. "Call Chelsea, tell her what's happened."

"I will," Madison said through clenched teeth. If Phelps wanted a war, he'd get one.

"Maddy," Terry's voice reached her from a faraway place.

She looked at him but said nothing.

"You're shivering. Let's get your coat."

Madison didn't move. "The girl was distracted, Terry. She was on her phone, crossing the street. If Jim said he had a green light, I believe him."

"Then it will be fine."

"You don't believe him," she accused, teeth chattering.

"How did you get that from what I just said?" Terry responded defensively. "I get it. Jim's family, and you wouldn't trust anyone but yourself right now, but traffic's not your job. Besides, the truth will come out. It always does. Statements will be taken from eyewitnesses."

"People can't be trusted, and when emotions come into play..." Her heart squeezed in her chest as if it were being compressed in a vise. "I've got to call Chels." She rushed to the restaurant and beat Terry inside. She stomped her boots and brushed the snow off herself on the move. She grabbed her coat and took off toward the restroom. She could call Chelsea in front of Terry, but she also wanted to reach out to Leland.

"Madison, what are you doing?" Terry's

question brought her to a halt.

She gestured a thumb toward the restroom. "I've just gotta—"

"Maddy?"

She spun. "Yeah." Irritated.

"Give me the car keys, and I'll clean off the car and get it warming up after I pay for our lunches."

"You sure?"

Terry nodded. "Just remember this moment if you're ever inclined to say I don't do anything for you."

"It might be cheaper to give you some money now."

"Go before I change my mind." He held out his hand. "Keys."

She tossed them to Terry and carried on. Inside the restroom, she locked the door and pulled out the burner phone first.

One ring. Two rings. Three—

A few seconds' silence followed by, "Hello?"

"He just as good as arrested my brother-in-law," she rushed out. Leland would know she was talking about Phelps. "Do we have a problem I should know about?"

"I don't think so." Leland wasn't oozing confidence, and she felt like collapsing onto the floor.

"Please. Is there *any* way he could have found out we're looking into him?"

"I really don't see how."

Madison pinched the bridge of her nose. "Just think. Please tell me. I'd rather know so I can deal with it."

"I don't know how he'd have found out." Leland was starting to sound aggravated. "You said he arrested your brother-in-law?"

She didn't want to get into all of it right now, but she wasn't feeling reassured by Leland. "You're sure?"

"I'd stake our lives on it." There was a lightness to his voice.

"Not in the mood," she retorted.

"Wow."

"I'm sorry. I didn't mean to..."

She pictured Jim in an orange jumper and her sister blaming her—and she'd be right. Phelps would do whatever he could to nail Jim just because he was Madison's family. There was no other explanation for his dragging Jim downtown other than an underlying vendetta against Madison. Good cops had other cops' backs, and they didn't cart their family members into the station.

"Do you want me to lie super low for a while, maybe stop—"

"No. Stick to the plan." She didn't trust that Leland would let the matter go even if she told him to, and it was another reason she'd chosen him. There'd be no backing out.

"In that case, I already have a bit of an update. I paid a visit to the private school where his kids go. There's no way anyone's affording that place on a cop's salary."

"Like I thought. Keep following the money, but I've gotta go." Terry would be starting to wonder if she'd fallen in.

"Before you go," Leland said, catching her just before she ended the call, "if it makes you feel better, he doesn't need to know about our little investigation to hate you. He probably blames you for driving you-know-who, and his payday along with it, out of town. I'm just getting started, but the guy's got to have some sizable financial obligations."

Why didn't that make her feel all warm and fuzzy? "Thanks." With that, Madison ended the call. She swapped phones and had a finger over Chelsea's name when her phone started ringing.

The caller ID wasn't one she recognized, but she answered.

"Hello? This…Craig…lone." The connection was breaking up. "I was…to…you."

Molly Reade must have just relayed her message without calling Madison back. "Sadly, I have bad news about your mother." Madison sank against a wall of the restroom, hating to deliver the news she had over the phone. "She was found dead this—"

"*What?*" Craig exclaimed.

"I'm so very sorry for your loss," Madison offered. "Do you think you could return to Stiles?"

"I'll be on the…available flight out…rent a… if I have to." With that, Craig hung up.

The doorknob on the restroom door jostled, followed by a rap on the door. "Someone in there?" an older woman called out.

"Yeah, just give me a second." Madison made use of the facilities and left. She still had to call Chelsea.

She found Terry outside, the department car running and him finishing up brushing off the snow. He paused when he saw her, and his eyes bugged out as if to ask what had taken her so long, though not daring to verbalize the inquiry.

"Did you reach your sister?" he asked.

"Not yet." She paused at the surprise evident on his face. "But Craig Malone called. He's coming home." Her phone chimed notification of a message. She read it and shared the gist with Terry. "Richards is conducting the autopsy in an hour. When it rains, it pours."

Fourteen

Madison debated letting Terry attend the autopsies solo while she dropped by her sister's house, but with the worsening driving conditions, the round trip would take longer than she'd like. "I'll touch base with my sister, then we'll go to the morgue. We'll get there when we get there." Typically, Richards was a stickler for starting on time, but hopefully he'd find himself a little more lenient given the last-minute nature of this situation. "Can you text Richards and let him know we might be longer than an hour?"

"I can." Terry proceeded to pull out his phone, while she called her sister through hands-free.

"Madison?" Chelsea sounded as if she was bracing for bad news.

Madison's back stiffened. "Are you home?"

"On the way. Just got the girls from school. What's going on?" Dread filled her sister's voice, but Chelsea operated on a fine trigger since her kidnapping. Madison had referred her sister to her shrink, and it seemed to be helping her, but there was still a long road to recovery. "Is everything all right?"

"Everything will be fine."

"Now, I'm worried."

"Just trust me." Madison wondered if she'd be able to do so if the roles were reversed. "Just drive carefully, and I'll see you soon." Madison hung up, hating to think of her sister behind the wheel right now. The accident played out in Madison's mind in vivid recall. The woman being scooped up onto the hood and then being tossed off, her fluttering eyelids, her eyes rolling back, her blacking out.

Madison took what was technically the fastest route to Chelsea's house, but with the hazardous roads, the going was painfully slow. It was a wall of white outside the windshield, and she didn't dare go much faster than fifteen miles per hour. As it was, she had barely squeezed the brakes at a stop sign and they slid about four feet into the intersection. Tension was knotting in the back of her neck and across her shoulders. If the driving wasn't enough, the situation with Jim made it worse, as did Troy's reaction to Lorene's murder.

The sign for her sister's street came into view, and Madison let out a deep breath. Chelsea's Ford Fusion wasn't in the driveway, though, and no tire tracks led into the garage. She should have been home by now. Apprehension tightened in her chest.

"I'm sure she's fine," Terry told her, as if reading her mind.

She parked at the curb in front of Chelsea's house, pulled down the overhead visor, and opened the mirror to see behind them. Headlights reflected at her. They were at the right height and the right shape for her sister's vehicle. Chelsea's garage door opened, and Chelsea pulled inside. The door closed behind her.

Madison was out of the department car and halfway up the walk when the front door opened.

Chelsea was standing there in her winter coat and boots and stepped to the side to let Madison and Terry enter. Chelsea didn't take her eyes from Madison, even when she went around Madison to close the door.

"What's going on?" Chelsea blurted out.

"Auntie Madison?" Brie, Madison's youngest niece who was four, came running over to her with a backpack that was larger than her body. She dropped the bag onto the entry tile.

"Hey, sweetie." Madison got onto her haunches to accept the incoming hug and squeezed her niece.

"Honey—" Chelsea ran a hand over her daughter's head "—go get a snack in the kitchen with your sisters."

Lacey and Marissa came to the front.

"Is everything okay, Mom?" Marissa, the eldest, asked. She was ten going on sixteen. She looked out for her mother like a protector, but Madison couldn't blame her. Especially after Chelsea's brush with a Mafia hit man.

"Just take your sisters to the kitchen," Chelsea said, "and get them a snack."

Marissa didn't move and neither did Lacey.

"Go." Chelsea flicked her hand toward the kitchen, and this time, the girls left. With them gone, she fixed her focus on Madison. "What's happened? Don't make me ask again."

Madison put a hand on her sister's shoulder. "Take your coat and boots off, and let's go talk in the office."

Chelsea's eyes beaded with tears. "You're scaring me."

"I told you, everything will be fine."

Chelsea nodded, took a deep breath, and did as Madison had directed. Madison and Terry wiped their boots on the front mat and followed Chelsea into the home office on the second floor.

Chelsea closed the door behind them and stared at Madison, waiting for her to speak.

"There was an accident—"

Chelsea dropped into a sofa chair in the corner of the room. "The look on your face is making me sick."

Madison held out a reassuring hand. "Jim's fine, but he struck a woman with his car."

"Omigod." Chelsea's lips quivered, and she snapped a hand over her mouth. "Is…is she okay? My god, Jim must be—" Her eyes locked with Madison's. "Is he being charged?"

Madison's eyes filled with tears. "It will all get worked out. Jim said he had a green light, that she came out of nowhere. Eyewitness testimony will be gathered, and I'm sure other people will back him up." She wished she could offer more assurance.

"Is he being charged?" Chelsea repeated and got to her feet.

"He's been taken down to the station for questioning."

Chelsea swiped tears from her cheeks. "What's going to happen?"

"Jim's statement will be taken. What he says will be compared to eyewitness testimony."

"What if…" Chelsea pinched her eyes, and fresh tears squeezed out and fell down her cheeks. "No, I don't even want to go down that path." She dropped back into the chair. "You said everything will be fine, but you don't know that."

"I'll do whatever I can to ensure that it is," Madison declared, meaning every word. "I was there when the accident happened."

Relief swept over Chelsea's face. "So, you can testify that what he's saying is the truth. You saw that he had a green light?"

The van in the left-turn lane was stopped, so

was the SUV in the middle lane. The woman stepped off the sidewalk. What color was the blasted light? Madison balled her fists at her sides.

"Madison," Chelsea pleaded, desperation filling her voice.

"I saw the impact, but not the color of the light," she confessed.

"Oh, no!"

"There will be people who did see the light," Madison said.

"What am I supposed to do? Should I go down to the station?"

"Just stay put for now. The questioning shouldn't take too long, and there's nothing you could do at the station."

"Can I call him?"

Madison thought back to how Phelps had snatched Jim's phone. "He'll probably be unreachable for a while. Just do your best to stay positive, okay?" Madison's heart was breaking. She'd protect her sister from anything. She was her little sister, after all, and Jim was family.

Chelsea pinched the bridge of her nose. "I'll do my best."

"Call me if anything comes up," Madison told her as she reached for and squeezed her sister's hand.

Chelsea got to her feet, and they hugged.

"Should I get him a lawyer?" Chelsea asked, pulling back.

Madison cupped the side of her sister's face, made sure to look her in the eye, and said, "If it comes to that, I'll take care of it."

Chelsea nodded and sniffled.

Madison and Terry saw themselves out. Her fists were still clenched, and she longed to punch something—better yet, *someone*.

Fifteen

Madison's stomach was tossing after leaving Chelsea. She felt as if she'd dropped a bomb on her sister and had run. She hated feeling that way, and she also hated feeling so helpless in the situation. If only she'd seen the traffic light.

"I know family means everything to you, but what if things didn't transpire as he'd said?" Terry's voice was gentle, but the message still cut like a knife.

They were headed through hallways to the morgue. She walked as fast as her legs would allow, hoping that the faster she went, the further she'd be able to push the accident and any possible repercussions behind her.

"Jim would never hit a woman on purpose," she said.

"I never said he did it on—"

"Really? If everything didn't happen as he said, you're alluding to the fact Jim could have avoided hitting her or that he's trying to shift the blame from himself. If Jim says he had a green light, I believe him," she punched out.

Terry held up his hands in surrender, but she wasn't sure if he had done so to placate her or if he really was on her side in all this.

They reached the elevator bank. She pushed the down button and was about to suggest they take the stairs when it dinged. They loaded onto the car, and she selected the button for the basement.

"Hold the doors." She recognized the voice of Andrea Fletcher, the police chief and Troy's sister.

Terry got to the doors before Madison and held one side back.

Andrea stepped in, looking as put together as always. "Headed to the Malone and Doe autopsies?"

"Yeah," Madison answered. "You?"

"Same."

Madison wondered if the chief's interest was professional or personal. Rarely did the police chief attend autopsies, but one of the victims was high profile and, according to Winston, a generous benefactor of the Stiles PD. Andrea wasn't superficial like the sergeant, though, so if she was there for professional reasons, it was just to get answers. Though it stood to reason if Troy knew the Malones, Andrea probably did as well. Maybe Madison could ferret out information from Andrea about why Troy may have reacted the way he had. Now wasn't the time, though.

The elevator dinged its arrival, and the doors opened.

Terry gestured for Madison and Andrea to step out ahead of him, and the three of them bustled down the hall.

"Is there a reason we're practically jogging?" Andrea laughed.

"Richards is very much about the clock," Terry replied.

"He's threatened to lock me out for being late before," Madison added.

"Well, he better not be pulling that today. He was to wait for me to get there." Andrea winked at Madison.

Being police chief really has its advantages.

RICHARDS BARELY LOOKED UP WHEN Madison, Terry, and Andrea stepped into the morgue. Madison was surprised there was no sign of Winston, especially considering he'd ordered the rushed autopsies.

The bodies of Lorene Malone and John Doe lay side by side on two gurneys. Doe was under a sheet to the medical examiner's right and Malone was to his left, her naked form on display. There certainly was no modesty in death.

The wounds on both of their foreheads had been cleaned, and the mask of death had turned their skin a dull blue.

Richards was wearing his lab coat and a hat with a shield. The latter was still up in the air. "Before I proceed with the female vic, I will share evidence that I've collected thus far. Both victims were shot by one bullet to the head."

"Is that the cause of death?" Madison asked.

"I'll let you know COD once I'm finished here." Richards resumed his assessment. "The bullets used were .357-caliber as I had initially thought. X-rays show the bullets fragmented in their skulls. I will retrieve these and hand them over to the lab for analysis."

"Do you know how far away the shooter was when the shots were fired?" Andrea asked.

"There isn't any stippling, so that puts the shooter beyond two feet away. I'd say within four to six feet."

"Our killer could have gotten blood on him- or herself," Madison said.

"Quite likely," Richards replied, "but not a lot."

Still, Madison imagined the killer leaving the house, blood on the clothing, possibly dripping. She'd check with Cynthia to see if they'd recovered any errant drops of blood anywhere else in the house or outside—though the weather would make that next to impossible.

Richards continued. "I've swiped under their fingernails and pulled epithelial from the female victim's."

Lorene Malone, Madison said in her head. She hated identifying the deceased by a label. They'd once been living, breathing people, after all, and she never wanted to lose sight of that fact. Even if she was supposed to play things from a detached standpoint, she feared if she ever forgot the dead were loved, the spark of urgency to find justice would somehow diminish.

"I'm going to caution you not to get too excited about this find. Beyond this, there wasn't any indication of a struggle."

"The killer was armed," Terry began. "There wasn't the need for one."

"The wrists on both victims look like this." Richards lifted one of Malone's arms, and bruises marred her wrist like a bracelet. "Based on the coloring, I'd say the contusions were caused not long before death."

"They were tied up," Madison concluded, glanced at Andrea, but then turned to her partner. Missing phones and ID, and now bondage.

Terry said, "If they were—"

"Not *if*, Detective," Richards started. "They *were*. No question about it."

"Huh." Terry's brow furrowed in concentration. "Was our killer trying to get information out of them? And if so, what?"

Madison tossed out another possibility. "Or they were tied up to keep them from escaping while the killer looked for something."

"Something on their phones perhaps?" Terry suggested.

"But then it seems the shooter took them," Madison countered.

Terry shrugged. "I don't know."

Something about the situation wasn't sitting right with Madison. The bondage, the missing phones, and ID. At the scene, Winston had taken a leap and suggested a hired hit. Maybe it hadn't been that far of a leap. It would seem the killer was after something—either tangible or information. If that was the case, had the killer meant to take out Mrs. *and* Mr. Malone? John Doe and Steven Malone were the same stature and age range, and both had silver hair. Maybe Doe's murder was the result of mistaken identity.

Madison turned to Terry. "Get officers positioned on Malone."

He looked confused, so she explained her theory and added, "We still don't know who the true target was, and we can't take chances."

Terry stepped aside to make the call.

"If there is a hired gun after Malone, why?" Andrea asked and put her gaze on Madison, concern for Madison's wellbeing in her eyes. "Surely this has nothing to do with the Russia Mafia. As far as we know they left Stiles."

As far as we know. The room for error in that statement curdled Madison's gut, but she sided with logic. "Even if it was a hit man behind the murders, it doesn't mean he or she has to be associated with the mob. Maybe someone was after money owed to them." The fact Steven didn't seem pleased about them looking into his financials was still clearly in mind. Madison continued. "We'll figure out who's behind this, but it will just take time. Knowing Doe's identity would really help." She motioned with her head toward the body under the sheet. "Any luck on that?"

"There wasn't a hit with fingerprints," Richards said. "His photo will be run through facial recognition software. That same photo has been forwarded to a sketch artist, so you'll have something to show around, too." The latter only confirmed what Madison already knew to be standard protocol.

"So, right now we're banking on him having a record." She felt deflated that the situation was outside of her control. Unfortunately, facial rec had limitations and only worked if someone had a previous conviction and was stored in a database. If only they could run an image through the Department of Motor Vehicles, but many would protest that such a thing would violate their human rights. As far as she was concerned, it might give criminals reason to pause and not break the law.

Richards cleared his throat and gestured toward the bodies. "As much as I love spinning hypotheticals, I should get started. Any more questions before I begin?"

"Can you tell what they might have been bound with?" Andrea asked.

"As you can see, the contusions were rather narrow bands," Richards said.

"Zip ties?" Terry proposed, pocketing his phone.

Richards shook his head. "I'd expect to see cuts in that case. I'd lean more toward it being a fine rope or string." Richards met Madison's eyes and smiled, probably because he'd gotten sucked into sounding off hypotheticals, after all. Richards lowered the shield in front of his face and pulled out the Stryker saw.

The three of them stood back at a distance as Richards moved toward Lorene's body. This was her least favorite part of autopsies—the actual autopsy. It wasn't for the blood or the guts—it seemed the former only bothered her when it was in a massive quantity or fresh at a scene—but rather just how the human body was broken down and cataloged as a bunch of parts. Richards had told her before that humans were basically machines, and that analogy never became clearer than on the morgue table.

When Richards removed Lorene's lungs, he weighed them, squeezed them, and sniffed. "They are full of liquid. I detect chlorine. Lorene Malone was alive when she went into the water. She drowned."

Madison felt as if she'd been struck. A bullet

to the head followed by a quick or instantaneous death was one thing, but drowning? That had to be one of the worst ways to go.

"So, the killer shot them, and they either fell back into the pool or were pushed," Terry summarized.

Madison paced. Her empathy for Lorene giving way to anger. "We need to find the son of a bitch who did this."

The rest of them remained quiet, and Richards gave it a few seconds before he continued with the autopsy. The three of them stood by as Richards worked through the process on Lorene and then John Doe.

It was a few hours after they'd first entered the lab when Richards lifted his shield. He'd talked throughout the autopsy, more to his recorder than to them, but now was the time for questions.

"You said you found growths on the female victim's vital organs," Madison started. "Cancer?"

"I'd need to send them off for biopsy to know if they're malignant."

Terry nodded. "Any evidence of recent sexual activity for either of them?"

"Not that I saw," Richards said. "I'll make sure you're kept posted on any of the findings here, but that's all I have for you now." With that, Richards essentially showed the three of them the door.

In the hall, Terry said, "I got ahold of Winston, and he's placing a couple of officers on Steven Malone."

"It doesn't surprise me he's acting fast on that," Madison jabbed, and Andrea angled her head, but Madison wasn't going to get into Winston's micromanaging of the case right now. She switched her thoughts back to Richards's last conclusion. "No evidence of sex, but they could have used a condom and flushed it, or the killer could have interrupted them."

"Or it really wasn't an affair, and there's another explanation for the fact they were naked," Terry countered.

Terry had brought up that possibility before, and it could fit with the bondage. The killer wanted to assume complete power and control over them, and having them strip would also serve to humiliate them.

Andrea led the way down the hall toward the elevator. Madison called for her, and she turned around.

"Can I talk to you for a minute?" Madison then said to Terry, "I'll catch up with you in a bit."

"Sure." Terry kept on walking.

Madison caught up to Andrea and asked, "Do you know the Malone family personally?"

"You could say that. Why do you ask?"

For a fraction of a second, Madison felt horrible for what she was about to ask and the reason she was going to ask it, as if she were violating a trust between her and Troy, but she needed answers and this route might be easier. Andrea had helped Madison understand Troy's reaction to a fellow officer's death last fall, and from what Madison witnessed then, grief tended to shut Troy down.

"You can talk to me about anything," Andrea encouraged.

"It's about Troy." A disclaimer, an upfront warning, that if his sister didn't want to talk about her brother, now was the time to cut and run. Andrea stood still. Madison went on. "I happened to mention to Troy that Lorene Malone was murdered. He ran off, told me we'd talk about it tonight, but I'm not holding my breath. To be honest, I'm having flashbacks of how he'd responded when Barry was shot. Troy is close to the family, isn't he?"

"Was, anyway." Andrea's face fell somber. "He was good friends with Brad Malone."

"Brad? Kimberly's son?"

Andrea shook her head. "He was likely named after Kimberly's older brother. Brad was the Malones' firstborn, and he died in a car accident at the age of eighteen."

Madison staggered backward. "That must have killed Troy."

"It was Troy's first time dealing with loss. It was really rough on him."

"So hearing that Lorene was murdered—"

"Probably brought it all up for him again," Andrea finished.

"Poor guy."

"Just be patient with him and be there for him when he's ready to talk."

Madison bit her bottom lip and nodded. "Always."

Andrea touched Madison's arm and left Madison standing there. She was hurting for Troy but also for herself. She wished he'd have opened up to her about all this on his own, but the pain must have been too much. She'd do as she promised Andrea and give Troy the space he needed, but she felt inclined to just touch base and let Troy know she was here for him. She took out her phone and found a new text from Chelsea telling her that Jim was home.

Good news, she keyed back, breathing a lot easier. It's possible the tension between her and Phelps had all been in her mind. She shook that aside, a feeling in her gut telling her that her initial assumption had been spot on, but at least Phelps had released Jim.

She opened the text thread with Troy and texted him, *Thinking of you. I'm here for you.*

She left it at that, even though she wanted to let him know about Jim's accident. She felt pained and a little put off that Troy was her go-to person and she wasn't his.

She went to put her phone away and noticed two things: it was going on seven thirty, and she had missed call from Tiffany's Bridal.

Shit! She'd forgotten all about calling to reschedule the fittings. At least they had her number and not Cynthia's.

She called the bridal store and apologized repeatedly. They rescheduled for seven o'clock tomorrow night. She hung up, breathing easier. Damage control was done.

Next, she called Canine Country Retreat Boarding, the kennel where she boarded Hershey during the day. They'd be closing at eight. She arranged for Hershey to stay overnight and then fired off one more message to Troy.

> *Hershey's at the kennel overnight. I'll*
> *be home late.*

She stared at Troy's name and was tempted to call him. If only she could strip his pain away.

Her phone pinged with a response from Troy.

> *Ok. I love you.*

She held the phone to her chest and pinched her eyes shut. He was the best thing that could have happened to her. She'd be right by his side, now and always. She'd never felt this strongly about any man before, not even her first fiancé. Now, that bit scared her.

Sixteen

A woman in her late forties answered the door at the Darbonnes' house, dressed in a black-and-white maid's uniform and saw Madison and Terry to a front sitting room. Apparently, Mr. Darbonne was out, but that was fine, as they wanted to speak with Sabrina. She and Terry remained standing as they waited for her.

Darbonne swept into the room as if she floated above the floor rather than walked on it. "Detectives?"

Madison held up her badge and introduced herself, and Terry and gestured toward a couch.

Darbonne sat and cocked her head, looking from Madison to Terry, back to Madison. "Is something wrong?"

Either she was a good actress or she had no idea about Lorene's murder. Madison had just assumed that she would have heard something from Steven or the Malone children. This visit had taken a sour turn to a death notification.

It was the most loathed part of the job and something she and Terry took turns doing for the simple reason that neither of them liked being the one to deliver the news.

Madison glanced briefly at Terry and said to Darbonne, "We thought you might have heard, but Lorene Malone was found murdered in her home this morning and—"

Darbonne gasped loudly, and her eyes pooled with tears. She fanned a hand in front of her face. "I'm sorry for…." She cleared her throat and placed her hands on her knees, which she held tightly together, and sniffled.

Madison felt uncomfortable watching the woman trying to squash her emotions. "Your reaction is completely understandable," Madison assured her. "We understand the two of you were close friends."

Darbonne's chin quivered, and she nodded.

"We're sorry for your loss." Madison let the sentiment sit for a few seconds, then said, "We're hoping that you can help us with something."

"Anything you need."

Madison wondered if Darbonne's enthusiasm would last after hearing her question. "Mrs. Malone wasn't the only one found." Madison watched that sink into Darbonne's eyes, and they gave way to deep sorrow.

"Steven, too?" Darbonne's voice cracked.

"No, Mr. Malone is just fine," Madison said.

Darbonne blew out a breath and looked

upward. Her legs were bouncing.

"She was found with a man, though," Terry interjected, taking Darbonne's gaze. "We're hoping you'd be able to help us figure out his identity."

"Do you have a picture of him?"

Madison shrank back. Sketch artists took too much time for her liking. "We're waiting on a rendering from an artist."

Darbonne's eyes widened in horror, as if she'd pieced together that any crime scene photos would be too graphic to share. "I see."

"He was a man of Mr. Malone's age, gray hair, trim," Madison began and slipped her gaze to Terry. There was a warning in his eyes to play this delicately. "Does this sound like anyone you might know? Maybe a friend of Lorene's?"

Darbonne's brow wrinkled in concentration, then she shook her head. "I'd need more than that."

Madison took a deep breath. There'd be no way around the question she had to ask, but she didn't need to share the details that Lorene and John Doe were found naked. "Did Lorene ever tell you or give you the impression that she wasn't happy in her marriage?"

"What? Absolutely not," Darbonne spat and splayed a hand over her chest.

Madison leaned forward. "So, Lorene never told you that she was seeing someone else?"

"She would never do that to Steven."

"But if she did, would she have told you?" Madison countered, and Darbonne looked like she'd been slapped, her cheeks turning a bright red.

"I would think so, yes." Darbonne squared her shoulders.

"As far as you know, then, the Malones had a happy marriage?" Madison watched as Darbonne's confidence faltered. She ran her bottom lip through her teeth, and her posture sagged. "They never had disagreements?" Madison continued, hoping to nudge her into speaking.

"Certainly they did," Darbonne said with a little heat and her face contorted in agitation, "but what couple doesn't? It doesn't mean that either of them was cheating on the other."

"Fair enough," Madison said.

Darbonne crossed her legs and ran a hand over her pants, smoothing out the fabric. The closed-off body language was revealing: Darbonne was withholding something. She certainly didn't take well to any hit—supposed even—against Lorene's character.

"Is there something that you want to tell us?" Madison cut to the point.

A glint flickered across Darbonne's eyes, and she took a deep, heaving breath.

"If you know anything that might help us find her killer…" Madison prompted.

Darbonne's gaze snapped to meet Madison's.

"Very well, but everyone has secrets. The lucky ones have someone they can confide in, and I was that person for Lorene."

Madison sat back, taking what Darbonne was saying as an insight into the Malones' marriage. Maybe Madison had a distorted view of marriage, but her ideals would have her believing that husband and wife should be each other's confidant. It could have been this ideal that had Troy's shutting her out affecting her so deeply.

Darbonne jutted out her chin, and she looked at Madison's bare ring finger. "You look surprised, like you thought that Steven would be that person for Lorene. Let me tell you something, Detective. Marriage kills conversation."

Terry grunted, albeit barely perceivable. While Darbonne didn't seem to notice, Madison certainly picked up on it.

Darbonne continued. "That's my experience, anyhow. I'm not saying that Lorene didn't share anything with Steven, but he was always busy with the business, like he had no time for her, so she kept herself busy. She volunteered for charities and did all she could to help the causes near and dear to her heart. She didn't deserve to be… What happened to her?"

"She was shot," Madison said.

"I see." Darbonne wiped the tip of her nose with a finger.

"What sort of secrets did Mrs. Lorene confide in you?" Madison asked after a few seconds.

"Lorene was diagnosed with cancer," Darbonne rushed out and exhaled deeply as if the purge finally let her breathe again, and the entire room fell into silence.

Terry was staring off across the room, his eyes wet.

"When was she diagnosed?" Madison asked.

"A month ago." Darbonne sniffled and dabbed her nose again. "She was only given a few months to live. She didn't want her family to suffer and be put through false hope—"

Terry leapt from the couch and walked out the front door, the door slamming shut behind him.

Darbonne flinched.

"I'm sorry about—"

Darbonne dismissed Madison's apology with a waving hand and carried on about Lorene. "It wasn't an easy choice for her—not telling her family—but she just wanted to pass with grace and dignitary. And with all her hair."

Anger flushed through Madison at the thought that Lorene Malone wasn't given that chance.

THE HEAT EMANATING FROM TERRY could have melted the ice and snow on the windshield. At least the snow was barely falling now and what was were small flakes. His nostrils were flaring when he looked over at Madison from the passenger seat. "She kept cancer from her family. Unbelievable."

"I got your feelings on the matter when you stomped out of the house," Madison shot back. "Lorene had her reasons not to tell her family."

Terry shook his head, his jaw clenched. "No excuses for that," he snapped. "If Annabelle did that to me…" He turned to face his window.

It was all coming together now: his moodiness, his reaction to the cancer, and to Lorene's secretiveness. Madison put her hand on his shoulder, but he jerked it off. "What's going on?"

He looked at Madison, his eyes pooled with tears. "Fine, you want to know? Annabelle's got a mole on her back."

"It's probably noth—"

"No, don't tell me it's nothing or could be nothing because you don't know. Heck, we don't know. She won't even go to the damn doctor and have the thing checked."

"Just tell her how much it would mean to you for her to go to the doctor."

He mocked laughter. "You don't think I haven't done that already? She's just being stubborn—and selfish."

She was probably terrified of facing her worst nightmare, but Madison dared not verbalize that as it seemed Terry just needed her to be on his side right now and listen.

"We have to let the Malones know about Lorene," Terry said, detouring from his personal life. "They deserve to know."

"No, we're not going to do that."

"What do you mean we're not going to—" He snapped his mouth shut, and his pulse ticked in a cheek.

"The cancer has nothing to do with her death, and Lorene didn't want them knowing."

"You don't know that the cancer didn't factor into motive somehow," he boomeranged. "Regardless, I still think the family deserves to know."

She could empathize that Terry's heart was in the right place, but this was one of those times they had to peel away emotionally and act objectively, in the best interest of the case and those involved. "Don't you think this family's going through enough already?"

"I think they have the right to know."

Madison was starting to feel like this was an argument she wasn't going to win, and she wasn't even sure if she wanted to—that was part of the problem. "I'll make you this promise. We'll tell them, but only when it's the right time and not until we confirm her diagnosis from her doctor. Fair?"

"Fine." Terry shifted position, his body leaning more toward the door.

"I'd appreciate it if we kept this to ourselves for now. There's no reason the sergeant even needs to know."

"Fine," he mumbled.

She set the car in the direction of Patty Beaulieu's house. Neither of them spoke another word, but the air sparked with tension and regrets. Madison felt for Terry and what he was going through personally, and it was harder than hell to separate the personal from the professional, but she needed him to—and so did Lorene Malone and John Doe.

Seventeen

Patty Beaulieu answered her door, all five feet of her, with a smooth complexion and wearing a red bandanna as a hairband. Beaulieu's background told them she was fifty-five, but she looked like she must have found the fountain of youth.

Madison held up her badge and introduced herself and Terry. "Is there somewhere we could sit and talk?"

Beaulieu backed up, keeping her gaze on both of them as she did so.

The house was compact, and the living room came off the entry to the left, the kitchen on the right. It smelled of fried eggs and rice and had Madison's stomach growling.

"Sorry if we're interrupting your dinner," Madison said.

"No, it's fine. Mike's at work. He gets more upset over interrupted meals than I ever would."

"Mike's your husband?" Madison guessed.

"Yes." Beaulieu rubbed her stomach. "Besides,

I'm not very hungry. I heard the news about Lorene on TV. Terribly sad."

"We're sorry for your loss," Madison offered.

"Thank you," Beaulieu lamented. "I was shocked. Mr. Malone must be out of his mind?" she said more as a question than a statement.

"It's difficult on him, for sure," Madison empathized, pulling from a soft spot inside of herself. "They were married for quite a few years. How long have you worked with the Malones?"

"Thirty years." Beaulieu kneaded her hands in her lap.

"It's safe to assume that you knew them very well, then." Madison smiled pleasantly.

"You could say that, but I probably overheard more than they shared with me."

"Did you work for the Malones last night?" Terry asked.

Beaulieu slid her gaze to him. "Yes, well, for Mrs. Malone anyhow. Mr. Malone was on a business trip out of town."

She might have worked for the Malones a few decades, but she still referred to them formally. Is that how the Malones preferred things or something intrinsic to Beaulieu?

"Was Mrs. Malone alone last night when you were there?" Madison asked.

Beaulieu's gaze drifted to the floor, and she frowned. "She had company." Slowly, Beaulieu met Madison's eyes. Her loyalty to the family seemed fierce, and Madison sensed the company had been John Doe.

"What time were you there?" Madison asked.

"I showed up at five and stayed until about eight."

Sometime between seven and ten o'clock. The time of death circled in Madison's head.

Madison nodded. "Who was her company?"

Beaulieu bit her bottom lip.

"Whatever you tell us is safe with us," Madison prompted, trying to cut through employer loyalty.

"It was a man," she said, then quickly added, "but she wasn't cheating on Mr. Malone."

"I understand. Can you tell us who he was?" Madison asked, playing diplomat.

"Mrs. Malone never introduced him."

"Can you describe him?"

"Silver hair, in his sixties. A white man. He kept himself in great shape."

That would fit their John Doe. "Did you ever see him before last night?"

Beaulieu shook her head.

"Do you know what the nature of their relationship was?" Terry asked.

"Friends? I didn't read anything improper. They were laughing a lot when I was cooking dinner." Beaulieu rubbed her arms. "The news mentioned a man was found murdered. Was it him?"

"Did they allude to an affair?" Madison

choked out the question. She hated it when the media got involved.

"Heavens, no, they kept things very vague, but that's where most people's minds go when a woman is found with a man who isn't her husband."

Sergeant Winston must have been in the dark or he'd have called Madison. Thank God for small miracles.

"What did the news say about him?" Madison asked.

"Just that police didn't know who he was at this time."

At least the media had gotten that right.

"You said Lorene and this man were having a good time together," Terry interjected. "Is there anything else you can tell us about their interactions?"

"Well, I found it strange that every time I'd come into the room, they'd go quiet. Up until then, they'd be chatting away. They also kept looking at the clock like they were expecting someone."

Madison sat up straighter. "Do you know who?"

"No," Beaulieu rushed out, "and it's not my place to ask such things. Besides, I could be wrong about why they kept looking at the clock, but that was just the impression I got."

Beaulieu's gut could be off. They could have been counting down to Beaulieu's absence, so they could be alone, get cozy with each other and a bottle of wine, but if Lorene was having an affair with John Doe, why have Beaulieu cook? They'd have gone out or made do on their own. "You left about eight you said?"

"Yes, after serving dessert. Pecan pie, Mrs. Malone's favorite." Beaulieu's face became serious.

"What is it?"

"Mrs. Malone sent me home before I finished my duties."

"And that's unusual?" Terry asked.

"Yes. She even told me she'd take care of things and not to worry. I didn't argue and left. She went back to the living room with the man, where they'd retired after eating. I could hear them laughing when I left."

"You said earlier they'd stop talking when you came around," Terry began. "Did you happen to catch anything they were saying?"

"I'm sorry, no."

"Was Mrs. Malone generally a happy person?" Madison asked, taking a slight detour in the direction of the conversation.

Beaulieu worried her lip. "She had her moody moments, but don't we all?"

Madison wasn't going to let the cook hide behind her off-the-cuff comment. "Does a particular instance come to mind?"

"Yesterday, I got to the Malones' about five. I told you that already, but Mrs. Malone was on the phone with someone, and she was really mad. She was upstairs, but I could hear her."

"What was she saying?" Terry asked.

"Something about 'you can't do this.'"

Madison perched on the edge of her chair. "Anything else?"

"All I feel I should say."

"Okay," Madison said, though not persuaded to leave the matter alone. Maybe she could work Beaulieu's loyalty to the family against her. "If there's something you know that could help us find Mrs. Malone's killer, I'm sure that Steven and the Malone children would be thankful. It's extremely hard on all of them losing their mother like that. It doesn't matter if a kid's grown; their mother is still their mother."

Beaulieu sniffled, and her chest heaved. "She also said she wasn't going to be bullied into anything, but that's it. That's all I heard."

"Bullied into anything...You can't do this." What did it all mean, and was it pertinent to the case?

"How was she when she came downstairs?" Terry asked.

"She was weary, and her eyes spoke of pain."

Lorene's phone records would be coming in, and then they'd be able to confirm who she was talking to yesterday at about five o'clock, but it didn't hurt to ask Beaulieu if she knew. "Do you have any idea who she was on the phone with?"

"I hate talking about the Malones like this."

Madison jumped on Beaulieu's reply. "Do you think she was on with her husband?"

Beaulieu shook her hands in front of herself. "No, no, please. I have no way of knowing."

"Mrs. Beaulieu," Madison said gently, "did the Malones have a rocky marriage?"

"They had a lot of lively discussions." She wasn't even looking at them now, as if she were a traitor to the family that had employed her.

"Any of their 'lively discussions' take place recently?"

"Last Tuesday," she said. "It was their forty-seventh wedding anniversary. Mrs. Malone had forgotten all about it and didn't come home until eight thirty. I'd already put everything away. Mr. Malone had retired to the study and was drinking scotch."

"I can't say I'd blame him for being upset," Terry empathized.

"Where had she been?" Madison asked.

Beaulieu shrugged and held out open palms. "I don't know. She apologized to Mr. Malone but also told him that he wasn't her father, and she was a free spirit."

Whoa. That was an entirely different picture of Lorene than had been painted of her up until this point. Rowe had said Lorene would do anything for Steven. "Had she ever spoken to him like that before, that you know of?"

"Heavens, no. She was usually very doting. Mr. Malone had asked what had gotten into her, and she'd yelled back that life was bigger than the two of them."

Terry winced. "How did Mr. Malone react to that?"

"He was livid and stepped out."

"And Mrs. Malone's reaction to that?" Madison inquired.

"She was calm, told me to have a good night. She was headed up to bed. She looked exhausted."

"Did she ever tell you or him where she'd been?" Madison asked.

"Nope."

Madison nodded, heading to another line of query. "When you left, around eight, did you lock up behind you?"

"Yes."

"And after you left the Malones last night, where did you go?"

"I had a friend over to watch Netflix," Beaulieu offered without hesitation.

Madison leaned forward. "Could we get your friend's name, for the record?"

Beaulieu gave them the name and number of her friend, and Madison and Terry saw themselves out.

In the department car, Madison said, "I'm beginning to think that Lorene Malone had this entirely separate life her family had no clue about."

"Starting with the cancer and ending with

John Doe," Terry stamped out.

"Let's confirm the cancer." She pulled out her phone and called Cynthia on speaker.

Cynthia answered on the third ring. "Thank God, someone from the outside world."

Madison smiled. "I take it you're still bagging and tagging?"

"Photographing, videotaping, yeah, you name it, but I'm dying for something to eat."

Madison's stomach responded with a growl. She hadn't gotten much of the salad down before things had turned sideways with Jim's accident, and that Hershey's bar from this morning was nothing but a faded memory. Not that chocolate ever had holding power unless she was talking about how it stuck to her hips—and how was that fair?

Madison glanced over at Terry, and he nodded. "We could eat," she said. "How about we pick something up and swing by?" Madison proposed, hoping her friend would bite.

"I won't say no. Mark?" Cynthia's voice waned in volume as she turned away from the receiver and called out, "Interested in dinner?"

"Oh, yeah, I could eat," he said in the background.

"Are Sam and Jennifer still there?" Madison asked.

"No, I sent them back a few hours ago to start processing."

"What are you feeling like?" Madison asked.

"Chinese? Thai? A burg— *Ah, ah, achoo!*"

"Uh-oh. You could be getting sick," Terry said.

Madison hit his arm and gave him a scowl. The last thing a bride needed to hear was her maid of honor was coming down with something four days before her wedding.

"You're not," Cynthia exclaimed. "Tell me you're not. The wedding's only in—"

"I'm not," Madison said, narrowing her eyes at Terry.

"Tell yourself what you wish," Terry said.

"What's going on?" Cynthia's pitch was one octave away from shattering glass.

"She probably caught a chill today when went outside without a coat," Terry said.

"What? Why would you—"

"It's a long story," Madison started, "but I'm not getting into it right now."

"Okay," Cynthia dragged the word out, but Madison felt uneasy. Her friend never let things go that easily. "I could do Greek," Cynthia finally said.

She flashed back to lunch. Maybe this time she'd actually eat an entire Greek salad. "Works for me," Madison told her. "Now could you check on something for us?"

"You're bringing food. Your wish is my command."

Madison was tempted to laugh, picturing Cynthia bending with steepled hands.

"Terry and I need to know if Lorene has any prescriptions in the house, and if she does, we'll need the doctor's name from the label," Madison said.

"I'll check it out and let you know."

"Please."

"I'm on it, but please hurry. I'm starving."

"We'll be there as fast as we can," Madison assured her and was thankful that the snowfall had eased up a bit.

She pulled out of Beaulieu's driveway, headed in the direction of Sammy's, Stiles's go-to for Greek.

"What do you make of Lorene asking Beaulieu to leave before she was done with her duties?" Madison asked.

"Lorene wanted her out of the house for some reason. What about the looking at the clock? I think Lorene and John Doe were expecting someone like Beaulieu had said."

"Me too. Only thing is I don't think they expected whoever it was to tie them up and kill them."

"I doubt they did."

Eighteen

That I could kill for." Cynthia wandered into the front entry of the Malones' house, nose to the air and sniffing. "Now, don't tell me." She inhaled, eyes closed. "Chicken souvlaki, rice." More sniffing. "Greek salad, fried pita, and tzatziki."

"You might have been tipped off." Madison laughed and handed Cynthia and Mark a bag.

"Thanks." Mark unfolded his and looked inside. "Breakfast was a long time ago," he added.

"Don't make me think about it," Cynthia said and nudged Madison's shoulder. "What's this about you getting sick?"

Madison looked at Terry. "You happy now?"

He recoiled.

"I'm fine," Madison told Cynthia. "Let's eat."

"This way." Cynthia led the way into the kitchen. "It's been processed."

Madison noted the dirty dishes on the counter and stove. Beaulieu had said Lorene had sent her on her way before she'd cleaned up, and that seemed to be true.

Cynthia tore into her bag. "Fork? Knife?"

"All in the bag, along with napkins," Madison said, her gaze now going to two pill bottles that were on the counter. "Those Lorene's?"

"Read...the..." Cynthia was chomping away, her cheeks bulged like a chipmunk's.

Madison read the labels. Both prescriptions were made out to Lorene Malone by a Dr. Kendra Cohen. It seemed safe to conclude that it would have been Lorene's doctor who had diagnosed her with cancer. She held a bottle toward Terry. "We'll pay her a visit first thing tomorrow." Turning to Cynthia, she asked, "What are the meds for?"

Cynthia swallowed what looked like a sizable rodent. "One's for acid reflux and the other is a decongestant."

She hadn't been expecting that Cynthia would find any meds to treat cancer, given that Lorene had wanted to keep the disease to herself. After all, medications would show on the family's medical plan, and Steven would see it. "That's all you found?"

"Yep. I'd say Mrs. Malone was a healthy lady overall. Stressed probably, but who isn't?" Cynthia lowered her fork for the first time since she'd unpacked her food. She looked at Madison's untouched bag. "Are you going to eat?"

"Ah, yeah." Madison said it as if that was a no-brainer, but she'd temporarily forgotten about the food. Her mind was swimming with the case and the poor people who'd lost their lives. It was Cynthia's prompting that had brought her back to awareness of her own body and the fact that she was starving.

Madison tore into her bag and got to work on her souvlaki. The four of them mowed down the food as if they hadn't eaten in days. Madison put another forkful into her mouth, savoring the facets of flavors that danced on her tongue. Greek food trumped Chinese food—almost as dreamy as milk chocolate.

Cynthia was the first to put her empty container into the paper bag in which it had come and scrunched it closed. "Now's probably a good time to talk, seeing as you're preoccupied and are less likely to interrupt." She smirked at Madison.

"Real nice," Madison mumbled around a mouthful of food.

"It's true, but listen," Cynthia began. "We're collecting a lot of evidence, so that's good. It will take time to work through what's actual evidence, though. You got to the autopsies, I'd suspect?"

Madison nodded.

"You know, then, there were no hits in the system for John Doe's prints?"

"Yeah," Madison said.

"Well, no good news about any others lifted around here. Ones from the wineglasses and wine bottle belonged to Lorene and John Doe."

Madison set down her fork and closed her container. She hadn't finished all of the food, but she'd had enough.

Cynthia's gaze went from the leftovers to Madison's eyes. "He would have told you they were shot at close range, but something we've just determined with blood spatter is they were lined up side by side when they were shot."

"Backs to the pool or facing?" Madison asked without much thought, not even sure if it mattered, except that Lorene had drowned. If she'd fallen in face first, she might not have been able to turn around or—Madison's heart sank—she was held under.

"It would seem they both had their backs to the pool," Mark said. "Again, that's based on the blood patterns that we had to work with."

"'Had to work with,'" Cynthia mumbled and crossed her arms. "You really don't want to get me started on the firemen again."

"No, we don't," Madison was quick to say.

"They were just doing their jobs," Terry inserted.

Cynthia gave him a heated look.

"Do we know how Malone ended up drowning?" Madison asked. "Did the killer hold her under?"

"Your guess is as good as any," Cynthia said.

"We might not ever know," Madison sighed. And did it matter? Lorene was dead either way.

"We do have something else for you," Mark said, stealing the floor. "We did a blind static lift for shoeprints in the area around the pool ladder and the blood."

Madison knew that meant they set a thin sheet of mylar on the floor and zapped it with an electric charge. That magnetized the mylar and drew dust and particles to it, outlining the pattern in which they were left. It was the perfect process for lifting prints invisible to the naked eye.

Madison perked up. "And?"

"*And*," Cynthia cut in, "it was actually Mark who did this, so credit goes where credit is due. I'll let him tell it." She bowed out.

Mark's cheeks flushed, and he dipped his head slightly forward in thanks. "We got a good print. A man's size eleven. It's a common tread, but, as you know, each print is unique."

"Almost like fingerprints," Madison said.

"That's right." Mark smiled. "Treads wear differently given how people walk. Imperfections happen. Well, these prints are from a running shoe, and there's a definite slash through the tread near the large toe on the right shoe."

"None of the shoes in the Malones' closet match," Cynthia started, "and that goes for John Doe's. We found Berlutis in the front hall.

They're a match to Doe's size-twelve feet. Mr. Malone's shoes in the bedroom walk-in closet were thirteens."

Terry whistled. "Berlutis don't come cheap."

"Nope. About eighteen hundred a pair," Cynthia said, "and the expense doesn't stop there. His clothes are designer."

"And we're sure the men's clothing near the pool were his?" Terry asked.

Mark nodded. "The clothes were tailored to him, and he's a couple sizes smaller than Mr. Malone."

"John Doe had money," Madison summarized.

"To throw away that kind of cash on clothing? I'd say so." Cynthia blew out air. "There are so many better things to spend your money on."

"All right, so who is Mr. Eleven?" Terry asked.

"A question we'll need to answer," Madison stated firmly, though overwhelmed at the thought of the task. "We'll need to rule out everyone who had access to this house that we know of and see if any of them are Cinderella."

"I don't want to be a killjoy," Cynthia started, "but we know that first responders trampled all over the scene. The shoeprint could belong to one of them."

"I know." Madison sighed.

"And it's not like there's a way to time-stamp a shoeprint. What are we supposed to do? Go down to the firehouse and check everyone's shoes?" Terry looked at Madison.

"Good idea."

"You're kidding me," Terry retorted drily.

"I am." She smirked.

Terry let out a deep breath, and she laughed, but her amusement was cut short.

Lorene and John Doe had been bound, and if the killer had gone through the house in search of something... "What if you checked more of the house to see if you can find the same shoeprint somewhere else? There'd be no reason for first responders to be anywhere else but on the path to the pool and around it. Terry and I were thinking the killer could have been searching for something."

Cynthia tilted her head to the side. "You do realize how big this house is, don't you? Where would you have us start? We don't even know if the killer was after something tangible."

"I love you, Cyn." Madison blew her a kiss and hurried out of the house as fast as she could.

Nineteen

By the time Madison and Terry were leaving the Malones' house, the weather had taken a turn for the worse again. It was as if they were inside a snow globe that had been violently shaken, and the sky held an eerie glow as the lights of the city met the cloud cover. There would be a lot more snow before this storm was over.

"The roads aren't in any shape for driving." Terry looked at her over the roof of the car, and his phone rang. He held the screen toward Madison, not that she could read it. "It's Annabelle," he told Madison before answering and getting into the car.

She gave him the keys, and she wiped the car down while Terry sat in the warming vehicle, talking to his wife. She hoped that Annabelle wasn't calling to have Terry call it a day. Madison appreciated that the roads weren't the best, but they had a double homicide to solve. Treacherous roads or not, they weren't going to stop her from doing what she had to do.

She finished up and hopped into the car with Terry. He was off the phone.

"Anything to worry about?" she asked.

Terry shook his head. "She just wants me to come home."

"I can't say I blame her, but—"

"But," he cut her off, "I told her I can't."

She jerked to look at him. Typically, her partner found it a lot easier to clock out than she did. "Really?"

He narrowed his eyes. "No need to act so surprised."

"Who, me?" She passed him a goofy smile, one he returned.

"I told her we've been working a case all day and have barely scratched the surface. I also told her she's being a hypocrite worrying about me when she's refusing to see a doctor."

Madison winced. "I don't even know if I want to ask."

"She told me she'd think about it."

"Well, that's good, right?"

"It's a start. So, where to next?"

"Well, take your pick. We can either go talk to Lorene's parents or the housekeeper." Madison fastened her seat belt.

"What time is—" Terry looked at the clock on the dash, drawing Madison's attention there. *9:30 PM.*

"I doubt they're going to sleep tonight,

anyway, but let's go to the parents first." Madison made the executive decision. Though the hour wasn't the most favorable, Lorene's parents might be able to offer them insight into their daughter's marriage.

She looked up their address and hit the gas.

The tires spun as they got going down the street. Stiles resembled a ghost town, but in the place of blowing tumbleweeds, there was just snow, snow, and more snow.

They arrived at a large, two-story brick home on the curve of the cul-de-sac that belonged to the Griffins, Lorene's parents.

"Another big place," Madison observed.

"Did you expect anything less?"

"They're, what? In their eighties? So, yeah, I figured at least a bungalow or something."

"Why simplify when you can just hire more help?" Terry smiled at her, trying to pass off what he'd said as casual, but he'd likely hit the bull's-eye.

They were let inside the home by a woman in her midthirties and shown to an elaborate sitting room touched by the hands of someone who loved the Victorian era. Lace doilies were on the arms of the couch and the two wingback chairs. Large, ornate brass frames housed oil paintings with broad strokes depicting fields of flowers.

"Mr. and Mrs. Griffin will be in shortly," the woman said in a somber tone.

"Thank you," Terry told her.

The feel of loss saturated the house, and the air was heavy with grief. Madison's nose was drippy, but not from emotion, and her throat was a little scratchy. It had to be in her head, thanks to Terry telling her she was getting sick. Surely, she wouldn't be showing signs of a cold this fast. She'd just caught the chill that afternoon.

"Detectives?" An elderly man entered the room, a petite woman to his side.

The couple held hands, and he guided his wife to the couch before sitting himself. They gave the picture of what Madison wanted out of her relationship with Troy. The thought struck so decisively, it stole her breath. Where had things taken the turn from casual to head over heels? When she'd moved in with him?

Madison cleared her throat and sat in one of the chairs. Terry sat in the other. "We're very sorry for your loss," she said, an ache settling into her chest, the grief so palpable.

"She was our..." Mrs. Griffin sniffled and dabbed her nose with a well-used tissue.

The husband put an arm around his wife. "As you can imagine, this has been terribly taxing on the two of us. To find out that our only child was killed." His voice tremored from emotion and age.

"We'll just be brief," Madison said kindly. "We know it's late, too," she added as if it could attempt to soften the blow of what they needed to discuss.

"Whatever we can do to help," the wife said, finding her strength.

The woman who had seen Madison and Terry in peeked through the doorway. "Would anyone care for some tea or coffee?"

"We'll be having tea," Mrs. Griffin told Madison and Terry. "You are both welcome to join us."

Typically, Madison would decline such an invitation, but she felt that Mrs. Griffin might be more at ease if she accepted the offer. "Sure, that would be nice." Madison smiled politely. Terry confirmed he'd have some, too, and the woman left.

"She won't be long." Mrs. Griffin took her hand back from her husband's and rubbed her two together as if attempting to warm herself.

Her husband got up, turned on the gas fireplace, and then sat back down beside his wife. "This front room gets a chill to it sometimes." He wrapped his arm around his wife again and crossed his legs. He looked at Madison and Terry, lines crisscrossing his face and tears beading in his eyes.

"Do you know anyone that might have had anything against your daughter?" Madison asked as delicately as possible.

"Enough to kill her?" Mr. Griffin shook his head. "I can't even imagine."

"She volunteered for a lot of charities. She was a sweet, sweet person." Mrs. Griffin tucked into her husband's side.

Hearing mention of the charities reminded Madison that Kimberly hadn't gotten the names of any to Terry yet.

"The truth is we don't know if she was the main target or if her companion was," Madison confessed. She also put it out there as a tester to see if the parents had heard about John Doe.

Mrs. Griffin looked at her husband, and he was the one to respond. "I can't imagine anyone targeting Lorene." His voice caught, and he took a few seconds to compose himself before continuing. "This man she was with, do you know who he is yet?"

"Unfortunately, we don't," Terry said.

"Well, Steven told us she was naked and that this…this man…was naked, too." Mrs. Griffin looked at them for answers.

Madison had to wonder what Steven would gain by telling the poor parents that. Was it some sick way of laying blame on them or Lorene for the murders? If that were the case, it made it sound as if Steven was aware of an affair and not a grieving widower.

"He was," Madison said, "but we're not sure of the nature of the relationship between the man and your daughter."

"She wouldn't be sleeping with him," Mrs. Griffin spilled quickly, the words bubbling from her. "She'd never do that to Steven."

"From the moment she first met Steven in college, she was smitten," Mr. Griffin elaborated. "We tried to help her see that she would meet a lot of men and she didn't have to rush to a decision to settle down."

The help entered the room with the tea already poured into four cups on a silver tray, along with a sugar dish and a milk server. She made up the drinks to everyone's liking, distributed them, and left again as quietly as she'd entered.

"As far as you know, it stayed that way over the years?" Madison pressed. "Lorene loving Steven?"

"No doubt of it." Mrs. Griffin puffed out her chest, then blew on her tea and took a sip.

Madison smiled at her. "They just celebrated their forty-seventh, too. That's a big accomplishment."

"Huge," Mr. Griffin said, earning the stink eye from his wife. "Let's be truthful here: Steven can be a handful."

Madison angled her head. "And how's that?"

"He's a businessman, and that's always come first, even before his furniture store came into existence. He's all about the almighty dollar." Mr. Griffin was taking on a serious tone, and Madison sensed there was some tension between him and Steven. Lorene might have doted on Steven, but she couldn't see Mr. Griffin going out of his way for him.

Mr. Griffin went on. "Steven always thought highly of himself, and anyone who didn't share his view was cast aside and made to feel like dirt."

Madison sat up straighter. "Does anyone specifically come to mind?"

Mr. Griffin shook his head. "Not at the moment."

Madison got the feeling Steven had a way of making Mr. Griffin feel insignificant. "Do you and Steven get along?"

Mrs. Griffin set her tea on the coffee table in front of them and stared at her husband, almost as if daring him to answer the question.

"Mr. Griffin?" Madison prompted.

He gave a fleeting glance to his wife and looked at Madison. "He always provided for Lorene and provided well. She had no monetary concerns."

"But emotionally?" Madison squeezed out.

"That's another story."

"You are not being fair to the boy," Mrs. Griffin said to her husband.

"Sweetheart, I'm just telling the detectives what I saw."

Mrs. Griffin settled back into the couch, staring straight forward as if she were willing herself to be somewhere else.

"He never saw to her emotional needs," Terry concluded.

"Not as far as I'm concerned," Mr. Griffin started. "She used to be such an open girl. She'd tell her mother and me anything, more than we even needed to know. She married Steven, and all that stopped."

"I'd say that's normal to a degree," Madison countered.

"To a degree, yes," Mr. Griffin agreed, "but even as a new mother, she never asked our advice on matters, to weigh in on preschools, etcetera."

"She became an independent adult," Terry concluded.

"She became controlled," Mr. Griffin spat.

"Larry, stop it this instant." Mrs. Griffin got to her feet and spun around near the doorway. "I can't sit here and listen to you tell these people that Steven …that Steven…" She covered her mouth and started crying.

Mr. Griffin rushed to his wife and offered her comfort, which she accepted, leaning against him and sobbing.

"We can go," Madison offered, regretfully. Things were just becoming interesting. She wanted to know if there wasn't more to the rift between father- and son-in-law. She watched as husband and wife hugged, seemingly frozen in time together in a world of their own. Mrs. Griffin's words finally sinking in: *I can't sit here and listen to you tell these people that Steven… That Steven what?* Had killed Lorene or they had reason to suspect that he had?

Madison got to her feet, and Terry followed. She stopped next to the couple and asked softly, "Mr. Griffin, do you believe that Steven Malone killed your daughter?"

Mr. Griffin drew back from his wife. She was trembling, her hand held up to her chin, tears streaking down her cheeks. She was staring in the direction of her husband but seemed to be looking through him.

"I think it's possible." Mr. Griffin admitted in a near whisper.

Mrs. Griffin gasped and went to pound a fist against her husband's shoulder. He got her hand and pulled her against him and rubbed her back as she sobbed.

"We'll see ourselves out." Madison maneuvered past them and outside, Terry at her heels.

"My heart's breaking for them," she told her partner when they'd reached the car.

"It's got to be hell having your child murdered," Terry said. "I don't even want to think about it."

"Don't blame you. Let's hope you never have to live with that pain." With her words, it struck her how Lorene's murder had upended the Griffins' lives forever while she and Terry would eventually move on to their next case.

"He really thinks it's Steven." Terry was somber as he did up his seat belt. "Your gut might be right this time."

"I just don't think we can let a couple aspects of the guy's alibi give him an out." She started the car. "We need to know without a doubt that Steven Malone was out of town and that he didn't orchestrate his wife's and John Doe's murders."

"Okay, I'm going to stop fighting you on it." He dipped his head, but he might as well have shaken her hand and made a pact.

"Thank you." She put the vehicle into gear. "One more stop before the station."

"The housekeeper?"

"You got it."

Twenty

Caffeine was the perfect companion for a murder investigation, and while Madison had requested a tea at the Griffins', she hadn't taken a single sip. She pulled into the parking lot of a Starbucks and said, "It's going to be a long night—just a feeling."

Terry reached for his door handle. "A venti caramel cappuccino?"

"You got it, partner." She'd have handed him money, but this location and several others in the city gave cops free drinks. The gift was technically a violation and something that could be seen as bribery, but the brass looked the other way in this case. Behold the power of caffeine.

Terry got out of the car, and she checked her phone. There was a message from Sam in the lab saying that Lorene's phone records had come through.

Yeah, it's going to be a long night.

She keyed back a quick *thanks* and then looked quickly at the file she'd printed with focus on Marie Rauch, the housekeeper. She was thirty-six, married, and had no criminal record. On the surface, it would seem there wasn't much to work with, but motive could be lurking beneath the surface. Rauch could have needed money and sold her key and code to the Malones' house. Really, the possibilities were only limited by the imagination.

Madison glanced up and saw that Terry was already placing their orders with the cashier.

She called Chelsea just to see how she was doing.

"Hey, Maddy," Chelsea was cheerful on the other end of the line. "You told me everything would be all right, and it was. The woman Jim struck was in the wrong. He could sue her if he wanted, and if she wanted to take him to civil court, she wouldn't get anywhere."

Madison was smiling. "That's great news."

"Yeah, she was crossing against the light, according to a lot of eyewitnesses."

That statement sank in Madison's gut. *A lot? Shouldn't it be all?* Madison didn't want to touch that and risk upsetting her sister. Besides, Jim had been sent home.

"Thanks for being there for him on scene and letting me know what happened."

"Of course." Madison tried to sound happy and casual but was finding it hard to breathe easy quite yet. Maybe it was just her paranoia. Surely if Phelps was going to work things against

Jim, he'd still be in holding.

Terry had moved down the counter to the barista and was talking with her and smiling.

"I should go, sis," Madison said. "Love ya."

"I love you."

Madison pulled out the burner and looked to see if there were any messages from Leland, but there weren't. She stuffed the phone back into her coat pocket.

Terry opened his door and got in. "Here you go." He extended her drink to her, which she gratefully accepted, and he closed his door. "I heard back from Kimberly about charities her mother volunteered at. She gave me one name."

"One?" Madison paused with her cup inches from her lips. "What happened to 'Mom volunteers all over'?"

"That I don't know, but I got Meals for You. They prepare fresh meals and deliver them to the elderly or infirm."

"Sounds like a great cause." One fear of getting older was being holed up in some home where a caretaker was abusive. It happened far more than Madison wanted to acknowledge. "Well, I reviewed the housekeeper's file. Not much there."

"Ah, she still might know something. Maybe the identity of John Doe."

"We can only hope." Madison sucked back on her cappuccino, soaking in the caffeinated goodness. She set her cup down in the console.

"All right, let's get over to her house."

The wipers moved quickly but not fast enough to clear the falling snow.

"And I promise I'll drive slowly," she added as she took off in the direction of Rauch's address.

"All you can do in this mess," he said.

Her progress was more like creeping along, any faster, and the wheels started to spin and slide. Thankfully, they made it to the Rauches' in one piece, but they had to park on the road. The Rauches' driveway was buried under a good foot or more of snow. No sign of any vehicles, but they could have been housed in the garage before the storm set in. Lights in the front room spoke to someone being home and awake.

"Here goes nothing," Madison said as she took her first step into the driveway. Snow spilled over the lip of her shoes, and she wished she'd dressed according to the day's forecast. Then again, the weathercasters hadn't announced that today would bring Snowmageddon. She glanced back at Terry who was doing just peachy in his boots. She should have let him lead the way and then walked in his footsteps.

The door was opened to them when they reached the top step of the porch. A man was standing there, towering a good six inches over Madison's five-foot-nine.

She pulled out her badge and announced their names and positions. "Are you Mr. Rauch?"

He nodded. "Oscar."

"We'd like to come in and speak with your wife Marie Rauch."

Oscar stepped back to let them inside but didn't say a word.

Madison stomped her shoes on the front mat and looked beyond the man at the modest home that stretched out behind him. It was organized and tidy as one might expect from the home of a housekeeper. Then again, there were always exceptions. Like the handyman who had a list a mile long to tend to in his own home, the plumber who had drainage issues, and the mechanic whose car needed maintenance.

"Why do you want to talk to my wife?"

Madison glanced at Terry. It would seem the news about Lorene hadn't reached the Rauch household. "We think she might be able to help us in an open investigation."

Oscar blanched. "You think she's involved in it somehow? Whatever it is?" His face scrunched up. "I don't know why you'd what to talk to her."

"We just have some questions," Madison said matter-of-factly.

Oscar held eye contact briefly with Madison, then spun and shouted over a shoulder. "Marie!"

Thumping came from the second level, followed by a shrill, "What?"

"The police are here. They want to talk to you." Confusion and curiosity married in his voice.

"Who?" Marie reached the top of the stairs and looked down at them, a scowl embedded on her face. She took the steps slowly as if approaching doomsday. At the base of the stairs, she stood close to her husband and asked him, "What do they want?"

"Ask them." Oscar gestured toward Madison and Terry.

"Is there somewhere we could sit and talk?" Terry asked.

"Sure." The single syllable was loaded with leeriness but peppered with curiosity. Marie led them to the living room that would have been the source of light they'd seen from the road.

Oscar sat in an armchair Madison would bet had been his perch when they'd arrived. A TV was directly across from it and muted. Marie sat on a couch, and Terry joined her while Madison took another chair.

Madison introduced herself and Terry to Marie.

"You're detectives?" Marie rubbed her arms and burrowed her gaze right into Madison's eyes. "I'm not sure why you'd want to speak with me."

"Lorene Malone was murdered," Madison delivered.

Marie leaned forward and clasped her hands between her knees. The sweater she was wearing puckered at breast level where a button was missing. "What happened?"

There was no sign of tears or real shock, rather a closing off of energy, given her clasped hands. She struck Madison as unattached and indifferent. It could also be a matter of her bracing for what was coming.

"She was shot," Madison said.

"Oh," Marie dragged out the word and leaned back against the couch.

"That's all? 'Oh'?" The words were out before Madison applied a filter between her mind and her mouth.

Oscar glared at Madison, then stared at his wife. "Honey?" Oscar prompted. "Are you okay?"

Marie blinked slowly. "I… I don't know what to say."

"Well, we're trying to figure out who would have killed her," Madison started, "and we have a few questions for you."

"I don't see how I could help."

"When was the last time you worked for the Malones?" Madison asked.

"I was there this past Saturday."

"And that's a normal day for you to work for the Malones?"

"Yes. I also work on Wednesdays." Marie looked to her husband, then back to Madison. "I take it I won't be there tomorrow."

Madison shook her head. "The house is a crime scene, and it will probably be sealed off for the next couple days."

"A crime scene," Marie parroted, the way people in shock often did.

"Did you come into contact with Mrs. Malone on Saturday?" Madison asked.

"Only in passing. She wished me a good day, and I'd responded in kind."

Madison's heart sank. "Nothing beyond a greeting, then?"

"No." Marie's gaze drifted to her husband, though it didn't seem she was really looking *at* him as much as *through* him. She added, "We don't have reason to talk much. If there's anything she wants me to pay close attention to, she'll leave it in a list that she puts out on the kitchen counter."

"Was there a list this past Saturday?" Terry inquired.

"Yes."

"And what did it say on it?" Madison asked.

"The regular things, but she also wanted the bed linens changed and for me to call the pool guy."

"Who is the pool guy, and does he have a key and security code for the house?"

"Heavens, no. The pool guy really isn't a person in particular. It's just a local business the Malones hire when they need any maintenance or repair work done to the pool."

"Do you know what was wrong with it?" Terry asked.

"It just required a top up of chlorine, etcetera."

Madison leaned forward, elbows to knees. "What's the name of the company?"

"Leisure World. Pool care and installation is only one part of their business."

Madison was familiar with Leisure World and had tagged along with Troy when he had picked up a new grill there last summer. It was possible someone at Leisure World had a beef with the Malones.

"Do you know if they came by?" Terry asked.

Madison assessed Marie. She still wasn't showing any signs of shock or grief. She'd settled into a rhythmic matter-of-fact approach. Was it just because she was shielding herself emotionally or was she devoid of emotion?

"They usually jump fast when the Malones call, but I can't tell you when they showed up. I wasn't around."

"What time did you leave on Saturday?" Madison inquired.

"Six in the evening." Marie glanced at her husband, who shook his head.

Madison flicked a finger between husband and wife. "What was that about?"

Oscar gestured for his wife to answer.

"Usually I'm done about three, but the place was a mess. Dirty dishes on the counter and around the pool. They're usually the kind to clean before the cleaner."

"Aren't dishes normally the cook's job?" Madison asked, pulling from their conversation with Beaulieu.

"I'd say usually, but not after the Malones have

parties."

"They had a party on Friday night?" Terry asked, beating Madison to the question.

"Not a party, per se, but Mrs. Malone did have a gathering. There were easily dishes for five or six people."

"Do you know who she had over or what the purpose of the evening had been?" Madison did her best to come across as conversational.

"Lorene doesn't owe me any explanations." Marie's chest expanded and deflated. "But she did mention that she had some friends over."

Madison's eyes snapped to Marie's. That was the first time she'd referred to her employer by first name. That might not mean anything. Then again, it might mean everything. She'd also caught onto Marie's conflicting responses. At first, all they'd shared was a greeting on Saturday, and now Lorene had mentioned the gathering? She'd let it go just because she didn't want to risk Marie clamming up. "Do you know who specifically?" Madison asked.

Marie shook her head. "She didn't say. I didn't push. Oh, she did happen to say they were *new* friends."

Had John Doe been a *new* friend? Had he been there on Friday night? Were one of these new friends Lorene's and Doe's killer?

"Were you close with Lorene Malone?" Madison reacted based on a hunch.

Marie let out a deep breath. "I was friends

with Lorene before she married Steven, long before. Back in Colton, where we did most of our growing up. All through public school, most of high school, the start of college."

Colton was a town north of Stiles and about a forty-five-minute drive away.

"Was your shared past why she hired you to clean?" Madison figured it would fit with what they'd learned from Bert Rowe about Lorene's personality. She had helped him get established.

"I'd so say, and she pays me quite well to do so. Far more than market value. I only clean for one other client, and that's because I want to, not because I have to."

Madison was measuring what Marie was telling them now against Marie's earlier claims that Lorene rarely talked to her and opted to leave written lists instead. "She pays you well and you have a history," Madison began, "but you said that you rarely talk, that she owes you no explanations. Did the two of you have a falling out?" Madison wanted to get a clearer picture.

Marie looked at her husband and frowned, then drew her gaze to Madison. "Let's just say we went down very different paths in life."

"So, you never had an argument or a blowup of any kind?" Madison peered into Marie's eyes, and Marie's body pulled back, sinking farther into the couch.

"I wouldn't say so, no."

Madison found Marie's wording strange but

would leave it untouched for now. "Would you be at all familiar with a male friend of Lorene's who had silver hair, was trim and fit, somewhere in his sixties?"

"That could probably describe a lot of people." She squinted and studied Madison's eyes.

Madison should probably tell her about John Doe being at the scene and also being a victim. Winston's caution about discretion paraded through her mind, but she disregarded it. "What's your opinion of the Malones' marriage?"

Silence. Seconds passed.

"All I'll say is the Malones weren't all they projected to the outside world," Marie eventually said.

Madison leaned forward. "In what way?"

"They argue more than any other couple I know. I could tell that Lorene hasn't been happy for years, but she didn't believe in divorce."

What about adultery? Madison bit her tongue and asked, "What about finding company with another man?"

Marie pulled her head back and tucked in her chin as if she'd been smacked. "I doubt it." She paused. "You think she was doing it with that silver-haired man you asked about?"

"I'm not at liberty to say," Madison responded. "But I can tell you he was found murdered along with Mrs. Malone."

Marie's mouth gaped open, and a few seconds later, she requested a photo again.

"There's a sketch in the works. I can show it to you once I have it," Madison said.

"Let me know."

"I will." Madison shifted position and straightened her back. "Just a few more questions before we go. Were you anywhere near the Malones' pool when you cleaned on Saturday or since then?"

Marie stiffened. "No."

"And last night. Where were you?"

"Here with Oscar." Marie pursed her lips. "Do you think I had something to do with her murder?"

"We're just covering our bases. Routine," Terry assured her.

Marie regarded him but didn't give the impression she was comforted in the least by his words. "There's probably something I should tell you."

The room fell quiet enough to hear the snow tapping against the windowpanes.

"When I was cleaning Mr. Malone's office on Saturday, Lorene came in and got real upset."

Madison tilted her head. "Why's that?"

"I don't really know. She just told me the mess wasn't in there, and that I was to leave at once. I did as she said."

"Do you normally clean the office?" Terry asked.

"I do."

Madison looked at Terry and stood. She

handed her card to Marie. "Call me if you think of anything else." Madison added her sympathies, and Marie showed her first sign of grief as tears sprung to her eyes and she bit on her bottom lip.

They saw themselves out, and Madison was on the phone with Cynthia before she and Terry reached the car. "I need you to sweep Mr. Malone's office. There's something in there we might want to see."

"More specifically?"

Madison unlocked the vehicle, and she and Terry got inside. "I don't know what you're looking for, but I'm hoping you'll know when you find it."

"Oh my God."

"Work with me, Cyn."

"You dumped the shoeprint thing on us and left," Cynthia grumbled. "It's late, I was supposed to go to the bridal store tonight, my wedding's only four days away, my maid of honor is getting sick—"

"I'm perfectly fine. Just please take a good look."

"Will do." Cynthia ended the call, and Madison tucked her phone into her coat pocket.

"You think whatever had Lorene in a tizzy over Marie being in the home office is connected to her murder?" Terry asked.

"I think it's possible."

Twenty-One

Madison's nerves were frayed by the time she reached the station. Navigating the treacherous roads were stressful enough, but she wanted some answers instead of just unearthing more questions. One thing was clear, though, there had to be something in Steven's office that Lorene didn't want anyone to find. Madison hoped that whatever it was would graciously reveal itself, but she wasn't naive enough to believe that would really happen. Things rarely worked out that easily with a murder investigation.

Lorene's phone records were on Madison's desk in a one-inch-thick file folder. She couldn't believe that was just for one month. She'd figured it would be most prudent to start with recent activity. After all, it would make sense that if someone close to Lorene had targeted her, it would be a person she was in contact with more recently. Madison had also assumed— obviously falsely—that the list would be short.

There was a sticky note on the front of the folder that read, *I am still working on accessing her social media accounts and email, Sam.*

Madison left the note where it was and separated the stack, giving Terry the slightly larger half. "You start scanning, see if you find any recurring numbers," she told him.

Madison flipped through the sheets she had in her hand and quickly discovered the stack she had contained the most recent activity. She went to Monday evening and found an outgoing call just after five o'clock.

Madison read off the number in her head and scanned across the page to the duration. Twenty minutes.

"I think I found that call that Mrs. Beaulieu told us about." She sat down and keyed in a reverse search for the number. The result came on her screen, and her blood ran cold. "Ah, Terry?"

"Yeah." He sounded groggy, like she'd just stirred him from sleep.

"Kimberly said that she talked to her mother for a few minutes on Monday night, right?"

"Sounds right, off the top of my head."

"Check your notes."

He rolled his eyes and pulled out his notepad, flipped pages. "She said, 'We spoke briefly on the phone yesterday.'"

"Do you consider twenty minutes brief?"

"Not really."

"According to this—" she held up the report "—Lorene called Kimberly, and they were on together for twenty minutes last night at five o'clock. Did the length of time just slip Kimberly's mind, or did she hold it back on purpose?"

Terry straightened in his chair. "Kimberly could have been who Lorene had been arguing with when the cook showed up. Well, you thought she was hiding something, but why lie about a phone conversation with her mother? It doesn't make much sense."

"Nope, unless it ties into the murders somehow."

"Whoa. Let's not take that leap just yet. It could have just slipped her mind."

"Convenient," she tossed back. "We've got to talk to her."

"We need more than something like this to interrupt her in the middle of the night. Even if she did leave it out, it might not have any bearing on the case."

"And it might." Madison wasn't going to let this go.

Terry shook his head. "It's not enough to justify our going over there right now. Tomorrow, sure, if we find it's still an avenue worth exploring." He buried his face in his part of the phone records.

"Fine, but I'm not forgetting this," Madison said. "We'll ask her tomorrow."

Terry didn't say anything, and Madison looked down at the sheets she had. She proceeded to highlight repeating numbers of which there were several. She'd do reverse searches for all of them, find out how they knew Lorene Malone, and go from there. The task might be something they'd need help with, especially if Terry was finding a lot of repeating numbers like she was. Then again, a clue might exist in the rarities.

She sat back in her chair and looked up at the ceiling. The fluorescent lights were buzzing, and the sound wormed into her head. Worse than Chinese water torture. During the day, with the station being a blur of activity, she never heard them. It must have been because she was tired that they even hit her ears now. The cappuccino was letting her down.

She took a different color highlighter and marked the numbers that didn't recur. After twenty minutes, the colors were blurring together. She looked back at Kimberly's number and committed it to memory. Revisiting the report, she noticed that Kimberly and her mother didn't talk that often.

"Terry."

He lifted his head, and she gave him Kimberly's number.

"Do you see that number on the pages you have?" she asked.

He shuffled through them, a few pages, a few

more, the entire pile. "I skimmed rather quickly, but, no, I didn't see it."

There was something there. She felt it through to her core. At the very least, it would seem mother and daughter hadn't been close. Yet they did yoga twice a week together? Maybe that negated the need to talk on the phone. "So, the only time Kimberly spoke to her mother was for twenty minutes on Monday, the night that she died, the call that Kimberly said only lasted 'briefly.' Now do you think we have enough reason to go over?"

Terry sighed deeply. "Let's leave her until the morning. Please."

He was just worried about Sergeant Winston; it was written all over his face and in his desperate plea.

She had little patience most of the time, but when she wanted an explanation on something, she was even worse. "Fine, but first thing."

She opened her email program and watched as a few new messages filtered in. One was from the sketch artist, and the subject line cited the case number for John Doe. She opened the message and clicked on the attachment. Staring back at her was the face of their John Doe.

Madison forwarded a copy to her phone and Terry's and told him they had Doe's sketch. She added, "It looks like I have another reason to pay Kimberly Olson-Malone a visit."

"You know what?" Terry lifted his hands in

a gesture of giving up. "If you think now is the best time—"

"If she knows him, we could be on the way to solving this case."

"Are you forgetting that she's the one who found him with her mother? She saw the man."

"Under traumatic circumstances. She might not have seen him close enough. She was probably more concentrated on having found her mother."

"Fine, you can go over there, but I'm staying put. I'll keep on the phone records."

"Okay." Madison stood and grabbed her coat. "Let me know if Sam comes back with anything on Lorene's social media or email."

"If she's smart, she'll be at home asleep already." Terry yawned as if on cue. "Just promise me one thing."

Madison tilted her head.

"You won't knock if the lights aren't on—and no doorbells."

Madison lifted one hand as if making a pledge. "Scout's honor."

She had her fingers crossed behind her back.

Twenty-Two

The front light was on as were a few inside Kimberly's house when Madison parked out front. Terry would be appeased. Madison knocked on the front door and waited. At least the snowfall had eased up, but the wind gusted around her, sending shivers tearing through her. She burrowed her chin into the collar of her coat.

No sounds or movements were coming from inside, and her finger was poised over the doorbell when her phone pinged. She jumped a little—as if Terry had eyes on her and was going to chastise her. There was a text from Troy.

Don't wait up for me. See you in the A.M. xo

She smiled at the "XO" but was curious what had him out so late. It could have been work, but if so, why not just say that? Wherever he was and whatever he was up to, she just hoped he was doing all right.

She keyed back a quick *okay*, and Kimberly's

door opened. She shoved her phone into her coat pocket.

Kurt was standing there, his eyes bloodshot. "Detective?" He looked past her, maybe searching for Terry.

"I'm sorry to be here so late—"

"No, it's fine." Kurt let her inside.

The warm air made her cheeks tingle, and she unzipped her coat.

Kurt leaned past her to close the door, and she caught a heavy whiff of scotch.

"No Detective Grant tonight?" he asked.

She shook her head. "He's busy with something else."

"Do you know who killed my mother?" Tears beaded in the corners of Kurt's eyes.

"I'm sorry but not yet."

Kurt sighed in frustration.

"There is something I'd like to show you and Kimberly," Madison started, "if you could get her? Is she awake?" She peered up the stairs to the dark upper hallway.

"Actually, she's not here."

Madison hadn't expected that. "Oh. Do you know where she is?"

"We're talking about Kim," Kurt said as if Madison knew her well. "She didn't say." He turned and walked to the parlor where she and Terry had talked with the siblings on their previous visit. He sat on an armchair.

Madison followed and took a seat on the

couch. Kimberly's being out actually presented a good opportunity to speak one-on-one with Kurt. "This is a stupid question, I know, but how are you holding up?"

He closed his eyes and pinched the bridge of his nose. "I still can't believe she's dead. It's like I expect her to walk through the door or call at any minute."

"I can only imagine how hard this must be on you." Madison leaned forward.

"It's incredibly hard."

"You were close to you mother? More than you made it sound earlier?" She was taking a risk approaching things this way. After all, Lorene had still been the woman who had given birth to him. That right there created a bond—and complications.

Kurt nodded.

What had made him bury his feelings in front of his sister? Was it because mother and daughter were at odds, and he didn't want to somehow hurt his sister by admitting he and his mother were close?

"When did you last see your mother? Was it more recently than you told us before?"

"I saw her on Friday night."

Tingles ran through Madison. "Where did you see her?"

"I just dropped by the house. She had a bunch of people over, so we didn't talk long. I thought she might have been lonely with Dad being away on business. That's why I'd popped over."

"They were just some friends?" Madison asked, pressing gently.

"Uh-huh. I'd never met any of them before." Kurt's eyes glazed over. "She introduced me to all of them, but I'd be pressed to tell you any of their names now." He looked at Madison thoughtfully. "You don't need that info anyway, do you?"

"Whatever you can remember could help," was all Madison said in reply. She didn't want to pressure him or cause his mind to go blank—if the scotch already hadn't to a degree.

"You think one of them killed her?" Fresh tears glistened in Kurt's eyes.

Madison remained silent, the quiet answering on her behalf.

"Oh." The utterance was full of pain.

"I'm not saying one of them did," Madison said, gaining Kurt's eye contact. "I'm saying if you can remember any names, that might help us. They could know the man we found with your mother." Madison pulled out her phone. "He could have even been at your parents' house the night you stopped by."

She walked her phone to Kurt, the sketch of John Doe up on her screen. "Do you recognize him? Either from Friday night or another time?"

Kurt tore his gaze from her and looked at the image. "This is the man who was found with my mom?"

"It is," she confirmed, attributing his question to the late hour, scotch, and an occupied mind.

Kurt studied the picture with intensity, his eyes squinting. "I've never seen him before."

"You're absolutely sure?" she tiptoed.

He expelled a rush of air. "I've never seen him before."

Kurt struck her as more angry with himself for not knowing than with her.

"That's fine, Kurt," she said, treading with caution, and sat back on the couch.

"It's not really." His bottom lip quivered. Tears filled his eyes. "Mom is dead. Murdered!" he spat. "Can you possibly imagine what we're going through?"

The alcohol, the grief, the shock, the anger of his mother's death were stripping him of his sanity.

"We heard from Craig," he blurted out. "Did Kim tell you?"

Heat simmered through Madison. "No. Craig and I did talk, though."

"Good. He's coming home. I'm glad, too. He's my favorite brother, and I was worried when we couldn't reach him."

She was just about to ask, *Isn't he your* only *brother?* when he winked at her, but his attempt at joviality sank heavily in the room. It could have something to do with the brother he hadn't even had a chance to know, the one Andrea had told her had died.

Somehow, the darkened path brought memories surfacing of Chelsea's kidnapping and how Madison had felt when she'd had no idea where her abductor was keeping her. Tears stung the back of her eyes. She was more than familiar with that ache in the chest, the one that squeezed her heart and sat as a heavy weight, making breathing next to impossible. "I know what it's like to have a loved one go missing," she admitted, thinking it wouldn't hurt to build up a bond with Kurt.

He scanned her eyes. "You do?"

"I do. It was only a couple of months ago."

"But you found them, your family member, and everything was okay?"

"My sister, and, yes, everything worked out." She didn't admit that there was still a long road ahead to full emotional and mental recovery. She smiled at him, touched that he'd care enough to ask, especially given what he was going through. "You and Craig are close?"

"After I started college. Before that I was in his way. Twelve years between us. I was the kid brother he couldn't shake."

"I know that feeling." Madison would hold back the fact that, in her situation, the roles were reversed, with her being the older sibling.

"Your older sister cut you out, too?"

"She's younger," Madison confessed with a smile. Three years younger, but who's counting?

"Ah, so you were cool, and she wasn't?" Kurt

stabbed at joviality, but it didn't reach his eyes. He got to his feet. "Craig has no idea that Mom was found with a man. Kim thought it best to tell him in person. I can't believe Mom would do this to Dad." His face balled into disgust, and he paced. "And after all those years and speeches about how when you made a commitment to someone, you stuck by it. She's a hypocrite." He clenched his jaw, and tears glistened in his eyes.

"I can only imagine how hard this is on you, your sister, your father," Madison empathized.

Kurt matched eyes with her when she mentioned his father. "Do you think Dad killed Mom and that man?"

Madison's breath froze. Did he really believe his father could have been the killer? Mr. Griffin had thought it possible, after all.

She studied Kurt's expression and body language, but both were hard to read. She had to be careful how she answered so as not to make him clam up or anger him. She also had to safeguard her own personal feelings on the matter of Steven's innocence or guilt. "I want whoever killed your mother to be put behind bars for the rest of their life." Safe, neutral ground, and she kept mention of Doe's murder out of it, focusing on Kurt's concern—his mother.

Tears fell down Kurt's cheeks. He was quick to wipe them. "And it's not Dad?"

"We will get the right person, I promise you."

That was the best Madison could do. She felt she'd exhausted her welcome and got up, pulled out a business card, and handed it to Kurt. "Call me if you need anything or think of something that could help find your mother's killer."

He palmed the card. "You can count on it."

She saw herself out and checked her phone for any messages that might have come in while she was talking with Kurt. She had a text from Terry.

> *Getting nowhere with the phone records. Morning was a long time ago. See you tomorrow.*

The clock on the car's dash told her it was approaching one o'clock; technically, it was tomorrow morning, but she'd let him have it. It was even tempting to let herself call it a day. She felt a dryness at the back of her throat and cursed Terry for even mentioning she was getting sick. She didn't have time to let some bug knock her on her ass, and with a double homicide, it was going to take a hell of a lot more than a little cold to stop her. For now, she'd listen to her body and crawl into bed. If she was lucky, she might even find Troy at home and awake.

Twenty-Three

Madison was dressed and nursing a coffee at the kitchen table by five in the morning. She was feeling miserable as heck—and angry. She'd tossed and turned waiting for Troy to get home. One, she was worried about him and curious where he was, and two, she'd adjusted to sharing the bed with someone. Regardless, her body gave up somewhere around three thirty. When she'd woken up at quarter to five, he'd been in bed next to her. She had been tempted to shake him awake but thought she'd let him sleep for a bit. She didn't want to come across as a psycho, jumping to conclusions. She could have misinterpreted his message, and he hadn't been out for fun at all but had been called to a job.

She cleared her throat and hated the fact it was still scratchy like last night, if not a little worse. Maybe it was just exhaustion, and she'd feel better once she got some real sleep. Who knew when that would be, though?

Troy staggered into the kitchen, his hair sticking up at the front. Dark circles underscored slightly bloodshot eyes. His green irises that were usually such a fierce hue were subdued. Usually, Troy was much like his sister in that he always looked good. This was the most disheveled she'd seen him.

"You look like shit," she said, a little heat sneaking into her voice. He'd obviously been out drowning his sorrows without her, without so much as opening up to her about the feelings he was having, about his grief.

"Gee, thanks." He rubbed a hand over his mouth and headed straight to the coffeepot.

"I take it you weren't working last night." All confrontational and unapologetic. He made a finger gun, pointed it at her, and pulled the trigger. "You made detective."

If he'd done it to be funny, he'd failed. "What time did you get in?" She'd leave the "Where were you?" part out for now.

"Late. Early. Depends how you look at it." He poured some coffee into a cup and sloshed some onto his hand in the process. He shook his scalded hand like a mad dog, then grabbed the cup as it was, partially full and black, and crossed the room to join her at the table.

He stopped next to her, put his free arm around her, and bent over with the intent to kiss her. She pulled back.

"Whoa, I guess somebody's pissed." He

dropped into a chair. "I just didn't want to wake you up."

"It's not about..." She gritted her teeth. He really had no clue it wasn't where he'd been or for how long as much as it was that if he was hurting, he wasn't sharing that with her. That hurt. More than she'd like to admit. "You smell like a distillery."

"A guy can't have a couple of drinks?"

Madison angled her head. "I think it's a safe bet you had more than a couple." He was still drunk from what she could tell.

"So what if I did?" He stared at her blankly as he put his cup to his lips and took a slow draw on the coffee.

"Out with the guys?" She hated that even the thought of him being unfaithful had flitted up from her subconscious. Her mind knew that Troy wasn't the cheating kind, but her heart that had been hurt before ached in her chest.

Seconds passed, and he said nothing, and with each tick of the clock on the wall, she became angrier. "What the hell happened last night?" she snapped.

He choked on some coffee and coughed. "I just went out for some drinks with a friend."

"Some?" There was an icky feeling crawling under her skin, and she didn't care for it one bit. He might not be lying to her, but he wasn't exactly being forthcoming.

"What is it, Maddy?" There was a sharpness

to his voice that sliced through her. "I don't get on your case when you go out and drink with friends."

"I rarely do that."

"Still. When you do, I say nothing. You're a grown fucking woman." He drank more coffee. "I'm a grown man."

She stared him in the eyes, tempted to retort with something hurtful, but she slammed her mug on the table instead. Her heart was pounding, and she was finding it hard to breathe. He never talked to her like this. Pain or not, she deserved better than to be treated this way.

He reached for her, and his big hand encircled her wrist, his touch gentle. His eyes softened. "I'm sorry."

Her chest was heaving to catch air.

"I know you have trust issues," he said.

"What?" She glanced away from him briefly, then returned her gaze. "Where did that come from?"

"Where did—" He let go of her and looked up to the ceiling, his jaw tight. He then met her eyes. "It's not an unfamiliar topic of conversation around here. We usually revisit it every few weeks, for God's sake, but I'm not your cheating ex-fiancé."

The coffee in her stomach had churned into battery acid. Why was he going there? Why was he assuming she thought he'd cheated on her last night? Was he guilty of having an affair? She swallowed roughly, nearly choking on her own saliva. "Why are you bringing this up?"

"Why am I? You're grilling me like I'm one of your suspects."

"Why are you acting like this?" She gripped her side where a stitch had latched on with a fierce grip. This conversation was quickly spiraling out of control.

His eyes drifted to where her hand was. He went to touch her, but she pulled back.

"Maddy, I—"

"What's going on?" She crossed her arms. "And be honest with me." God, she begged for honesty, but she feared that it might bring news that would end their relationship. If so, she'd never get involved with anyone else again. Men just wouldn't be worth the pain.

"I just had drinks with a friend. I should have stopped at one, made it an early night. Come on, forgive me." He was looking her in the eyes and put his hand on the table, palm up, wanting her to put hers in his.

She didn't comply. "Who? What friend?"

He sighed and raked a hand through his hair.

"You do realize that your not telling me is suspicious, Troy. What are you hiding?" She hurled the question at him, knowing at least part of the answer. He was holding back his feelings about the Malone family, about the grief he'd endured so many years ago and how

Lorene's murder had brought it all back with startling freshness.

"I'm not hid—"

She coughed, ripping it from the base of her lungs. "Fuck. Shit."

Troy was looking at her with concern in his eyes. "Are you all right?"

His affection, in the light of his secrecy, made her bristle. "Nope, I feel peachy keen." She coughed more.

"Liar."

"Sounds like—" She bit her tongue. Speaking of lying, why couldn't he just say who he'd been having drinks with? She got up, intent on heading into the station.

"Please," Troy petitioned and patted a hand on the table.

"Are you going to talk to me?" She hated being put in this position. People might think she lived for confrontation, but she'd prefer to go through life without any.

He slid his jaw from side to side. The room suddenly felt heavy. "It's been a while since I saw her."

"*Her*?" Madison dropped back into the chair. He was being cagey about who he'd been drinking with…and no wonder. His friend had been a female. She had to be naive to think Troy wouldn't cheat. He was a man, he was vulnerable, he was grieving. The woman had to be someone he shared common ground with, a history, someone who would understand what he was feeling… The woman's identity presented itself in a flash. "You were with Kimberly Malone," she concluded.

He grimaced.

"Troy, are you serious?" Had it just been an innocent reunion or something more? She couldn't think about it too deeply. She just couldn't.

"It's not what you might be thinking," he beseeched her. "Kim and I are just friends—"

"*Kim*," she interjected loudly, speaking over him, but he continued speaking. "Sounds like you're close."

"Just friends. I swear to God, Madison, that's all. I'd never do anything to hurt you" His green eyes were wet and piercing through hers. Her mind wanted to believe him, but her heart wasn't as brave.

She held eye contact, letting his vulnerability sink in; he was hurting, too. And she knew that Troy had been devastated when his wife had cheated on him—surely, he wouldn't become the cheater. Her heart started to calm down as logic seeped in, and her mind shifted to another reason that would have had him withholding who he'd been with last night. "Oh, Troy." She stood and paced. "Kim hasn't been cleared as a suspect in her mother's murder, in John Doe's."

"Kim didn't kill them," Troy stated firmly, his body tensing as he got up.

"I appreciate that you might think so—" she held up a hand, hoping he wouldn't interrupt like he seemed braced to do "—but she could be involved, things could still get messy. Heck, don't you see how this could be a huge conflict of interest for me and have me thrown off the case?"

"That's why I didn't want to tell you who I was with."

"Does she know about us?" A random question, but Madison was curious.

"She does after last night."

"Oh." Madison took a deep breath. "Please don't see her again. At least not until the case is solved."

"I'm not sure if—"

"Please. I know you want to be there for her," Madison told him. His fierce loyalty, something she normally found attractive, would make her request difficult, but it was necessary.

"I don't know if I can promise that," he confessed.

"Just try." She took a steadying breath. "Did you talk to her about the case?"

"We talked about her mother's murder." He was calm. "That's why we met."

"So you did talk about the case?" Heat fired in her earlobes, and a damned tickle danced in the base of her throat. She coughed again.

"I don't know much about the case, Maddy, besides the vague amount you told me and what she shared," Troy began. "She just needed someone to talk to."

"Did she ask you about the investigation or how it was going?"

"You're asking if she's trying to keep tabs through me? No." There was a simmering heat underlying his voice.

"How can you even be sure that Kimberly isn't involved in the murders?" She cut right for the sore spot.

"Come on." He was unamused.

"No, really, Troy, how could you know? You admitted you haven't seen each other in a long time. She could be an entirely different person from who you knew."

Troy flailed his hands in the air. "And we're back to this."

"Back to *what*?" she rebuked.

"You think she charmed me somehow, or that I was unfaithful to you."

Ice laced through her veins. "I don't know why you're bringing that up again, but there's a lot I don't understand right now, and as long as we're on the subject of Kim, you as much admitted to knowing I wouldn't be pleased you'd met up. And while we're revealing secrets, I'd also like to know why you never told me about Brad."

He staggered backward, and his cheeks flushed as if he'd been slapped across the face.

"I'm sorry, I—"

"No." He pointed a finger at her. "You don't

get to go around my back and talk to my sister about me."

"Maybe if you'd just talk to—"

"I was going to talk to you. Remember? I even told you we'd talk about it last night, but you had a job to do, and that's fine. Trust me when I say that I want you to catch this killer more than most, but you have no right to put this in my face, play the woe-is-me victim."

She gripped her stomach as if she'd been hit there. "I just wish you'd talk to me when something upsets you," she said quietly.

"I was going to last night as I said, but—"

"I wasn't here," she finished.

He didn't say anything.

"It's just when Barry died, you pulled away from me. I thought I was going to—" Her voice hitched, and she wished she could blame it completely on the scratchy throat and not emotion. "To lose you," she finished.

He frowned and pulled her in for a hug and held her tight. He put his face into her hair, and just above her ear, said, "I've told you before, I'm not going anywhere, and I mean it."

She soaked in his love and chastised herself for doubting even for the fraction of a second that he'd been unfaithful, that he was even capable. She kissed him and pulled out of the embrace.

"I'd gotten up this morning planning to talk to you about Brad, the Malones, all of it, even though I'm still feeling last night and could sleep for the week."

"Well, I'd say we got off to a bad start this morning."

"That's an understatement."

Her mind drifted back to Kimberly and Troy's relationship. "Did you sleep with her?"

"Really? We're back to that?" He turned to walk away, and she grabbed him by the elbow. His eyes were daggers when he looked at her.

"I meant in the past," she clarified.

"No, Madison. We were friends. That's all we ever were." He glanced at where her hand was still on him. "I'm going back to bed for a few hours before shift."

She watched him walk away, and pain splintered her heart, making it hard to breathe. Bryan Adams knew what he was saying when he sang about love cutting like a knife.

Twenty-Four

There wasn't anything that could get Madison's mind off Troy. Paperwork—mind-numbing, most of the time—certainly wasn't cutting it. She still tried to scrutinize Lorene's phone records, conducting reverse searches on a few of the numbers. She decided it would probably be more effective to call after eight o'clock and inquire as to how they knew Lorene Malone, but as soon as Terry got in, she had something else she wanted to take care of first.

Terry walked into the bullpen and staggered back when he saw her. "You beat me here?"

"Always a smartass."

"You bet." He smirked, and she was happy to see that her partner seemed to be in a good mood this morning. Maybe Annabelle had agreed to see a doctor.

"Someone got a good night's sleep," she said, not daring to ask about Annabelle.

"Annabelle is going to make a doctor's

appointment today," he volunteered as if he'd read her mind.

"That's good news."

"Yeah. Let's just hope she *gets* good news."

"Whatever it is, you'll have each other, me, friends, and family." Madison gave him a reassuring smile.

"You're right," he said somberly, and she wished she'd just spewed sunshine, but life had taught her to be cautious.

Madison glanced at the clock on the wall. *8:10 AM*. She got up, grabbed her coat, and said, "Let's go."

"I just got here," he sulked and pointed toward the coffee machine. "I haven't even poured a cup—"

"We'll get one on the way."

"Where are we headed?"

"Kimberly Olson-Malone's." She walked past him, not waiting for a reaction, not even wanting to see one. Speaking with Kimberly about the phone call was the next logical step, and it was a respectable hour of the day, even though Kimberly might not feel the same way if she had drunk anywhere near the amount Troy had. There was a tiny part of Madison that would find some pleasure in waking her. After all, she didn't think Kimberly was the innocent little thing the woman would have some people believe. Call it a gut feeling.

IF A HOUSE COULD LOOK like it was sleeping, that's about the amount of energy Kimberly's was emitting. The driveway had been cleared, but no lights shone from inside, and the front light was off. Everything looked sealed up. No vehicles were parked in the driveway, but Madison figured they were in the garage.

She rang the doorbell and waited, Terry beside her.

The door cracked open, the seal around it sounding as if it were resisting. Kurt peeked his head out and squinted into the morning sun.

"Good morning, Kurt," Madison said. "We need to speak with your sister."

He opened the door for them to step inside.

"She's sleeping," he said.

"I'm afraid we're going to need you to wake her."

"This can't wait until later?" The Kurt from last night was gone and replaced by a protective younger brother—and possibly a hungover one. "If it's about that man's picture, I doubt she'll recognize him."

"We're here about something else as well," Madison started. "Something only she can help us with."

Kurt held Madison's gaze as he took a staggering breath. "I can go see if I can rouse the dead. Wish me luck." He went up the stairs, mumbling something about being thankful homicide detectives were in the house.

Terry turned to Madison. "We probably could come back later."

"No, we're here now." Her obstinance was partly coming from Kimberly's meeting with Troy last night, circumventing the system and breaking an unspoken rule by doing so. She had essentially inserted herself into an active police investigation. Whether Kimberly had done so intentionally or not, Madison had yet to determine. It wasn't like she could come out and confront Kimberly in front of Terry, though. If she did, she'd call Troy's character and integrity into question.

A door creaked open upstairs and footsteps padded toward the upper landing. Kimberly looked down at them. Her dark hair was tousled and fell over her shoulders as if she'd just had it blown out at the salon. Her eyes were weary, as was the expression on her face. "What can I do for you, Detective?"

Detective? Singular? As if Terry wasn't even standing there. Kimberly seemed to be making this personal. To what end?

"We have a sketch for you to look at—of the man who was found with your mother."

Madison would get to the phone call, but she'd start with more neutral territory first. Otherwise, Kimberly would probably get all defensive and call for a lawyer faster than kids run around a candy store.

Kimberly tied the belt on the silk robe she was wearing and slinked down the stairs. For an instant, Madison hated the woman with every fiber of her being. She was beautiful, and no doubt knew how to use it to her advantage. Madison hated to think of her manipulating Troy for her own agenda.

Kurt started down behind his sister but passed her. "I'll go put on a pot of coffee, sis."

"Thanks," Kimberly barely mumbled and flipped some hair out of her face. She reached the entry and leveled a glare on Madison.

"We thought you'd like to see the man's picture as soon as possible," Madison said.

Kimberly regarded her with suspicion. "His face is burned into my mind, actually," she said drily. "I can take a look, but I didn't recognize him when I found him with my mother."

Terry took out his phone and extended the sketch of John Doe toward Kimberly.

She leaned in toward the screen, studied the image for long enough to memorize it in detail, then shook her head. "I've never seen him before." There was disappointment in her voice.

"You're sure," Madison pressed.

Kimberly matched gazes with Madison and spoke very slowly. "I've. Never. Seen. Him. Before."

Why did this woman have such an edge to her when all Madison was trying to do was solve her mother's murder?

Kurt edged up to his sister and put a steaming mug of coffee into her hands.

Kimberly looked on her brother with affection, but her eyes turned to ice when she turned back at Madison. "Kurt said you had something to discuss with me." It was as if she were daring Madison to bring up Kimberly's rendezvous with Troy.

"We do," Madison said coolly.

"Okay." Kimberly sauntered into the sitting room. Madison, Terry, and Kurt followed.

Kimberly sat crossed-legged on the couch and flipped her robe over her legs. Madison regarded her skeptically. She'd found her mother murdered yesterday morning and there didn't seem to be any grief coming from her at all—no emotion, really—unless rage counted.

Madison sat on a chair. "We're just wanting to verify something." She turned subtly toward Terry.

"The last time you spoke to your mother was Monday night," Terry said.

"That's right," Kimberly said slowly and sipped some of her coffee.

"And it was only briefly," Madison baited the hook for a liar, using Kimberly's own words.

"That's right."

Kimberly's tone was relaxed, as was her posture. Either she was really good at lying, or the length of the phone call totally slipped her mind.

"Huh." Madison just let that sit out there for a few seconds, utilizing the power of silence. It could drive some people mad with the need to fill the dead space.

"She was my mother, we talked. So what?" Kimberly licked her lips, and her body stiffened ever so slightly. "I don't know for how long!" she snapped.

"You don't think that might be important?" Madison asked.

"I don't see how." Kimberly glanced at her brother, eyes widened as if Madison were a crazy person.

"It was hours before she was killed," Madison softened her approach with the intent of throwing Kimberly off guard and opening her up. "What did you talk about?"

Kimberly hugged her mug with two hands and nestled into the couch. "I don't see how what we talked about matters."

"How was she?" Terry interjected, taking Kimberly's gaze.

Kimberly didn't say anything for a few seconds, and the underlying current of tension and animosity was easy to feel.

"Were you and your mother at odds about something?" Madison raised her eyebrows.

Kimberly glanced at Kurt, who was watching her intently. After a bit, she said, "Let's just say that Mom and I weren't seeing eye to eye on something."

Kurt leaned over and put a hand on his sister's forearm. "Why didn't you say anything to me?"

Kimberly put her hand over her brother's. "I didn't want to burden you with that." She looked at Madison. "It would have gotten sorted out. It was just a silly matter when I think back on it." The dullness in her eyes belied her claim. Whatever they had been talking about was far from being the "silly matter" that Kimberly was trying to pass off.

Madison leaned forward, just slightly. "Where were you Monday night after eight o'clock?" This would have been after Beaulieu, the cook, had left for the day.

"I believe last time you asked a similar question, I'd said we'd have a lawyer present. I've been pleasant, Detective, speaking with you even after having my sleep disturbed." Kimberly stood. "If that will be all. There are some things I need to take care of."

What was Kimberly hiding? Didn't she know that her behavior was just making her appear more suspicious? She'd had the opportunity to kill her mother and John Doe, but what was the motive? Did it have something to do with their disagreement? By extension, where had Kimberly gotten the gun? She didn't have any registered to her.

Terry got up, but Madison hesitated. If only there was something more conclusive to justify bringing Kimberly downtown. Unfortunately, her refusal to provide an alibi wasn't enough. It seemed there were secrets in the Malone household, and it led Madison's mind to Lorene's reaction to Rauch cleaning the Malones' home office.

"We spoke to your parents' housekeeper," Madison started.

Kimberly shook her head. "Okay." She might as well have said *sooooo?*

Madison went on. "She said that the other day your mother got quite upset that she was in your father's office. Would you happen to know why?"

"I wouldn't have the faintest."

"Mrs. Rauch said that she's cleaned in there before without issue," Madison said.

Kimberly crossed her arms, but light flickered across her eyes. "I can't answer for my mother, Detective, and unfortunately she'd dead, so she can't answer for herself."

Madison turned her attention to Kurt, who was still around but more as an observer. "Would you happen to have any idea why your mother wouldn't want the housekeeper in there?"

"That's where Dad kept confidential files. Mom probably didn't want his privacy invaded."

But she'd cleaned in there before...

"Have either of you been in your father's office?" Madison asked, trying to get a better feel for how the room was normally treated:

Fort Knox or open door.

"When I lived at home, sure," Kurt said. "You, Kim?" He prompted his sister.

"Yeah, I've been in there." She fidgeted with the tie on her robe and ended up stuffing her hands into its pockets. "But it was a long time ago for me, too."

"Okay." Satisfied for now, Madison dipped her head and got up.

She and Terry were seen to the door, and it was closed heavily behind them.

Madison glared over a shoulder toward the house. "What is that woman's issue?"

"She lost her mother."

Madison stared at her partner. "That doesn't explain why it feels like she's fighting us every step of the way. We're trying to find her mother's killer, and she treats us like we're the bad guy. Threatens to call a lawyer every time we ask where she was Monday night. She doesn't want to tell us what she was arguing with her mother about. That's suspicious, too. If it had been my mom, I would do whatever I could to help detectives find her killer. I don't get it."

"Well, not everyone thinks like you do."

"Ain't that the—" Her phone rang, cutting her off, leaving "truth" unsaid. The caller ID told her it was Cynthia. "Whatcha got?"

"Good morning to you, too," Cynthia said unamused. "Sometimes I feel so used."

"You know I love ya." Madison bit her tongue

and resisted the urge to ask her friend what she had for them a second time.

"I just wanted to let you know that we've finished up the preliminary at the house. I haven't released the scene yet, but I'm at the lab with some updates for you guys if you want to—"

"We'll be there in five."

Twenty-Five

Madison and Terry found Cynthia in the lab at her desk. She swiveled to face them. Cynthia's eyes were red and underscored by dark circles.

"Whoa, and I thought I looked rough," Madison said.

Cynthia grimaced and pointed at Madison's face. "Looks like we have matching luggage. You're not sick, though, right? Tell me you're not—"

Madison put a hand on her friend's shoulder. "I'm completely healthy." A white lie.

"Good, I don't need any bad news." Cynthia popped to her feet. "The wedding is in three days."

"I'm fine," Madison assured her again.

"Uh-oh, it never is when you say 'fine.'" Cynthia stared in Madison's eyes.

"Okay, I'm not one hundred percent, but I will be."

"Oh, no," Cynthia groaned. "The pictures are

going to be ruined. You'll have puffy eyes and a red nose—"

"I'm sure I can take a pill or something." Madison looked at Terry for help, but he was smirking and shaking his head. So much for her partner backing her up.

Cynthia's brows drew down, and she fixed her bead on Terry. "You let her get sick."

"Hey, what? No." Terry's smirk was gone.

"You're my maid of honor. I've told you that you can't be getting sick," Cynthia whined.

Madison loved her friend, but she was starting to lose it. "It could blow off. Let's just focus on the case. You have some findings for us?"

Cynthia didn't move, didn't say a word, just peered into Madison's eyes. "Sam got into Lorene's social media accounts. She only had Facebook and Twitter accounts. Had a significant following. Mostly tweeted about human rights and charity movements."

"The daughter said she volunteered at Meals for You," Terry squeezed in.

Cynthia glanced at him. "The name is familiar. I recall seeing some retweets from them on her feed."

"What about on Facebook?" Madison asked.

"She shared community events and photos from them. Her posts always received a number of reactions and comments. She didn't post often, though."

"Did she share anything for other charities?" Madison was curious, as Kimberly had said her mother was involved in a few of them.

Cynthia shook her head. "Not that I remember."

"Any luck finding our John Doe among her friend list?" Madison asked.

"If we had, I'd be a little more hyper than I am now."

Madison sighed. "Fair enough."

"Now, Sam got into Lorene's main email account, too. She logged right onto the hosting server and was able to recover some deleted emails. Two of interest," Cynthia paused. "You listening closely?"

"On the edge of my seat," Terry said, and that got Cynthia laughing.

"Ready?" Cynthia looked at Madison.

"Yes," she rushed out, not handling suspense well.

Cynthia smiled at Madison's impatience. "They were deleted yesterday."

"Yesterday?" Madison blinked slowly. "You're sure. Lorene was—"

"Dead? Yeah, I know, but someone must have access to her email and deleted those two."

"What were they?" Madison asked.

Cynthia snatched a couple pieces of paper off the printer and extended them to Madison. "Here's one."

Terry leaned in next to Madison, his elbow

hitting her stomach.

"A little personal space might be nice," she said.

He moved a fraction of an inch.

Madison looked at the printout. Page one was the email message, complete with the sender's information. The subject read, *Your Invoice*, and the body read, *Please find your invoice attached.* There was no salutation and no signature.

Page two of the printout was the attachment. It was an invoice and didn't provide much in the way of details. The description was, *For services rendered.* The letterhead just had a name and a tax ID, no phone number or address.

Madison looked up from the page. "Did you look them up?"

"Haven't gotten there yet," Cynthia confessed.

"Well, it must be important," Madison said, tension knotting between her shoulder blades and burrowing into the back of her neck. "Important enough that someone saw fit to delete the email. They weren't counting on it being recovered."

"I agree that it could be important, and trust me, it's a priority—along with a lot of other things. We also have the Malones' financials to review."

Progress was being made, but Madison wished for more just a little faster. "Please. As soon as possible."

"Yes, Maddy, I promise."

Terry raised his brows toward Cynthia. "You said there were two emails."

"The second." Cynthia handed them a third piece of paper.

"The sender was Kimberly Olson-Malone?" Madison gasped and searched for Cynthia's reaction.

Cynthia butted her head toward the printout, directing Madison's attention back to it.

Madison read the brief message aloud. "'You have the proof! Now do the right thing or I will.'" Madison looked up. "What's that mean? And proof of what?" She paced a few steps. "Kimberly and her mother were in a disagreement about something. I eventually dragged that out of her. Did that lead her to killing her mother and John Doe?" She faced her partner as doubts snaked in and coiled around her chest.

"What do you think the chances are Kimberly was the one to delete the emails?" Cynthia theorized.

"Quite good." Madison looked at Terry. "We've got to bring her in right away."

"Hold up. There's no need to jump on this so quickly," he replied, holding up a hand. "It could have been the killer who deleted these messages for some reason, someone other than Kimberly who had access to Lorene's email. And may I remind you that we don't even know if she has access."

"Then we ask her." Madison was halfway to

the door.

"Oh, God. Here we go." Terry hustled after her.

"Wait, guys," Cynthia called out and drew them back to her. "I haven't even told you everything yet. I see you're in a hurry, so I'll email the list of evidence that we've collected thus far."

"Cyn, you're killing me." Madison jacked a thumb toward the door. "We've got to bring Kimberly in for questioning, and she needs to start talking."

"Before I arm you with more ammo against Kimberly, let me just tell you that both Kimberly and her father were negative for gunshot residue."

Madison couldn't say the results surprised her, but she latched on to Cynthia's promise of "more ammo against Kimberly. "What else do you have?"

"We checked out the home office like you'd asked me to," Cynthia began, a smirk on her lips. "It's hard to find something when one doesn't really know what they're looking for."

Madison tapped a foot.

"We did collect a few USB sticks, along with the home computer, thinking there might be something electronic that would give us something useful. We still need to work through all that, but we lifted fingerprints from the desk drawer." Cynthia let a pregnant pause play out, and Madison was about ready to throttle her friend when she resumed, "They were Kimberly's."

"Kimberly said she hadn't been in the office for years." That part might be true, as there was no way to date prints, but if the housekeeper typically cleaned the office, as they were told she did, it would be assumed she'd wiped down the desk, including the handles. "What was in the drawer?"

"The USB sticks I mentioned, among other things."

Had Kimberly gone into that drawer in search of one of the drives or something else, and had she found it?

"Let me know what's on them as soon as possible," Madison said, then hit the door running.

Twenty-Six

Madison entered the interview room in front of Terry. Kimberly had put up quite a fuss when they'd returned to bring her downtown, and she followed through on her threat to secure a lawyer. Blake Golden was sitting next to Kimberly, hands clasped on the table in front of him and reeking of smugness. Sergeant Winston was holed up in the observation room, likely waiting for an opportunity to pounce.

"Kimberly and I have been talking, and we believe there's been a misunderstanding," Blake said.

Madison sat across from them. "Oh, really? Please enlighten me." She had little patience for the defense attorney at the best of times. She'd already wasted months in a relationship with him. She wished she could say it was forever ago, but the fact it was within the last five years just confirmed how far she'd come in so little time.

Terry took position against the wall behind Blake and Kimberly, leaning against it and jingling the change in his pocket.

Blake looked over a shoulder at Terry and smirked. "Up to the same old tricks, Grant."

Terry shrugged. "Whatever works"—and he kept jingling the change.

"You said there was a misunderstanding," Madison began. "I'm still waiting to hear what you feel that is." She stared Blake in the eye.

"Ms. Olson-Malone is in grieving. Her mother was murdered. It's understandable that she simply forgot how long the conversation was that she had with her mother."

"Only one small part of why she's here."

"Then we haven't received the full story. Please, enlighten us." Blake adjusted his tie without breaking eye contact.

Madison turned away from Blake only because she wanted to look at Kimberly, not because she was giving him a win in the stare down. "Do you have access to your mother's email?"

Blake faced his client and nodded for her to answer.

"Why would I have?"

Madison wasn't impressed that she'd counter with a question. "Some older people don't have the same understanding of technology," Madison said nonchalantly. She'd given some thought to how Kimberly might have had access to her mother's email server. "My mother's first smartphone, and she was ready to toss it within minutes. She couldn't figure out how any of it worked, and my sister had to help her set it up." She was hoping to rope Kimberly into the relatable scenario.

Kimberly's gaze drifted briefly to the table.

"Did you by chance help out your mother with her email?" Madison asked.

Blake placed a hand on Kimberly's forearm and said to Madison, "What is this about, Detective?"

"Two emails were deleted from your mother's email server," Madison started, claiming Kimberly's gaze. "One of them was from you."

"I don't see how this—"

Madison held up a hand to silence Blake and was pleased that it had worked. She continued. "This one." She pulled a printout of Kimberly's message from a file and extended it across the table.

Kimberly retrieved it and looked at it. "So? I emailed my mother." Her brows made a V. "Even the fact it was deleted, as you say, doesn't mean I'm the one who did it. What reason would I have?"

"In the email, you said she has proof, and you ask her to do the right thing," Madison said, not about to be swayed by Kimberly's innocence act.

Blake leaned forward. "Parents and children

argue all the time. It doesn't mean one is going to murder the other."

Madison tightened her jaw. "Your client told us that she spoke with her mother for a few minutes the night she died. It was actually *twenty* minutes. Your client also found her mother and that man. She had all the time she wanted before calling nine-one-one."

"Now you're suggesting I tampered with—" Kimberly burst out and stopped short when Blake touched her arm.

"If you were going to say 'tampered with the crime scene,' Ms. Olson-Malone, yes, I think it's entirely possible." Madison was working her way up to confronting her on the home office and why her prints would be in there. "Did you go into your father's office on Tuesday morning?"

"I told you. I haven't been in there in years." Kimberly's body was quaking ever slightly.

Madison relaxed into her chair. "Why did you go in there…back then?"

Kimberly's eyes turned cool. "It was years ago, why would I remember the reason?"

Madison shrugged her shoulders like it didn't matter why she had, hoping it would goad Kimberly.

"I went in to see my father, that's all." Kimberly crossed her arms and extended her neck to one side. "I was over for dinner on a Sunday night and went up to get him to let him know the meal was ready. Mom had asked me to."

Madison nodded, noting how "clear" Kimberly's memory had become. "And that's all? You didn't touch anything?"

Kimberly seemed to think about it and then said, "I might have put my hand down on the corner of his desk?"

"Okay, makes sense. You went up to get him for dinner, so there was no need to go into his desk or anything."

Kimberly latched eyes with Madison and slowly shook her head.

"So, this 'proof' you mentioned to your mother had nothing to do with anything in your father's office or his desk?" Madison asked, fishing and hoping for a catch, finally being able to circle back to the email and its meaning as well as to see if she could connect Kimberly's prints on the desk drawer somehow.

"I don't know what you're talking about," Kimberly claimed.

Madison pointed a finger to the printout. "In this email you mentioned proof. Proof of what? I asked you before. I'm asking again."

"And you can keep asking, Detective," Blake spoke firmly. "Unless you have some *proof* that this is in any way connected to the murder of two people, then, by all means, we'll hear you out, but I'm failing to see what even warranted bringing my client down here."

Madison glanced to the one-way mirror,

thinking that Winston was probably on his way to call an ending to the meeting. "We're here to solve your mother's murder, but you're fighting us every inch of the way. Why?"

Kimberly's face softened a tad. "You keep looking at me and my family as if we killed her. The world doesn't have the right to know all our family secrets—and, yes, I admit we have some, but what family doesn't? You don't need to know everything."

"That doesn't apply when there's a murder investigation," Madison countered.

"Well, I'm refusing to disclose our secrets to protect my mother's reputation. I do have that right." Kimberly jutted out her chin.

Madison and Kimberly locked in brief eye contact. The woman's eyes were a storm. Madison pulled the invoice from Your Best Friend from the folder. She wanted to see Kimberly's reaction. She barely looked at it before her gaze flicked away.

"Do you know what they did for your mother?" Madison asked.

Kimberly's cheeks flushed, and she shook her head.

Lie.

"But you've heard of them before?"

"Yes."

Madison leaned forward. "How?"

Silence.

"Did your mother mention them to you?"

Madison kept pushing.

Kimberly turned to Blake and whispered something in his ear. He scowled and shook his head.

"I'm just going to tell them," Kimberly said to him.

"You're the client, but know I strongly advise against your doing so."

Kimberly faced Madison and tucked a few strands of hair behind an ear. "I deleted the emails. The one I sent and one from Your Best Friend. Only reason I've heard of them."

Madison sat up straighter, her heart racing, but she dared not say a word at the risk of shutting Kimberly up.

Kimberly went on. "You were right to assume I had Mom's email login information. She had me set it up for her."

Madison worked to suppress her smugness from showing. "Why did you delete the emails?"

"Because…" Kimberly sighed heavily. "I don't want things to come out about the family, what Mom and Dad are really like behind closed doors."

Blake put his elbow to the table, his hand against his forehead.

"And what are they like?" Madison asked, feeling euphoric, on the brink of a lead.

Kimberly crossed her arms. "I refuse to say. I know that you might not understand that, but it's just the way it is."

Madison couldn't force her to speak, though she wished she could. Whatever the family secret was, it was substantial. It involved some sort of "proof" and affected Kimberly.

"I believe we're finished here." Blake collected his briefcase from the floor beside him and stood. Kimberly followed suit. "Don't call my client back in unless you have proof that she's involved in the murders, or we'll be filing a complaint," he warned.

Blake and Kimberly left the interview room and shut the door behind them. Terry came to stand next to Madison, the change jingling at an end.

"We need to know what's in her head," she said.

"Well, we're going to need to do it without her help," Terry replied soberly.

"Isn't that abundantly clear." It wasn't a question. She didn't mean to be snide or sarcastic, but she was frustrated. She would have to focus on the fact that they had *something*, even if they didn't really know what that something was— just that the Malones had a secret, and that might be exactly what had gotten Lorene and John Doe killed.

Sergeant Winston stormed into the interrogation room. "That could have gone better, don't you think."

"We were questioning a suspect," she responded calmly. "We kept you in the loop, and we were just going where the evidence took us."

"You heard Mr. Golden. He'll sue the department for harassment. I've been too lenient." Winston clenched his jaw. "No more talking to members of the Malone family unless you're able to put the murder weapon in one of their hands," he spat. "Dragging that poor girl in here and putting her through this circus. Besides, wasn't it at your request that I put protection on Mr. Malone? I took that as you having released him of your suspicion. Now you're focusing on the man's daughter."

Her earlobes shot up to high temperature. "She refuses to answer simple questions. She hasn't even provided us with an alibi for the time of her mother's murder, yet she admits to having had a difference with her." She paused, her anger making her lightheaded. "If this was any other case—"

"But this isn't any other case, and the Malones aren't just anybody."

"I know," she spat. "They're one of the largest contributors to the Stiles PD."

He held up an index finger. "One more word, Knight, and I'll suspend your ass. Don't think I won't."

He'd done it before, so she believed the threat was real, but she was sick of defending herself for doing her job. It might be time to take the matter over his head and talk to Andrea. Before she did that, though, she would attempt to appeal to him from another direction. "You keep—"

He glared at her and grimaced.

"You keep," she started over, unpersuaded, "telling me how important the Malones are to the community, to the Stiles PD…well, then doesn't that make it all the more important to find out who killed one of them sooner than later?" She hoped the appeal to logic would work because the stress was speeding up her heartrate and causing the tickle in her throat to worsen.

Winston clenched his teeth and put his hands on his hips. "I don't like the way you're trying to mess with my mind, Knight."

"Yeah? But it's true. We owe it to them, one of the Stiles PD's largest contributors, to find out what happened."

She felt Terry shrink beside her, wilting, if he could, into the floor.

Winston eventually said, "What's the next step?"

"We still need to find out who John Doe is," she affirmed. "I was going to pay Steven Malone a visit now that we have a sketch and see if he recognizes the man."

"Good," Winston said. "But keep your hunt for a killer outside the Malone family."

She wasn't even going to waste her breath anymore. He would have heard everything

Kimberly had said, or at least had alluded to: the Malone family had secrets. Winston just seemed to have the Malones secured to a pedestal, and they weren't toppling down any time soon.

Twenty-Seven

If only it were possible for the nip in the air to cool her temper. Madison's insides were quaking with rage from having her hands tied with this case. At least Winston was getting himself to the hotel where they'd be talking with Steven Malone and not tagging along with her and Terry.

The sky was clear of clouds and the sun bright, a true contrast to the storm that passed through yesterday.

She parked the department car in the drop-off area, and a man in an overcoat, who worked with the hotel, walked toward them.

He smiled pleasantly. "Good evening, miss." He glanced at Terry but poured his charm on Madison.

She flashed a badge, and his expression died. She brought misery wherever she went—and she didn't give a crap right now. "We're here on police business."

"Oh," the man said with surprise.

Madison brushed past him and was the first through the automatic sliding doors, Terry and the hotel employee close on her heels.

"They can help you at the front desk, ma'am," the hotel employee said. "Just on the right."

She still had her badge out and held it up for the male clerk at the desk. "The room number for Steven Malone?"

"One moment." The clerk clicked some keys on the keyboard and went for the phone.

"What are you doing?" Madison asked.

"I'm calling to let him know the police are here to see him." The clerk pointed to his monitor. "There have been specific instructions that he be notified when someone comes to see him."

Madison let out a deep breath. "Of course there was."

"Excuse me?" The clerk's tone made his remark sound genuine, but his eyes told her he'd heard her just fine.

Madison flailed a hand toward the phone. "Go ahead. Do what you have to do."

The clerk picked up the receiver, pushed the buttons to call Malone's room, and a few seconds later, he was saying, "Mr. Malone, the police are here to see—"

"Detectives from Major Crimes," Madison clarified.

The clerk shared that information, paused as he listened to Steven, then said, "Yes, I'll tell them." The clerk hung up. "He's asked me to tell you to wait down here until his lawyer and a Sergeant Winston arrive. You can make yourself comfortable in the lounge or take a seat." He pointed behind Madison and Terry to the lavish lobby with its posh seating and floor-to-ceiling waterfall.

So much for getting in ahead of Sergeant Winston and Blake Golden. "It's imperative that we speak with him immed—"

"I'm sure you're not used to being told 'no.'" With that, Mr. Congeniality went out the window. "But Mr. Malone is our client, and we put our clients first. Please, take a seat." This time, the clerk gestured to the sitting area with his entire hand.

Madison didn't budge but stared the man down. Terry tugged on her elbow.

"Come on, let's just do as he said."

She glowered at her partner. "I don't like this, Terry."

"You can't really be surprised by this. Blake Golden's not about to sit this out. He'd be on his way—"

"You felt the cold front, too?"

He smirked. "I don't like the guy, either. Heck, I like him less than you do."

Debatable...

"But he's just doing his job for the Malones," Terry added and dropped into a chair with red cushions.

Madison paced next to the fountain. She eyed the coins at the basin and considered throwing in some change herself, then remembered she didn't have any. Even if she did, wishes rarely came true anyway, so why bother?

Twenty minutes passed, and she huffed to the front desk, wound up and ready to pitch a—

"Madison? Twice in one day. Heck, twice in a couple hours." Blake was standing there dressed in some designer full-length trench coat and wearing Berlutis like their John Doe.

"Yes, how wonderful," she said drily. "But there's no need for you to be here."

Blake dipped a head toward Terry in greeting, who didn't give any reaction.

"You're wrong about that," Blake said. "Mr. Malone called, and I'm in the habit of doing as the client requests. It's better for business that way." He sounded a lot like the clerk, snide and pretentious. What had she ever seen in Blake? Sadly, she would never get back the few months she'd wasted dating him.

Blake stepped up to the front desk and raised a finger in the air.

The clerk smiled at him. "What can I do for you, sir?"

"Please let Mr. Malone, room 2056, know that Mr. Golden is on the way up with the detectives."

Not ideal, but maybe she'd still have more clearance to say the things she needed to without Winston present.

"And Sergeant Winston," Winston bellowed from behind them.

Madison turned to see Winston stomping his snowy boots on the hotel's mat inside the sliding doors. He didn't even look at her but smiled at Blake. Too bad drinking on the job was frowned upon because a shot of whiskey would hit the spot perfectly right now.

TWO OFFICERS WERE POSITIONED AT the door to Malone's presidential suite. Somehow, Winston had justified providing Malone with what was essentially a mini apartment complete with a full kitchen, living room, and separate bedroom.

Malone had answered the door dressed in slacks and a collared shirt, and he smelled of scotch. He let them in and dropped into one of the armchairs in his suite, crossed his legs, and grabbed his rocks glass from a side table. He might as well have been a king on a throne, except for tangible grief emanating from him.

Terry, Winston, and Blake all sat down, but Madison remained standing. She was too anxious and tense to sit.

Malone pointed toward a bottle of Balvenie PortWood twenty-one-year-old scotch sitting on a credenza. "Blake? Sergeant? Help yourself."

Apparently, she and Terry were excluded from the invitation.

"Don't mind if I do." Blake got up, tugged

down on his jacket, went over and poured himself two fingers' worth into a rocks glass. "Sergeant?" He turned to Winston.

"Why not? Just a little." Winston pinched his fingers to within a quarter inch apart.

Was this investigation a joke to all of them, including Lorene's own husband? She clenched her fists, and her earlobes simmered.

Blake delivered Winston's drink and took his seat again. All heads turned to Madison, including her partner's, but unlike the other men who seemed brace to fight, his gaze offered support.

"I identified my wife last night," Malone started. "It's the hardest thing I've ever done. Tell me you've found her killer." He leveled his gaze on Madison.

"We're still looking into the murder of your wife and the man she was with." Madison felt Winston watching her, probably trying to beam her a mental message to watch her steps, but she didn't need a babysitter. She considered offering Steven a sign of peace, letting him know they'd confirmed his alibi and that his GSR test was negative, but she wasn't ready to give him that quite yet. "We still haven't been able to identify the man, but we have a sketch for you to look at." She pulled out her phone and brought up the image of John Doe, then walked over to Malone and extended the screen to him. "Recognize him?"

Malone set his drink down on the table, uncrossed his legs, and smoothed his slacks with his hands. He took her phone and studied the image. "No, never seen him before." He handed her phone back to her.

"You're sure?" she asked, just to be certain.

"Detective," Winston cautioned.

She might as well have been on a leash or wearing a shock collar. The sarge didn't agree with something, then *zap!*

"We're trying to find out what happened to his wife, and knowing who this man is could help," Madison said.

"I'd tell you if I knew who he is, but I honestly don't." Malone picked up his drink, took a sip, then set it back down on the table.

"He could have just been a new friend of your wife's," Madison said. "It seems she's made a few lately."

"My wife was a lovely woman." Malone almost sounded like he believed it, but his eyes were vacant. Was it grief, or had their love run cold?

"We understand that you and your wife had an argument last Tuesday," Madison started, "on your anniversary."

Winston stood. "Madison, what does this have to do with—"

"She missed a nice dinner that you'd arranged for the two of you." Madison barreled ahead. "That must have been upsetting."

Winston glared at her but sat down again.

"A misunderstanding is all." Malone lifted his drink but didn't take a sip. He just cradled it in his hands.

"It sounded like she was out with a friend that night. She's been spending quite a bit of time with different friends lately. She had a gathering at your house on Friday night." She smiled at Malone. "You knew about that, I'm sure."

"I didn't know, but that's nice that she had fun before…" Malone pressed his lips to his glass.

"Detective Knight, I'm not sure what you're getting at with all this," Blake said.

"Me neither," Winston seethed.

"I'm just trying to determine how well Steven knew his wife," Madison explained. "It might help us."

"You find out who that man is, and I'm sure you'll get a motive for her murder," Malone rushed out. "My Lorene couldn't have brought this on herself."

John Doe was repeatedly a victim: cast aside, blamed.

Something changed in Malone's eyes and hinted at rage. "How did you find out about the gathering?"

"Marie Rauch," Madison said, deciding that by naming the housekeeper, it would be a good lead-in to discussing his home office.

"I'll have to speak with her," Malone said coolly. "She shouldn't be telling you anything about the household."

"Well, she has," Madison said, unapologetic.

"She also told us that she and your wife were close friends," Terry added.

"Close friends?" Malone scoffed. "Hardly."

Spoken as if Malone saw himself above the help. "Are you calling Mrs. Rauch a liar?"

"I am. Lorene was kind to her, but she was kind to most people. Then again, I suppose everyone has a different definition of friendship," Malone said.

"Fair enough." Madison wasn't convinced it was the definition that was the issue here. Marie Rauch said they went back to public-school days, but it would seem that Malone didn't know anything about that. Lorene kept secrets from her husband, and maybe her history with Rauch was one of them.

"While we're on the subject of Mrs. Rauch," Terry continued, "we were also told that your wife didn't like her cleaning your office."

Madison noticed how Terry had worded that as if it was a regular thing and not the one-off that Rauch had said.

Malone seemed to consider his response before speaking. "My office is a private area." He glanced at Blake, who nodded.

"So, you didn't let other people in there?" Madison questioned.

"If necessary, but not unattended."

"That you know of," she countered.

"Suppose that's true. I'm not there twenty-four/seven."

"Do you ever remember your daughter going in your office?" Madison asked.

Malone slid his jaw side to side. "Kimberly has no reason to go in my office."

The tension in the room would be hard to cut with a saw, let alone with a knife. Everyone but Malone knew why she'd asked.

Madison took a few steps. "You seem quite definite on that."

"I am." Malone puffed out his chest and set his drink down. "She would have no reason to go in there."

"And the maid, Mrs. Rauch?" Terry interjected.

Malone put his gaze on Terry. "Again, no reason."

Terry went on. "She told us she regularly cleans it, but your wife—"

"Apparently, the maid does a lot of talking."

"Your wife," Terry picked up, "apparently got quite upset when Marie Rauch tried to clean the office on Saturday. Would you know why?"

"Besides the fact she shouldn't be in there in the first place? I have no idea." A twitch began in the man's cheek, and if he'd been anyone else, Madison would call him out on that, but with Winston's watchful eyes, she dared not.

"Do you know if your wife and daughter had any disagreements lately?" Madison feigned innocence.

"Detective," Blake cautioned.

Malone turned to the lawyer. "What is it?"

"Don't let Detective Knight mislead you. She's aware that Kimberly and her mother had words, but nothing more. It was a family affair and has nothing to do with the murders." Spoken as a smooth-talking attorney. "And I believe we've been over this—" Blake made a show of twisting his arm and looking at his Rolex "—not long ago."

"We're done, and we'll see ourselves out." Winston stood.

"Are you going to harass my son when he gets in?" Malone asked before she reached the door.

Madison spun.

"You haven't heard?" Malone asked. "He's flying in today and should be in sometime around two o'clock this afternoon. Be kind to him. He's got nothing to do with any of this."

Madison got the feeling she knew who the favored child was: Craig Malone. Steven Malone had never told her to be kind to his other children.

"The detectives don't think your son did this. They just want to solve your wife's murder. Come on, Knight, let's go," Winston urged her.

Pucker up!

Madison left the room before she'd say something to Winston she couldn't take back and headed straight for the stairwell. Who cared that she had twenty stories' worth of stairs to take? She'd be away from Winston, and he'd be too impatient to wait for her in the lobby. It would give her a chance to cool off and him a chance to, hopefully, get a grip.

Twenty-Eight

Madison and Terry's next stop would be Lorene's doctor's office, but she hadn't shared that fact with Winston and expected his call any moment.

"Thanks for leaving me alone with him, by the way," Terry grumbled, referring to Winston. "The man was bitching the whole way down."

"Good for him." She glanced apologetically at Terry. "Not for you."

"*Not for me* is right!"

If her partner was expecting an apology, he'd be waiting forever. The journey down the stairs had given her time to think about whether she should elevate matters to Andrea. Madison concluded that she'd avoid that option for as long as possible, if not altogether. Everything would eventually hit the fan with Phelps and the other corrupt cops she had on her radar, and the fewer enemies she had to start with, the better. It was one thing that she and the sergeant weren't getting along on this case; it would be another if he saw her as overstepping and backstabbing him.

"You'd think Winston doesn't even want the case solved." She was pouting. She heard it in her tone of voice, but she was so sick of Lorene's family being indifferent and difficult. By nature, murder investigations churned dark secrets to the surface, stripping the deceased of any privacy they'd had in life.

"I just think they're overly concerned with image."

"You think?" she snapped. "Wait, you said '*they're*'?"

"We know Winston cares how things look, but the Malone family does, too. They have a certain image in the community to uphold, and unless you're in someone's shoes, you can't understand how they're coping with grief. Everyone is different."

She was well aware that people handled their grief differently and didn't need Terry telling her that. When her grandmother died, she didn't want to talk for weeks. Her mother wanted to talk about it nonstop. Her sister busied herself with raising a family.

Her phone rang, and she handed it to Terry. "It's going to be Winston, but I can't answer. I'm driving."

"How mighty convenient."

"Thanks."

Terry sighed. "Detective Knight's phone."

She could hear Winston's voice coming through from the other end of the line, demanding to know where they were going and why.

"We're checking on a lead…Yes, I know you'd like more detail, sir, and—" Terry put him on speaker and held out the phone. Madison scowled at her partner.

"Knight, here," she said. "Terry told you we're following a—"

"I want specifics."

Madison stopped at a red light, and the engine idled, as did she, standing still with this case, needing to explain herself like a child. "We're going to speak with Lorene Malone's doctor."

"Why are you doing that?"

"We believe she might have had cancer," she served out rather indelicately.

"Why is this my first time hearing about this?"

"We're following a lead," she said as if to imply they'd just happened on it.

"And does her having had cancer tie into her murder?"

"We don't know if it does. We're following a lead," she repeated slowly.

"I don't like the attitude, Knight."

Well, you don't seem to want to listen.

The light turned green, and she hit the gas.

"I'm just preoccupied. Two homicides to solve, sir." She almost choked on *sir*—especially at the tail end of making excuses—but when all else failed to appease the sergeant, it didn't hurt to remind him of what was at stake.

"I am very well of aware of what you have on your plate, but if you keep up the attitude, that can be remedied."

And there he went, spewing off more threats. If he really thought he had any grounds to suspend her, he would have done so already.

"I'll keep you posted on what we find out," she said to pacify him as she turned into the clinic's parking lot where the doctor, Kendra Cohen, worked.

"Be sure you do."

With that, he clicked off, and Madison resumed breathing.

"You really know how to get under the man's skin," Terry poked.

"It's not hard," she agreed sourly. "One just has to fight being his puppet."

She parked the car, and they went inside. A receptionist with stunning blue eyes greeted them with a warm smile.

"Your insurance card, please?"

Madison pulled her badge instead. "Detectives Knight and Grant. We're here to speak with Kendra Cohen."

The receptionist nodded, her expression now serious. "She's in with a patient at the moment, but she should be finished soon. I can squeeze you in before her next appointment. Will that work?"

"That works." Madison was grateful for the receptionist's willingness to accommodate them, especially when she'd expected a fight.

"If you wouldn't mind taking a seat." The receptionist gestured toward the waiting room where there were a few vacant chairs.

Madison and Terry stepped away from the counter, making way for a patient who was approaching the receptionist with her medical card at the ready.

Madison looked around the room. People of all ages were waiting for their appointments. A couple of children, both under the age of six, played together with a set of building blocks, making Madison cringe at the thought of the germs clinging to the plastic. People were coughing and sniffling, and it made Madison more aware of her scratchy throat and burning eyes. If she closed them for a second, they might stay that way for several hours.

"Madison Knight," a nurse called out from a side hallway.

Madison and Terry joined the nurse and followed her to a room where Doctor Cohen would join them.

The door had barely shut when a woman stepped into the room holding a clipboard.

"I'm Dr. Cohen. You can call me Kendra," she said without much modulation, closing the door behind her. She was petite with brown hair pulled back into a loose bun and had a small mole on her left cheek. Her face was oval, and her dark eyes were deeply set.

"We're detectives with the Stiles PD," Madison said. "I'm—"

Cohen held up a hand. "Rebecca told me your names. Knight and Grant?"

"Madison and Terry," Madison said, feeling it would put them on a more even ground, though she'd still think of the doctor as Cohen. "We have questions about a patient of yours."

"I'm sorry, but unless you brought a subpoena, I can't help you."

"It's about Lorene Malone," Madison said, as if that would be enough to change the doctor's mind about the subpoena.

Cohen glanced at Terry, back to Madison. "Who it is doesn't make a difference." She crossed her arms with the clipboard hugged to her chest. The closed body language implied she wouldn't willingly or easily be parting with information.

Madison wasn't too surprised by Cohen's reaction and had actually expected it. There were other ways of getting the information she needed, though. "Let me ask you this question. If you diagnose a patient with cancer, do you recommend any support groups or therapy for them?"

Cohen blinked and pursed her lips. She hadn't seen that question coming. "I do."

"Which ones?" Madison was hoping to come away with a support group and, from there, a possible lead on John Doe's ID.

"Well, there's one that meets in the basement of St. Peter's Catholic Church on Rideout Street."

"And when do they meet?" Terry asked.

"Every Wednesday at seven o'clock."

Madison glanced at Terry, back to the doctor. "So, tonight."

"Yes."

"Any others that you recommend?" Madison asked.

"There's another one that meets in the rec center downtown on Saturday afternoons at three o'clock."

"Which one did you suggest to Lorene Malone?" Madison asked.

Cohen went rigid, and her eyes turned to steel. "I don't appreciate what you're trying to do here."

"We have come to learn from one of Lorene's friends that she was diagnosed with cancer and given only a few months to live, but Lorene was found murdered on Tuesday morning," Madison laid out.

"I remember seeing that on the news, and I'm sorry to hear that. But I'm not sure how my confirming she had cancer would help with your investigation in any way."

There was something in Cohen's eyes—the way hers held Madison's—that told Madison

Lorene had, in fact, been diagnosed, but if Cohen didn't say it, it wouldn't count as breaking patient confidentiality.

"One more question before we leave." Madison pulled up the picture of John Doe and angled her screen toward the doctor. "Do you know this man or recognize him?"

Cohen assessed the photo for a few seconds, then shook her head. "I've never seen him before."

"Thank you for your time, Doctor," Madison said and stepped toward the door, disappointed they weren't necessarily any closer to Doe's identity.

Cohen opened the door and gestured for Madison and Terry to go out first. They made their way through the waiting room and caught the door another patient was holding for them. She was in her fifties and was eyeing them as if she wanted to say something but was hesitating. Madison smiled at her as she walked past with Terry.

"Excuse me," the woman said.

Madison turned back to her. "Yes?"

"Were you just in with Dr. Cohen?" the woman asked.

"We were," Madison confirmed.

"You're detectives?" Her eyes seemed to be searching for their badges. Madison helped her with the endeavor by lifting hers. The woman nodded. "You were asking about Lorene

Malone? I have excellent hearing, and the walls aren't very soundproof in there," she added as an explanation.

"You know Lorene?" Madison intentionally asked in present tense.

"I did, yes." The woman huddled into her coat as a gust of wind swept around them. "My name's Meghan Cantwell." She adjusted her purse strap that had slid down her shoulder.

Madison recognized the name instantly from digging into Lorene's phone records that morning. "You and Lorene were friends?"

"You could say that. We went to the same cancer support group."

"Which one?" Terry asked.

"The one that meets on Wednesday nights at St. Peter's Catholic Church."

Madison had a dress fitting, but it was probably a good idea to send Terry to scout out the support group. She hurried to pull up the picture of John Doe, feeling like running into this woman was too good to be true. "Do you know this man?"

Meghan glanced at Terry, back to Madison, then she looked at the phone. "I've never even seen him before."

Madison pocketed her phone, disappointed.

"I heard about her…how she was murdered," Meghan said, her gaze drifting to the ground. "Horribly sad."

"It is," Madison empathized. "Did you know

her well?"

"As I said, we were in the same support group. She'd only been going for a couple of weeks, but I believe we became quick friends. I was just over at her house on Friday night."

Madison wished everyone was as open to talking as Meghan. It would make their jobs a heck of lot easier. "What did you do there?"

"She had a few from the group over." Her brow scrunched up. "I think there were six of us. Her son showed up for a bit. Kurt? He seems like a great kid." Meghan frowned. "My heart goes out to him and the rest of the family. Cancer's one thing, but murder?"

"We have reason to believe that Lorene wasn't planning to take treatment for her cancer," Terry said.

"Yeah, I'm aware of that. She didn't hide that fact from anyone in the group."

Yet she'd held it back from her own family. Madison still wasn't sure if that was loving and selfless or quite the opposite.

"So, she got along well with everyone from the group that you were aware of?" Madison asked, just to gauge if there were any possible murder suspects lurking there.

"Everyone admired her," Meghan smiled. "She was an inspiring woman and will be missed." A shiver ran through her, and she shrugged deeper into her coat. "I should get going, get someplace warm."

"Of course. Take care," Madison said, "and thank you for your time."

Meghan half-jogged to an idling Chevrolet sedan and got behind the wheel.

Terry turned to Madison. "Okay, so we've as good as confirmed the diagnosis. I think it's time we tell the family."

"No." She was firm on that. "After we catch the killer, then we'll do it."

"It's not fair that they carry on in the dark."

"They have it hard enough as it is right now," Madison said, though sadly felt the only Malone she'd met so far with any diehard grief was Kurt. "We don't want to muddle things by telling them just yet."

"How would it 'muddle' things?" Terry put air quotes around *muddle*.

"There's just enough going on. We don't even know for certain that none of them were involved with the murders."

"I'm still quite confident we can mark Steven Malone off the list."

"And Kurt Malone," she voiced.

"Really? We don't have his alibi, just like we don't have Kimberly's."

"He's genuinely upset by his mother's death. I feel it here." She touched her chest.

"Well, then, it's set in stone. He's innocent."

"Hey, don't be snide."

"We can't just go on gut feelings."

She sighed—and they were back to this. It

was something that came up periodically. "They rarely steer me wrong."

"Do you want me to list off the times they didn't?"

"Don't be a smartass."

He held up his hands. "Just saying the gut's not always the most reliable source."

Madison's phone rang, and she answered without consulting the ID.

"Craig Malone's come in." It was Sergeant Winston. "You about finished with the doctor visit?"

She rolled her eyes. "We're on our way."

She hung up and looked at Terry. Their conversation about gut feelings and the reliability of them would be benched—for now.

Twenty-Nine

Craig Malone was sitting on the sofa next to his father, and both men looked eerily alike. Blake Golden and Sergeant Winston were seated in chairs, turned to face the sofa. It was pretty much a regular ol' party down at the station.

Craig wasn't as handsome as his younger brother, but there was an attractive and mature quality about him. He kept his black hair closely cropped and had a short, boxed beard. He was wearing a plaid shirt in shades of blue, as if he'd come straight from the woods.

Craig looked up when Madison and Terry shadowed the doorway. His rectangular face was drawn tight, and his eyes studied her.

Steven Malone stiffened, and Blake stood, on the defensive.

On the table in front of the sofa was a .357 Smith & Wesson.

She entered the room first, Terry behind her. "Craig Malone?" she said, feeling all the men's eyes on her and not quite comfortable with the situation, given it hadn't been that long since they'd drawn blood.

"I am." He held out a hand, and she shook it, feeling slightly awkward for doing so.

"I'm Detective Madison Knight, and this is Terry Grant."

"Also a detective," Terry said in a lighthearted manner.

Craig's eyes pooled with tears, as if their presence was driving home the stark reality that his mother was dead. "I brought Dad's gun." He made no gesture or movement toward where it sat on the table.

"I appreciate that," she said. Terry scooped it up in gloved hands and left the room.

"He'll be taking it to the lab for testing," Madison explained, not even sure if it was necessary.

"Dad said you still don't know who did this to my mother." Craig squared his gaze on her, and she closed the door to the room.

"It's still an open investigation, but we're doing all we—"

"You can save the speech, Detective," Craig interrupted her, but his tone wasn't harsh in the least. "I know you're doing all you can do." He gestured toward Winston. "I've been told that the Stiles PD is viewing the capture of her killer as their top priority."

Madison wasn't sure how other detectives in

Major Crimes with open murder cases would feel about that, but she doubted they'd be pleased. "It's certainly mine." There would be no easy way to bring up what she had to next, but she didn't have much choice. Craig might tell them more without the audience of his father, lawyer, and Sergeant Winston. "Would we be able talk privately?" she asked Craig.

Winston's eyes snapped to her, but she ignored him.

"Anything you have to say to my son, you can say in front of us," Steven spoke up.

"It's fine, Dad." Craig nodded to his father. "I have no problem answering her questions."

Steven's face took on hard lines. "I'd rather—"

"Dad," Craig said firmly.

Madison sensed a battle of wills in the sizzling eye contact between father and son. Steven eventually relinquished.

"At least let Mr. Golden stay with you."

"I don't need a lawyer. I've done nothing wrong."

A pulse ticked in Steven's jaw, but he stood and left the room. Blake followed Steven, but Winston stayed parked in his chair.

"You can go, too, Sergeant," Craig told him.

Winston gave Madison a long look as he passed by her and leaned in to whisper, "Discretion."

She took a steadying breath and waited for the man to leave her personal space. With him in the hall, she closed the door and resisted the urge to give him a smug smile before he went from view.

"Sorry about my father. He can be overbearing at the best of times. Suffocating most of the time," Craig said.

Madison sat down in one of the chairs. "I get it. Some parents are that way." She was thinking about her mother and her distaste for Madison's career choice.

"I wish I could say his heart's in the right place," Craig deadpanned.

Tingles went through Madison. More trouble in the Malone ranks? "It's not?"

"My father is about my father. He always has been."

"So your parents' marriage was…" Madison started, hoping that Craig would take over.

"Solid," Craig replied. "That's because Mom basically worshipped Dad. She always took his side in things and wouldn't back down."

"We've heard they've had their disagreements—even more, recently." Madison put it out there as delicately as possible.

"Oh, they would butt heads from time to time, but Dad always wins." He put finger quotes on *wins* to imply there wasn't any real victory. "I heard that Mom was found with a man, and you don't know who he was."

"Who told you that?" She recalled that Kurt said Kimberly hadn't.

"Dad."

Madison nodded and brought up the sketch.

Craig looked at the image, and a few seconds later, he said, "I've never seen him." He looked at her as if he anticipated she'd say something, but she remained silent. "I know how they were found," he added.

His knowing lifted a burden from Madison's shoulders. "What are your thoughts on that?"

The door opened, and Terry walked in. "Don't let me interrupt." He sat down in a chair.

"On Mom being naked with another man? Disturbing. Shocking."

"You don't think she'd cheat on your father?" Madison asked, sneaking in a quick look at Terry. She wasn't sure he could read in her eyes that Craig was quite open to talking about his parents, but he would have noticed that Steven, Blake, and Winston had left the room.

Craig tightened his jaw and shook his head. "There's no way she would."

It was written all over Craig's body language, words, and tone—he stood strong in his stance regarding his mother's loyalty.

"Your mom had a good relationship with your father," Madison started, "but what about with you or your siblings?"

A touch of amusement danced across Craig's face. "You probably know all about my past, my acting out as a teenager. I hated my parents then—both of them—but what teenager doesn't?"

"None of that animosity carried on through your life?" Madison regarded him skeptically. He obviously had a tenuous relationship with his father.

"No. Only thing I resent is Dad pulling out how he helped me get out of my jams when it was really Mom."

Madison sat straighter. "We were under the impression it was your father."

"Doesn't surprise me. It was actually Mom who pulled the necessary strings. She's..." Craig paused, took a deep breath. "She *was* the strong one between the two of them, if you ask me. Dad's probably going to fall apart now she's gone. It's only a matter of time. I'm not looking forward to sticking around."

"You'll leave Malone's?" Terry asked.

Craig faced Terry. "Probably not, but it might become more out of a sense of duty than it already is."

Craig didn't seem to want to admit as much in so many words, but Madison was getting the distinct impression that he didn't care for his father. It could just be that they were both strong-willed men of differing opinions on many things, but there might be more to it than that. It brought to mind Kimberly's holding back the details on her disagreement with her mother. Maybe Craig would be able to shed light on the matter.

"You said that your father is very much about himself," Madison began. "It must have taken a lot of time to build Malone's into the business it is today. There would have been missed games and activities for you and your brother and sister growing up."

"Mom attended for Dad, made excuses for him not being there, too," Craig confessed.

"Kurt seems to have a close relationship with your father and like he had one with your mother." Madison shared her observations in a conversational style, hoping it would keep Craig talking.

Craig licked his lips, but then his expression hardened. He said nothing.

Madison continued. "Kimberly does give the impression she's close to your father, but she's admitted to being in some sort of disagreement with your mother the day before she was murdered."

Craig's eyes snapped to Madison's. They flashed cold. Still, he remained quiet.

"She won't tell us what it was about," Madison approached cautiously. "Do you know?"

"That's not my story to tell, Detective." His voice was harsh. "As for Kurt, leave him out of all of this. He doesn't know anything."

"Anything about what?" Madison asked.

"Nope, I'm not saying anything." He crossed his arms and his ankles. "If I believed it was tied to Mom's murder, I'd tell you, but trust me when

I say it isn't."

Madison leaned forward, elbows to knees. "You don't think she's involved with your mother's—"

"Absolutely not," Craig shot back.

Silence fell over the room and hovered there for at least a solid minute.

Terry broke the stillness. "Do you know of anyone that might have hated your mother enough to do this?"

"If I did, I would have told you already. Mom made people light up." Something bitter tinged his statement.

"What was it about her?" Madison followed a hunch that he didn't understand why and might have even felt the opposite about her.

"She was a people-pleaser," Craig offered quickly. "One way to your face, another behind closed doors."

"You had a difficult relationship with your mom?" Terry inquired.

"You could say I hold my judgments toward her."

A moment ago, Craig had praised his mother, calling her the strong one. His flip-flopping made Madison curious, but she could feel Craig shutting down. There'd be no more conversation right now, no more insights to be had.

"We'll be checking the gun you brought in and comparing it to bullet fragments pulled from your mother and John Doe," she said, all business.

"I understand, but you're not going to find a match."

Madison nodded. After speaking with Craig, she had a feeling he'd be right about that.

Thirty

Madison and Terry went back to their desks to review the phone records and the paperwork side of the case. She made her way down the evidence list Cynthia had emailed and spotted something that struck her.

She reached over and slapped a printout on Terry's desk as he hung up his phone. "Check out page two."

"Okay," he said slowly and picked up the report. "A button?"

"Not just any button. Don't you recognize it?"

"Ah, no."

"When we spoke to Marie Rauch, she was wearing a sweater, and it was missing a button. The other buttons look just like this one."

Terry leaned back in his swivel chair, and it creaked as it always did, with little provocation. "Not that big a deal, is it? She does clean their house."

"Look where it was found."

He consulted the report. "Next to the pool. Still—"

"Terry, it had blood on it," she spat.

He must have been preoccupied with something else to miss what was right in front of him.

"This is a lead. Rauch told us she didn't clean near the pool on Saturday."

"The button could have come off at any time. It just needed to be on the floor at the time of the murders to get blood spray."

"But she has access to the house. She told us she was close to Lorene, but the husband didn't believe so."

"Steven seems to be in the dark about a lot of things," Terry countered.

Madison rocked her head side to side. "Okay, I have to agree on that, but I still think that a button would have been seen and picked up before the murders, even if it was by Steven or Lorene Malone."

"So, you're suggesting that Rauch might have been there? She might be our killer? There could have been a struggle and the button came off then?"

"Why not?" she challenged her partner.

"What about motive and means? Doe and Malone weren't killed by a button."

"You're such a brat."

He patted his chest. "I don't even have to work hard at it, either."

"A natural gift," she said drily and moved next to him and pointed to his monitor. "Does she have any registered guns?"

Terry groaned but proceeded to check the gun registry. "Nope," he said once the search results filled the screen.

"What about her husband?"

More key strokes, then, "Nope."

Madison crossed her arms. "Huh." She paced. "So, where did she get the gun?"

"Let the gun go for now. Where there's a will there's a way, but what could have been Rauch's motive?"

"I have no idea," she admitted.

"Well, until we've got that, I say we scratch her off the suspect list."

"In pencil."

He was shaking his head.

"No way is she off altogether."

"However this shakes out, you seem to be forgetting the male, size-eleven shoeprint found near the pool," Terry said.

"Not forgetting, just disregarding it for now. Besides it could have been left at any time." She recalled that Cynthia had not said anymore about another shoeprint being recovered that matched, and it wasn't on the list. "Or…" She widened her eyes. "Maybe we're looking at this wrong, and two people took out Lorene Malone and John Doe."

"Okay, fair enough. In the fashion of

continuing to spew out hypotheticals...Rauch's partner in crime could have been the one with the gun." He smirked, no doubt at his playful choice of words: *partner in crime*. She guessed he didn't buy for a second there were two killers.

"Yep, you're definitely a brat." She loved how he'd flipped—when convenient to himself—and finally gave credence to the possibility that Rauch was involved in the murders.

"Takes one to know one."

"Hey, guys." Cynthia was coming toward them—looking like the walking dead—with a file in her hand.

"Not enough coffee in the world?" Madison asked.

"Not even close." She held the folder out to Madison.

"You could have just called," Madison said. "We would have met you in the lab."

"I need to keep moving, or I'll fall asleep. I tell you how much I'm looking forward to the honeymoon?"

In reality, Cynthia had hardly said anything about it. All Madison knew was that they were planning to go to Cancun for a week. Now, she wasn't sure if Cynthia was being sarcastic, but why wouldn't she be looking forward to time away, sipping a fruity drink, lounging next to the ocean, and soaking up the sun?

"It can't come soon enough." Pointing to the folder she'd given Madison, Cynthia added, "I found something in Malone's financials. The business pays out fifty thousand a month, but I haven't been able to track to where."

"We could call and speak with Emily. She might know or be able to find out," Madison suggested. "It could allow us to put off questioning the Malones and even make it unnecessary."

"If we can avoid 'em, let's," Terry said.

"Although..." Madison glanced at her partner. "Rowe told us there was something he and Steven didn't see eye to eye on. It could be tied to these transfers. Either way, it's an awful lot of money."

"But it could be for anything," Terry said.

Madison faced Cynthia. "I hate to agree with him, but keep on it and see what you can find out."

"I plan to," Cynthia said somewhat bitterly. Hopefully, Madison could cheer her friend up tonight at the dress fitting and dinner afterward.

"Any update on the items collected from Mr. Malone's office?" Madison wasn't sure she should ask, but she couldn't help herself. She was greedy for information at this point.

"Still working on it, Madison," Cynthia said coolly.

Ouch. Cynthia rarely called her by her full first name. Usually, it was Maddy. She felt like she was in trouble. "Are you mad at me for some reason?" Madison hated to ask this in front of

Terry.

"No, I'm just tired and cranky. The wedding's only a few days away and—ah!" Cynthia waved her hands. "It just feels like everything's in the air. I don't want to leave with this case just hanging out there."

That caused Madison to smile. She loved Cynthia's devotion to the job. She was about as possessive about cases as Madison. "Terry and I are doing what we can. With any luck, the case will be solved before you go, but even if it isn't, you have good people working for you." She was referring to Mark, Sam, and Jennifer who reported to her in the lab.

"I know." Cynthia bobbed her head. "I still would like it all wrapped up. Good news is I think I have something that might help." Her face cracked into a smile. It was like watching a gargoyle transform into a teddy bear. "We found John Doe's ID. Well, Mark did, specifically. Obviously, Sam's busy with the ballistics of the case, including running comparisons between the slugs pulled from the victims and Malone's Smith & Wesson."

"I don't care who found it," Madison blurted out. "Who he is?" How could Cynthia not have led with this information? Talk about burying the lead!

"It's all in the file. Happy reading." She laughed and spun on her heels.

Madison wasted no time digging into the file.

The name was next to a remark that there was no next of kin and highlighted in yellow.

"Who is he?" Terry asked.

"Saul Lynch," she said slowly, "and I know that name."

Terry buddied up to her shoulder and peered into the file.

"One of the numbers on Lorene's phone report tied back to a Saul Lynch," she said.

Terry's finger went to the page. "He's the owner of Your Best Friend."

"That was the company who invoiced Lorene. The one email that was deleted," Madison pieced together.

"Uh-huh."

Madison read a comment Mark had left regarding the business that told her the only way he could find Your Best Friend was by looking it up through the tax number noted on the invoice.

They have zero online presence.

Madison found that strange. After all, being active on social media and having a website were key for most businesses' survival.

She flipped the page to a second sheet, and there was Saul Lynch's DMV photo staring back at them in color. She froze on the face that she'd only encountered in flesh and blood as a bloated corpse and pinched her eyes closed briefly.

"Your Best Friend, what do they do?" she mumbled as she searched the file, flipping through more pages. "Ah, here it is. It's a private investigation firm in Colton."

"Colton? That's about forty-five minutes' to an hour's drive from here," Terry squeezed in.

"It's also where Lorene Malone grew up, as did Marie Rauch," she said, remembering that Rauch had told them that.

"But you said Your Best Friend is a PI firm? Lorene was poking her nose in where it didn't belong?" Terry suggested. "It backfired?"

"Or Lynch was, and Lorene was an innocent victim?" She hurried to her chair and grabbed her coat. She pointed at Terry. "The file says Lynch has a Mercedes E300. Call the sarge, see if he'll approve a BOLO."

A be-on-the-lookout bulletin.

"The car could be in Lynch's driveway," he said.

"Possibly, but if it's not, we're another forty-five minutes to hour behind the game."

"On it." Terry put his cell phone to an ear, and she listened as he pleaded their case on the way to the lot for a department car.

He was still talking five minutes later and didn't hang up until the vehicle had time to warm up and she was pulling away from the station.

She glanced over at him. "So?"

"He'll get it done immediately."

She should have just rejoiced, but she couldn't help but think snidely that of course Winston had approved the BOLO quickly. It meant they would start looking somewhere other than the Malone family.

"Probably not a good time to bring it up," Terry started, "but I'm starving."

His complaint had her stomach growling. "We can do a drive-thru."

"Suppose it's better than nothing," he grumbled.

"You could have grabbed something from the vending machine before we left."

"I know that you consider chocolate a meal, but I don't."

"I've told you before—"

He held up a hand and smiled. "Yes, yes, chocolate comes from a bean, and it's technically a vegetable. That means it's good for you."

She'd brush her hands together if they weren't on the wheel. "My work here is done," she teased.

"Um, I just thought of something." Any joviality was gone from his voice. "If Lynch is a PI, wouldn't his prints be on file?"

And there was the rain for her parade, just when it seemed the clouds had cleared.

Thirty-One

Madison balanced a burger in one hand while driving. Her nose was so congested she could hardly taste the meal, but thank heaven for small miracles—the thing was dripping with grease and probably tasted like a vat of oil. Terry scarfed his food down without complaint, surprisingly, and was working on getting a search warrant for both Lynch's business and residence.

Throughout the drive, she and Terry had been over the matter of Saul Lynch and his missing fingerprints several times. It was possible he wasn't a licensed PI but simply owned the firm and worked from an administrative prospective. The only thing with that was it wiped out a strong motive quickly. If it had been an employee stirring up a nest, why did Lynch get a bullet in his head? But she wasn't ready to let go of their theory just yet.

"You know, Lynch and Lorene poking their noses into the wrong person's business could explain the missing phones and Lynch's ID," she said, feeling good that they had a plausible explanation for both. It had been one of the many facts in the case that was gnawing away at her.

"Absolutely. The killer wanted to cover their tracks," Terry agreed. "It could explain them being tied up. The killer could have been testing to see how much they'd uncovered, who they told. The fact they were naked could have been to humiliate them, as we touched on before."

"I'd also say the killer was motivated for personal reasons."

"Was it personal with Malone, Lynch, or both?"

Madison shook her head, unsure. "Whoever's behind the murders had to know they were both at the Malones', and he or she would have waited things out until the cook left."

"Whoever they were expecting could have turned out to be their killer," Terry wagered. "All this"—he flailed his hands to imply their discussion—"sounds good in theory, but if the killer was motivated because Lynch uncovered something, why go to the trouble of tying both of them up? I don't think she was collateral damage."

"So, we're either back to it having something to do with them having an affair, or they were investigating something—more importantly, *someone*—they should have left alone. And the killer held them both responsible."

"I think so."

Madison turned into a residential neighborhood at four fifty-five in the afternoon and looked for a sign announcing Your Best Friend. None existed, but the address they were seeking had an "Open" sign displayed in the door's window. No online presence and no real signage; it was a miracle they had any customers.

"They're pretty private about their business." Terry snickered at his own joke. "Get it? Private investigation firm...*private* about their business?"

"I get it. Wish I didn't." Madison rolled her eyes at Terry's play on words and parked around back. As she passed along the building, she looked inside the front window. "There's a light on."

"Now, is anybody home?" Terry jested.

Her partner was obviously full of beans, but she rather preferred him like this than upset and moody. She recalled that Annabelle had agreed to go to the doctor. Considering he was rather upbeat, maybe it was a good time to ask.

"How did Annabelle make out at the doctor's? She get an appointment?"

"Yep." He undid his seat belt and got out of the car. She followed suit.

Terry continued as Madison locked the vehicle. "She saw him this afternoon, and we should have the results by Friday."

"Oh, that's quick."

"Made me happy to hear. I'd rather know what we're dealing with sooner than later, but I'm just going to keep positive."

She feared saying something that would jeopardize his optimism, so she went with a simple, "Best way to be."

He looked at her, tilted his head. "I appreciate your saying that, but I know you're wired to think negatively."

"That's not really fair," she said, his comment stinging a little.

"It's true, though. We both know that." He offered her a small smile, and they walked around to the business's front door.

She stopped outside the door and peered through the window. A twentysomething brunette stood behind a desk stuffing items into a lunch bag. She was probably getting ready to go home and just hadn't gotten around to flipping the sign on the door yet.

Madison turned to Terry. "Just remember that whoever we talk to in there has no idea Lynch is dead."

"Hey, I'm the nice one. The fact you even thought to tell me that is surpri—" He was toying with her, and he stopped talking the farther down her brows went.

Madison got the door for them, and a chime rang.

The brunette stopped what she was doing, frozen with her hand in the air holding a Tupperware container that had been en route to the bag. She smiled at them and then put it into her bag. "Good day. Is there something I can help you with?"

Madison hated that they were about to strip this girl's happiness. She held up her badge and approached the counter with Terry. "We're detectives with the Stiles PD. I'm Madison Knight, and this is Terry Grant. Would there be a manager in that we could speak with?"

"It's just me and Mr. Lynch around here, and he's not in, so I'm it," she said, zipping up her bag and watching them as she did so. "How can I help you?"

"What's your name?" Madison asked.

"Stephanie Bateman."

"Unfortunately, we have bad news about Saul—"

The phone on the desk started to ring, and Stephanie didn't answer it. Her eyes pooled with tears, and she dropped into her chair. "I had this horrible feeling when I couldn't reach him." Her voice held a tremor. "What happened to him?"

"He was found yesterday morning. He was murdered, gunshot to the head." Madison laid out the details with sensitivity in her tone.

Stephanie's face contorted as she fended off crying.

"We're very sorry for your loss," Madison

empathized.

Tears fell down Stephanie's cheeks, but she remained speechless.

"Have you worked with Mr. Lynch long?" Madison asked.

Stephanie palmed her cheeks and sniffled. "For a couple of years now. Saul took me on right out of college. He treats me—*treated* me—" She stopped there and looked toward the ceiling as if gathering strength to continue. "I just can't imagine who would do such a thing. He was an amazing man. He loved life and helping other people."

That claim all depends on perspective.

"We think it's possible that his killer might be someone he was investigating," Terry said, worming his way into the conversation.

Stephanie looked at him. "I really can't think of anyone."

"What sort of things do you investigate?" Madison asked. "Is it possible someone didn't appreciate Mr. Lynch poking around?"

"Well, for the most part, we look into insurance scams and cheating spouses." Her cheeks still damp and her eyes pooled with tears, she met Madison's gaze. "I guess it's possible that someone…"

Cheating spouses…

Lorene Malone and Saul Lynch were found naked together. This was a stretch, but maybe they were made to look like they were having an affair to draw attention away from someone else who actually was. Steven Malone, perhaps? Had Lorene had been looking into her husband, suspecting him of cheating? Steven could have found out and flipped things. It was quite a leap, as nothing so far pointed to Steven being unfaithful to Lorene. "You said insurance scams and cheating spouses are what you look into 'for the most part.' Anything else?" *Though both clientele bases could be ripe with motive.*

"Really, whatever a client needs." Stephanie's gaze drifted to her desk. "We have looked into cases the police couldn't solve."

Stephanie's grief was blinding her to the fact their client list was rich with suspects. They'd be best to focus on what Lorene Malone was having investigated and then, if necessary, spread out from there. There'd be no putting off Lorene's murder any longer. "Mr. Lynch was found with someone—"

"Oh." Stephanie pushed back from her desk. "Was he the unidentified man found with Lorene Malone?" Her voice raised an octave. "I read about it online. She was found in her house?"

Madison nodded. "We just discovered his identity before coming here and have reason to believe your company did work for Lorene Malone. Would you be able to tell us what?"

"Let me just verify it in the system." Stephanie rolled her chair up to the desk and started working on the keyboard and moving the mouse around.

"We have an invoice number if that helps," Madison offered.

"That would make this much faster." Stephanie moved her mouse, then stopped, looked up at them. "Maybe I should be asking for a warrant?" Simply posing the question made her visibly nauseous. She continued. "I'm probably being stupid requesting one. I mean, if I can tell you something that will help you catch his killer... It's not like I have to worry about protecting the clients so much anymore." Her eyes were glazing over, concentrating. "What's going to happen to the business now? Without him, it's just me, and I'm not an investigator. I've never worked anywhere but here."

"I can imagine the next while will be tough for you," Madison said gently, "but whatever you can do to help would be appreciated." Madison glanced at Terry who had his phone out.

"Actually, the warrants came through," Terry said.

"Okay, that helps." Her chin quivered, and she bit her bottom lip. "But it doesn't bring Saul back."

"Like you said, you have a chance to help us catch his killer," Terry repeated as he extended his phone to her to show her the warrant for the business records as they pertained to Saul Lynch and any electronics.

Stephanie glanced at the screen, and her gaze hardened to steel. She put her attention back on the monitor. "He did bill Lorene Malone for work, that you know already."

Madison leaned on the counter. "What was she having him investigate?"

"That might be trickier." Stephanie took a deep breath. "Saul wouldn't tell me the details of open investigations. He said it was out of respect for a client's privacy."

Apparently, when Stephanie said she was verifying what work Lorene had hired them for, she was simply confirming she was a client. "How can we find out what he was looking into?" Madison asked.

"He keeps everything on his laptop, and he protects the files with passwords." Stephanie frowned. "He keeps that laptop on his person all the time, like most of us cradle our phones."

Madison glanced at Terry. Did that mean that not only was Lynch's ID and phone missing but so was his laptop? The killer was trying to cover all of his or her steps.

"I take it by the looks on both your faces, you didn't come across his laptop." Stephanie split her gaze between the two of them.

Madison shook her head.

"I'm sorry, then. I don't know what else to do for you."

"He didn't back up his files to a server here or to a cloud, perhaps?" Terry asked.

Good thinking, Terry!

"Oh, maybe…" Stephanie slid her bottom lip through her teeth as she moved her mouse around, clicking here, clicking there. Her face darkened. "It was a reach. He wasn't good about updating to the mainframe computer here, but then again, he was rarely in the office. He very well might have backed up to a cloud, but if he did, I know nothing about it."

One step forward, two back. That stood to define the entire case so far, but how frustrating to have John Doe's identity and still feel like their hands were tied.

"We're going to need to bring the office computers with us," Madison said.

"Whatever you need." Stephanie sniffled. "Just please catch whoever did this to him."

Madison touched the woman's forearm. "Don't you worry. We intend to do just that."

Tears fell down Stephanie's cheeks. "Thank you."

"Before we go, you might be able to help us answer something else," Madison started. "Most PIs have their prints on file. Do you know why Mr. Lynch's wouldn't have been?"

Stephanie's brow furrowed. "I have no idea."

"He was a registered PI?" Terry inquired.

Stephanie pointed to a framed certificate on the wall that declared Saul Lynch just that with the state.

They might have had a name for their John

Doe, but they had no idea who he really had been.

"We're going to need to take that with us, too," Madison told her.

Thirty-Two

Madison and Terry had collected the computer from Your Best Friend and hit Lynch's house for a quick search. It didn't yield Lynch's Mercedes or laptop, just as their trip to Colton didn't bring any answers they were after but only raised some new questions.

She drove like a mad woman back to Stiles, determined to make the dress-fitting appointment at seven. The clock on the dash read six fifty as she pulled into the station's lot. She was going to be late. "She's going to kill me," Madison said.

"Nah, I don't think she'd go and do that with the wedding being so close." Terry paused to smile at her. "Though she's probably already killing you. Making *you* wear a dress. Have fun being all girlie."

She scowled at him. "You, my friend, are living dangerously."

"I like it that way."

"You won't when I kick your ass." Madison parked, and they got out.

"Come on, Maddy, you'd never hurt little ol' Terry," he called out. He was laughing, and it got her started, which led to some coughing.

"Oh—" she tossed him the keys for the department car "—so you're not hanging around here bored or not knowing what to do, there's that cancer support group…"

"We know who Lynch is now, so I'm not sure why I'd go."

"Lorene could have opened up to one of them about what she was investigating. You might get answers faster than we would waiting on finding Lynch's laptop. We might not even find his laptop."

"Fine," he mumbled and stalked back to the department car while she headed toward her personal Mazda. "You go have fun, and little Terry will be working his ass off."

She smiled as she got into her car. He'd referred to himself in third person twice in about as many minutes. He had to be running on fumes. He was certainly wrong about one thing: tonight probably wouldn't be any fun at all. Well, except she'd be spending time with her best friend. The dresses, the crinoline, the girlie-girlie—*ack*. All that she could live without.

TROY CALLED HER ON THE way to the bridal shop. "Just so you know, I broke Hershey out of jail.

We're home safe and sound and cuddled up on the couch in front of the TV."

"Thanks." She'd called him on the way back from Colton to see if he could get Hershey from the kennel. Hearing about their relaxing evening, jealousy wound through her. The domestic life she'd fought against for most of her adult life was now something she craved. This morning—and their conversation—had been a long time ago, and she just wanted to forget all about it. In fact, she'd love to be there in Troy's arms and petting Hershey's velvet ears.

"Enjoy every minute," she said.

"I wish you were here."

She thought to the near future, of herself parading around in her maid-of-honor dress. "Trust me, so do I."

"You working the case late again?"

She realized then she'd never told him why she needed him to pick up Hershey beyond mentioning she was out of town investigating the case. "I will be…*after*." It came out sounding as if she was facing the end of the world.

Troy's end was silent for a few seconds. "Oh." One small utterance, and she could detect his amusement. "You have the dress-fitting thing tonight."

Dress-fitting thing. She could relate to that. She laughed. "Yep." She pulled into a public parking lot next to the bridal shop. "I just got here, so I better go."

"Well, have fun." There was no mistaking his pleasure in their conversation now. He was just as bad as her partner.

"Oh, yeah, I don't know if I can contain myself." She scanned the lot but didn't see Cynthia's car.

He laughed. "That's my girl, sarcastic to the end."

"Bye." She was smiling.

"Maddy," he rushed out, "about this morning. I should have just been forthcoming with you. About Kimberly, the Malones, meeting up with her."

She wasn't going to correct him because he should have been, but hearing him put it like this had her thinking about Leland King and the little side investigation she had going. She hadn't shared any of that with Troy. "It's fine."

"We are okay?"

"We're good," she assured him and looked toward the bridal store, "but I've really got to go."

"Yeah, of course. Love you."

"Love—"

He'd ended the call.

"You," she finished to the interior of her car, and her insides twisted. She hated being so tied up in this relationship just as much as she loved it. She didn't remember being this in love with Toby Sovereign even when they'd been engaged.

She stepped out of the car, thoughts of her

love life swirling in her mind as she headed to the front door of Tiffany's Bridal. She could wait outside in the cool night air or go inside and get acclimated to all things bridal. She braved option two.

"Good evening." A slender woman whom Madison hadn't dealt with previously greeted her. The woman's gaze ran over Madison. "Welcome to Tiffany's Bridal. Are you a lovely bride-to-be?"

Madison's heart began racing, and her breathing deepened. She couldn't get a solid lungful of air. She went to swallow, and saliva went down the wrong pipe. She started coughing, and the clerk waited patiently.

"I'm here—" Madison cleared her throat "—with the Cynthia Baxter party."

The woman angled to look around Madison and had this expression on her face that read, *but you're alone.*

"The bride and bridesmaid are just running behind." Madison gave the woman a tight smile, feeling suffocated by the racks and racks of wedding dresses.

"May I take your coat?"

Madison shucked her jacket and laid it in the woman's waiting arms.

"Please remove your outside shoes over there." The clerk's eyes fell to the carpet, and Madison followed her gaze. Wet shoeprints tracked from the door to her feet.

Madison winced. "Sorry."

"No problem." Her words said one thing, while the glint in her eyes told Madison another. "Would you like a glass of champagne while you wait?"

"Yeah, that would be—" Madison caught movement outside the front window. It was Cynthia and her sister Tammy walking down the sidewalk. What a relief!

Madison jacked a thumb toward them. "Looks like they're here. Make that three champagnes."

"Certainly," the clerk said but didn't move.

Cynthia and Tammy entered the store.

"Welcome to Tiffany's Bridal," the clerk said. "One of you is the lovely bride to-be?"

Hearing that expression again knotted Madison's gut. After all, she'd just been thinking about how serious she was about Troy and how she loved the depth of their relationship. Marriage was even something that came to her mind periodically. It was the next logical step to take, but it felt like taking a nosedive off a tall cliff. If she took that jump, would she meet with jagged rocks or water as hard as cement, or would she just simply go beneath the surface and come out unharmed? She gulped.

"Oooh, aren't you excited?" Tammy rushed over to Madison and shook her shoulders. "The wedding's only three days away. Can you believe it?" She wrapped her arms around Madison and squeezed her hard enough that Madison feared bones popping out of alignment.

"Hi, Tammy," Madison said. She'd only met Tammy once before, but from comparing then to now, Tammy operated on fully-spun. It might not be a bad thing that she lived in Alabama.

"You stay away from her," Cynthia told her sister and kept her distance. "She's got a cold."

"Oh." Tammy crossed her fingers and backed up, putting feet between her and Madison.

The clerk was still standing there, holding Madison's coat, and smirking at the interaction. She didn't show any indication that she was aggravated Cynthia or Tammy hadn't acknowledged her yet.

"She's the bride," Madison said, directing the clerk's attention to Cynthia.

"Welcome," the clerk said to Cynthia. "Tiffany, sadly, had to leave early this evening, but she left me everything that I should need to know."

"Good." Cynthia was smiling.

The clerk held out her arms to Cynthia and Tammy, and they handed over their coats.

"I'll be right back, and we can get started." The clerk's gaze went from Madison's eyes and led to a rubber mat near the door.

Message received. Madison took her shoes off and placed them on the mat.

"Oh, I didn't think to take mine off before…" Tammy's voice trailed off as she studied the mess she'd made of the carpet.

Cynthia also slipped out of hers.

Tammy was back in front of Madison but had left more space between them than before. "I can't afford to be catching any cold. You should really go pick yourself up everything you can from a pharmacy tonight: echinacea, orange juice. If you talk to a pharmacist and tell them about the wedding, they could probably recommend something to get rid of it faster." The words were hurling from Tammy's lips and seemed to bounce from concern for herself to things going smoothly for the wedding. It was hard to say which she really cared about more.

"I'm fine. It's just a little scratchy throat," Madison replied. If she told herself enough times that she was healthy, then she'd be healthy. She wouldn't be going down the bitter path of echinacea again, no matter what. She'd almost thrown up when she tried the drops in the past.

Madison and Cynthia caught each other's eye, and Cynthia mouthed, *Sorry*. Madison sensed the apology had to do with Tammy and her exuberance.

"Here you go, ladies." The clerk returned with a silver tray and three flutes of champagne, each of which was garnished with a strawberry.

Madison and Cynthia plucked a glass, but Tammy didn't. She started flapping her hands again.

"I was going to tell you after the weddin', Cyn,"

Tammy started, practically squealing, "but Ken and I are expecting."

Cynthia's mouth gaped open, closed, opened, closed, opened, closed.

"Eek," Tammy added, failing to read the room.

The clerk stepped back.

"Congratulations," Madison said, but Cynthia's face didn't read celebratory. "That's exciting news, isn't it, Cyn?" Madison prompted.

"Yeah, that's...quite something." Cynthia's eyes went blank, the way they often did before she'd lose her temper.

"Congratulations," the clerk offered in a near whisper. "I'll give you some time." The woman walked off with the other champagne, and Madison wished she could follow.

"You're pregnant?" Cynthia spat, eyeing her sister.

"Yes!" Tammy flashed a huge grin.

"I didn't think that you and Ken could have children."

Oh? Oooh. "Maybe we should take this someplace else?" Madison suggested. "Outside? Talk about it later?"

Cynthia shook her head at Madison.

"It's a real miracle, sis." Tammy went to hug her sister, but Cynthia raised an arm to block the embrace, then flung back her champagne.

Tammy's shoulders sagged, deflated, as if she'd finally clued in that Cynthia wasn't happy about the news. "I thought you'd be excited for us."

Cynthia pointed at Madison's champagne. "You didn't touch that yet?"

"No, I—"

Cynthia shot it back and handed Madison both empty glasses.

"What is your problem, sis? Are you jealous?"

"Hardly." Cynthia leveled a cold glare at Tammy. "Is the baby his?"

Yikes. Madison wilted and wished herself invisible or, better yet, somewhere else. Cynthia's temper didn't come out often, but when it did, it was best to steer clear of her. Obviously, there were deep roots that were being ripped out.

"Of course the baby's his," Tammy snapped. "Who else's would it be?"

Madison looked down at the empty glasses in her hands. Where was the champagne when you needed it? "I should probably just leave you al—"

"Madison, stay right there," Cynthia said.

Full name again. Okay, then, I'll stand right here. Lord, help me.

"You have a history, Tammy," Cynthia accused.

Tammy's left leg was bouncing. "I told you it was only that once."

"Don't you mean *twice*?" Cynthia countered. "Or has it been more than that?"

"I haven't cheated in a long time."

"How long?"

Somewhere a pin dropped, probably in a dressing room at the back of the store. Madison was sure she heard one.

"Is it Ken's kid?" Cynthia asked before her sister answered her last question.

Madison took another few steps back from the sisters. Cynthia's temper was marked by stages: the blank stare, the hot boil, the retreat, and the comeback. The last was the worst stage.

Tammy glanced at Madison. If she was looking for an intervention, she was out of luck. She was on her own. There was no way Madison was getting involved.

"I think so?" Tammy whispered.

"Now the truth comes out. You *think* it's Ken's kid?" Cynthia put a hand to her forehead, paced a few steps, and spun back around. "Ken doesn't deserve this. He's never deserved the way you treat him."

"The kid is Ken's. I can feel it. It's not—"

"Not what? Not some other guy's? And now you can *feel* whose baby you're carrying?" Cynthia snarled.

"And how would you know? You've never been pregnant."

Ouch! "Tammy, there's no reason to—"

Both sisters glared at Madison, and she held her hands up in surrender.

"Neither have you," Cynthia snarled.

"Until now." Tammy crossed her arms.

Cynthia expelled a rushed breath and opened her mouth to say something, but Madison blurted out, "Let's go try on the dresses and then grab a bite to eat." She had to risk jumping in again before either sister said something she'd regret—if they hadn't already. "Come on. It will be fun," she urged them. If there was a heaven and hell, this had to go in her heaven column. When neither sister responded to her, she said, "It's only three days away." She playfully nudged her elbow into Tammy's shoulder. It felt like she'd come in contact with a corpse.

Madison continued, struggling to find the right words. "Tammy, it's your sister's big day. Seconds ago, you were so excited about it. You both love each other—"

Tammy started crying and turned to Madison. "Get me my coat."

"Tammy, what are you doing?" Madison had a horrible feeling.

"What do you think? I'm leaving."

Anger bubbled close to the surface. "You're not going to leave your sister hanging like this."

"Watch me. Coat!" she bellowed for the clerk.

"Come on. Think this through. You'll both get past this," Madison grasped. "Someday you two will be laughing about this."

Tammy and Cynthia slid Madison cutting glares.

Or maybe not…

"My coat!" Tammy yelled out again, but the

clerk was already on her way. Tammy took her coat, slipped on her boots, and stomped out the door.

Cynthia watched her sister leave. "Good riddance. I don't need that slut in my wedding party anyway." Sadness and regret seeped into her voice, the bravado a fragile front that was already breaking down. Tears glistened in her eyes. Madison put an arm around her friend and squeezed.

"We're going to need more champagne," Madison told the red-cheeked clerk.

"I'll be right back."

"And she's going to need to try on her dress," Cynthia added. With the clerk gone, she turned to Madison. "I'm sorry you had to witness all that."

"Don't mention it."

"Try on your dress, and we'll just walk down the street for dinner and drinks. My treat."

"If you insist." Madison grinned, and Cynthia laid her head briefly on Madison's shoulder.

"Why can't everyone's sister be Chelsea?" Cynthia said. "You guys have an amazing relationship."

"I don't know about—"

"Don't lie to me."

"It was because of me she almost died at the hands of a Mafia hit man, or do you have selective memory?"

Cynthia laughed, and in contrast to the last

few minutes, it might as well have been the sound of an angel. "But she forgave you."

Madison was seeking a way out of this conversation when she saw the clerk signaling for them to go to the back of the store to the dressing rooms. Madison waved to let the woman know she'd be right there. "Dress-fitting time."

"Nice switch of subject."

"Hey, me in a dress. This should be fun for you." Madison flashed a goofy grin, and Cynthia smiled.

Yep, let's get that dress on and off, and let the drinking commence!

Thirty-Three

"S he's the most selfish person I know." Cynthia was gripping her beer bottle so hard that her knuckles were white.

Madison sat across from her, drinking a coffee that was closely comparable to the mud from the bullpen. Stir it with a spoon and hope it comes out intact. They'd already eaten dinner, and the five ounces of steak and a scoop of garlic mashed potatoes were sitting in her gut like a lead ball.

"I'm sure she'll be back in time for the wedding." It was a lame offering, and Madison knew it, but she wanted to at least try to cheer up her friend. Madison was prepared to do whatever she could to turn things around between the sisters in time, but she wasn't a miracle worker, either. Some pretty nasty things had been said.

"I'm not holding my breath." Cynthia fanned her hair back from her face and adjusted her black frames. "She's always been so self-absorbed. It's all about Tammy."

Was Cynthia jealous at Tammy's news coming at the time of her wedding? Madison didn't think Cynthia would be petty like that, but it seemed likely there was something deeper going on that Madison wasn't privy to.

"Well, tonight, this week, and this weekend are all about you." Madison gave her friend a smile before she braved another sip of brew.

"Apparently, Tammy didn't get that memo," Cynthia sulked.

"Okay, what is it between you two?" Madison leaned across the table, caution be damned. "Has it always been this way for you guys? I sense this goes back much further than tonight."

"It's the story of our lives." Cynthia lifted her beer bottle. "I just wish you'd drink with me."

Detour tactic, but Madison wasn't biting. She'd already been through the fact with Cynthia she might be headed back into work and had curtailed her indulgence to a couple of beers. "Just talk to me. Isn't that what you say to me when something's weighing on me?"

"I don't want to talk about it."

"Huh. I usually say the same thing, and it doesn't get me far."

The friends locked gazes.

"Fine," Cynthia said. "She's just…she likes guys too much to be married. Ken is a great man, and he doesn't deserve the way she treats him."

Madison remembered Cynthia saying as much to her sister. "So, Tammy's cheated on him before?" A question to which Madison had an answer, but hopefully it would stir Cynthia to open up more.

"Yeah, and she didn't see anything wrong with it, either." Cynthia rocked her bottle and peered inside. She flagged down a waitress and said, "Another."

The waitress left, and after she returned and dropped off a new bottle, Madison said, "Tough to stand behind that."

"Right?" Cynthia lifted her beer in a toast gesture then gulped a few chugs. "I figured you'd understand where I'm coming from."

Cynthia didn't need to say that she was referring to Madison's past and her subsequent views on cheating and infidelity.

"I do, but...don't hurt me." Madison drew back. "Are you willing to lose your sister over how she lives her life?" There was no easy way to ask.

"She's just so rude."

It was best Madison stay quiet. Silence was really a response, too. She certainly wasn't going to point out that she had found Cynthia's response—in a public place, at that—to be inappropriate and rude as well. She could excuse the behavior seeing that emotions ran high between the sisters, and Madison was well aware that family could be complicated.

"You think I was rude, too." Cynthia drew a circle around Madison's face, implying her reaction was written there.

"I just think that the two of you could have found a better place to talk," Madison admitted.

"Probably, but sometimes things come up, and we're not given the luxury of choosing when and where." Cynthia gulped back the rest of her drink and signaled for the check.

"You're mad at me now?" Madison asked the question, hating to do so for the second time today.

"No, I just need to get to bed. My head is swimming." Cynthia looked blankly at Madison. "She just ran out on me, three days before my wedding." There was regret and emotion in her voice, a vulnerability.

Madison took her friend's hand. "I'm sorry." As much as Cynthia may have overstepped, Madison's heart ached for her. It was her perfect wedding at stake, and Cynthia was like family to her.

"It's bad enough Mom's no longer around." Cynthia's eyes glazed over.

Cynthia's mom had died not long before Madison had met Cynthia, going on nine years ago.

"That has to be tough," Madison empathized.

"Yeah." Cynthia pinched her eyes shut briefly. "She can just be so stubborn. More than you."

How did I get pulled into this?

Madison jutted out her chin. "I'm proud of that quality."

"As you should be."

Well, that's a first. Madison had always thought she was alone in viewing her stubbornness as an asset.

Cynthia continued. "If you weren't so stubborn, you'd let things go, turn the other way. Killers would walk. Stiles PD, the city, the world would feel the loss."

"I don't know about the world," Madison said modestly, "but thank you."

"You're welcome."

The waitress brought the check, and Madison scooped it off the table. "I know you said tonight was on you, but I won't have it." She slid a credit card in the check folder and put it at the edge of the table.

"Thanks."

"For you, the world." Madison laughed, and Cynthia smiled.

"Hey, how did you make out with Your Best Friend and notifying them about Saul Lynch?" Cynthia asked.

Madison proceeded to tell her about Stephanie and how they still had to put their hands on Lynch's laptop. "We think that something Lynch was investigating resulted in his murder and you-know-who's." Madison didn't want to mention Lorene's name in case anyone overhead.

"Let's hope his laptop shows up," Cynthia said.

"You're telling me. All we have right now is their billing, which doesn't really tell us anything." Madison shrugged. "They kept the details vague, but it gives us some names."

"Huh. Hard to figure out motive and line up suspects without knowing what Lynch was into."

The waitress came by and took off with the check folder.

"Isn't it? Impossible really, short of contacting everyone he was working for and asking them."

"You might not have another choice," Cynthia stated.

"Might not, but I'm hoping we will."

The check returned with Madison's credit card. She added a tip and signed off. She realized, as she did, that she was utterly exhausted. It had been an eventful day, and a long one. Tag on her symptoms that hinted at a cold settling in, and she felt more drained.

"You heading back to work at—" Cynthia consulted her phone "—ten thirty at night? You can't exactly be calling around."

"I can get their names and numbers ready for tomorrow. Besides, Terry was working tonight." For her partner, for the name of teamwork, she couldn't give in to the temptation to just go home and snuggle in with Troy and Hershey, even if she desperately wanted to.

"Then he should have that all done," Cynthia joked.

"I'm not holding my breath. He had to check out a cancer support group. He was going to ask around and see if anyone there knew what you-know-who was having investigated." As Madison said the words, she felt like smacking herself in her head with her palm. If anyone would know what Lorene was investigating, it would be Sabrina Darbonne, her best friend. After all, Darbonne knew about the cancer when no one else did. How had she and Terry not thought of this before?

"There's also a little mystery," Madison started, "related to Saul being a PI but not having his fingerprints on file."

"Right. I never thought of that."

"Terry gets the credit."

"Guess he has to sometimes."

"Sometimes." Madison agreed. "We brought back a framed certificate saying that Lynch is licensed as a PI with the state. It's right there in black-and-white, but something's off."

"I'd be verifying its authenticity." Cynthia shrugged.

"Definitely part of the plan." A tickle at the back of her throat caused her to cough.

"You told me you're not going to get sick."

"I'll be fine."

"I sure hope so. Without you, no one will be standing up with me at my wedding."

Madison had every intention of reaching out to Tammy to see if she could smooth things out on that end, at least patch things up enough so that the wedding could go on as planned. "Everything will work out."

"You say that like you know for sure, but you don't."

Madison hesitated to let Cynthia know she planned on talking to Tammy, fearing Cynthia would hate the idea. Madison opted for honesty. "Let's just say that if there's anything I can do about—"

"You're going to talk to her? Well, good luck." Pain flicked across Cynthia's eyes.

"Are she and Ken staying with you and Lou?"

"Ha! Heavens no! Are you kidding me? You saw how well we did in the store. The tight quarters of our apartment? We'd probably kill each other," Cynthia teased though amusement didn't touch her eyes. "They've got a room at the Marriott."

"That's where Steven Malone's set up. It's a nice place," Madison said, her mind drifting. If the two sisters butt heads often, why had Cynthia invited Tammy to be part of her wedding? Was it out of a sense of obligation? Madison couldn't imagine Cynthia doing anything because she felt she had to.

"Yeah, the place is all right."

She obviously hadn't seen the presidential suite.

Cynthia slipped out of the booth. "You really think Terry's back at the station? He probably hit the support group, then his pillow."

"He could have," Madison conceded. "He'd probably cut out for a bite to eat, but I can't blame him for that." She started coughing.

"Please go home and get some rest."

"I've got to solve this case, Cyn."

"At what cost?"

"I'll be fine for the wed—"

"Not just that. You're no good to the investigation if you're bedridden."

"Bedridden? It's just a cold. It hasn't even fully set in, and you and Terry make it sound like I'm dying." She felt like it at times, but that was beside the point.

"Yep, there's the stubbornness." Cynthia laughed and got into her coat.

Madison stood and put an arm in one sleeve of her jacket, and something fell to the ground. Cynthia bent over and picked it up for her.

"Here you—" Cynthia was holding the burner phone.

Son of a bitch.

"Thanks." Madison snatched it from her and stuffed it back into the pocket.

"What was that?"

"A phone."

"Don't be smart with me, girl. That's not your normal phone. Why do you have a second phone?"

She couldn't tell anyone about what she was doing with Leland King or her need to take down corrupt cops, how it was becoming a side mission in her life. "I could have replaced the one I had."

"Spill," she said and slid back in the booth.

Madison sat down again, too. "I can't tell you why I have that phone. Please trust that it's in your best interests not to know."

"Whoa. That sounds serious. And mysterious."

"Just forget you saw anything." While Madison pleaded for Cynthia to look the other way and forget what she'd seen, there was a part of her that would love to unburden herself.

Cynthia studied Madison's eyes. "Just promise me you're not getting yourself into trouble and that you're not in danger."

Madison's shoulders slumped, and Cynthia clenched her jaw and shook her head.

"What is it with you? You need to face danger to feel alive? You were hunted by a Mafia hit man just a couple of months ago," she spat. "You barely survived that!"

"Please, Cynthia, just let this go."

"If you end up dead because you're digging where you shouldn't be, I'll never forgive you."

Her friend's statement stabbed her in the heart and briefly stole her breath. "You know I'd only look into something if it needed to be looked into." She held Cynthia's gaze. "I promise that I'm taking all the necessary precautions, and one of those makes it necessary for me to not tell other people what I'm doing."

Cynthia didn't say anything, and seconds ticked off on a clock somewhere. "Fine, but please just stay safe."

"I'll do my best. That's all any of us can do." Madison sure hoped her best efforts to keep herself and loved ones safe and to get corrupt cops off the street would be enough.

Thirty-Four

Madison had stopped by the station and worked a few hours with Terry before calling it a night. He'd told her everyone at the support group had good things to say about Lorene Malone, but none of them knew Saul Lynch, and Lorene hadn't opened up to any of them about why she'd hired Lynch. Terry had thought to pay Sabrina Darbonne a visit, but Lorene hadn't told her best friend anything about Your Best Friend.

She and Terry had gone on to compile a list of people Lynch had billed recently, complete with phone numbers and addresses. If the investigation wasn't given another curveball, they'd be picking up there in the light of a new day.

When she got home, it was nearing one in the morning, but she found Troy and Hershey on the couch.

"There she is," Troy roused Hershey, who whined with excitement, jumped off the couch, and ran to greet her at the door.

"At least someone's happy to see me." She hurried out of her boots and hung her coat on the doorknob, then bent over and rubbed Hershey behind the ears. "Momma's missed you. You're such a good boy."

"You never rub my ears and goo-goo gaga over me." Troy slipped his arms around her waist and kissed her lips.

"I'd imagine there are other places you'd prefer I rub."

"Rrrr." Troy pretended to growl and backed up to give her space to enter farther into the house. "By the way, the closet's right there next to the door." He flicked a finger toward her coat.

"So it is," she said but didn't make a move to put her coat away. Hershey was nudging his nose into her leg, looking for more affection. She doled out more head rubs. "Hey, buddy. Hey."

"I see the dog gets the most attention."

She hitched her shoulders. "He was the first to greet me, to make a big fuss over me."

"Oh, is that all it takes?" Troy pulled her to him, planted his mouth on hers, slipped his tongue into—

She pushed on his chest and pulled back. "You might be sorry you did that."

"Why?" Revelation dawned in his eyes before the entire question left his lips. "The damn cold. *Pfft. Pfft.*" He pretended to spit as if he'd eaten dirt and wiped his tongue on his hand.

She laughed. "Now you're being dramatic."

"I'm being—? No, if you get me sick, I'm going to—"

"Going to *what*?" she challenged, her voice husky.

"Take it out of your hide." He lunged for her and grabbed her sides. His height towering over her, his energy possessing her.

"What if I—" she coughed "—said I'd welcome that?" She tried to recover from the rasp in her throat, angled her head upward some more, looked him in the eye, and licked her lips. Trying her damnedest to be sexy but feeling any chance of that slipping away as another cough erupted from her chest. "Ah, son of a—"

Troy smiled. "Come on, let's get you into bed."

"You'd like that, wouldn't you?" She refused to accept the inevitable: sex had officially been swept off the table.

"You bet I would, but you're not feeling well. I'll have to take a raincheck."

"Oh," she groaned.

Troy turned off the TV and went around the living room turning off the lights.

"Did you stay up waiting for me?" she asked.

"Let's just go to sleep. We'll talk in the morning." He put a guiding hand on her lower back, and they went down the hallway to their bedroom, Hershey trailing them. He dropped onto his pillow in the corner of their room, and Madison and Troy went about their nightly routines. After getting into bed and saying their goodnights, she stared at the ceiling.

She flicked on the lamp on her night table. "What do you want to talk about?" She rolled on her side to face him.

"Maddy, we can talk in the morning," he stressed. He was squinting, his eyes averse to the light.

Her gaze went to the alarm clock. *1:25 AM.* "Technically, it is morning."

"Ah, you know what I mean."

"Please, just talk to me now. I'll sleep better."

"Anyone tell you you're stubborn?"

"Just tonight." She shuffled into a seated position and crossed her legs.

"Fine, let's talk *now.*" Troy sat. "I…" He expelled a deep breath. "I haven't been fully forthcoming."

Imaginings of him kissing Kimberly flashed through her mind, and she stiffened. "In what way?" she forced out.

"And I should have been straightforward when it came to having drinks with Kim," he replied, avoiding her direct question.

Dear God, he did do something he shouldn't have.

"I'm all yours. Heart, soul, and mind." He reached for her hands and squeezed them. "And you're right about the fact we should communicate, even when it's not easy."

Her heartbeat was thumping in her ears. She couldn't take it if he was going to tell her he'd cheated.

Troy continued. "Relationships fail when the doors of communication are closed."

She pulled her hands back. "What do you need to tell me?" She steeled herself to hear the worst possible news she could imagine: that they were over and he'd fallen for someone else.

Troy pinched his eyes shut briefly and nodded. "This isn't going to be easy to share."

She braced herself.

"I've never told anyone this before."

Wait a minute—that didn't sound like he was about to confess to cheating. "What is it?" she asked.

"When Brad, Kim's brother, died…" His eyes glistened with tears. "I should have been with him that day." He was peering into her eyes as if seeking strength to continue.

She put her hand on his arm. "You can tell me, whatever it is," she said softly.

"He died in a car accident." His voice turned gravelly, and he sniffled. Tears fell down his cheeks, and she wiped them with the pads of her thumbs. "He was driving. He hated to drive." He met her eyes. "Usually, I drove us anywhere we needed to go, but I…" He paused to collect himself. "I needed to study for an algebra test. If I failed it, I'd have to take math the next year, start from scratch. I hated math," he said with contempt. "It seemed like a small sacrifice, stay home this one time, and it should have been me—" Troy broke down then, sobbing. She scooted over to him, took him into her arms, and lightly rocked him.

"I'm so, so sorry," she consoled him, emotion welling up in her own throat as she saw the strong man she loved falling apart.

She held him until his tears ran dry and rubbed his back. She put her forehead to his and cupped his cheeks. "I'm so sorry," she repeated, "but I'm so very happy you're here, today, with me." She tapped a kiss on his mouth, intending to keep the display of affection to just that. He parted her lips with his tongue. She didn't resist him but did what she could to take his pain from him.

When they parted afterward, she put a hand over her racing heart and turned out the light. She felt like such a fraud. She loved this man with her entire being. He'd just opened his heart and confessed something that he had to tear from his soul, yet she was withholding from him. She was a sham, demanding they talk and be open with each other. If she told him what she was doing with Leland King, would she put Troy's life at risk? Would he try to talk her out of the investigation? But if she didn't tell Troy, was she jeopardizing their relationship?

Thirty-Five

When Madison woke up, Hershey was in Troy's spot on the bed.

"What are you doing up here, boy?" She petted him and glanced at the clock. *7:30 AM.* "Son of a—!" She jumped up. So much for getting an early start this morning. She'd hoped to go over to the Marriott and talk with Tammy before heading into the station.

She found a note Troy had left on the kitchen counter next to the coffee machine telling her he'd gone into work and that he loved her. It was written on a printout for a craftsman bungalow. She'd take it with her and look the listing over later. She glanced longingly at the coffeemaker, but decided she'd get ready and grab something on the way into the station.

She hurried around the house, Hershey at her feet anywhere he could follow. She suffered through a few coughing fits and calmed them with some lozenges that were hanging around in the medicine cabinet. She couldn't bring herself to check the expiration date on the packaging, figuring she didn't want to know. A quick shower helped her feel a bit more human, but the cold was definitely doing its best to settle into her chest. She wondered how Troy was feeling this morning.

It was about eight thirty when she was at the kennel dropping Hershey off for daycare; eight forty-five by the time she had a venti Starbucks cappuccino in hand; and nine by the time she walked into the station.

"I was just wondering if you were making it in," Terry chided when she reached their desks.

"Very funny." She set her cup down and got out of her coat, slipped it on the back of her chair.

"Actually, I wasn't here much before you."

She could feel him watching her every move.

"How was last night?" he asked in a sing-song voice.

"I'd prefer not to talk about it." She sipped some cappuccino and pulled out the listing Troy had left her. Cute place, priced right, in a good neighborhood, close to work—all selling points—but her attention was more drawn to the heart that Troy had drawn in the top corner with the words, *I love you.*

"What have you got there?" Terry rounded her desk.

She folded the sheet and tucked it back into her pocket. "It's none of your business." She hadn't told her partner that she and Troy were looking to buy a house together, because she'd never hear the end of it. He'd pester her about them getting married every day, and life could be stressful enough.

"Okay." Terry stepped back. "Why so touchy this morning? Not feeling well?"

Salt to the wound.

She hated that the cold was doing all it could to best her.

"I'll take that as a no," he said and went back to his desk.

She took a drink of her cappuccino, hoping the caffeine would calm her down. Ironic considering that the stuff was meant to stir her up, but what the hell. "We should probably pay Marie Rauch another visit," she said, agitated through her core, "see if she can offer any explanation for her sweater's button being found near the Malones' pool."

"Not to even mention why it was covered in blood," Terry added. "And I can't help but find it interesting that Lorene Malone and Marie Rauch both grew up in Colton, where Your Best Friend is located. Is there a connection there? Something that Rauch might be able to help us piece together?"

Madison sat back in her chair. She wished she'd thought of that much.

"Detective Knight."

She swiveled at hearing her name.

Detective Alex Commons from Guns and Drugs was headed straight for her. They weren't exactly the best of friends but managed to work together okay if circumstances required.

"What is it?" She expected he was there to ask a favor of some sort.

"My team made a big bust last night. We seized more than a hundred K in meth, not to mention fifteen illegal firearms."

Madison took a slow sip from her drink, lowered her arm. "Looking for an attaboy?"

"The raid was on a body shop in the downtown core," Commons continued unfazed. "It's a chop shop, really."

"I'm still waiting for the part that has to do with us." Madison glanced at Terry.

Commons clenched his jaw. "I'm here because, in the process, we found a vehicle you're looking for. It's registered to a Saul Lynch of Colton."

Madison shot to her feet. "Where is it now?"

"Now, she's interested in what I have to say," Commons huffed indifferently. "It's been brought in to for the lab to process, but you'll also want to know that we brought in an Edward Adach, thirty-seven along with it." He paused there as if he thought the name would mean something to them. When it was evident it didn't, he went on. "Adach served time for armed assault. Was released about ten years ago now, but some guys just never adapt to life on the outside after prison. He might just want to go back and get his three squares a day."

"Where is he?" Madison rushed out.

"In holding. He was also brought in with a .357 Smith & Wesson. Found it in the trunk. Adach claims it isn't his, but everyone says they're innocent."

She was partway down the hall before Commons finished talking. She waved a hand over her head and called out, "Thanks."

Terry caught up to her. "Shouldn't we pull Adach's background before we just go off rushing to talk to him?"

Her steps slowed. All she wanted to do was get Adach in an interrogation room and draw out a confession to a double homicide. But going in prepared would work stronger for the case and yield more results. "Fine, you go pull Adach's record," she said. "If we're lucky we'll find a connection between him, the Malones, or Lynch—beyond him having Lynch's car."

"We? It sounds like I'll be doing the work. While I'm solving the case, what are you going to be doing?" He raised his eyebrows.

"I'm going to see if I can get some things rushed in the lab." She stepped toward the elevator. "Maybe they'll have some updates for me, too."

"Yeah, find out if the S&W Craig brought in is a match," Terry called out.

WHEN MADISON ENTERED THE LAB, she found
Cynthia peering through a microscope. Cynthia
looked up to see who'd entered and smiled when
she saw Madison.

"How are you feeling?" Madison asked,
though her concern wasn't on how many beers
Cynthia had drunk last night. She never used to
hold her liquor well, but that had changed over
the years.

"I can tell by the look of you I'm much better
than you are."

Madison put a few fingers to her cheeks, and
they were hot to the touch even though she was
feeling chilled. *Ignore the cold, and it will go
away.*

Madison's gaze went to what Cynthia had
been looking at on the slide. It was a piece of
coarse fiber. "Is that from the Malone-Lynch
case?"

"Yep. You should have seen it on the evidence
list I sent you. Mark pulled it from the pool
filter."

Madison leaned in to get a closer look. "What
do you think it's from?"

"Best guess would be kitchen twine."

*"I'd lean more toward it being a fine rope or
string," Richards had said.*

"Could this be a piece of what was used to
bind Lynch and Malone?" Madison asked.

"That's what I'm thinking. We collected a spool from the Malones' kitchen. I'm working to see if the piece is from that roll."

"Finding anything definitive?"

"If I had, I'd say that. I'm working on it." Cynthia was a little sharp with her words. "I'm sorry. I didn't mean to be rude about it. It's just…" She took a deep breath. "I haven't heard a word from Tammy. I think she really went home."

"Really? Have you tried the hotel?"

"No." Cynthia's jaw tightened. "If she's going to be like this, why am I chasing after her?"

Because it's killing you not to…

"I'm sure you two can work this out if you just try talking again." Madison was taking a stab at optimism.

"We do, we don't. I'm still getting married. At least I have you." Cynthia smiled at Madison, but the expression didn't reach her eyes. She proceeded to remove the fiber with a pair of tweezers and put it into an evidence bag. She sealed it and made her notations of when she'd had it out and what she'd done with it.

With the shift back to business, Madison thought of the scrapings taken from under Lorene's nails. "Anything back on the epithelial from Lorene?"

"It's in the queue. I'll let you know when I do."

Madison knew better than to push Cynthia. There were several other things she'd love answers to as well, including knowing what was on the USB drives found in Malone's home office—but it was all about picking one's battles. "Has Sam finished processing the ballistics from the bullets found in Lynch and Lorene?"

"She should be finished soon. I can send her down with the results as soon as she has them," Cynthia said. "I know about Lynch's car coming in along with a .357 S&W."

"I just want to know whose S&W is the murder weapon—whether it's Malone's or this new one."

"We can only work as fast as we can work, Maddy."

"I know. It's just—"

"When we've got something for you, I'll send her down," Cynthia said firmly.

"Thanks." Madison smiled. "I'll be in an interview room. Have her check with Ranson for which one and have her interrupt me."

Officer Ranson manned the front desk most of the time, and sometimes Madison wondered if she ever left the station.

"Will do," Cynthia said, "and before you ask, Mark's processing Lynch's car. We'll let you know anything we find."

Madison nodded and left the lab. She found Terry lowering the receiver on his desk phone, a strange look on his face.

"What is it?" she asked.

"Adach has a colorful employment history.

The guy never stays anywhere for long."

"Can't be easy to hold down a job as an ex-con," she said, playing along but waiting rather impatiently for the meaty tidbit she felt he had to share.

Terry went on. "Adach was unemployed for a stretch of eight months before he got his latest job, but you're not going to believe it when I tell you where it was."

"Try me." *Just please* tell *me.*

"Up until last week, Adach worked as a chef at Meals for You."

"That's Lorene's favorite charity." *Or only one…*

"Yep. Adach had worked there for a month when he was let go and another chef brought in. I asked why Adach was fired, and the line went quiet. I thought the call had been disconnected. I never got an answer to that question, but I found out who his replacement was." Terry paused for dramatic effect. "Patty Beaulieu."

"The Malones' cook?"

"Yep, when she's not working there, she's at Meals for You."

"How does that tie in to the murders? Now you're thinking that Adach took revenge for losing his job?" She shook her head. "Why kill Lynch?"

"Wrong place, wrong time?"

"I've heard stranger things. Let's go question the son of a bitch."

Thirty-Six

Adach had been pulled from holding and plunked into interview room two. Madison looked at him through the glass in the neighboring observation room. She hadn't known what to expect of the forty-five-year-old ex-con, but she didn't expect him to be strikingly good-looking with a solid fireman's build. His biceps bulged beneath his long-sleeved tee, and he wore blue jeans. His blond hair was mussed, a look he probably spent time to achieve, and his face was scruffy. And he certainly had the glint in his eyes that told women he wasn't the man you brought home to Momma.

"That's Adach?"

"What?" Terry turned to her.

Shit! Did I say that out loud? What else did I say?

"Uh, nothing," she rushed out. "He didn't ask for a lawyer?"

Terry had been the one to get Adach pulled

from holding.

"Nope," Terry replied. "Said he's got the truth on his side."

"That's trusting, considering his record works against him, as does being in possession of Lynch's car with a .357 S&W in the trunk."

"Yep, the guy's either trusting or stupid. I'd bank on the latter."

"Good for us, then." Madison left the observation room and joined Adach. His gaze latched onto her immediately, blue eyes blazing like crystal. She felt her knees weaken and hated herself for the reaction.

"I'm Detective Knight," Madison said firmly, taking a seat across from him. She was armed with a file, and Terry had printed out Adach's background. Madison gestured to Terry, who was already leaning against the back wall. "That's my partner, Detective Grant."

Adach glanced over a shoulder, then locked his baby blues back on Madison. "I should have left that car where I found it," he said. "I don't want to go back to prison."

She hadn't waited around long enough for Commons to fill them in on Adach's side of the story, but sometimes it was best to just dive in and see where things went, though Troy would disagree. Then again, he was breaching buildings with criminals inside.

Madison opened the folder, clicked a pen she'd brought in, and pretended to study the reports. "How did you come to be in possession of the Mercedes E300?"

"Doesn't that tell you how?" Adach asked, pointing at what she had in front of her.

"Humor me," she said drily. "Tell me where you got the car."

She pictured it in her mind. He showed up at the Malones', killed Lorene and Lynch, and left in Lynch's car. Easey peasey—until he was caught. She was curious what story he would come up with, but it seemed he'd need more prodding. "Where did you pick up the car?" Madison stamped out.

"I found it idling over at Westchester and Maine."

That was nowhere near the Malones' house. "Bad neighborhood. What were you doing there?"

"I live there," he fired back, offended. "Not like I can afford much better when I can't hold a job."

Mr. Adach was bitter with the world. He was becoming less attractive by the second. "So you found it idling and thought you'd just take it?" she prompted.

"Cars like that never show up in my neighborhood, not unless they're already stolen or were used in a robbery or something." Adach's Adam's apple bobbed with a rough swallow. "I knew I was being stupid taking it, but I needed money for rent, food. I was going to sell the car for parts, and now I'm going to prison." His chin quivered.

"You took the car for money?" Madison asked, not fully buying Adach's story.

Terry started jingling the change in his pocket, but Adach didn't seem to notice.

"Yeah. I needed the cash. I was just getting around to selling it when I was dragged in."

"When did you find the car?" Madison asked.

"Monday night, around eleven."

"Yet here we are, Thursday morning. You must not need money that badly."

"Oh, I do." Adach leaned back in his chair and clasped his hands in his lap. "It's not easy getting work with a criminal record."

"I don't know," Madison said, "from what we could tell, you've gotten a lot of jobs."

"Pfft. None of them last. Thought the last one was going to, but…"

Madison leaned forward. "It didn't?"

"You have the file. You tell me," Adach slapped back, revealing another side to his character that didn't shy away from law enforcement. For the breaks in his composure, one might think Adach was vulnerable, but he was more hardened than he wanted to let on.

"Where was the last job?"

"Meals for You," Adach answered. "Some charity, though. They fired me." A pulse tapped in his cheek.

"That made you mad."

"It did."

"They had to have a reason for firing you."

"Nope. They gave me nothing. I'm pretty sure it has to do with my record, though."

Madison shrugged. "Why hire you in the first place, then?"

Adach seemed to chew on that question.

Madison pulled a photograph of Lorene Malone that was provided by her family from the file. It showed a grinning Lorene wearing a beautiful cashmere sweater. "Do you know this woman?"

Adach took the photo with a shaking hand. "She looks kind of familiar. I don't know why."

Madison didn't read any tells that Adach was lying, but he could have perfected the skill. "We think she might be why you lost your job," she put out there, looking to see how he'd react.

"Her?" Adach pulled back. "Why? Who is she?"

Either he was telling the truth or he was the best liar in the history of humankind. "Her name is Lorene Malone, and her cook got your job. Mrs. Malone was involved with Meals for You. She could have had a say in what happened to your position."

"Well, I don't know what I ever did to this Lorene lady." Adach's eyes darkened.

"What about this man?" Madison handed him a printout of Lynch's DMV photo.

Adach took the picture, again with a shaky

hand. "Never saw him before. Why are you showing me these people's pictures?"

"That man's Saul Lynch," she laid out, and Adach's expression was blank.

"Does the Mercedes belong to them?"

"It had belonged to Saul Lynch," Madison spoke slowly.

"*Had*?" Adach gulped.

"Saul Lynch and Lorene Malone were murdered Monday night, the same night you found the car."

"No, no, no!" Adach jumped to his feet, and he was trembling.

"Did you kill them, Mr. Adach?"

Adach paled, and his eyes widened. "No, I had nothing to do with their murders. I swear to God! I didn't kill anyone. I swear. I took a car. That's all. Shit! Shit! Shit!" He ran a hand through his hair.

"You can see how this looks from our side," Madison deadpanned. "You were in possession of a murder victim's car, and a gun, which fires the same caliber bullet as was pulled from his head, was found in the truck. And not just his head, but Lorene Malone's."

"No, I never…I never even knew the gun was there. I just took the car, drove off."

Madison slapped crime scene photos of Lorene and Lynch on the table. "Did you kill these people?"

Adach took in the pictures and belched as if

he was going to be sick. "No, I—"

"You're sure?" Madison barked, applying more pressure.

"No!" Adach cried out, and tears streamed down his cheeks.

"So, when we test the gun found *in your possession*," she emphasized, "it's not going to tie back to their murders?"

"I…I…"

"What, Mr. Adach? It's a yes or no answer."

"I don't know. I swear to you, I just picked up the car." There was something so desperate in his tone, in his appeal, it chipped away at Madison's suspicion that he was behind the murders, but she couldn't let herself lower her defenses, either. He had a record, and he was, at least, guilty of stealing the car.

"Where were you Monday night?" she asked.

Adach wiped his hands down his face. "Depends on what time."

"Don't get smart with me," she kicked back.

Adach held up his hands. "Trust me, I'm not." He dropped back into his chair.

"Say from six until ten." That would more than cover the time-of-death window.

"I was at the gym from six until eight."

"You have a gym membership?" she asked, cocking an eyebrow. "I thought you were in desperate need of money?"

"I pay fifteen dollars a month for a gym down on Fifth Avenue." Adach looked insulted. "Life isn't anything if you're not healthy and fit. You should probably start gulping back orange juice. It might help with the... I can hear the cold in your voice."

"Yes, thank you," she said curtly, not about to let him derail her. "Where did you go after the gym?"

"I went home and applied for some jobs online."

"I'm not sure how we're supposed to verify that."

"I use an online job bank. It logs the dates and times that I apply for jobs."

"Then we're going to need your login information."

"I didn't kill those people."

"So you keep saying, but if I'm going to get the double homicide charge off your head, we'll need more than your say-so."

Adach sobbed. "I just...I can't go back to prison again. Please help me."

She steeled herself and stood. "You should have thought of that before you stole a car."

Adach didn't say anything as Madison and Terry left the room. They went into the neighboring room and looked through the one-way mirror.

"He's certainly not what you'd expect of a man with a record who served prison time," Madison said. "Just when I think he's hardened, I change my mind."

"Do you believe his whole story about finding the car idling in his neighborhood?"

"I do, yes," she admitted. "The killer could have dumped it there in the hopes that some stooge would take the fall. They chose a bad neighborhood where it would be more likely to happen, too."

"So, you don't think he killed them?"

"No, I don't."

"Then this cold is affecting your head more than I thought."

"Hey, what's that supposed to mean?"

"Normally, you're very black-and-white and suspect everyone. Why not this guy?" Terry asked.

"You said for yourself that he's held numerous jobs since he's been out of prison."

"Sure. He's got a list of them."

"That tells me he's trying to turn his life around." She thought of Adach's assault charges and wondered if they'd been trumped up. Then again, her exhaustion could be making her weak. "Maybe the cold is getting to me."

"Like I said."

"I still don't think he did it."

Sam walked past the observation room door, and Madison went after her.

"Sam," Madison called out.

Sam turned and came back to Madison, and they slipped into the observation room with Terry.

"I have the ballistic results from Steven Malone's gun, and the grooves and striations are not a match," Sam said.

"What about the new one that was just brought in?" Madison asked.

"It's next on my list," Sam said. "I'll need some time, but I'm aiming to get an answer for you this afternoon."

Madison hated the waiting game, but sometimes it couldn't be helped. "Okay. Let me know the second you get the results."

"Yes, of course." Sam walked off.

Madison couldn't help but think Sam had a good job. Squeezing the trigger was a stress release, regardless of how she might have initially judged Craig Malone.

"I have a feeling about that Adach guy." Terry jabbed a finger toward the glass.

Adach was sitting there, his arms on the table, raking his hands through his hair. Everything from the guy screamed he was nervous as hell, but he should be nervous. A grand-theft-auto charge was coming down on his head, and a double murder charge hovered above him. Was it just a case of poor judgment, or was he spinning a story and trying to cover up murder? She could reconcile a few things with the former theory. "I really don't think he's our killer. You saw his reactions in there, to the accusation, to the crime scene photos, and you heard his pleas about not knowing Lorene or Saul."

"So the guy's a good actor."

"Before we convict him, let's wait and see what Sam finds out about the gun from Lynch's trunk." Madison observed how they'd reversed their regular roles. Usually it was she pushing for a person's guilt.

"Sure, but I'm telling you he's behind the murders."

"Okay." She widened her stance. "Put your money where your mouth is. Adach's innocent of the murders."

"Another bet? You come into money that I don't know about?" He held out his hand. "I say Adach's going to hang for the murders."

Madison chuckled and took his hand. "That's a bet I'm rigged to win. There's no capital punishment here."

"It's an expression," Terry said slowly. "Besides, you know what I mean: Adach's guilty as hell."

Thirty-Seven

Madison had Adach put back in holding, and Terry was following up on his alibi.

He was on the phone with the gym while she brought up the evidence list that Cynthia had given her. They still needed to speak to Rauch about why her button was found near the pool, with blood on it, but her eyes went to the line that noted the piece of kitchen twine. Had the killer come armed but not prepared to tie them up and improvised with what the Malones had on hand?

Terry hung up and looked over at her, a sour expression on his face. "Well, Adach's alibi's confirmed, but I'm still not convinced."

"Now who's sinking their teeth in?" she retorted, realizing how hard it was to let go of her suspicions against Steven Malone. She still wasn't sure she had.

Madison saw Cynthia approaching, laptop in hand.

Madison stood. "Is that what I think it is?"

"If you think it's Lynch's laptop? Then, yes." Cynthia handed it over to Madison. "Mark found it in Lynch's trunk with the spare wheel."

"Clever hiding spot," Terry interjected.

Madison looked down at the computer in her hands. "Why are you giving this to me? Have you gone through—"

"I thought you wanted this right away to see what Lynch was working on."

"I did, but…" Normally, Cynthia would root through evidence of this sort.

"It's going to be a while before I get into that. I still have the USB drives from the Malones' home office and a ton of evidence to process." Cynthia reached to take the laptop back.

Madison moved it out of her reach. "Never mind. We'll do it."

"Yeah, it's like Christmas all over again," Terry said sarcastically.

"You like the laptop," Cynthia said, disregarding Terry's comment, "you'll like to know that I found the fifty-thousand-dollar transfers have been going to a company called Blissful Enterprises."

"Who are they?" Madison asked.

"Don't know yet. Okay, well, I'm leaving." Cynthia hustled off.

"Someone's in a hurry," Madison mumbled.

"She probably wants to move before you tie her down and demand more updates," Terry teased.

"Very funny."

She sat down at her desk with the laptop and fired it up. There was a sticky note on the screen from Mark, noting the login password. At least the lab had gotten that far.

"You think we even need to bother with this?" Terry gestured to the laptop. "We've got the killer in holding."

"We'll see about that. Either way, we've got to build a case."

"If the gun in Lynch's trunk comes back as the murder weapon, I'd say that's basis for a case right there."

"Say that again."

"What?" He lowered his brows. "The gun comes back a match—"

"No, it was in Lynch's trunk," she said as if it were news she heard for the first time.

"Yeah, I thought you've been around, but—"

"I mentioned it before, that the killer left the car in the hopes of a stooge taking the fall for the murders. That makes sense on the surface, but why would the killer leave behind possible forensic evidence—prints, DNA."

"It's because Adach doesn't care."

"Or because the real killer doesn't have a record," she theorized. "And if Adach is the killer, why would he drive around in his victim's car?"

"Why wouldn't he? Adach told us he

suspected the Mercedes had been used in a crime, but he took it anyway. It comes down to one truth: criminals are stupid."

"Well, I can get behind that, but if Adach's guilty, we really need to find something to build that case against him." She turned her attention to the laptop and keyed in the password. She opened the file directory and quickly recognized some names. She pulled out the list she'd made with Terry last night of the clients Lynch was currently working for, and they matched the file folder names. She double-clicked on the one for Lorene Malone and inside were PDFs and one Word document.

She opened a few PDFs, and they were all invoices. The Word file was eighty-five pages long.

"He certainly had a lot to say."

Terry grabbed his chair, moved it around beside her, and sat down.

She started reading from the beginning, but the wording wasn't making sense. Was her cold messing with her mind?

"Okay, is this gibberish, or is it just me?" Terry asked.

She let out a deep breath. "Not just you."

"He must have used some sort of coding system for his notes. A type of shorthand? One that only he can understand? Sounds extreme."

"He could have been eccentric or overly cautious. He *did* have his laptop hiding in the trunk of his car."

Terry rocked his head side to side. "Good point."

"He could have been looking into more than cheating spouses and insurance fraud."

Terry was staring blankly at the screen and shook his head as if he had water in his ears. "I'm grabbing a coffee, then all this might make more sense."

He left in the direction of the coffee machine.

While she doubted coffee would have the power to translate what was in front of them, chocolate might. She had her drawer open before she remembered she hadn't replenished it, but she found three Hershey's bars and a note.

Was thinking of you. Love, Troy. XO

She held the note to her chest and looked up to the ceiling. "Thank you, thank you." She kissed the paper and heard Terry laughing behind her.

"I see that you found the gift left by the chocolate fairy," he said.

"Why are you back so fast?" Her cheeks heated with embarrassment, and she quickly exchanged Troy's note for a chocolate bar and shut the drawer. And if Troy was anything, he was a chocolate *god*.

"I'm just quick." He slurped some coffee and plunked into his chair next to her. "You figure all that out yet?"

"Ah, yeah, no." She tore into the packaging

and took her first bite. Heaven, heaven, heaven. "When did Troy come by?" she asked around a mouthful of milk chocolate.

"Really? Chew, chew, swallow, chew, chew, swallow, then talk."

Sometimes, it took so little to get her partner going.

She rolled her eyes and said nothing.

"Don't know…about seven this morning?" Terry answered her question.

"Thought you said you weren't here much before me."

"I might have said that to make you feel better about being late."

"And you just had to add that last part." She took another huge bite off the bar.

"You know it."

"Brat," she mumbled around another mouthful of chocolate—heavenly, glorious chocolate. "If you were here that early, what did you do?"

"I started a little digging into Saul Lynch and his PI's license."

"What about it?"

"Well, just the fact that his prints aren't on file is bugging me."

"But he's got the framed license."

"I'm just looking into its legitimacy."

"Why fake being a licensed PI?"

"I don't know, and that's what I'd like to find out. Assuming, of course, he was faking. Either way, there has to be some reason why his prints aren't on file."

She held his gaze, then nodded. She finished off her bar and tossed the wrapper in the trash. She looked back at Lynch's document on Lorene Malone. She scrolled down slowly, giving time for Terry to read the screen, too, not that there was much understanding.

"It's worse than pig latin," Terry mumbled. "At least I can understand pig latin."

She smiled but didn't look over at him. Something caught her eye, and she pointed it out to Terry. "Right there."

"Julia and Gene Boyd. Sounds like real names. Who are they?"

Madison switched screens, typed the names into a database, and sank back in her chair after reading the results.

"They're dead. Shot and murdered twenty years ago," Terry summarized.

"And look where they lived." Madison pointed to the monitor, and Terry leaned in more toward the screen.

"Colton," he said and looked at her with wide eyes.

"It can't be a coincidence that the case keeps taking us back to Colton."

"So who are the Boyds to Lorene Malone?" he asked.

"Good question."

"Were their murders ever solved?"

"Another good question." Madison skimmed the notes on the Boyd investigation, and her heartbeat bumped off rhythm. "No arrests were made in connection with the murders. It's a cold case."

"So…what? Lorene hired Lynch to solve their murders?"

"Based on the state of Lynch's notes, your guess is as good as mine," she said, admitting temporary defeat. "Maybe Stephanie could translate this for us."

"We can ask her," Terry said absentmindedly as he moved his arm in front of her and scrolled through the Boyd investigation notes himself. "They were in what looked like a home invasion gone wrong."

"Items were stolen?"

"One second." He leaned over more, and Madison rolled her chair to allow him better access to her mouse. "It doesn't look like much of anything. Investigators figured some cash, some jewelry. There's no noted value."

"Those things could have been taken by the killer to cover their tracks to make it look like robbery was a motive. Any suspects questioned?"

She coughed, and Terry pulled back.

"Please don't get me sick."

"I covered my mouth."

He eyed her as if he still wasn't convinced he was safe.

"Suspects, Terry?" she prompted.

"I don't see any, and it looks like they had no next of kin. Their estate paid for their burials."

"And the rest of the money? Did it go to children?"

Terry scrolled more. "According to the file, the couple didn't have kids."

"Well, I think it's time we talk to some people. Steven Malone, the Malone children, the Griffins again, Marie Rauch. We need to see if they know anything about the Boyds and why Lorene would have hired a PI firm to look into them or, at least, how they factored into what Lorene was having investigated." She got up and added, "Rauch still needs to account for that button of hers, too. When we're speaking with Steven Malone, we should ask about those fifty-thousand-dollar transfers as well."

"And tell him that his wife had cancer," Terry said. "Good time now?"

"Possibly."

"Let's not forget about Ed Adach, either."

"Grand Theft Auto?" She tossed out a smirk. "Not at all."

"Don't you think we should ask everyone you just mentioned if they know him, too?" Terry said, all business.

"Actually, that's a good point, partner." She put on her coat and hustled down the hall to the station lot.

"We might even want to stop by Meals for

You and see if they can tell us whether Adach knew Lorene. He could be holding that back to protect himself."

Madison didn't respond to Terry's recommendation, but she did take satisfaction in knowing that her partner could be every bit as stubborn as she could be.

Thirty-Eight

Madison made a call to Steven Malone to let him know that she and Terry wanted to talk to him about some developments in the case. She'd also asked if he could have Kimberly, Craig, and Kurt present for their conversation. Sergeant Winston's call came in five minutes later, when she pulled into the parking lot of the Marriott.

"I was just about to call you," Madison said, though not buying her claim herself.

"What is hard to understand about calling me *first*? Just stay away from the Malones until I arrive," Winston barked through her hands-free and hung up.

The man is always such a treat.

She and Terry went into the hotel and met a different front-desk clerk than was there yesterday.

A couple he'd just checked out stepped around Madison and Terry, each of them pulling a rolling suitcase behind them.

The clerk smiled at Madison. "Good day, can I help you?"

Terry pulled back on her arm. "We're supposed to wait."

The clerk shared his gaze between Madison and Terry, his eyes darting back and forth.

"Fine," she said to Terry and gave a pressed-lip smile to the clerk. "We'll just be over there for a few minutes."

The clerk nodded.

"Thanks," Terry said to her.

Madison's eyes went to the couple who was leaving, and it made her think of Tammy and her husband. She was in a holding pattern, so she might as well use the time God gave her. She jutted her chin toward Terry. "Why don't you call Stephanie, Lynch's assistant at the PI firm, see if she can help us with Lynch's notes?"

"Okay."

"And while you're doing that, there's something I need to take care of." She headed to the front desk.

"What are you doing?" he hissed.

She held her hand up at him and kept moving.

"Madison," he called out after her.

She reached the desk. "Could you connect me with the room for Tammy and Ken..." Oh, God, her mind went blank. Had Cynthia even told her Tammy's last name? She had to think back to the first time they were introduced, but it was years ago. Was it a color? White? Black?

Oh, those were shades.

"Last name, ma'am?" the clerk asked.

"Ah, Greene," she blurted out as the recollection hit. "Tammy and Ken Greene."

"One minute." The clerk clicked away and, a few seconds later, looked up at her. "I'm sorry to inform you, but they checked out this morning."

"They *what*?" When Cynthia had said she thought her sister went home, Madison didn't want to believe that Tammy would leave her sister in a lurch like that. It didn't matter how hurtful Cynthia might have been; family makes amends. Madison leaned across the counter. "You're sure? You're reading it right?"

"Madison?" Terry came up behind her.

She looked over a shoulder at Terry.

"As I said, they checked out this morning," the clerk repeated.

"Shit, shit, shit!" Madison clenched her hands into fists and spun and paced. She had to get Tammy back here. If only she'd made it here before going to work, she might have gotten to Tammy in time. She'd failed as a friend. She'd failed as a maid of honor.

"What's going on?" Terry asked.

She stomped over to the lobby area. "I've got to get her back. Cynthia's going to kill me. I'm the maid of honor. I'm supposed make sure everything goes smoothly and—"

"Slow down." He touched her shoulder. "Start from the beginning. I heard you asking about

Tammy and Ken Greene? Who are they?"

"Tammy is Cynthia's sister and her only bridesmaid, and she—" Madison pointed to the clerk "—has gone home."

"What am I missing?"

"She and Cynthia got into a huge fight last night, but I figured, heck, it's sisters. Sisters get into fights. They smooth things over. Life goes on. It doesn't go back to Alabama!" She took a few steps. "What am I going to do?"

"Okay, just breathe."

"Just breathe?" she scoffed loudly enough that people walking through the lobby looked at her. "What am I supposed to do? I can't go down there and drag her ass back. Well, I could, I suppose, but I need to work this case and—"

"Cynthia wouldn't expect you to."

"Cyn's counting on me. I told her I'd fix this."

"Oh."

"Yeah. *Oh*. I thought it might take a little talking, convincing on my part to aid the reconciliation. I never thought her sister would fly home!"

"All right, so before we go off the deep end—"

She glared at him.

"Never mind," he said. "We've already jumped."

"Ha ha."

"Just call Tammy."

"I don't have her number."

"Call Lou. See if he knows how to reach her,

or look her up in the system. You're not without ways of tracking people down."

"Gah." She put her fingertips to her forehead. "I just didn't think it would come down to this."

"But it has. Pull yourself together, woman."

Just the way he said it and looked at her caused Madison to start laughing. He was right. The situation wasn't entirely lost. She'd get Tammy's number from Cynthia's fiancé. Cynthia never had to know. She would talk to Tammy and work everything out. The wedding would go ahead as originally planned: one bridesmaid, one maid of honor.

Air was starting to fill her lungs again— satisfying, life-giving breath—until the tickle in her throat had its way.

ABOUT TWENTY MINUTES AFTER ARRIVING at the hotel, Winston strode through the front doors, Blake Golden at his side. They joined Madison and Terry, and the group of them went up to Malone's suite.

Kimberly answered the door without a word, but Madison felt the woman's eyes on her back as she walked through the suite to the sitting area, where they found Steven, Craig, and Kurt. Steven and Craig were sitting much alike with crossed legs, their backs straight. Kurt was leaning forward, elbows on his knees, but hopped up when he saw Madison.

"Do you know who killed my mother?" Kurt

asked.

"Unfortunately, not yet," she replied.

Grief deepened in his eyes, and Madison wished she had a better answer for him.

Kurt took his seat again on the couch next to his father.

Blake and Winston took seats, too, as did Terry. Kimberly and Madison remained standing.

"There have been some developments in the case," Madison started.

"Did you come here to tell me that my boy's a killer?" Steven rushed out.

She glanced at Craig and smiled. "Not at all. In fact, your gun has been cleared as the murder weapon."

Kimberly jutted out her chin and crossed her arms. "I told you that none of us would have done this to Mom."

Steven looked at his daughter, his eyes full of fire.

What is that about?

Madison dismissed it. She showed the Malones a photo on her phone of Ed Adach but withheld his name. "Do any of you recognize or know this man?"

One by one, the Malones shook their heads.

"I've never seen him. Is he the man who was with my wife? He looks different than the sketch you showed me before."

None of the Malones had met Adach before,

so it was possible that Lorene hadn't, either. His being fired from Meals for You really might not have been personal at all. Adach could have been telling the truth about not knowing Lorene, just as Madison had suspected.

"He's a person of interest in the case," Madison told them.

"A person of interest," Kimberly pondered that. "What does that really mean?"

Madison started, "It means we have reason to suspect he might somehow be involved."

Steven shimmied to the end of the chair's cushion. "He killed my wife."

"It's too soon to know," Terry said, beating Madison to a reply.

"But you think he might have?" Steven clenched his teeth.

"It's possible. That's all we can say. We're trying to figure out if he had any connection to your wife," Madison elaborated. She didn't want to risk giving Adach's name or that he had been in possession of Lynch's car with a gun in the trunk. Even if Adach were cleared, she wouldn't put it past Steven to get revenge.

"Well, he would have if he killed her," Steven spat, latching on stubbornly.

"We're just collecting our facts and building a case, wherever that takes us," Madison stated calmly. "Now, we've found out the identity of the man your wife was with, Mr. Malone." Madison pulled up the DMV photo of Lynch on her phone and made the rounds, starting with Steven, ending with Kimberly.

"Does he look familiar to any of you?" Terry asked. "He could be easier to identify that way than from a sketch."

"No, I've never seen him."

Kurt looked at his father, then his brother and sister.

Kimberly shook her head.

Steven answered for his family. "None of us know him."

"Well, his name is Saul Lynch, and he was a private investigator," Madison said, sitting down.

"A private investigator?" Kimberly spat. "Why would Mom be with—"

"Kimberly," Steven said in a warning voice.

Kimberly snapped her jaw and flushed red like a little girl who'd been scolded. Madison kept watching father and daughter. Kimberly had admitted to a disagreement with her mother, but there was definitely something simmering beneath the surface with her father as well.

"Do any of you know why she'd have hired a PI?" Terry inquired.

Kurt shrugged. Craig splayed his hands. Kimberly pursed her lips and shook her head. Steven hardened his expression.

"No idea, Detective," Steven deadpanned.

"Do the names Julia and Gene Boyd ring any

bells for any of you?" Madison asked.

The Malone children each said they hadn't heard of them before.

"The same goes for me," Steven said. "Who are those people?"

"It seems Lorene may have hired Mr. Lynch to investigate them," Madison said.

"Ah, I see, so this is one of those circles. You ask us if we know what Lorene would be investigating just to see what we know, then you tell us what it was?" Steven stood behind his chair and gripped its back.

"The truth is we don't know all the details," Madison said. "That's why we're here."

"Well, I can't help you." Steven met her eyes. "Every time I talk to you about my wife, I feel like I knew her less and less," he delivered with heat.

"We can appreciate her hiring an investigator must come as a shock to you," Terry said.

"It sure as hell does." Steven fired a glare at Terry. "My wife and I have—" he cleared his voice "—*had* a close relationship. Or at least I thought we had."

"It could be a matter of her not wanting to talk to you about the investigation." Terry stated this in a delicate and respectful manner, but it still had Steven clenching his jaw.

There was an inflection in Terry's voice that made Madison question if he was going to discuss the cancer, but he didn't add anything.

"I can't imagine why she'd want to keep this a secret," Steven countered.

"The Boyds are from Colton," Madison interjected. "They might have tied in to her past somehow."

"Grams and Gramps are from there." Kurt glanced at his father. "They might know."

"Where they're from makes no difference to me, Detective," Steven said, more likely referring to the Boyds than the Griffins. "I still don't know who those people are or why Lorene would be looking into them."

Madison glanced at Blake just to see if he was still awake. He hadn't said a word.

She showed the Malones old DMV photos of the Boyds. Still, no luck.

"They were murdered in their home," Madison said, feeling it was time to put that out to gauge reactions.

Kimberly crossed and rubbed her arms.

"Like Mom," Kurt said.

Craig remained quiet, as did Steven. Father and son might have butted heads, but they were more alike than they perhaps realized.

Madison put her phone away and passed a sideways glance to Winston and Blake. "There's another matter we need to ask you about, Mr. Malone." She let her gaze drift to his children.

"Whatever it is, you can speak to me in front of them," Steven replied.

"As you wish." Madison took a deep breath.

What she had to say next wouldn't be popular with either the sergeant or the lawyer. "We've discovered a significant amount going out of your business account on a monthly basis, fifty thousand to a Blissful Enterprises."

Steven sat back down and crossed his legs. His gaze ever so briefly went to Kimberly.

"Why are you looking at your daughter, Mr. Malone?" Madison was tired of holding back and tiptoeing. If Winston didn't like her calling out Steven, too bad.

"What I would like to know is why you're digging into my financials when I specifically declined this when we spoke on Tuesday," Steven served back and glared at Winston.

"I tried to tell you that it was a necessary step," Winston said.

"Money has been a powerful motive for murder for a long time," Madison added, though not sure why she was coming to Winston's defense. "We need to explore every angle we possibly can to find your wife's killer. You could have owed the wrong person, screwed the wrong person in business. It could be any number of things related to your finances," she said, reiterating yesterday's conversation.

Steven's cheeks were a deep crimson, and he glared at Blake.

Blake stood. "I think it's time for you to leave."

"We're just trying to find out who killed your wife," Madison said. "Surely, you want to do all you can to help."

Blake came over and touched her elbow to guide her to the door. She recoiled from his touch, surprised she'd ever found arousal or comfort from it.

She held up her hands, not feeling like it was the appropriate time to come clean about the cancer now. "We'll see ourselves out."

Madison hurried down the hall toward the elevators, Terry in tow.

"What do you think you're doing, Knight?" Winston called out.

She should have known that he'd follow. She pressed the down button between the elevator doors and spun to look at Winston. "I'm doing my job, Sergeant, and if you can't see that—"

"You come down here, *then* I'm the one to call you? I've made it clear I want you to run your next steps by me *before* acting with this case." A vein was throbbing in his forehead, like a fat, wriggling worm.

"And we did," Madison said. "We stayed in the lobby until you got here."

"I had to hear that you were going to speak to Steven Malone from Steven Malone."

"Speaking of him, you were in that room," she stamped out. "You heard his reaction to the fifty thousand? Saw it?"

"What I saw was you harassing a man who just lost his wife." Winston paused, took some deep breaths, his nostrils flaring.

"There's something he doesn't want us to know," she said.

"It's his own damn money," Winston spat.

The elevator dinged its arrival, and she and Terry loaded onto the car. Unfortunately, Winston did, too.

"You've always had a problem respecting authority, but this? This is too big to ignore. I've specifically told you—" Winston's cheeks were as red as Steven's had been, and he was shaking his head. "I'm putting this down in your record."

"Do what you have to do," she mumbled.

"Excuse me?" Winston leaned his head forward, lowering his face to the level of hers. "What did you say?"

Terry jabbed the toe of his boot into the side of her shoe, no doubt a plea for her to keep quiet, but she was done playing the sergeant's games and dancing around the Malones as if they were fragile glass. She met her sergeant's gaze. "I said, 'Do what you have to do.'"—*and I will, too.*

Winston straightened up, tugged down on his suit jacket.

Nothing more was spoken for the entire ride down to the lobby, and even when Winston stepped off, he didn't say a thing.

"I've never seen him quite like that," Terry said.

Winston might have been pissed beyond words, but so was she. Just the way the man spewed off threats was infuriating.

"What are you going to do?" Terry asked after a few seconds of her not saying anything.

"I'm going to keep doing my job, and if he tries to stop me one more time, I'm going to the chief." Enough playing nice. Her focus had been on corrupt cops taking a payday, but abuse of power also counted as corrupt. It was more clear than ever that while she and Sergeant Winston both wore the badge, they were not on the same team.

Thirty-Nine

It's said that rage has a way of blinding a person. Madison could see the truth in that as her vision was pinpricked with laser precision on nabbing the killer behind their two homicides. She'd never even seen the light turn red until she was underneath it and through the intersection.

"Maybe I should drive?" Terry looked over at her.

He had being a nervous passenger down pat, but she couldn't entirely blame him when she was behind the wheel—not that she'd ever admit that to him. She sometimes drove emotionally impaired, not as bad as being intoxicated, but close. She'd had her near misses before.

"I'm fine, but Winston's becoming more like McAlexandar all the time."

"A corrupt police chief who has a kinship with the head of the Russian Mafia?"

Madison considered Terry's words. What if Winston did have a tie to the Russians? His attitude toward her lately was nothing short of bitter.

"I wasn't meaning to say Winston's involved with them," Terry clarified. "Things between you might improve if you started talking to the man."

"Any other case, I might agree, but he's trying to control this case. And me."

"Well, he should know better than that. No one can control you."

She punched him in the shoulder as best as she could, given the confines of the car.

"Ouch," he howled and rubbed where she'd hit him.

Same ol' sideshow, but man, it had been a long time.

"You know that didn't hurt." She was laughing.

"How would you know?"

"I barely touched you. Besides, you deserved it for saying what you did."

"Put 'em up. Put 'em up." He raised his fists and mocked the lion from *The Wizard of Oz*.

She started laughing, and so did he.

"I'm here for you anytime you need a punching bag." He tapped the shoulder she'd hit.

She reached for him, and he moved out of the way. "Trust me." He came back within reach. She squeezed his shoulder. "Thanks."

"Okay, now, don't hurt me," he teased, "but do you think it's a good idea going to see the Griffins again, after what just happened at the hotel?"

"Did you notice there was zero warmth between father and daughter, and how Steven had looked at Kimberly when I asked him about the fifty thousand? Does it connect with her somehow?"

Terry leaned his elbow on the window ledge, hand to forehead. "I don't know."

"I think we need to find out what's going on there and whether it has anything to do with Kimberly's rift with her mother. The Griffins might be able to shed light on that and the Boyds."

"We have a lot to find out," Terry griped.

"Welcome to the life of a detective."

"Ha ha."

She took the last turn down the Griffins' street and parked in front of their house at the curb.

They were seen to the sitting room, and Mr. and Mrs. Griffin came into the room holding hands.

"Thank you for taking the time to speak with us again," Madison told them.

"Did you find out who killed our beautiful daughter?" Mrs. Griffin asked, her hand visibly trembling in her husband's, her eyes cool marbles.

"I'm sorry, but we haven't yet." Madison let that heartfelt sentiment sit there for a few seconds before continuing. "We have uncovered some things, though."

The Griffins sat on the couch; Madison and Terry each took a wingback chair.

"We've been able to identify the man who was with Lorene," Madison said.

"His name was Saul Lynch," Terry said and took out his phone and showed the couple Lynch's photo. "Do you recognize him, or have you heard of him?"

Mrs. Griffin nuzzled tightly into her husband's side. He looked down at her, and they both shook their heads.

That was unfortunate. "Mr. Lynch lived in Colton." Madison paused as the couple squeezed each other's hands and their gazes drifted to their laps. For one of them to react that way was one thing, but both of them? Madison continued. "He was a private investigator, and we have reason to believe that your daughter hired him to look into the Boyds."

The wife's chin quivered, and she squeezed her husband's hand so hard that he winced.

"You know them," Madison concluded.

Mrs. Griffin looked at her husband.

"If you do, whatever you share with us might help us find your daughter's killer." Madison didn't want to apply too much pressure to the older couple, but it was a fair statement.

"We should tell them, Larry," Mrs. Griffin said to her husband.

Mr. Griffin rubbed his wife's arm, but she

shook terribly, and tears streamed down her cheeks.

"Mrs. Griffin, I'm sorry to have upset you," Madison offered, feeling horrible for having done so, but she had hit pay dirt. If there had been any doubt whether or not the Griffins knew who the Boyds were, there wasn't any now. "How do you know the Boyds?" Madison asked, the pursuit of justice again trumping discomfort.

"We need to tell them, Larry." Mrs. Griffin was sniffling and letting the tears fall.

"Tell us what?" Madison wasn't relinquishing her stance on the matter.

The Griffins looked at each other but said nothing.

"We want to find the person responsible for your daughter's death," Terry pleaded.

"Then, go do that," the husband spat, "but leave us and the Boyds out of it."

"Unfortunately, we can't do that," Terry said.

"Oh, Larry," Mrs. Griffin said, "for our dearest Lorene." She blew her nose on a tissue she took from a pocket in her pants. "I think I need to tell them."

The husband took his wife's trembling hand again and held it over his chest. "Are you sure, sweetheart?"

Madison was afraid to say a word, let alone breathe too loudly for fear she'd somehow cause them to shut down.

The husband cleared his throat. "Lorene was—"

Mrs. Griffin sobbed.

"She was adopted," Mr. Griffin finished. "Julia and Gene Boyd were Lorene's biological parents."

What the—?

Madison looked at Terry, and he at her.

Had Lorene set out to find her birth parents and gotten herself caught up in a murder investigation? Why did she wait so long to go looking for them? Was it somehow tied into her cancer diagnosis and tying up loose ends?

"You didn't know that, did you?" the husband asked, taking in Madison and Terry.

Madison shook her head. Shock stitched her throat closed.

"She also had a brother, a twin. They were born with the names Michael and Melanie," Mr. Griffin said as his wife silently sobbed. "We gave her a new life and figured that should come with a new name."

"Understandable," Madison said, her mind racing with thoughts. Had Lorene proceeded to investigate the murder of her parents and gotten too close to their killer? Had the killer, in turn, found out that Lorene and Lynch were onto them and silenced them? Had Steven Malone not known about his wife's adoption and, thereby, nothing about the Boyds, or had he lied to them? And what had happened to

Michael Boyd?

"We heard many years later that Julia and Gene were murdered," Mrs. Griffin added to the conversation.

"They were," Terry affirmed.

"How very sad," the husband said. "They never had it good in life."

"In what way?" Madison queried.

"They had these beautiful children, but they were in no position to raise them. They were drug addicts."

Madison ran with an assumption. "The state took the kids and put them into the system?" They really needed to dig into the Boyd case files after they left here.

"No, they willingly gave them up for adoption at birth." Mr. Griffin's jaw trembled.

"Were they born addicted to drugs?" Madison asked.

"No, thank heavens." Mrs. Griffin signed the cross. "Julia stopped doing drugs during her pregnancy, but she—" The woman twisted the used tissue in her hand.

"She loved drugs more than her own children," Madison surmised.

Mrs. Griffin nodded.

"Do you know what happened to their son, Michael?" Terry asked.

"Just tell them, Larry," Mrs. Griffin elbowed her husband's arm.

"We tried." Emotion fluctuated his voice. "We

raised Michael until he was seven, but then we had to let him go."

Mrs. Griffin dabbed at her nose again, but no tears fell. This particular pain had scabbed over for her.

Madison turned to Mr. Griffin. "Why's that?"

"He was trouble. Violent," Mrs. Griffin was the one to respond. "Lorene would get cuts and bruises on her body. When we'd ask her what happened, she'd tell us it was Michael, but it was never easy to get out of her. He was born with the name of God's son," Mrs. Griffin said, "but that boy was the son of the devil."

Quite a harsh assessment of a child. "Did you change Michael's name?" Madison asked, thinking that since they'd changed Lorene's, they'd probably changed Michael's as well.

"We named him Leo," Mr. Griffin said.

"Do you know what happened to Leo after you had to…" Madison found it hard to say *give up*, as if Michael/Leo had been a lost cause. It was possible that Lorene had been searching for her brother.

The husband shook his head, frowning. "After we gave him up, we had to let him go."

"I can appreciate that," was what Madison said, but she was thinking that couldn't have been easy after raising the boy for seven years. It wasn't like returning an unwanted purchase to Walmart.

Madison redirected her mind to Colton. So

much in this case brought them back to there. "Do you know the name Marie Rauch?" she asked.

A smile touched Mrs. Griffin's lips. "Marie Evans? Her maiden name, yes. How is that sweet girl?"

"She's doing fine," Terry told her. "How do you know Marie?"

"Why, she and Lorene were best friends growing up." Mrs. Griffin's demeanor softened, and she turned to Madison. "Why do you ask about her?"

"Just covering all our bases," Madison assured her. There was no sense sprinkling suspicion on the housekeeper to the Griffins. They'd just confirmed the friendship did exist, at least at one time, between Lorene and Marie. "One more question before we leave," Madison said. "We understand that Kimberly and her mother had a falling out of sorts. Would you know what that was about?"

"If Kimberly won't tell you"—Mrs. Griffin shrugged—"I can't help you. As Larry told you the other day, Lorene stopped confiding in us after marrying Steven, and our granddaughter doesn't talk much to us."

"Okay. Thank you for your time, and again, we are truly sorry for your loss," Madison offered, saddened by the fact that Kimberly had her grandparents around to talk to and she didn't avail herself of the opportunity. Madison would give anything to talk to her Grandma Rose again.

Madison and Terry saw themselves out, and once in the car, she turned to face Terry. "I thought you said the Boyds didn't have children."

He splayed his palms. "Hey, that's what the report said. You saw it, too. It was in front of us both."

"Well, we need to dig into the Boyds much more closely, along with their murders." She put the car into gear and headed to the station.

"Don't we have two to solve already?"

"We do, but I'd put money on the cold case shedding light on ours."

"Another bet?"

She shook her head, serious. "Lorene and Lynch could have found the Boyds' killer and that person silenced them," she said, voicing the thought she'd had at the Griffins'.

"Well, the only way we're going to know what they found out would be by deciphering Lynch's shorthand."

"Thought you were calling Stephanie about that," she replied.

"I had to leave a voice mail."

"Let's hope she calls back, but we can't just wait around. We need to—"

"Someone's a little ambitious," he said. "We could stare at it all day and get nowhere."

"We do what we can do. We also have to find

out all we can about this Michael Boyd, a.k.a. Leo Griffin. Do you really think Steven Malone knows nothing about any of this?"

"He's been in the dark about a lot of things— the gathering on Friday night in his house, Lorene's friendship with their housekeeper, the PI investigation, probably Lorene's cancer. What's one more thing?" he tagged on bitterly.

"The turn things took at the hotel, it wasn't a good time to—"

"It's never going to be a good time to hear your wife has cancer."

Madison didn't know what to say to that. She imagined he was right. She just hoped he would never have to face it.

Forty

Back at the station, Madison ate a Hershey's bar and counted it as lunch. Terry had a bagged meal he'd brought from home—a wholesome turkey sandwich on whole-wheat with carrot sticks, sliced celery, and a small container of cottage cheese on the side. *Showoff.* If only she were that organized. Then again, it had probably been Annabelle who prepared the food.

Both of them chewed and worked. She'd started with searching for Leo Griffin and wasn't making much progress. Terry was hunting down the Colton PD detective who'd been in charge of the Boyd case. He would ask for any information that might not have made it to the electronic file and request the evidence boxes be sent over. Depending who made it there first, they'd also take another shot at Lynch's notes again. They still hadn't heard from Stephanie.

She stared at the blinking cursor on her screen, becoming slightly hypnotized by it.

She was congested, and the sinus pressure was giving her a headache. It felt as if she were wearing a cap and had a strap wound tightly across her forehead. What was she going to do? Maybe she was being blindly optimistic to think she'd be fine in time for the wedding. Not that it mattered how she felt—she'd be there. Thinking of the wedding, she pulled out her phone and dialed Lou. She might not be operating at peak performance, but she'd do her best to make sure Cynthia had a bridesmaid. And a teeny break from work wouldn't hurt. It could even help her come back with a refreshed perspective.

"Detective Sanford," Lou answered.

"It's Maddy," she said, her voice cracking.

"Not sounding so good. Does Cynthia know?"

"Oh, yeah, she knows, but she could have bigger issues than my cold."

"You're talking about Armageddon."

That was pushing it a tad.

"The fight she had with Tammy," Lou clarified.

"I figured that's what you were referring to. She told you?"

"We tell each other everything."

He sounded so sure, and it quieted Madison for a second. *Everything* was a big claim. She went on. "I need Tammy's phone number, but I can't have you telling Cynthia that I asked for it." She found herself sinking into her chair and looking around. It might not have been a good idea to have made the call from inside the station, where Cynthia could walk up at any moment.

"Okay," he dragged out the word, "why not?"

There was no way she could tell him that Tammy had indeed flown home as Cynthia had suspected.

"Maddy?" Lou prompted. "Can we talk about this later or—"

"Tammy went home," she blurted out. So much for keeping that part to herself. "She and Ken checked out of their hotel this morning and—"

"That selfish bitch."

Madison didn't say a thing and gave Lou a few seconds to calm down.

She continued. "I need to get her back for the wedding. I'm Cyn's maid of honor and—"

"She won't hold this against you."

"Listen, Lou, I have a sister myself." She paused, expecting to be interrupted, but he said nothing. "Sometimes sisters fight. Sometimes it gets ugly." Her mind went back to the bridal shop. "Sometimes *real* ugly."

"With these two, it's beyond simply explosive. It's nuclear. I've seen them in action before."

"Right? But they've always made up," she said, feeling that he had started making her point for her. "She was going to be Cynthia's bridesmaid. They have to love each other under all their…" She paused, the right words failing her. "I know Cynthia, and whether she'll admit it or not, she wants to work things out."

The other end of the line went quiet for a long stretch, and Madison was just about to check if Lou was there, when he started rattling off a number.

"Good luck," he added, "and I won't say a word to Cyn." He hung up.

Madison was left looking at her phone. "Wow."

Terry glanced over at her from his desk, his receiver to an ear. He had an inquisitive expression on his face, as if to ask what she was doing.

"I just need a minute." She got up, grabbed her coat, and headed for the privacy of the station's lot. Once there, she dialed Tammy.

"Hello?"

"Tammy, don't hang up," Madison rushed out.

"Who is this?"

"Madison."

There was an exhalation of breath that carried over the line, then, "If Cynthia told you to call, tell her to call me herself."

"Cynthia doesn't know I'm calling." Madison gave it a few beats. The line was quiet but still live. "I know what it's like to have a sister and how sometimes—"

"Then you know how they can judge you like they're God and condemn you? You know that?"

Madison and Chelsea only butted heads when it came to Madison's relationship with their parents. Chelsea thought she should be in touch with them more than she was. "Not fully, no, but—"

"Then you have no idea."

"I know that if you let her down like this, don't show up and be a part of her wedding, you'll regret it for the rest of your life."

Tammy didn't say a word.

"I could help you out with the airfare home," Madison offered, figuring Tammy's silence could be a good thing, an indication that she was leaning toward returning to Stiles.

"Wait. You know I'm home now?" she'd asked as if Madison had overstepped and violated her privacy.

"I went to the hotel, and they told me." Madison was tiring of tiptoeing. "You should be grateful Cynthia has asked you to be a part of her wedding. It's an honor."

"Well, I pass." Tammy hung up.

"Oooh," Madison raged. Her breath came out in huge puffs of white in the cold air. If Tammy were her sister, she might kill her. She dialed back and was redirected straight to voice mail.

Unbelievable.

"Tammy, this is Madison." She wanted to rush into a lecture but knew that wouldn't work. She had to approach things from a more understanding point of view, even if she had to work to imagine one. "I don't blame you for being hurt from everything that was said.

It could have been handled much better—and somewhere more private. I think it just came as a shock to Cyn, and she reacted. At the end of the day, you're sisters, and if you bail on her wedding, I'm certain that you'll regret doing so for the rest of your life, but it's not too late. You still have time to turn things around between the two of you. Your dress is still at the bridal shop, and they're expecting you. I hope to see you on Saturday." With that, she clicked off, hoping that she'd done enough and said enough to make Tammy rethink her stance.

Madison was on the way back into the station when her phone rang. Caller ID told her it was Chelsea. "Hell—"

"Madison." Panic pierced her sister's voice.

The skin tightened on the back of her neck. "What's going on?"

"They just picked Jim up from work."

"They?"

"The police, an Officer Phelps."

Madison tightened her grip on her phone and balled her other hand into a fist.

"The girl he hit," her sister continued, "she… she had a blood clot, and they think it…it…"

"What are you telling me?" Madison felt sick.

"She died in the hospital. Jim's being charged with vehicular manslaughter." Her sister was one octave away from screaming. "Did you hear me?"

Madison felt herself go cold. "I'll take care of

this."

"What are you going to do? They have someone who says that he ran a red light."

"All the cars were stopped." Madison was grasping, wishing that she'd just been looking at the damned lights, not Jim's approaching vehicle.

"So, everyone had a red?" Chelsea exclaimed. "Jim swears he had a green. Do you know Officer Phelps? You could talk to him? Reason with him?"

Madison rushed into the station. She passed her and Terry's desks. Cynthia was standing there with a file folder in hand, talking to Terry. They both stopped what they were doing and quickly followed Madison.

Chelsea went on. "There has to be something you can do, say. Madison?"

"I'm going to get this cleared up. Trust me." Madison was headed to booking. If she hurried fast enough, she might get there before Phelps had Jim processed.

"Madison," Chelsea petitioned.

"Yeah?"

"I'm scared."

She was going to ring Phelps's neck. He had a problem with her, so be it, but he was showing some brass balls to pick on one of her own.

"I feel like I need to be there," Chelsea said. "But the girls."

"No, just stay at home. There's nothing you

can do here."

"But, Maddy."

"Call Blake Golden. He's a lawyer. Tell him I need a favor."

"I remember Blake."

Madison had forgotten that she'd introduced Blake to her sister when they were dating. They'd even gone to Chelsea's for dinner one night. "Yes, well, tell him what's going on. Ask him to help."

"Okay." Chelsea's voice was trembling. "If he doesn't want to help?"

Madison pinched her eyes shut for a second, saying a silent prayer. "He will." She didn't even know how she knew that, but as corrupt as Blake could be, he did have a soft spot. He did pro bonos and favors—and not just because it made his firm look good. She had to believe there was a smidgen of good in the man she used to date.

"I've got to go, Chels, but I'll keep in touch. I promise. Stay strong."

They ended the call, and Madison was walking so fast she felt a burn in her calves and a small breeze. She entered the stairwell to go to booking.

"What's going on?" Cynthia asked from behind her. "Did I hear you say Blake's name and 'favor' in the same sentence?"

Madison turned, tears burning her eyes, anger welling up in her throat. Cynthia was there, as was Terry.

Terry angled his head. "What is it?"

"That son of a bitch, Phelps, is charging Jim with vehicular manslaughter." Madison had told Cynthia about Jim's accident somewhere between appetizers and the main course last night.

"That woman died?" Cynthia whispered.

"Yeah." Madison felt like she was living a nightmare. She could only imagine how Jim and Chelsea were feeling.

"Well, to hell with that," Terry snarled. "They let him go yesterday, based on witness testimony."

"Apparently—" she added air quotes to the word because she didn't trust Phelps one iota "—a witness says that he ran a red. So much for the truth coming out." She tossed a look at Terry, remembering how he'd tried to assure her that would happen.

"This ain't over yet," he defended.

"Jim gets charged, his life is over. My sister's, the girls'…all their lives will be over."

Cynthia put her hands on Madison's shoulders, and the warmth she felt from the contact was overwhelming. Madison bit her bottom lip to keep herself from crying. She'd told her sister that everything was fine, and they had nothing to worry about. Was her word good for nothing?

She tilted out her chin. "I'm going to kill that son of a bitch." She tramped down to the holding cells, which were in the basement, off the garage. She got there in time to see Phelps hauling in her brother-in-law. Jim lit up when he saw her.

"Phelps, a minute," she demanded.

Phelps met her gaze, and she swore there was the hint of a smirk on his lips. "Sure, in just a minute." He bobbed his head toward Jim. "I'm booking someone here."

She grabbed Phelps by the arm and yanked him aside.

Phelps glared at her hold on him. "Let go of me," he seethed.

"We need to talk."

"I don't think there's anything to talk about. Your brother-in-law ran a red light. He struck a girl, and she died. Now, if you'll excuse me." Phelps left her and rejoined Jim at the booking desk.

"Come on, Madison," Terry prompted.

She'd almost forgotten that he and Cynthia had followed her down. Madison's world was spinning out of control. Jim was looking at her, his eyes pleading that she say something, *do* something, but short of cuffing Phelps and getting suspended, she didn't have any recourse at the moment. She'd serve her brother-in-law better with her badge intact.

She mouthed, "*I'm sorry*," to Jim and pinched her eyes shut. Each heartbeat was the flap of a hummingbird's wings in slow motion.

Forty-One

What just happened down in holding?" Winston roared.

Madison hadn't been back at her desk for five minutes before he called her into his office.

"Why were you manhandling Officer Phelps? Not that anything you say is going to justify your actions."

Already judged and condemned before she'd opened her mouth to speak. Huge surprise. "My brother-in-law has been pulled in on charges of vehicular manslaughter, but the accident was not his fault. There's no criminal standing in this case." She'd take the high road here and be polite, even though she felt resentment.

"I'm sure Officer Phelps had just cause to bring him in."

"Or he made one up," she mumbled.

Winston leaned across his desk. "What was that?"

She made solid eye contact. "I'm sure you

heard me, but I can repeat myself if I have to."

Winston's cheeks flamed red. "He has a witness, Knight, that saw your brother-in-law running a red."

"*One* witness," she stamped out, holding up an index finger. "Whereas yesterday, everyone from the scene said he'd had the right of way."

Winston pulled back, steepled his hands under his chin. "Are you sure you're not just being blinded by the fact he's family?"

"You're implying that I want him to walk because of who he is?" Her earlobes were burning hot with anger.

Winston shrugged and splayed his hands as if to say, *Well?* Madison stood, too livid.

"I didn't excuse you, Detective."

She didn't give a shit and was on the way to the door when someone knocked.

"Not now," Winston barked, but the door opened.

It was Troy.

Winston slapped his hand on his desk. "No one listens around here."

Madison went to Troy, fighting the urge to throw her arms around him. "Jim's been arrested."

"I heard." Troy looked past Madison to Winston. "What's going on in here?"

"None of your business," Winston said hotly.

"Apparently, Phelps didn't care for being called into question," she told Troy.

"There was a little bit more to it than that," Winston chipped in.

"Which was?" Troy asked and took a seat.

Madison sighed. She'd almost made it out of this office. She sat down in a chair next to Troy.

"I don't see how this concerns you, Matthews," Winston said, using Troy's surname.

"Madison's family to me," Troy responded.

Madison turned to face him. *Family?* She gulped.

"And when my family's in trouble, I'm there for them, as I'm sure you can appreciate." Troy was all business and raw power.

"I sure can." Winston glared at Madison, and she received the underlying message that he thought she was crossing the line for hers.

Winston continued. "I will be putting a formal reprimand in your file, Detective Knight."

Here we go again…

She got up and left the office before saying something she might later regret.

Troy followed her into the hall, and Winston didn't say a word as they closed the door behind themselves.

"I don't know what I'm going to do." Madison gestured wildly. "Jim says he had a green light, and I believe him."

Troy was peering into her eyes, and the urge to let him hold her and take her pain away was impossible to resist. He put his hands on her upper arms. She felt so small next to him. She also regretted not telling him about the accident before now, but she'd thought it was all worked out. "I would have told you what happened to Jim, but—"

"It's okay," Troy assured her. "Your friends are here for you, and so am I."

She picked up on the separation he'd placed between friends and himself. "Thank you."

He placed a quick kiss on her forehead. "Anytime. I've got your back."

She nodded softly.

"Will you be okay if I go back to work?" He jacked a thumb over his shoulder. "We'll catch up later."

"Yeah."

"Call me if you change your mind or need anything."

"Actually, could you find out who Phelps's eyewitness is that saw Jim run the red?"

"Consider it done." He squeezed her hand, then left. She couldn't move.

Family? I'm in too deep to be helped now.

Forty-Two

Madison went to the lab to touch base with Cynthia. She must have had some updates, given she was speaking with Terry earlier.

She entered the lab and found Cynthia at her desk, Terry standing next to her. Both of them turned from what they'd been looking at on the monitor.

"How did that go?" Terry winced.

"I heard you were called to the principal's office," Cynthia teased.

"Oh, you know, formal reprimand in the file and a lecture: standard Winston issue."

Terry laughed, and Madison giggled, and then she got into a coughing fit.

Terry pulled a lozenge out of his pocket and handed it to Madison. She took it from him gratefully. Why he had them, she didn't ask.

Madison sucked the candy, calling on it to work its magic. "Okay, where were we?"

"You were going to call it a day, go home, get

some rest, heal up," Cynthia said.

"I wish." That was the truth.

"I can't have you not showing up on Saturday. Everything's already going to be a disaster."

"I'll be there unless I'm dead." Unfortunately, the same couldn't be said of Tammy, whom Madison just might have to drag back, kicking and screaming. She nudged her head toward the monitor. "What are you two looking at?"

"First, you bring us up to speed," Cynthia started. "That jackass actually brought Jim in? He's charging him with vehicular manslaughter?"

"He's going to try. We need to find out if they have traffic cams at that intersection." She hadn't seen any when she'd looked, but technology was making gadgets smaller and smaller.

Cynthia shook her head. "Sorry. I called the city, and no luck. What are you going to do?"

Madison was touched that Cynthia had taken the initiative to check.

"I don't know yet. I have Chelsea asking Blake for a favor. Hopefully, there's still some good left in the man." Madison was banking heavily on it.

Cynthia and Terry were watching her as if they felt sorry for her, but she wasn't going to have any of that.

"All I know is I'm not letting Jim go to jail for this," she said. What Cynthia and Terry didn't realize was *this* referred to far more than the accident and took in whatever vendetta existed between her and Phelps. "Earlier, you were talking with Terry at his desk. You had a file. Now you are huddled down here. Do you have findings from the case?"

"Yes, ma'am."

"Let me have them."

"Sam finished up comparing the ballistics from Adach's gun to the bullets pulled from Lorene and Lynch. They weren't a conclusive match."

Madison held out an open palm to Terry, ready to collect on the bet of Adach's innocence in the murder of Lorene Malone and Saul Lynch.

"Nope." Terry stepped back, held his hands up in surrender. "This isn't over yet."

"It is from my point of view." She arched her brows.

"Until someone other than Adach is charged with the murders of Malone and Lynch, my money stays right where it is." Terry patted his pants pocket.

Terry using the word *murders* made Madison think of the Boyds. They'd been shot, too. She looked at Cynthia. "Were the ballistics from the gun in Adach's possession run through the system?"

"Of course," Cynthia spat. "But there was no hit."

"So, it wasn't used in any previous crimes?"

"That's usually what it means," Terry said sarcastically.

Madison narrowed her eyes at him. "What else?"

"Do *I* have for you?" Cynthia surmised.

Madison faced her friend. "Yes, you. I know you probably have more."

Slowly, Cynthia smiled. "Well, you'd be right. I have big news and huge news. Now, the big news won't bode well for you, Terry, and your conviction that Adach's guilty, but Mark found a third set of prints on the wheel of Lynch's Mercedes."

"A third set?" Madison asked, feeling that she'd missed something.

"Oh, I was telling Terry that two others were lifted," Cynthia started. "One matches up to Lynch, one to Adach—"

"Ah, so, Adach just might simply be a car thief, after all," Madison chided Terry, despite knowing that it had never been in dispute.

"Ha ha," Terry said.

Madison turned to Cynthia. "Who does the third print tie back to?"

"Your killer?" Cynthia jested. "I don't know, but it might."

"Huh," Madison said. "What's the huge news?"

"The epithelial taken from under Lorene Malone's fingernails was a familial match to her. Maybe from one of her children? You were suspicious of Kimberly and Craig."

"Lorene's brother," Madison said, looking at

Terry. "She found him."

"Lorene's *what*? Obviously, I've been cut out of the loop." Cynthia drew a finger between the two of them. "Spill."

"We found out that Lorene Malone was adopted, and she had a brother," Terry explained.

"Lynch was investigating Lorene's biological parents," Madison elaborated. "At least that's what we gather, based on what little we can interpret from Lynch's files."

"The Boyds," Terry jumped in, "and they were murdered by gunshot as well."

"That's why I asked if the gun in Adach's possession had ever shown up in the system before," Madison explained.

"Damn." Cynthia's eyes widened. "I figured that I was bringing you case-breaking news that would point you to one of the Malone children."

"You've narrowed things down," Madison assured her.

"I really think you should bring this brother in. He could be the killer." Cynthia had found her spark and was all animated again.

"He could be a killer four times over," Madison stated somberly.

Terry looked at her. "Let's not leap there just yet. Besides we're just assuming he didn't want to be found."

"He's not making it easy, but I hadn't gotten far in the search before everything unraveled with Jim."

"It could be something as simple as him changing his name again," Terry reasoned. "But one would think it should still be easy enough to find him anyhow, if that's the case."

"When were the Boyds murdered?" Cynthia interjected.

"Twenty years ago," Madison replied.

"Obviously the case was never solved," Cynthia said.

Madison nodded. "That is correct."

"Whoa. You catch this guy and you could close four murder cases."

"Wouldn't that be good news," Madison exclaimed. "And I'm going to make sure no defense attorney will be able to spin the evidence we present."

"Always best to do your homework." Cynthia winked at Madison.

Madison turned to Terry. "How did you make out with the lead investigator on the Boyd case?"

"He's getting the files sent over," Terry said, taking a few steps toward the door. "I'm going to get started on finding Michael Boyd, a.k.a. Leo Griffin, a.k.a. who knows?"

Madison went to follow him, but Cynthia stopped her. Terry kept going.

"Tell me what's going on," Cynthia said.

"With regards to?"

"Last night, and the burner phone."

The way her friend was watching her now,

Madison was tempted to confess that she had Leland King investigating Phelps, but that wouldn't help anyone. "It's fine, Cyn."

"No, it's not." Cynthia put a hand on a hip. "Last night I let it go, but with what's happening with Jim, I just have a bad feeling. Does whatever you're involved in have anything to do with Phelps?"

Madison stared at Cynthia as if she were a mind reader.

"There's something going on there," Cynthia continued. "No witness against your brother-in-law, and now, all of a sudden, there is. He shouldn't even have been brought down to the station yesterday. Phelps is crooked, isn't he?"

Madison wouldn't be able to hide her thoughts if she wanted to under this scrutiny. "I believe so."

"And you're going after him somehow."

Madison glanced away.

"Madison, if this guy is crooked like you think, I'd watch your back."

"Trust me, I am."

"Did Phelps concoct this witness against Jim to somehow get at you? If so, that means he knows you're looking into him. Why are you doing this?"

Madison stumbled backward. Of anyone, Madison would expect Cynthia to understand. "He doesn't deserve the badge."

"It's your job to clean up the Stiles PD now?"

Madison could read the concern in Cynthia's eyes, but her friend had to know she couldn't just turn her back on crooked cops. "I've got to go."

"Sure," Cynthia grumbled.

"Don't be mad at me over this," Madison said. "You know the type of person I am."

"I know that you've almost gotten yourself killed—more than once, by the way—for doing the right thing." The latter part came out bitter and in finger quotes.

"I'm taking precautions, as I told you last night."

The door to the lab swung open, and Troy rushed in. "I've got the ID on the eyewitness. Name's Lonnie Dunn, thirty-five, single, no record."

Madison glanced at Cynthia, back to Troy. "That was fast."

"That's how I roll."

Troy hadn't said it again, but the word *family* went through Madison's mind.

Madison reached out for Troy's hand. "Thank you."

"Don't mention it."

Cynthia brought up Dunn's DMV photo on one of the monitors on her desk. He had shoulder-length brown hair and eyes that didn't speak of a high intelligence.

"I've got to go talk with him." Madison barreled toward the door.

Troy grabbed her arm on a backswing. "What will that accomplish?"

Madison flicked her gaze to Cynthia, and Troy caught it.

"What is it?" he asked Madison.

She'd preached to him the last couple of days about how they should communicate openly with one another. Maybe it was time to open up to him, but all she could squeak out was, "Phelps."

"What about him?"

"Jim's innocent," Madison said, deflecting. "I'm going to prove it."

"And *how* are you going to prove it?" Troy asked calmly.

Cynthia mouthed, *Tell him.*

Madison took a steadying breath. "I think that this eyewitness is a fake."

Troy's face contorted into sharp lines. "Why would Phelps do something like that?"

"He has a problem with me, and he's taking it out on Jim."

"Why would he have a problem with you?"

Man, Troy has a hundred and one questions.

"This doesn't leave this room," Madison started. "You understand that?"

"Sure." Troy glanced at Cynthia, who directed him to look back at Madison.

"He's corrupt, Troy. I feel it." Madison put a hand to her chest.

A few seconds of silence passed.

"That doesn't explain why he has a problem with you."

"I think he worked with the Mafia. Now they're gone…" *Or assuming they are…*

"So is his payday," Troy finished. "You think he holds you responsible for their leaving town?"

Madison nodded, though she still wondered if Leland's investigation had gotten back to Phelps somehow.

"Madison," he prompted.

"Yeah, that's part of it."

"And the other part?"

"A conversation for another day?" She was hoping for a pass, but his green eyes turned to ice.

"Huh. I see what's going on here. You want me to open up to you, but you're allowed to keep secrets."

"Um, I'm just going to go grab a coffee." Cynthia brushed past them, her gaze on Madison as she did so.

Troy watched after Cynthia. "You told her what's going on, didn't you? But you're not telling me?"

"I didn't mean to tell her," Madison pleaded. "It just came out."

"So, let it come out to me. God, Maddy." Troy raked a hand through his hair. "You don't want secrets between us, so get talking."

"As I said, I'm pretty sure that Phelps was

working with the mob. Still might be."

He stared at her impatiently, waiting for her to reveal something new.

"I am having him looked into, to gather proof to use against him."

"Like what? A PI? IA?"

"No, not IA. Not yet anyway. I have someone helping me to build a case against him, though."

Troy's body went rigid.

"I didn't want to tell you any of this in case it endangered you in some way."

"I can take care of myself," he snapped.

"I know you can. I'm sorry."

"You think Phelps found out and has found someone willing to help him stick it to Jim, to stick it to you?"

"I do."

"My God, Madison."

He wasn't saying it, but Madison sensed he wished she'd just leave it alone.

"Phelps is sending me the message he's not to be messed with," she said, breaking the silence.

"The guy's not too smart if that's the case."

"So he's cocky," Madison tossed out.

"No, he's stupid. When we expose his eyewitness, he's going to have to defend himself, and he won't be able to."

"We? Oh, no. I don't want you involved with any of this." She was shaking her head.

"It's too late for that," he said in such a way that left no room for negotiation.

"I mean it, Troy. I don't want you involved."

"Phelps is going after your family…well, he's also going after mine. If we have to, we'll get Andrea involved."

This was spiraling out of control too quickly for her liking.

"We could talk to her first," he added.

"No," Madison said firmly. "I'm talking to Dunn."

"And what?"

"I'm going to get him to confess that Phelps is paying him off to lie—or whatever it was Phelps used to coerce him into lying." She was grasping, but she was being run by her gut right now.

"Well, if you're going to talk to Dunn, I'm coming with you."

She put a hand on his arm. "You don't have to do that."

"I know I don't have to, but I'm going to." He led the way out of the lab.

Forty-Three

Madison was torn between getting back to her murder investigation and attending to the matter of Dunn. Regardless, she found herself on the sidewalk in front of Dunn's apartment building with Troy.

"You sure you want to do this?" Troy asked.

"No doubt in my mind." She trudged up the walk with confidence. Shoulders held back, head held high. There was no way she'd let Phelps take out his vendetta against her through Jim. More than that, she wanted to see Phelps taken down for this stunt.

Troy knocked on Dunn's door with a heavy hand. Someone was moving around inside, but no footsteps approached.

Troy knocked again.

"I'm coming, I'm coming," a man called from inside. Dunn opened the door and slinked back into his apartment when he saw Madison and Troy holding up their badges, and they followed him inside.

To call the place a "sty" would be an insult to pigs. Clothes were strewn all over the place. Dirty dishes were on tables. There wasn't much available surface area.

She went straight for the jugular. "Do you know why we're here, Mr. Dunn?"

"You're probably here about that girl, the one who died."

"We're here to verify the statement you made to Officer Phelps," she said in a kinder manner. Best that he think she was a friend, maybe even working with Phelps, if Dunn was on the take, as she suspected.

"Everything I told him was true." He gave a placid smile.

"And what was that?" Madison asked. "Just so we make sure we have it down right."

Dunn's expression slipped, and his brows pinched together. "That I saw that man strike that girl."

"And she was crossing against the light?" she inquired to slip him up.

"Against?" Dunn shook his head. "No, she had the right of way."

"You're sure?" Troy asked.

"Yeah." Dunn sniffled. "Absolutely."

"Wonderful." She plastered on a fake grin. "You're really making the case."

Dunn drew his shoulders back proudly. "I do what I can to help."

Troy leaned in toward Dunn. "Where were

you at the time of the accident?"

"I was on the sidewalk." Dunn went on to tell them that he was standing in front of Petals Floral. The boutique was about five storefronts down from the corner.

Madison proceeded with caution. "That's a fair distance from the corner. You saw the accident clearly?"

"Yes, and there was a red light when he hit her. The driver went through a red light."

She nodded, forced another smile. "We will need you to testify to everything you saw in court."

"I was told I might have to do that."

"Good. It's great to have a witness who's not afraid of taking the stand." Madison's stomach was turning over just speaking the words, playing the role, but she was trying to shake Dunn into a confession, appeal to his conscience even. That was assuming Dunn possessed one.

"Should I be afraid of—" Dunn didn't finish. His voice was shaky.

"Only if you're lying, but you're not, so…" She turned toward the door.

"What could they do to me? If I was a liar? Purely curious." Dunn's forehead glistened with sweat as he looked up at Troy, who was at least four inches taller.

Troy clasped his hands in front of himself. "Liars go to prison. It's called perjury."

"It's…it's a…g-good thing I'm not a liar,

then." Sweat had begun to bead on his brow.

"Good thing," Troy assured him. "But you might want to work on your presence before you go to court."

"Wh-why that?"

Troy pointed to Dunn's face. "You're stuttering. You're sweating profusely."

Dunn's face was a mask of fear.

"You were telling the truth about what you saw?" Madison pressured.

"Yeah."

"For certain, the red light you saw wasn't the one facing you when you looked toward the intersection?" Based on where Dunn had said he was standing, Jim would have adhered to the opposite light.

Dunn sniffled again, ran an arm under his nose. "I know what I saw."

"Okay, then." Madison smiled again, trying to put Dunn at ease, but all she wanted to do was crack the guy—even if that involved shaking him until all his nuts and bolts fell out. "I'd just hate to see you question yourself on the stand, like you are with us."

"I'm not…" Dunn was shaking.

"You know it's not too late to back out of this, tell Phelps that you were mistaken. No harm done," Troy offered.

"Yeah? You sure? I'm not the best person to take the stand."

Madison looked at him curiously. "And why's

that?"

"I…I'm shy, and I…I st-stutter some-sometimes when I'm nerv-nervous."

"Oh." Troy winced. "Yeah, like I said, that could be a problem. A judge might question whether you're telling the truth. Of course, you are, but it will look like—"

"I may have lied," Dunn confessed, "just a bit." He pinched his fingers to within half an inch.

Satisfaction weaved through Madison, but so did rage. Phelps *had* manipulated this man. "What do you mean 'just a bit'?"

"The light I saw directly was red." Dunn blinked rapidly.

"So, the light the driver would have come through was…" Madison prompted.

"Would have been green. I mean, come to think of it. But that officer made me question myself, like you guys are doing."

"What's the officer's name?" Troy asked just for clarity.

"Phelps?"

"That's all he did?" Madison raised a brow, skeptical. "You sure he didn't pay you to say what he wanted to hear?"

"No." Dunn madly waved his hands. "He didn't give me money."

"Did he threaten you in any way?" Troy asked, coming across as the man's ally.

"He said that it was my duty as a citizen to be

honest with the police."

More abuse of power. "When did he say this?"

"Late last night," Dunn said. "And again today."

Last night was before the girl had died. Phelps was planning to frame Jim regardless of the girl's fate. She clenched her jaw.

"Am I in trouble?" Dunn was frantic.

"You lied to police," she seethed. "You're going to go down to the station and retract your statement, and we'll forget this ever happened." It felt horrid giving Phelps a pass for what he'd done, but he'd get his own in the larger picture.

"Should I mention your names?"

"Not necessary," Troy replied.

"Who are you guys, anyway?"

"The right side of the law," Madison stated bitterly and left Dunn's apartment.

Back in the car, she was shaking, and tears of indignation burned her eyes. She'd been playing things too safe with Phelps and should just send the matter up the ladder, call in the IA and call it a day.

"A penny for your thoughts?" Troy put his hand on her lap.

"It's going to cost a lot more than that." She was attempting to be humorous but couldn't get herself to smile. "Why is it I feel like everyone who should be on my side is against me? I mean, other people on the force. We all took a pledge, but some of us just fight each other."

"Unfortunately, not everyone's like you."

"I appreciate that you're trying to make me feel better, but…"

He took her hand and squeezed it. "I'm by your side the entire way. I'll fight for you. I'd give my life for you."

She met his gaze and leaned over to kiss his mouth, then drew back. "Because we're family?"

"Because we're family," he drove home.

She watched him for a bit before settling back against her seat. The thought of being his family was less scary than it had ever been. In fact, it was a concept that made her feel warm inside.

Forty-Four

Madison found Terry at his desk just as her phone rang. Caller ID prepared her for Blake Golden.

"You had your sister call me," he said when she answered. "I never thought the day would—"

"Don't let it go to your head. I just figured you could help, but we probably won't be needing it. Thanks anyway."

She had her finger over the button to end the call when Blake spoke up. "You might want to be careful about who you finger."

The hairs rose on the back of her neck. Did he know about her investigation into Phelps, and if so, how? Blake had prior connections to the Mafia. Was that still the case? "What do you mean by that?" she hissed.

"I think you know."

"Are you threatening me?"

"No, it's just me telling to watch your back, as a friend." He ended the call.

What the hell have I set in motion?

She shook off the shivers tearing down her spine and dropped into her chair, opposite Terry.

"Find Lorene's brother yet?" she asked him, hoping for something gripping enough that would take her mind off the phone call with Blake.

"Nope. Finding him's not proving to be easy."

"Huh, seems I said that."

"Not in the mood."

"Did you try child services?"

"Michael, a.k.a. Leo, was never adopted, and their records don't show where he ended up after aging out of the system."

"Okay, so social security number. Track him through that."

He squinted and angled his head. "Do you think I was born yesterday? I tried that, too."

"So now what?" She spun a pen on her desk.

"Mr. Griffin was really upset about the need to get rid of Leo. Maybe the Griffins kept an eye on him, you know, to see how he was doing?"

Madison met her partner's eyes. "It's possible, but it would probably have been far too painful." The wisp of a thought lingered on the edge of her mind that hinted at an epiphany. She thought through the case to date and how it kept leading them to Colton. "Let's go talk to Marie Rauch. She might know something about Leo, and we can finally talk to her about her button."

Marie Rauch opened her door in a bathrobe that she wore over flannel pajamas. It was six thirty in the evening, but she could have been feeling under the weather or grieving. Unlike Tuesday when they'd delivered the news about Lorene, Rauch was showing possible signs of sorrow with puffy eyes and messy hair.

"Detectives?" Rauch's gaze covered Madison and Terry.

"Can we come in?" Madison asked.

"Sure." Rauch stepped back inside and closed the door behind them. "Have you figured out who—" She stopped there, as if "murder" was too painful to say.

"The investigation is ongoing," Madison started, "but we have some questions for you."

"Do you want to sit down?"

"It's probably best," Madison replied.

Rauch stepped into the living room and sat on the couch. Madison and Terry took chairs.

"We found out the man's identity, the one who was with Lorene," Madison said, thinking it might be best to start there before getting to the matter of the Boyds.

"Oh?"

Madison took out her phone, brought up Lynch's DMV photo, and walked it over to Rauch. "He was a PI from Colton. His name was Saul Lynch. Ever hear of him?"

Rauch looked at the screen. "No, and I've never seen him before." She lifted her gaze from the phone. "You said he was a PI? Why would he be with Lorene?"

"She'd hired him," Terry said.

"Whatever for?"

"From what we can tell, it was to find her birth parents."

Rauch shifted and wrung her hands. Uncomfortable.

"You knew she was adopted," Madison surmised.

Rauch nodded. "I did. I was one of the few who did, but it was a secret that Lorene entrusted me with."

Her admission made Madison realize they'd never broached the matter with the Griffins about whether they'd told Lorene she was adopted. "So, her parents were honest with her about the fact she was adopted?"

Rauch flipped the tassel on her robe, doing so repeatedly. "After..." She looked Madison square in the eye. "Only after they sent Lorene's brother away. The Griffins must have felt they needed to tell her, to explain why Michael was gone all of a sudden."

"Did you know Michael...I mean, Leo?" Madison asked.

"Yes, I knew him, and Lorene blamed herself for him going away. Said if she'd just kept her mouth shut about him hurting her, she'd still have a brother."

"Do you know what ever happened to Leo after he left the Griffins?" Madison asked.

"Not really."

"You never saw him again after they sent him away?" Madison pressed.

Rauch kneaded the hem of her robe. "I saw him at least once. I lived right across the street from the Griffins as a girl. It was late one night, already pitch dark. I saw him standing in front of the Griffins' house, facing it."

Madison sat back down in her chair but leaned forward. "What did he do?"

"Nothing. He just stood there watching the house while I was watching him. He must have sensed my eyes on him, though, because he turned in my direction, and I swear, he looked right at me." She shivered.

"How old would he have been?"

"Say sixteen, seventeen? That memory still gives me the willies." Rauch became contemplative. "You don't think that Lorene's looking into her birth parents somehow resulted in her death?"

"We think it's possible," Terry said.

"We're still investigating," Madison retorted. "We'd like to question Leo but can't seem to find him. You really have no idea where he'd be these days?"

"Well, my brother, who's older than me, used to be friends with him."

Madison sat straighter, wondering why Rauch had bided her time to share this information.

Rauch continued. "He might be able to help you find Leo." She reached for her cell phone that was on the table next to her. "I'll get you my brother's number."

Less than a minute later, Madison had her brother Roger's number stored in her phone, but she was curious about something. "Did Lorene ever express interest in finding her biological parents when you were growing up?" Madison asked, trying to understand why Lorene had been looking for them as an adult and whether her earlier hunch that the cancer diagnosis had been a motivator to seek out the Boyds may have been correct.

"Not really. She said she'd never want to hurt the Griffins by doing that, but I always felt she must have been curious about her real parents."

Madison nodded. "There is something else we need to ask you about."

Rauch crossed her legs. "Whatever you need."

"Investigators found this in the Malones' home." Madison brought up a photo of the blood-covered button, less the blood, which Cynthia had photoshopped out for the purpose of this visit. She took her phone to Rauch. "Does this button look familiar to you?"

Rauch glanced at the screen, then looked in the direction of the front door and gripped her robe tighter. "It looks like the buttons I have on one of my sweaters."

"Are you missing one?" Madison asked.

"I might be." Rauch scowled, but the expression lasted briefly. "What are you getting at, Detective? The button was in their house, but you do remember I work there, yes?"

"It was found in the solarium and covered in blood." Madison replaced the photo with one taken by Mark at the crime scene.

"I think it's time for you to go." Rauch stood and gestured toward the front door.

"You don't have any ideas?" Madison asked.

"I had nothing to do with what happened to Lorene Malone and that PI." Rauch crossed her arms. "If you found my button there, covered in blood, as you put it, it certainly wasn't because I was present at the time of the murders."

Madison held eye contact with Rauch and then left the house with Terry. Rauch closed the door firmly behind them, and the sound of deadbolts thunking was clear. Ironically, the more Rauch attempted to shut Madison out, the more it ignited her determination to get to the bottom of whatever the hell had happened in the Malones' house. And she'd put money on something happening in Colton many years ago factoring into the murders.

Forty-Five

Madison had been determined to find Leo Griffin if it took her all night, but she lost the battle with exhaustion at about two in the morning. She'd tried calling Roger, Rauch's brother, a few times since she and Terry had returned to the station after speaking with Rauch. Finally, she'd resigned herself to leaving him a voice mail, stating that it was urgent he call her back immediately. He never did return her call, and now the light of a new day was blinding her as she drove to the station.

She had woken with congested sinuses, a groggy head, but ready to catch a killer—beyond ready. She was also ready to get this issue between Cynthia and her sister resolved. Assuming it was something she could fix. This could be the fight that separated the sisters for good.

She called Tammy through her car's onboard system and listened again to Tammy's voicemail greeting. "Tammy, it's Madison again. Can you at least call me back?" She paused. It was really starting to feel like she was having a one-way conversation. "The wedding's tomorrow, and your sister's counting on you to be there. The bridal shop closes today at six, but they reopen tomorrow morning at nine. I told them you'd be picking up your dress in the morning at the latest. Please don't make me a liar." With that, Madison hung up.

She pulled into the lot and went to her desk and found Terry at his.

"What have you got?" She slapped her coat on the back of her chair.

"Good morning, Terry," he said. "How are you doing today, partner? Oh, I'm fine. How are you?"

Seemed she wasn't the only one talking to herself.

"Terry," she said firmly.

"The Boyd files still aren't here, but I got through to the investigating detective again this morning, and he assured me he'd get them over today."

"Did you ask for him to rush them?"

He looked at her blankly.

"I'll take that as a yes," she said, wishing he had but guessing he hadn't. "Any miracles happen overnight? Have we found Leo Griffin?"

"No leprechauns working the desks while we were gone, so I'd say no."

"Good morning, guys." Cynthia came to the side of Madison's desk, all smiles and bubbling energy. She held a file in her hand.

"Someone's in a good mood," Terry commented.

"Tomorrow, I marry my perfect man, and today's the last day at work for a week."

"That's a good reason."

Cynthia smiled. "I also have some more findings you'll want to know about."

"Gimme, gimme." Madison held out her hands and wriggled her fingers.

"Patience," Cynthia cooed. "First up, the blood spatter on the button found by the pool."

"The one from the housekeeper's sweater?" Madison asked, running with that theory. After all, Rauch never denied it was her button.

"That very one. Well, the blood came back a match for Lorene."

"Just proves the button was around when she was shot," Terry interjected. "It doesn't prove Rauch killed her."

Madison let his comment go. They'd gone over Madison's thoughts on the housekeeper last night. Rauch seemed to be withholding something, and it left Madison with a niggling feeling in her gut.

"We also found blood that's a match to the epithelial DNA taken from under Mrs. Malone's fingernails."

The epithelial could be explained away, but

matching blood *and* epithelial?

"Where was that blood found?" Madison asked.

"Near where the victims were shot," Cynthia said.

"So next to the pool?" Terry asked.

"Yes," Cynthia replied.

"Lorene and Leo, or whoever else this familial match belongs to, got into an altercation before the murders," Madison spewing hypotheticals. "Lorene scratched him, and he bled afterward."

"It's possible, but I think there'd be less blood than we found. I was actually thinking that maybe whoever it was had cut themselves," Cynthia suggested.

Madison perked up. "Okay, I'm listening."

"We figure they were bound with kitchen twine. Who's to say this person didn't slice themselves with a knife or scissors when they went to cut some from the roll?"

"Were you ever able to confirm if the roll from the Malones' was a match?" Madison asked, recalling that Cynthia was going to check on that.

"Yeah, I did, and it was. Now, toxicology has come back on both of the victims as well."

"That was lightning fast." Madison was used to it taking at least a week. She had no doubt Winston's hands were in that pot.

"Uh-huh," Cynthia agreed. "First of all, Richards wanted me to pass along that Lorene was full of cancer."

"We tell the family now," Terry declared, and Madison nodded.

Cynthia went on. "There was no sign of any drugs in their systems."

"Guess having a gun pointed at you is enough to force cooperation," Madison concluded.

"It would work for me," Cynthia agreed.

"Got anything else for us? A content update on the USB drives taken from the Malones' home office? More information about Blissful Enterprises and why the corporate account for Malone's was paying them fifty grand every month?" Madison spewed the questions.

"If I had something useful for you in that regard, I'd tell you."

"Okay, fair enough." Madison sighed and retreated.

Cynthia tapped the edge of her file on the edge of Madison's desk. "Remember, the rehearsal dinner's tonight."

"Of course I remember."

"I know you get caught up in your cases sometimes, but I wouldn't want you to miss—"

"You have my word. I'll be there," Madison promised with a smile, and Cynthia left. Madison turned to Terry. "Call that detective again."

"What?"

"We need those files. If he doesn't want to bring them to us, we'll go pay him a visit in

Colton."

"Just give the guy some time. Besides, let's focus on finding Leo Griffin."

"Oh, because that's going so well," she seethed and pulled out her phone. "Rauch's brother never did call me back, either." She dialed his number, and this time, he answered. She pointed to her phone. "Roger? This is Detective Knight with the Stiles PD. I need to talk with you about Leo Griffin. Your sister said you were friends with him."

"When we were kids," Roger shot back. "Listen, I never called because I don't see how I can help."

"Let me determine that," she said, trying to squelch her temper. "You ever see him as an adult?"

The line fell quiet.

"Mr. Rauch?" she prompted.

"Last weekend. He was at Publix buying groceries."

"Which location?" There were a few in the city.

"The one in the east end," Roger said. "At least I'm pretty sure it was him. He stopped when I called out his name and turned around. He was looking right through me as I told him who I was, then he walked off without saying a word."

"And you're sure it was him?"

"Those eyes I'd know anywhere, no matter how many years have gone by."

"What stands out about them?"

"They're dark, like peering into a void. But there's something you should know, now that I think about it. He happened to be checking out in front of me later, after our run-in. He'd forgotten his credit card, and the cashier called him Mr. Carter."

Forty-Six

Roger had provided them with the key they needed: Michael Boyd had become Leo Griffin had become Michael Carter, or so it would seem. The DMV showed an address for Michael Carter within a few blocks of the Publix where Roger had seen him. Unfortunately, the DMV also showed that his license had expired three years ago and had never been renewed.

Regardless, it was a lead, and she and Terry were racing toward that address now. Terry was gripping the oh-shit bar and wincing every time she got to within a couple feet of the vehicles in front of her.

She was going to bring Boyd/Griffin/Carter—whoever he was—in and get some answers.

"Maybe we're rushing to a conclus—" Terry stopped talking as she took a sharp curve around a slow-moving car.

"He was in the Malone residence, *bleeding* in the residence. He needs to explain that."

"I think you're losing sight of the fact that it's just *someone* who is related to Lorene who was bleeding in that house. We don't know that it's Michael's blood." Terry winced when she slammed the brakes to avoid rear-ending the SUV in front of them. "Even if it is his blood, it could have had a nose bleed, brought on by stress. Being reunited with his sister after all these years wouldn't have been easy."

"Sure, but why were his skin cells found under Lorene's nails?"

Terry sighed. "We don't know who the DNA belongs to just yet. We just know it was a familial match to Lorene."

He was right, but she wanted something to fixate on besides her personal life and the seeming threat from Blake Golden, and having a suspect to pursue fit that bill.

She pulled into the driveway for Michael's townhouse, got out, and banged on the home's front door.

"You might want to dial it down just a bit," Terry said. "More bees with honey…"

She rolled her eyes and banged again. "Mr. Carter, it's Stiles PD."

The door to the adjacent townhouse opened. A man in his fifties poked his head out, then stepped onto the front porch in blue jeans, a T-shirt, and socked feet. "What's going on?"

"We're detectives with Stiles PD here to talk with Michael Carter. We understand he lives here."

"Michael who? I've never heard of him." Clearly irritated. He disappeared back inside his house for a few seconds. He reemerged wearing a big coat and a pair of boots. He stomped across the front patch of lawn to Madison and Terry.

"We show this address for a Michael Carter," Terry told the man.

"He could have lived here before my time."

"And who are you?" Madison asked.

"Will. I own this building. I live over there—" he pointed needlessly to his townhouse from which he'd come "—and I rent out this one to a young mother. Good thing she's at work, or you would have scared the shit out of her and her kid with your banging."

"How long has she rented here?"

"Three years."

"She live with a man?" Madison asked.

"Just her kid."

"You ever see a man come around?"

"She's had dates, some overnights, but I'd know if someone was shacking up with her." Will was standing there regarding her and Terry as intrusions on his day. His brows were corkscrews.

She pulled up the DMV photo of Carter. "Do you recognize him?"

Will took her phone and held the screen at arm's length. "Don't recognize him."

She stuffed her phone back into a pocket.

"How long have you owned the building?"

"Four years."

Carter would have had to receive his license in the mail, so he had to have had access to this property at some point. Given that his license expired three years ago, it could have been here longer than four years ago that he was here. She asked, "Who owned it before you?"

"Lady, I don't remember their names. Can't you look that up somehow?"

She skulked off toward the department car. They had ways of hunting down who'd owned the property previously.

"You're welcome," Will called out.

Madison waved over her head, not turning around. She should have known that it wouldn't be as easy as just showing up and cuffing a killer.

They were down the road a few minutes, headed back for the station before either one spoke.

"Okay, so he used to live there, and he doesn't now," Terry said calmly. "We just do as Will said and find out who owned the townhouse before—"

"I got it, Terry." She knew her comment came off a little snide, and she was somewhat sorry for that, but she just wanted this case tied up.

Terry went on. "He could have provided a fake address, but I doubt that since it was connected to his license at one time."

"All he needed was access to the mail being

received at that address," she countered.

"So, you think he provided a makeshift address? To what purpose?"

"Well, criminals do things like that all the time." She glanced over at him.

"I know you're starting to latch onto this guy now but—"

"We need to track down the son of a—"

"Less with the swearing," Terry reprimanded with a smile.

"Oh, yes, my partner and his sensitive ears."

THE DAY WAS PASSING AT a crawl. Madison had started out trying roundabout ways of finding another address or an active phone number for Michael Carter until it struck her: Roger had said that Michael forgot his credit card with the cashier. She pulled up his credit records and saw another address other than the townhouse. A quick visit yielded the same results as the townhouse had: *nada.*

She returned to the credit report and found that Michael Carter had one active credit card. She'd subpoena the credit card company to obtain the address they had on file for him. She hoped theirs would be up-to-date, but if not, they might have a current phone number. She didn't care how she found him, only that she did.

Madison got to work on the necessary paperwork to build a case for why it was important that the credit card company disclose the information on the cardholder so that it would hold up to a judge. Suspect in a double homicide should cover a lot of that ground.

Madison stretched out her neck. Even the kinks had kinks.

She glanced at the clock and saw that it was going on five in the afternoon, and she had to leave soon for the rehearsal.

She caught up with Terry in a conference room where he'd holed up with the Boyd investigation files that had come in somewhere around ten o'clock that morning, not long after they'd returned from the townhouse. She walked in and found Terry behind the table that was covered in papers and files.

Terry looked up at her, holding a report in his hand. "We knew they were both shot. Now we know it was also .357-caliber bullets."

"That can't be a coincidence."

Terry continued. "They were killed in the dining room and found tied to chairs."

"Tied? Like Lynch and Malone." She dropped into one of the conference chairs. "What were they bound with?"

"Report doesn't conclude. The ME noted that the contusions were rather small in width, indicative of a narrow restraint."

"Twine could fall into that category."

"Possible, but that might be a reach, given we have nothing else to lead us there."

"Besides Lorene and Lynch and one person we know that is connected to both murders."

"And maybe just as a relative," he cautioned.

"Were any prints lifted from the Boyd crime scene?" She ignored his comment.

"If the ones from ours met with a hit in the system, we'd already know if they were the same," Terry said. "I take it that's what you're getting at?"

"Were there any prints?" she repeated. Prints left behind at the Boyd crime scene could have been absent from theirs only because the killer had gotten smarter.

"Ever consider that there wasn't, and that's why it's a cold case?"

Madison shot him a glare.

"I'm just saying if their murders had been easy to solve, they would have been already."

"Except that now we're going at this with a suspect in mind. I'm guessing the locals back then didn't note Michael Carter as a suspect."

"You're right about that. They'd concluded it was a home invasion gone south, as you know, and didn't have any viable suspects. I thought I told you that part already."

Knowing how her head felt, that was quite possible. She'd let the matter of prints go for now, even though Terry hadn't really answered her. "Okay, well, the Griffins told us the Boyds let their children go because of the drug addiction. Were dealers ever considered?"

Terry's face paled. "The Boyds had cleaned up their act again."

"You're kidding me? After giving up their kids?" Madison was disgusted by how an addiction could rip apart and destroy lives.

"Ten years later, but still."

"Did they ever try to get Michael and Lorene back?"

"Don't know."

"The Griffins didn't say the Boyds came after Lorene," Madison kicked back, attempting to answer her own question.

"They'd have nothing to gain by telling us they did, if they had."

"Suppose that's true."

"Now, in reading the medical examiner's report, it was noted that their eyes were intentionally closed, and they did pull prints from the victims' eyelids."

Good things do *come to those who wait.*

"And for the record," he said, "they don't match any in the system."

Madison's mind slipped back to how the Boyds had turned their lives around. "Can you imagine if you were Michael? Kicked around, foster home to foster home, never adopted. Then you come to find out that your biological parents could have kept you?"

"That could make me angry enough to kill," Terry reasoned.

"And sad enough to feel remorse afterward."

"Possibly, but either way, just leave me with the files for a bit longer. I'm not sold on Michael being behind all the murders yet."

"Okay." Madison rose. "I've got to go to the rehearsal dinner. If I'm a no-show, you'll be solving my murder next."

"Sure, whatever it takes to get out of paperwork."

"Hey, I've done my share this afternoon, thank you very much." She let him know what she'd done and how she was just waiting on the subpoena to be signed before going after the credit card company.

"I'm all out of gold stars," Terry joked.

"Dang. I was hoping for a big, fat, shiny one, too." She laughed.

He grinned. "Go, have fun. I'm going to keep digging and hoping that something reveals itself."

"Sounds good." She turned to leave.

"Oh," Terry began, and she spun around. "Stephanie got back to me. I got her email address and sent Lynch's file on Lorene to her. She's going to essentially translate it into English."

"Good news. By the way, call me if the subpoena comes back while I'm out."

"I'll text," he corrected. "I don't want Cynthia mad at me."

"Wuss. Oh, and follow up with Mark on Lynch's car, too. Forensics might tie evidence found there to the Boyd case."

"Maybe." Terry didn't sound convinced, but she was certain the murders were all connected. *How* exactly remained to be seen, and while she'd never been one to love paperwork, she didn't want to leave. She felt like they were so close to wrapping up this case, and she wanted to be there when it all came together. She wasn't even going to think about the fact that even if Terry could tie Michael Carter to all four murders, they still had to find him.

Forty-Seven

Seeing Cynthia's bright smile at the church at six thirty was enough to calm Madison's anxious energy. Before that, all she could think about was getting the rehearsal and the dinner over with and returning to the station.

Cynthia hugged her and kissed her cheek. "Eek! Can you believe that I'm getting married tomorrow? Me?"

"Sometimes, no." Madison laughed, not about to point out that Cynthia should have kept her distance, just in case she caught her cold.

"Me neither." Cynthia sucked in a deep breath and looked across the nave at Lou, who was talking with Toby near the altar.

Toby near the altar... In another life, she and Toby would be married, but her thoughts turned to Troy being the one waiting for her as she walked down the aisle in a white dress. She gulped.

"Madison?" Cynthia touched her arm. "You okay? You're pale."

Madison fanned herself and plastered on a smile. "I'm good."

"I know it must be awkward thinking about walking down the aisle with Toby." Her friend, the mind reader.

"I admit it's a little strange, but what we don't do for those we love."

Cynthia's face fell, and Madison felt it had something to do with Tammy's absence. If she were within reach, Madison might have decked Tammy for putting Cynthia through this drama.

"I'm sorry that Tammy's not here."

Cynthia dismissed her with a wave of her hand. "It's not your fault."

Madison had done all she could to get Tammy to come back to Stiles. She'd even called the bridal shop on the way to the rehearsal in the hopes that they'd tell her Tammy had picked up her dress. No such luck.

"Well, I'm here for you. Always." Madison took her friend's hands.

"Hey, should we get this party started?" A man's voice had Madison and Cynthia turning.

Garrett Murphy was making his way down the aisle toward Lou.

Lou cried out, "About time you got here."

Madison's stomach soured. Murphy was as corrupt as Phelps as far as she was concerned. He was the next name she'd be providing to Leland to investigate. "Why is—"

Cynthia was smiling when she turned to look

at Madison. "Garrett Murphy. He's one of Lou's groomsmen."

"Why—" she touched her throat "—why didn't I know that before now?"

Cynthia screwed up her brow. "What's up with you? He's a good friend of Lou's. Patrick had to back out due to a family emergency. Garrett's been good enough to step in. What's up with you, anyway? You look like you've seen a ghost."

"No, no, I'm fine." Madison placed a hand over her stomach. "Just a little hungry. You know me on an active case."

"You survive on Hershey's bars." Cynthia chuckled.

Madison smiled, though she felt it falter. "Things could be worse."

"Well, we'll get to the food part of the evening soon enough."

As if on cue, the priest positioned himself behind the pulpit and called for the rehearsal to begin. From that point, for the better part of an hour, everyone in the wedding party was directed here and there, told when to move, etcetera.

Madison kept watching Murphy, but he never seemed to look at her, at least that she noticed.

When they got to the "food part of the evening," Troy joined them at the restaurant, and Madison was thankful for his presence.

Madison leaned in toward Cynthia's ear

sometime after the first round of drinks were served and the appetizers were forthcoming. "So how long has Lou known Garrett?"

"Since they were kids." Cynthia drained her glass of champagne. "Why?"

"No reason. Just curious."

Cynthia peered into Madison's eyes, raised a quizzical brow, and was about to say something when Toby tapped his flute with a fork.

Madison listened as Toby went on about Lou and Cynthia and their romance. Troy squeezed her hand and smiled at her. She returned the expression and tried to let herself relax into the present moment, but she couldn't help but think a storm was on the near horizon. How could she investigate Garrett—potentially bring him down—and retain Cynthia's friendship? She'd been understanding about Madison bringing down corrupt cops, even if she didn't like the associated risks, but Madison had a feeling that might change if the cop whose badge Madison sought was closer to home.

Madison drank champagne, hoping to numb herself somewhat, but still wanting to keep enough of her head to return to work.

There were more rounds of toasts, the appetizers were served, the main course, then dessert. Madison couldn't eat another bite and was ready to go back to the station.

She turned to Cynthia.

"Oh, no, you're not getting out of here. You're

my maid of honor."

"Speech. Speech. Speech," Lou chanted, staring right at Madison, and proceeded to rouse his best man and groomsmen to join him.

Cynthia was smiling at Madison. "You don't have to if you don't want to."

Madison sensed her friend was saying one thing but wishing for the exact opposite. She wanted a speech, a testament of friendship and well wishes. Wasn't it enough she'd be saying some words tomorrow?

Troy nudged her elbow. "You should say something before you go."

Madison's heart raced as she took everyone in. She could never make the claim that she was shy, but she detested public speaking.

People at the table were starting to clink their wineglasses to demand a speech. Waitstaff fluttered about Madison with encouraging smiles as they cleared dishes.

"Okay, why not." Madison stood.

The clattering stopped. Everyone looked at her expectantly. She caught Garrett's gaze, and their eyes locked briefly. He glanced away first.

Madison's legs were weak, and she just wanted to leave the place and not look back, but Cynthia was counting on her. Cynthia took Madison's hand. Madison could do this.

"I've known Cynthia for…well, a woman never shares her age," Madison injected to defuse her nerves. "Anyway, she's the strongest, most hardworking woman I know. She's independent and beautiful." She paused and gestured down Cynthia's form. A couple of Lou's groomsmen whistled, and Lou flashed a playful, dirty look toward his future bride. "She's reliable and such a true—" Gratitude rushed in on her, and tears threatened to spill. She smiled to suppress the urge to cry. "A true friend. I've been so lucky knowing her, and now, Lou—" Madison turned to him "—you are lucky. This woman has decided she loves you and wants to spend her entire life with you."

"Here, here," Toby barked out and raised his glass.

Lou was grinning as if he'd won the largest prize—and he had.

Madison turned to her friend and put a hand on her shoulder. "I don't tell you this near enough." She sniffled, battling with emotions and the will to hold herself together. "I love you."

"Aw," Cynthia cooed and pressed a fingertip to her eye to still the tears from falling, and that was all it took for Madison's wall to fall along with her tears.

Cynthia stood, and they hugged. Everyone clapped.

So much for getting out of this evening unscathed.

"I know you want to get going," Cynthia said to Madison as people returned to their own conversations. "I understand, but I will see you tomorrow."

"Not even a question." Madison kissed her friend on the cheek.

Madison and Troy left the restaurant together. She'd had a few drinks and would leave her car in the lot and arrange to get it in the morning.

"That was a heartfelt speech you gave about Cyn," Troy said as they waited on his Ford Expedition to warm up.

"I meant every word."

Troy shuffled to angle his body toward the passenger seat. "That's why it was heartfelt." His green eyes were peering into hers. The way he'd grabbed her hand when Toby was talking about Cynthia and Lou's love and how, yesterday, he'd called her family…it all made her feel so vulnerable.

"You know that I'm lucky to have you." Troy leaned over and hooked her chin with a thumb. "There's not a day goes by that I don't know that."

She didn't know what to say. She felt frozen, and her lungs expanded with a breath waiting for release, but she worried that if she exhaled, this moment would forever disappear.

He leaned over, placed a gentle kiss on her lips, and then drew back. "Tell me you're coming home with me."

She dipped into his beautiful eyes, letting her gaze trace his face. There was nothing she wanted more, but… "Terry's expecting me back at the station."

Troy put a hand on her cheek. "Just one night. Come home with me."

Her mouth couldn't form words, and she was drawn to his power, his raw maleness, his gentleness. She nodded.

"Good." He settled back into his seat and put the vehicle into gear.

She sat there, gripping her purse in her lap, feeling like the world was whizzing by around her. Her phone pinged notification of a message.

"Don't—" Troy reached out a hand, but she already had the text screen up and was reading a message from Terry.

> Blissful Enterprises is owned by Kimberly Olson-Malone

Madison looked at Troy, her mouth open. Her mind was trying to process what that meant, if anything, to the case.

Before she could say a word to Troy, another text came through.

> Mark discovered something on Malone USB drive

Troy leaned back against the headrest. "You need me to drop you off at the station?"

She studied the profile of his face, the hardened lines, the etch of disappointment. She reached for his hand. "After."

He lifted his head and smiled at her. "That I can do."

She watched him for most of the drive back to their place. *Their place.* It had taken her so long to come to the point that she even referred to it that way. As recently as two months ago, she was still calling it *his* place, but the dynamics of their relationship were changing—and fast. She could only hope that she was brave enough to keep up.

Forty-Eight

It was after eleven o'clock by the time she got into the station. She found Terry at his desk, slurping back on a vile brew from the bullpen.

"About time you got here," he complained.

"I got here as fast as I could." Partially truthful anyway. Or was it one hundred percent the truth? After all, there was no way she possessed the strength to leave Troy without making love to him before she came in.

"Uh-huh. You have that look about you." He drew a finger around her face. "The one you get after—"

"Don't say it," she groaned.

"The after-sex glow."

"Oh, Lord." She rolled her eyes. "You said that Kimberly owns Blissful Enterprises. Why did it take so long to find that out?"

Terry put up his hands. "I'm just the messenger."

"Why is Steven paying his daughter fifty

thousand a month?"

"One of the many questions we'll need answered." He slurped some coffee, and she waited patiently, while tapping a foot beneath her desk. "Mark found out something else," he continued. "Kimberly's in the process of changing her name, and get this: she's dropping Olson-Malone in exchange for…"

"Blissful?" Madison guessed.

"Bliss."

"Okay, so what makes a Malone change her name?"

"Ah, see, I told you there would be more questions."

"The name has clout in this town. She went to the trouble of keeping it after she got married." Madison got up and paced a few steps. "What happened to make her do that?"

"Another good question. Now, Mark also found out the withdrawals have only been going to Blissful Enterprises for the last six months. Before that, the money was just going to a personal account under Kimberly's name."

"She doesn't work for Malone's, so why is her dad paying her all this money?" She knew she was circling back to her original question, but she was still stuck on it.

"Something else that Mark discovered might explain."

Madison regarded him curiously. Why hadn't he just said as much a moment ago? "Something to do with a USB drive?" she asked, recalling Terry's text message that Mark had discovered something there.

"Yep, and it's pretty nasty."

"Spit it out."

His face soured. "It was a video of Steven Malone assaulting a young girl. It appears that it was Kimberly when she was about eight to ten years old."

"Oh no, don't tell me..."

"I wish I had better news."

Madison felt sick for the woman she'd spent most of the last few days disliking. But did the abuse somehow tie into the murders? Kimberly would have motive to kill her father, but if she did, the money would stop. Why kill her mother or Lynch?

"I can tell you're running through everything I did. Does Kimberly have motive to kill her mother? The conclusion I came to was—"

"Lorene always defended Steven."

"Yeah, thanks." Terry sounded deflated.

"Even Kimberly told us there was a family secret she wouldn't share and something that caused arguments between her and her mother."

"Uh-huh, and Lorene didn't want Rauch cleaning in the office. Probably didn't want that USB drive to be found."

Madison took a few steps, spun back around. "That was on Saturday. Before that, she let her clean in there."

"So, Kimberly recently provided them with the video and used it to blackmail her parents?" Terry spitballed.

"Maybe that's why she's been so defensive? Threatening a lawyer? She knows if we found this out, we could be looking at her," Madison concluded. "How did she get the video?"

"We're going to have to talk with her about that, but I want to point out something else. You might have lost sight of this, because I know you were pretty confident that Michael Carter, Lorene's brother, was behind the murders, but—"

"I know." Madison frowned. "Kimberly could very well be a match to the epithelial pulled from under Lorene's nails and the blood droplets in the Malones' house."

"I think we should consider that possibility."

"Better than that, I say we collect a sample from her."

"Not sure how Winston will take to that."

"It's too bad if he doesn't like it, Terry. I'm sick of his bullying on this case. He's worried about appearances. I'm worried about finding justice for two people, possibly four." Madison scowled, hating that she might be pushed into a corner. "If I have to, I'll go above his head to the chief." She was tired of making the threat, too, and about ready to follow through.

Terry scanned her eyes and, after a few seconds, nodded. "I'll stand behind you."

"Appreciate it. Did you receive the signed subpoena yet for Michael Carter's credit card company?"

"Not yet."

"We're going over to Kimberly's now. I'm not running it by the sergeant. You're sure you want to—"

"I'm in. Let's get this case wrapped up."

She hustled from the station, Terry trailing her. There might be hell to pay for this, but she was willing to pay that price if it meant justice would be served.

Forty-Nine

W hy are you changing your name?" Madison asked directly.

She and Terry were in Kimberly's sitting room. There was no sign of Kurt.

Kimberly was sitting cross-legged and picked at the arm of the couch.

"There's no sense lying to us," Madison said, hoping to prompt Kimberly to speak.

"I just wanted out from under my father's name." Smooth, like a politician.

"Did it have something to do with the abuse you suffered as a child?" Madison asked, and was haunted by Winston saying *discretion*.

Kimberly's eyes snapped to Madison's. "You know about that?"

"We do, and, unless you start talking, you look like you have motive for killing your mother." The hour was late, and Madison was beyond diplomacy. "If you want, we can wait for Mr. Golden to show up."

Kimberly sniffled. "I never killed my mother."

"There was DNA found in the home that was a familial match to your mother. Will we find that it belongs to you?" Madison asked pointedly.

"I've been in my parents' home many times. It's possible, of course."

Madison's question had been a bit of a test. Kimberly hadn't jumped to an assumption it was blood, but that didn't mean she was innocent. "Tell us about Blissful Enterprises."

"You found out?" Kimberly's body shook, and she started to sob.

Madison, not expecting that reaction, glanced at Terry. "Why does this upset you so much?"

"Even after all that my father did to me... I felt horrible for..."

"Blackmailing your parents?" Terry asked.

Kimberly nodded slowly.

"When did this start?" Madison inquired.

"I sent them a video of Dad last week." Tears filled her eyes. "It was of him molesting me as a girl."

That explained why Lorene had become protective of the office on Saturday, but it didn't align with many payments of fifty thousand. "Your father's been paying you fifty thousand for months now."

"Years actually," Kimberly corrected.

Cynthia must have missed the other transfers, or they had been better at disguising them.

Kimberly continued. "Dad threatened to cut me off. That money is my only source of income besides a pittance of child support I get from Joe."

Madison felt for the situation Kimberly had been subjected to with her father as a young girl, but as an adult—and a mother—it was time for her to take some accountability for her own livelihood. "So you sent him, what? A video you've had all these years for security?"

"Yes." Kimberly sighed. "I'm not proud of it, okay? But he should have to pay damages for what he did to me," she spat out with heat. "Really, I only took what was mine."

"So, when you were talking with your mother on Monday, it was about the video?" Madison asked.

"Yes."

That explained why Lorene could have been overheard saying something about being bullied.

"Your mother took your father's side," Madison said. "That must have killed you." *That* could play into motive.

Kimberly palmed her cheeks and shook her head. "It wasn't a surprise. I swear Mom knew what was going on years ago and did nothing to stop it."

"What prompted your father to threaten cutting you off?"

Kimberly jutted out her chin, a sign of

strength, but her shoulders sagged. "I caught him...dear God." She swallowed sobs. "He was showing 'affection' to Brianna. I snapped. I snatched her away from his reach, and we left. I told him he'd never see me, Brad, or Brianna again."

"You were at their house when that happened?" Madison asked.

Kimberly nodded. "I've always been so careful, watching over the two of them with eagle eyes. I know men like my father are sick, and they either never rehabilitate or don't want to."

Madison wasn't here to argue that some pedophiles turned their lives around—though, sadly, too few.

"Did you kill your mother and Saul Lynch?" Madison asked directly.

"No. I mean, why would I?"

"She took his side, hid what he had done," Madison said gingerly.

"Why didn't you tell us about the abuse and all of this before?" Terry inquired. "You see how it looks."

Kimberly gestured toward Madison. "Just like Detective Knight just said, it seems like I'd have a motive, but think about it. What would I gain from killing my mother? Dad's going to stop the payments to me now. You can be sure of that. He's even told me as much."

Madison thought back on the tension between

father and daughter yesterday afternoon in the hotel room. "You can report your father for what he's done. Go through the justice system."

"With what?" Kimberly sounded absolutely defeated. "He's got money to keep the fight going for years. I don't have money for an attorney, and the stress..."

"One reason you tried to handle it the way you did," Terry concluded.

Kimberly looked at him. "Exactly."

Madison studied Kimberly and let her gaze fall to Kimberly's hands. There were no nicks or cuts that could have bled. Maybe the killer—Kimberly?—was cut somewhere other than her hands, but Madison didn't think they were looking at their killer.

She stood to leave. "I'm sorry for all you've been through."

"Thanks." Kimberly sank her face into her hands and started to weep.

It would have been easier to just leave, but this woman was a friend of Troy's. He was a good judge of character. After all, he loved Madison. She stepped back to Kimberly and squeezed her shoulder. She pulled out a card with her other hand and extended it to Kimberly. "Call me if you need anything."

Kimberly thanked her again.

Back in the car, Terry turned to her. "We're just going to leave her here? We didn't even take a DNA sample."

"You heard everything that was said. She didn't kill her mother or Lynch. I believe her."

"Hmm."

"You don't?"

"Not that. It's just that you don't normally let go so easily."

Madison didn't have any response to that and let her mind drift from Kimberly. "Did the results of Annabelle's test come back from the doctor's?"

Terry grinned and nodded. "Negative."

"Oh." Madison expelled a deep breath. "I'm so happy for you guys. That's awesome news."

"Yeah, it's such a relief."

She dropped Terry off at the station and then took the department car home. At least there was some good news packed into this week, and it would help offset some of the disappointments. For one, they still didn't have Lorene and Lynch's killer, and two, she'd be going to Cynthia's wedding with the investigation still open and hanging over her head.

Fifty

Madison looked at her reflection in the mirror. A cosmetician was buzzing around her chair in the salon, like a hawk swooping around its prey. The woman held a makeup brush in slender, manicured fingers and was poised to take action.

Cynthia sat in the chair next to Madison with her hair in curlers. She seemed to be having the time of her life, and the primping was just getting started. She'd always taken more kindly to the girlie stuff than Madison had.

Cynthia's photographer, Harold, was bouncing around taking random shots of the beautifying process, and Madison would have loved to bop him on the nose. It was one thing to be caught up in the whole girlie thing and another for it to be recorded. She guessed that was the price she'd have to pay for being the maid of honor.

With that thought, guilt snaked through her. She should focus on how grateful she was to be a part of Cynthia's big day. If Cynthia had chosen wisely, it would be her *only* wedding day. That was the plan, but as the saying went: man plans, and God laughs.

Madison was doing her best to keep her mind from veering to the case, but it was hard. Terry was at the station, and he was to notify her the moment he received the subpoena or got anywhere with tracking down Michael Carter.

"So...I'm thinking shades of plum for your eyes." The cosmetician stepped back, sizing up Madison. "It will match your dress and your nails," she added, as if looking at Madison for input.

Madison looked down at her hands—her nails already decked with polish—and tucked them under the cape the hairdresser had on her, even though she wasn't getting a haircut.

"What do you say?" the cosmetician asked.

"Sure." She'd trust the lady's judgment. After all, beauty was this woman's arena while Madison's was solving murder. Something she was feeling like a bit of a failure at right now.

"Excellent," the woman cooed and started applying the warpaint. "We always do makeup first, then hair."

A useless piece of trivia Madison discarded immediately.

"Except for the bride." Cynthia's hairdresser spoke up as she was working her magic with Cynthia's long, dark locks and starting to unravel the curlers.

"She's right," Madison's cosmetician agreed. "I'll be using a powdered foundation for your friend. We'll want a natural glow, yes?" The woman turned to Cynthia.

"Please," Cynthia said, passing a smile to Madison.

She returned the expression, though Madison didn't really know anything much about makeup. She applied *liquid* foundation in the morning, but otherwise, it was out the door *au naturelle* including her wake-up-and-wear-it short hairstyle. On good days, she ran a comb through it.

Another hairdresser came up to Madison as the cosmetician was working on her face. The hairdresser put her fingers through Madison's hair and ran them up the length, which was only a few inches. Disappointment soured her expression. Madison didn't have anywhere near the locks Cynthia had.

Nothing like time at the salon to make one overly self-conscious about her appearance. For Madison, being here was the equivalent to sitting in the dentist's chair—just as uncomfortable and pretty much as painful as a root canal without Novocain.

"It shouldn't take any amount of time to style your hair," the hairdresser declared.

That conclusion sparked hope. She could be out of this chair before she knew it.

Madison's phone pinged, and she worked to get it out of her jeans pocket. It was a text message from Terry.

Third set of prints from Lynch's car just added to the system and it ties to the Boyd murders

Madison wriggled, wanting to get up.

"Just sit still, please," the cosmetician told her, coming at Madison's face with a makeup brush. "You have very dry skin, especially around your nostrils."

"I have a cold." At least she was feeling a lot better today. Whatever was in the decongestants she was taking seemed to be working.

"Ah, well, that explains it."

Her phone blipped again.

Are you getting this

Madison texted back a quick *yes*.

Her cosmetician set down the brush, dipped her finger in moisturizer, and dabbed it around Madison's nose. Sitting here for this was torture. She shifted in her seat again.

"Still, please," the woman repeated, a little heat to her tone.

After two hours of being primped and prodded, a stranger looked back at Madison in the mirror. There was enough makeup on her face to do her for the next several years.

"You're beautiful, Maddy," Cynthia told her.

She looked over at her friend, and her breath caught. The curlers had all been taken out, and her friend's long hair fell in beautiful twisted strands.

"Lou's going to faint when he catches sight of you." She smiled.

A bell on the salon's front door chimed, and Madison looked that way to see her partner coming toward her.

"Terry?" she gasped, and glanced over at Cynthia, back to Terry. "What are you doing here?"

Cynthia scowled. "Yes, Terry, what are you doing here?"

"We've got a location on Michael Carter."

Madison ripped off her cape and got to her feet. "How did—"

"Oh, no, you're not going anywhere," Cynthia said preemptively, looking at Madison. "You can't leave me."

"The subpoena came back, and I heard from the credit card company," Terry said, "I got a working phone number and tracked it down."

"Why not just go to the address? You know what? Never mind."

"Well, if I had, he wouldn't have been there."

"Where is he, then?"

"You might not believe me when I tell you, but let's go pick him up."

"Terry," Cynthia barked and snapped her fingers, "*you* go get him. She's busy."

Madison regarded her friend with the softest of eyes. "I'll make this quick. Catch the bad guy, get back in time for the wedding." Madison formed prayer hands.

"Fine, go. I should know better than to stop you. Go catch the bad guy," Cynthia grumbled but flashed a half-smile.

Madison kissed her friend's cheek. "I'll be back in plenty of time. I promise."

"You better be, or you'll be dead."

Madison ran from the salon with Terry and jacked a thumb behind her. "You heard her."

"Yeah, and I believe her."

"Me too. Let's hurry."

Fifty-One

"You're not going to believe where Carter's phone traced back to." Terry was doing the driving and speeding through the city streets.

Yet he gives me a hard time about my driving.

"So you've said, but I'm really not in the guessing mood," Madison fired back. She smelled like a damned powder puff with a hint of vanilla. She sniffed down her arms, then her hands. The fragrance was probably coming from the makeup and lotions, but it was filling her head. On some days, it would be easier if she'd been born a boy.

"You look nice, by the way."

She scowled at him.

"And smell good."

She balled a fist and waved it in his face. "Take it all back."

Terry started laughing.

"Where are we going?" She was on the road to a painful, agonizing death.

"Marie Rauch's."

"Say what?"

"Yep. I did some more digging into the Boyd investigation files. Rauch's name came up as someone who was questioned. It turns out she lived two doors down from the Boyds at the time of their murders."

"Holy shit." She'd known that Rauch had lived close to the Griffins as a girl, but she didn't know she'd lived near the Boyds as an adult, but then again, she hadn't had a reason to go looking for that.

Terry continued. "Rauch lived there by herself until she got married ten years ago to her current husband."

"Yet, she didn't bother telling us any of this." She turned to Terry and held out her hand. "My gun?"

"Back seat."

She undid her belt and reached back for her gun and holster. She worked to get it all in place. "What are your thoughts on why Carter's phone is at the Rauches' house? Are they having an affair?" Madison tossed out.

"Exactly what I'm thinking. I called the Colton detective about the Boyds after finding Rauch in the file, and he remembered her being sort of twitchy. He thought she was hiding something but had no way of proving his suspicions."

"She knew her boyfriend had killed his biological parents," she concluded.

"Could be."

"Anyway, Carter's phone traced back to the Rauches' home as of thirty minutes ago. Units are watching the house at a distance. Back and front are covered, so we'll know if anyone comes out." Terry took the turn down the Rauches' street, and they passed a couple of patrol cars.

Terry continued. "The warrants came through just before I picked you up, but remember, it will be SWAT that breaks down the door."

Standard procedure, so she wasn't sure why he was telling her.

"I thought you'd have more to say. Something along the lines of, 'Thank God, I won't break a nail,'" he teased, playing the role of a diva, then burst out laughing.

She glared at him and stuffed her hands into her coat pockets.

"They look nice, too, by the way."

She snarled at him. He laughed again.

Madison saw the SWAT command vehicle. Troy and his men were approaching the door. Obviously, she wasn't the only one being waylaid from today's plans.

Terry slowed the car, and she got out.

"Where are you—"

She slammed her door and started advancing on the house.

Terry caught up to her and nudged her in the back, extending a bulletproof vest toward her.

She was wearing a bulky coat. There was no

way she was getting the vest on over it. "What am I supposed to do with that?"

"Put it on. Ditch the coat. I don't care."

"Fine." She snatched the vest and lost the coat, just leaving it to lie on the Rauches' front lawn.

"And where do you think you're going, anyway? SWAT's got this."

"I left Cynthia to get this clown, and I'm bringing him in." She kept her eyes forward, realizing that was probably why Terry had reminded her of the protocol.

Nick Benson, a member of Troy's team, was knocking on the door, announcing the Stiles PD's arrival. He was armed with a shield, which he retreated behind after knocking.

"Recap on our jobs," Terry interjected. "SWAT goes in first, clears the scene, then you and I sweep in, save the day. *Voilà*. Textbook. Heads stay on shoulders. Everyone goes home."

She stormed up to the sidewalk to Troy and stood behind him.

Troy kept his face straight forward, but he must have felt her presence. "What are you doing?"

"I'm taking down a killer."

"You keep her back until we've done our thing." He must have sensed Terry, too.

"As if I can control her."

"Stay behind me," Troy directed her.

She did as he asked.

Benson knocked on the door once more, and

then quickly lifted the shield in front of them again.

"Stiles PD!" Troy roared.

There was shuffling in the house, and Madison was close enough to Troy to hear a voice coming over the comm in his ear.

"Move in, now," Troy commanded.

The sound of wood tearing from the door frame in the rear cracked like thunder.

Troy, Benson, Madison, and Terry moved out of the way, and Mark Copeland, who was built like a tank himself, rammed the door. All of them went in, guns at the ready.

Madison's heartbeat was pounding in her ears, adrenaline in full force. Everything seemed to take place in slow motion, including the sound of the heavy footsteps of the SWAT team heading in the back door and up the stairs.

Michael Carter stepped out of the sitting room into the front entry, holding a .375 S&W on them. "Just leave me alone." His hand was shaking, as was his voice. Desperation in his tone, a plea more than a directive. But Madison noticed something more: a cut on the back of his hand.

"We can't do that, Michael," one of Troy's men said in a soothing manner.

"One target acquired. There's still another," Benson said into his comms. "A female. May be armed."

At the same time, Troy yelled to Carter, "Put

your gun down now!"

As Madison watched the standoff, her mind raced. Where the hell was Rauch? With Troy's men spread throughout the house, why hadn't they found her yet?

"Clear," one of Troy's men shouted at the same time she heard a motor grinding.

What the—

Then the sounds of metal gave the source of the sound away—a garage door was opening. Madison wanted to bolt out the front door, but she couldn't risk startling Carter. He seemed twitchy enough already for someone holding a gun.

Troy was advancing on Carter, one painfully slow step at a time, but Carter didn't seem to notice. "Put your gun down, Michael, or—"

"What? Are you going to make me?"

"Things don't need to go that way."

If she slowly backed up toward the door, Carter might not notice. His focus was on Troy.

The motor stopped, which meant the garage door was open. Sure, there were other officers around who could stop Rauch, but—

Madison stepped backward out the front door, leaving Terry there in the entry, Troy and Carter still talking. She cleared the front steps without incident.

In the garage, the taillights of Rauch's SUV were lit, and she was backing up.

Where the hell does she think she's going?

Madison headed toward the driver's side, and shots rang out the opened window.

Madison ducked and returned fire.

Rauch gunned the gas and the SUV barreled down the driveway in reverse, but Rauch wasn't looking where she was going. She was looking ahead, her eye on Madison, her gun lifted.

Madison squeezed her trigger.

Direct hit.

Rauch fell forward. Her body slumped against the wheel, but her foot was still on the gas. The SUV swerved across the street, barely avoiding the parked cars and came to rest on the front lawn of the house across the street.

The wheels were spinning in the deep snow, spitting ice. Officers moved in on the vehicle—*Now they show up*—and Madison went toward the driver's door.

"Put your hands up where I can see them," she cried out to Rauch, running on the assumption that she was still alive. She couldn't take the risk she wasn't. "I said, 'Put your hands up!'" Madison huffed to the door and swung it open, her gun on Rauch.

Rauch put her hands up, groaned in pain, and took her foot off the gas.

Madison cleared Rauch's gun, handing it off to an officer who had come up behind her, and cuffed Rauch to the steering wheel.

"You're under arrest for shooting at an officer and harboring a murderer."

Rauch started to laugh, blood seeping from the corners of her mouth as she did so. Madison turned to call out for an ambulance and found a small army of Stiles PD officers there to assist. *Finally*, she thought again, but still experienced a moment of pride. This was the life she'd chosen, and she'd do anything to protect it.

A gun report shattered through the air, and Madison's heart stopped. It had come from the Rauches' house.

Troy! She ran across the street, taking the front steps two at a time. Her worst fear would be finding Troy shot and dead. She blinked the tears away when she came to find it was Michael Carter lying on the floor in a pool of blood—a bullet between his eyes.

Madison knew it wasn't standard or even necessarily professional, but she threw her arms around Troy. "Thank God, you're okay."

"Yeah, well, you and I need to talk about your lack of listening."

She touched his cheek. "Just happy we're both around to talk."

He leaned down, putting his forehead to hers, and for a moment, she forgot she was at a crime scene.

Fifty-Two

Madison had one thing to see through before the wedding, even if it meant Cynthia might kill her. She still had a few hours before the wedding.

Michael Carter had been taken off in a body bag, but Rauch was taken to the hospital and slated for surgery. Madison's bullet had hit her in chest. Doctors thought she'd live, but Madison would make sure Rauch spent those remaining years behind bars.

With Terry at her back, Madison stood next to a groggy and heavily-medicated Rauch.

"You shouldn't have killed him," Rauch said.

"Do you really think you're in any position to threaten me?" Madison tossed back. "Michael Carter was a murderer, and you were hiding him from the police. I'd like to know why." She glanced at Terry, who stood at the end of the bed. She'd stretched the truth, because the final word wasn't in yet. There was still the matter of getting the unregistered .357 S&W tested—the

one with which Carter had been armed—along
with Rauch's unregistered Glock. Carter's prints
were being compared to the third set pulled
from Lynch's vehicle—the ones connected to
the Boyd murders. His DNA would also be run
through the system, but that would take much
longer than the prints.

"I think you should have just minded your
own business," Rauch spat out, her eyes briefly
rolling back into her head. "You and Lorene."

The way Rauch had hissed out that statement,
the glint in her gaze, her reaction to Madison's
telling her she was under arrest for harboring a
murderer sprang to Madison's mind. Rauch had
laughed, heartily, after just being shot. Madison
went cold and backed up from Rauch even
though the woman was cuffed to the bed.

Rauch sneered.

Madison recalled their visit to Rauch when
they'd asked her about Michael. Rauch had
asked, *You don't think that Lorene's looking into
her birth parents somehow resulted in her death?*

"You knew all about Lorene investigating her
parents' murders," Madison accused.

"Wouldn't you like to know?"

Madison moved in close and applied pressure
to Rauch's wound.

Rauch cried out in pain.

A nurse peeked her head in, and Terry told
her everything was fine.

Rauch grimaced and gritted her teeth. "They

got what was coming to them."

"Are you confessing to killing Mrs. Malone and Saul Lynch?"

Terry's phone dinged a notification, drawing Rauch's and Madison's gazes.

He consulted the message and said, "Detective Knight, can I see you in the hall?"

Her partner looked and sounded like he'd just been struck by a truck.

In the hallway, he held up his phone. "Mark just texted on behalf of himself and Sam. Everything's been rushed and quickly reexamined—"

"Terry, I know we'd asked him to—"

"The shoeprints lifted from the Malone crime scene? They matched the shoes Carter was wearing when they brought his body into the morgue. It's conceivable that he was present at the murders of Lorene and Lynch—the familial DNA match to Lorene and all."

"I saw that he did have an injury on his hand."

"I saw that, too, but we know there's no way DNA results will be back today. But that third print on Lynch's steering wheel tied back to—"

Madison could see the answer in his eyes. "Rauch," she concluded.

Terry nodded. "They were also on the .357 S&W found in the trunk of Lynch's car."

"The gun that wasn't a conclusive match to the bullet fragments taken from Lorene and Lynch."

"Yup, that one. Well, there's more." Terry's face took on shadows. "Those prints also match the ones left on the Boyds' eyelids."

"She killed them, too?"

"At the very least, she was present. Now Sam super rushed the ballistics testing on the .357 S&W that Carter was armed with today. That gun was a match to the bullets extracted from the Boyds."

"So it's likely either Rauch or Carter pulled the trigger," she concluded.

"It would seem. Now, Stephanie from Lynch's PI firm also got back with the translation of his notes. Lorene had hired Lynch to find her brother, not her parents."

"But Lynch had uncovered the parents' murder and— Wait a minute. The cook told us that Lorene and Lynch were happy on Monday night, like they were expecting someone they were looking forward to seeing. Was it to be a reunion?"

"Yep. Lynch had arranged for Carter to meet him and Lorene at the Malones' on Monday night at eight thirty." Terry tucked his phone away. "There's more, though. Lynch's notes indicate that he felt Rauch might be dangerous."

"Did he pass that message along to Lorene?"

"No way of knowing for sure."

"So, what are we looking at here? Michael killed the Boyds for giving him up as a boy— though we can place Rauch there, too—and

Rauch killed Lorene and Lynch because they could have exposed the man she loved for murdering the Boyds, and we assume we can place Michael at the Malones' house."

"Or he killed all four victims, and she was along for the ride."

Madison shook her head. "Not the way she reacts so smugly to my saying she's harboring a murderer. I wouldn't doubt she pulled the trigger for at least one of them."

"That's so *not* how I saw this all going down. Guess our bets even us out."

"Guess they do." She'd lost the bet about Steven Malone's guilt/innocence, and Terry had lost the bet where he saw Adach as the killer.

"Now, I also found out why Lynch's prints weren't in the system," Terry began. "The simple answer is he was a fraud."

"But that framed—"

"A fake. I finally got a hold of the state and their certificates have gold *foil*. Lynch's was just printed gold."

"Huh. Guess his reason for doing all that has gone to the grave with him."

"Best as I can tell."

Madison took a step toward Rauch's room, then circled back. "That's all?"

"Yes, Christmas is over."

"No, it's just beginning." She looked forward to telling Rauch they had her, not just for the attempted murder of a police officer, but for her role in four murders. If she pushed hard enough, maybe she'd get a confession.

Madison took the deepest breath she had in days when she reentered Rauch's room. Not only had they solved the murder of two people, they'd cleared a cold case. That always made for a good day.

Fifty-Three

Madison pulled into the church parking lot, and the dash clock read four twenty. She'd made it with ten minutes to spare. Troy had gone on ahead of her, and Terry was probably going to be running in after the ceremony started.

Cynthia had been blowing up her phone, and each time Madison responded, she did her best to reassure her that she'd make it on time.

A vehicle's door shut, and Madison looked over her shoulder.

"Tammy?" Madison went over to Cynthia's sister. She was holding her bouquet, something that had been picked up weeks ago—a win in the superficial flower column. Tammy was wearing her bridesmaid's dress with a waist-length coat over top of it. "I didn't think you were—"

"I didn't think I was, either." Tammy bit her bottom lip. "But she is my sister, and I would regret letting her down like this."

"I'm happy you came," Madison said,

meaning it and hoping that Cynthia would feel the same way.

Madison looked back over the parking lot once more before going through the church's doors and saw Leland King leaning against the hood of a sedan. He signaled her over.

"I'll be in in a minute," Madison told Tammy and headed to Leland. "I don't have time to talk right—"

"I have proof of Phelps's corruption," Leland rushed out. He handed her an envelope. "Don't open it now, but I have pictures in there that I took at Club Sophisticated. It's a—"

"A bar," she cut in, feeling peaked. It had been where the Russian hit man who'd come after her had met with another Mafia contact. Her suspicions had been right: the Russian Mafia hadn't left Stiles. "Let's just say I know of it," she added.

Leland went on. "When you look at the pictures, you'll notice there's another familiar face from the Stiles PD family. A Garrett Murphy," he said lowly.

Shit! Just as she'd suspected, he was corrupt, but sometimes being right wasn't a good thing.

Leland pursed his lips and his face took on hard lines. "This is where we must part ways."

"I don't under—"

"Someone found out about what I've been doing. I don't know how, I don't know who, but if I don't stop looking into you-know-who..." Leland toed his shoe into some snow. "I received a threat."

"It's just me telling you to watch your back..." Shivers snaked through her body at the memory of Blake's threat that he'd tried to package as a precaution by saying he was basically warning her *"as a friend."* But Leland was a hardened investigative reporter, he didn't just back down from a story. "What was it?"

"I got this." Leland reached into his coat's interior pocket and pulled out a piece of paper and extended it to her.

She folded the envelope and put it inside her coat pocket, then she tucked her bouquet under an arm and unfolded what Leland had given her. Her heart took pause at each word she read.

> *I see everything you're doing, and I see you. Stop or I'll make you stop.*

"They sent that with a picture of my mother, Madison."

Leland wasn't married, and he didn't have kids. His softest target would be his mother.

"She's in a home, she's vulnerable. I can't be there all the time. I'm sorry, but I've got to cut out here. No story's worth her life." He took her hand with the note and put his burner phone on top of the paper.

She met his eyes, held the contact for a few seconds, and then nodded.

"Madison!" Tammy called out.

Madison glanced back at the church, and

by the time she turned back to Leland, he was behind the wheel of his car and driving away. She watched after him for a few seconds, then stuffed the threat into her coat pockets.

She was sick to her stomach. It was her fault his mother had been threatened. If she hadn't roped him into investigating Phelps—

"Hey, Detective," Phelps said, getting out of a car, "shouldn't you be inside already?"

She willed herself to move toward the church, but her legs wanted to carry her to him and beat the living shit out of him. You didn't fight the devil with evil, though; you fought him with love and kindness. It would be those qualities that would see good triumph. She had to believe that, just as she respected her badge and all it stood for.

"You're right about that." She turned heel and entered the church. Once inside, her legs froze. Joel Phelps, Dustin's brother, the one they'd met at Craig's gun range, was a freelance writer. Did he contribute to the *Stiles Times*, and had he been the one to uncover what Leland had been working on? He'd mentioned sticking around for an interview he wanted to conduct in person. Did he actually have an interview, and if he did, was it at all connected to the mob?

"Madison!" Cynthia pulled back from an embrace she'd been in with Tammy and hurried toward Madison, her train floating behind her. "Where have you— You know what? Never mind." Cynthia looked all around. "Someone take her coat."

An attendant came over, and Madison gave him her coat.

Toby Sovereign, Garrett Murphy, and Cynthia's dad were positioned at the other end of the entry.

"Cutting it a little close, aren't you, Knight?" Toby jested.

"Don't stir things up, Sovereign," Cynthia barked, but it was no teeth. She touched Madison's face and then squeezed her hand. "Thank you for getting Tammy here."

Madison's eyes burned with tears that wanted to fall, but she blinked them back—even though, after what she'd just learned outside, she had even more to cry about.

"Oh, you chipped a nail." Cynthia pointed to Madison's hand that held the bouquet.

Madison looked down, and sure enough, polish was missing from the tip of her left index finger. Her trigger finger. Madison smiled at Cynthia, seeking mercy.

Cynthia laughed. "Just hide it in the pictures and tell me you caught the bad guy."

Madison swayed to calm her nerves and cleared her throat. "*We* caught the bad guys."

"More than one?"

Madison expected that what she'd said would be enough to satisfy Cynthia's curiosity, but she wanted to hear the whole story.

Guess it's her day.

Madison went on to lay everything out for her as quickly as possible, going through the shootout with Rauch to the forensic findings to her confession to the murders of Lorene and Lynch. She'd killed them, and Carter had killed the Boyds, his biological parents, but she'd been present.

"Rauch said Lorene deserved to die, even if her little investigation wasn't going to send Michael to jail. She'd found out about the cancer Lorene was hiding from her family and the child abuse she helped cover up."

"Tell me Steven Malone's going away for that," Cynthia said.

"He's been brought in, and he'll be charged," Madison assured her and carried on.

"So…Rauch and Michael Carter?"

"Having an affair, going on twenty-two years," Madison ran with a guess as to what Cynthia was getting at.

"Whoa." Cynthia let out a whistle.

"Yeah, Rauch was an excellent liar. Her husband had no idea, but now that he does, he told her to expect to hear from a divorce lawyer."

"She deserves that. I can't even feel sorry for her."

"Me neither."

"So, I'm guessing Lorene Malone and Saul Lynch weren't having an affair?"

"No."

"Why were they naked?"

"I asked Rauch a similar question and she said it had to do with humiliating her boss and the man who quote 'could ruin everything.'"

"Huh. Some people."

"You can say that again, but enough about work. Let's get you married." Madison touched a point on Cynthia's tiara. "You're absolutely stunning, by the way."

A tear dripped down Cynthia's cheek.

"So, are we doing this or what?" Toby said.

"Yes, we are!" Cynthia palmed the tear and motioned for her father to join her.

Everyone got into their positions as an usher ran off to signal the music to start.

Madison looped her arm through Toby's. He straightened his posture and said, without looking at her, "You're beautiful."

"Thanks."

"Hard to believe that another lifetime ago this could have been us taking this step."

He looked at her now. There was a softness to his eyes and a demeanor that he'd demonstrated to her over a couple years ago when he'd made a play to get her back—but life was meant to be lived forward, not backward. If anyone had learned that tragic lesson, it had been Lorene Malone.

"Another lifetime ago," Madison reiterated.

Toby nodded slowly. He didn't say it, but Madison sensed he was thinking that he'd messed up with her—and he had. But things have a way of working out even better than we can imagine. After all, she had Troy now. A man who loved her, who was faithful, who was *family*.

"Well, let's do this," she said as she and Toby led the way through the doors and down the aisle.

Fifty-Four

Madison dropped in her chair at the head table. She'd never had to smile so much for the camera in her entire life as she had so far today. Her feet were killing her, and if she ever found the man who invented heels, she'd give him a firm talking to. Though better punishment would be to force him to wear heels twenty-four/seven.

The catering staff was cleaning up the last of the dinner dishes, and soft music played. The happy couple would have their first dance soon, followed by the wedding party, followed by an outright party, but she wasn't feeling entirely celebratory. She'd managed to slip away briefly and looked at the photos Leland had given her in the privacy of a restroom stall. They depicted just what Leland had said they did and, by extension, confirmed that she wasn't being paranoid: the Mafia was still operating in Stiles.

Troy walked into the reception hall, and her breath hitched. He was too handsome to believe, and he was hers. What had she done to deserve him? She stood and helped close the distance between them.

He took her hand and spun her. "Look at you." He whistled. "Gorgeous."

Her impulse was to fight the compliment, but it felt good to hear. He'd never seen her like this before, and he'd never see her this decked up again unless… Her heart thumped.

He put his arms around her waist and pulled her to him.

"I could say the same about you," she said. "You're very handsome all buttoned up in a tux."

"Oh, yeah?" He brought his nose to hers.

"Yeah."

"Yeah," he parroted and took her mouth. He left her breathless and flashed one of those rare smiles as if he were the devil who'd gotten his way. "You know, you and me, we're a good fit."

"I think so." Her heart beat off rhythm.

"One day, this will be us."

Her stomach turned to lead. Her chest felt heavy. She suddenly felt very, very hot. Her head was spinning. Sure, she'd thought about taking things to the next level with him for a while now, but being faced with the fact that he was thinking along the same lines…shit was getting real. "I should sit down," she said.

Troy chuckled. "Didn't you just eat a five-course meal?"

"Uh-huh." She spun, feeling lost. She could

see the head table, but her legs weren't moving.

"I'm not letting you get away from me, Knight." Troy wrapped his arms around her from behind, nuzzling his face against an ear.

She pinched her eyes shut. She needed oxygen or she would faint.

"Did you hear me?" Troy asked.

"I…I need to go to the washroom." She shuffled across the room as fast as she could.

Inside the restroom, she put her back to the wall and gasped for air.

One of the stall doors opened, and Cynthia emerged.

"You okay?" Cynthia went to the sinks.

"Fine."

Cynthia lathered her hands, rinsed, and dried them on paper towel. "If I could eliminate that word from your vocabulary, what would you say?"

"Terrified."

"Intrigued." Cynthia sidled up to Madison.

Madison felt dizzy.

"Are you really not going to talk to me? You do realize today's my day, and I—"

"I think Troy might be proposing to me."

"What?" Shock gave way to a grin. "How romantic! One, it's Valentine's Day, and two, at a wedding."

With everything that had transpired this week, Madison had forgotten all about it being Valentine's Day.

"Yeah, it will be all roses until he wakes up and regrets his decision, blaming it on some rash emotional moment."

Cynthia laughed. "We both know Troy doesn't act rashly. You're the rash one in your relationship."

Madison exhaled. "What should I do?"

"What do you think you should do? You love him?"

"Not a quest—"

Cynthia grabbed her by the arm and yanked her from the washroom.

"What are you doing?" Madison tried not to panic but was losing the fight. Cynthia was guiding her through the hall toward a small stage where Lou was standing next to the emcee.

"And there's the bride," the emcee said in a dramatic voice. They must have been waiting on Cynthia for the first dance.

Cynthia turned and directed Madison, "Stay put."

"Tell me why," Madison begged.

"Let's leave it to fate, shall we?" Cynthia gave her a smile that made Madison's stomach clench and went up on the small stage. Cynthia said something to Lou, then the emcee.

"At the bride's request, there's been a change in the order of tonight's proceedings," the emcee announced. "We were going to do the first dance, but—"

Oh, no. Madison suspected what was coming.

That's if the sick, swirling feeling in the pit of her stomach wasn't leading her astray.

The emcee continued. "All you single ladies, come out to the floor. The bride's doing the bouquet toss now."

I'm going to kill *her!*

"No, no, no." Madison was shaking her head.

Cynthia leaned over the stage. "My day, my say. You play, Madison Knight. Let fate decide."

"You know I don't believe in fate." The child inside of Madison was stomping her feet.

"And you know I do. Remember, this is my day." Cynthia was wielding the power of a guilt trip quite effectively.

Women started crowding the dance floor.

"Fine," Madison spat.

"Ready, ladies?" Cynthia called out over the microphone, her gaze meeting Madison's, then darting to a direction on the floor. She was trying to tell Madison where to stand.

To heck with that!

Cynthia turned, and Madison was on the move, weaving to the back of the room. Along the way, something was coming right at her head, and before she could think, she reached out. As she did, she caught eyes with Troy, who was standing on the sidelines. He was smiling and pointing at her hands.

She looked down. She was holding the damn bouquet.

Acknowledgments

Writing may be a solitary endeavor, but publishing is not. My husband has always been my greatest ally, supporter, cheerleader, and business partner. His presence in my life means everything to me, whether it's an encouraging hug, a Starbucks latte delivered to my desk when I'm neck-deep in words, or the kickass covers he designs for my books. Thank you, George Arnold, for everything, for shining your light and being you!

I'd also like to thank Detective Edward Adach of Toronto Police Service for his selflessness and patience in answering my innumerable questions about forensics! Not only that, but he took time out of his weekend and gave me and five others a tour and hands-on experience in the lab. His enthusiasm is contagious! Thank you for your service, too, Ed. You help put the bad guys behind bars.

Also, my amazing editing team has outdone themselves again and helped me take a diamond in the rough and polish it for publication. Thank you!

Congratulations to those who won character namings: Marie Rauch, Patricia (Patty) Beaulieu, and Sabrina Darbonne. I hope you had fun seeing your names in print and the characters you "became" in fiction.

Catch the next book in the Detective Madison Knight Series!

Sign up at the weblink listed below
to be notified when new Madison Knight titles
are available for pre-order:

CarolynArnold.net/MKUpdates

By joining this newsletter, you will also receive
exclusive first looks at the following:

Updates pertaining to upcoming releases in the
series, such as cover reveals, book descriptions,
and firm release dates

Sneak peeks of teasers and special content

Behind-the-Tape™ insights that give you an
inside look at Carolyn's research and creative
process

Read on for an exciting preview of
Carolyn Arnold's FBI thriller
featuring Brandon Fisher

ON THE COUNT
OF THREE

Prologue

Three years ago
Miami-Dade County

*O*p-Ed columnist Pamela Moore passed away today after a violent home invasion left her for dead. Pamela was..."

The reporter droned on, sensationalizing Pamela's redeemable qualities while shoving all her faults, misgivings, and mistakes into a closet of obscurity. But it was a fine representation of Pamela's real life: she had spun perspectives to make a headline. More than that, she had been so obtuse that she had painted his family as *idyllic*.

She knew nothing!

His heart was thumping in his ears, his mind replaying the reporter's words: *left her for dead.*

As if he'd done that on purpose.

He clenched his fists and focused on his breathing, on slowing his heart rate. Sometimes he wondered why he put himself through watching the video over and over. The incident had taken place just over three years ago.

Still, he settled into his chair to journey back in time. To listen to what the newspeople had said about his victim, her masked assailant, and what had looked like a home invasion gone horribly wrong. It reminded him of what he'd done right and where he'd failed.

Pamela's fiancé came on the screen. He was the picture of calm put-togetherness in his pressed suit, standing in front of the camera with a microphone to his lips. He, too, was singing her praises and calling for justice.

But poor Pamela. There would be no justice for her. Her case was as cold now as her body in the ground.

He focused on the TV again and listened.

"Sadly, police have no suspects at this time but say the man who did this is considered to be especially dangerous. They don't believe that robbery was the motive, and they warn women to remain vigilant."

Her confirmed death and the reporter calling him *especially dangerous* were takeaways he rather enjoyed. He leaned forward, a smile playing on his lips as he stopped the recording and rewound the VHS tape. He was determined to dwell on the good that came with the botched murder of Pamela. He'd learned from his mistakes and his second murder had gone much better. While they say practice makes perfect, he didn't greedily indulge. No, he only took out those he deemed worthy of his attention. It was enough to quiet the darkness inside him. But there were times that the burning need to take a life was all-consuming. He called that side of him the Night.

It was an authentic part of himself, having lingered in the background for some time, calling out to him, taunting him to listen to its petitions. And now, as a man of thirty-seven, he was no longer afraid or leery of this facet of himself. He entertained the blood-filled fantasies of the Night when it was prudent, and no more would he be robbed of the fulfillment that came with taking someone's last breath. His preferred killing method assured that now.

The VCR whined down to a *thunk*. He got up from his recliner and ejected the tape. He returned it to its cardboard sleeve and put it back under a floorboard near the TV set. It was safe there.

He laced up his boots and headed out to the shed—where he was holding his latest victim. The Night purred within him, yearning to be satisfied. His heartbeat pulsed beneath his skin, anticipating what was to come.

He reached the shed and entered. The woman was naked and fixed into a guillotine that he'd crafted with his own hands. The woodworking skills his dad had taught him turned out to be useful after all. The blade was suspended and ready to be called into action. There'd be no escape for her; any movement would upset the delicate balance of the apparatus. Ah, yes, he'd finally concocted the perfect murder weapon, one his victims couldn't come back from.

He creeped closer to her, the floorboards creaking under his steps.

Her long, straight hair cascaded from the crown of her head around her face. She cried out in dry, heaving sobs, "Please…no." As if she knew what was coming.

He ignored her pathetic protest, went over to his tripod, clipped his cell phone into place, and started recording.

"Smile for the camera." He swiped her hair back, and she arched her head up the small amount the restraint around her neck would allow.

Terror streaked through her eyes. "Please… don't…do…this." Her mouth gaped open and shut, open and shut.

"You know why you're here," he said.

She wept, but it came out weak and pitiful, lacking conviction—merely gasps for breaths and hiccups in her throat. "I… Please forgive me."

He smiled. She was right on schedule: three days out here and she'd lost her fight to live, hope extinguished and her survival instinct gone. This was when they became boring to him. He much preferred when they clung to hope without reason.

And now, there she was, requesting absolution. But he was neither a priest nor a redeemer.

"We'll start on the count of three," he said in a singsong voice. The Night pulsed beneath his skin with a heartbeat of its own.

"No, no, please!" the woman screamed.

It pierced his ears, but he smiled, moving into position next to her. "One…" He reached out for the chain that suspended the blade. "Th—" His phone rang. His body quaked, the tremors of the Night snaking through him.

He grabbed a roll of duct tape from a nearby utility shelf and slapped a piece across her mouth. He normally didn't have to worry about their screams out there, but he wanted to answer this call. The ringtone told him it was his girlfriend, Roxanne. She fit into his life plan—at least for now—and he didn't want to mess things up with her.

He kept his eyes on the woman as he answered his phone. "Hey, sweetie."

He listened as his girlfriend prattled on about their plans for the following evening—dinner, then a movie. Nothing new there. She said maybe dancing afterward, but they'd never make it to a club. She'd be ready for bed by ten, and he'd tuck her in. She was as predictable as drying paint and about as exciting. But she played along with his sexual fantasies without contention, and she'd do anything to make him happy.

"You'll pick me up? My place at six o'clock?" she asked.

"I can do that. I'm looking forward to spending some time with you."

"Love you," Roxanne told him.

"Love you, too." He hung up, smiling, and let the expression carry for his victim to see. He set up his cell phone to record again and walked toward the woman. "Let's pick up where we left off, shall we?"

She was screaming behind the tape and bucking her head wildly. She was clearly trying to slide back, as if she could worm her way out of the guillotine.

Yes, fight. It makes it so much more fun...

"One," he roared above her. "Two..." He wound the chain around his fingers. With a flick of his wrist, he released it. "Three."

He smiled at the camera as the woman's head fell to the floor and rolled. It settled faceup, her eyes looking right at him. He'd heard that the mind went on living for minutes after decapitation.

He got down next to her head, swept some hair out of her face. He then put his hands over her eyes and lowered her lids. "Sleep well."

One

I sure as hell hoped there was no truth to the idea that the way a day started set the tone for everything that followed. Or I was screwed. My day had started at five o'clock—before the alarm—with me waking up to my girlfriend Becky's arm lying across my chest and my leg dangling off the edge of the bed. My phone was buzzing and dancing across my nightstand, its lights flashing like some sort of crazed disco ball. It was like trying to rouse the dead to get Becky to move, but eventually she groaned and rolled over.

My boss, Supervisory Special Agent Jack Harper, didn't even say hello, just got straight to business. "We've got an urgent case. Wheels up in twenty."

I barely grunted, but he must have taken that as agreement because he said, "Good. See you there."

I sighed and tried telling my still-asleep appendages that it was time to move. Easier said than done. I staggered out of bed, tripped on the corner of the comforter that had spilled mostly onto the floor, and narrowly avoided slamming my nose against the doorframe. Making it to the hallway unscathed had been cause for celebration, not that I had the time to revel in the accomplishment.

I was in and out of the shower in less than two minutes. Even though I ran a comb through my hair, it was as unruly as my attitude this morning. The red tufts didn't want to lie down in the back. Becky came into the bathroom and sat on the toilet while I brushed my teeth.

"Mor...ning," she said, the word fragmented by a yawn.

I continued brushing, my gums taking the brunt of my frustration. Since we had become exclusive about two months ago, I'd pretty much kissed my privacy goodbye. We didn't live together, but she was taking over my house. Her toothbrush was even in the holder.

"Where are you off to this time?" she asked.

Becky knew all about my job as a special agent with the Behavioral Analysis Unit, and as a police officer in a nearby county herself, she respected that a job in law enforcement didn't always have set hours. And with mine in particular, I could receive a call to move at any given moment. Sadly, serial killers—the type of criminal we primarily hunted—didn't adjust their schedules for our convenience.

"Did you hear me, Brandon?"

I peeled my eyes from her toothbrush and set mine in the slot next to hers. The layers of sleepy fog were finally clearing, and I realized just how brief Jack's call had been. "He didn't actually say…"

"Text me once you land? Let me know you got there—wherever *there* is—safely." Becky wiped and flushed. She inched up next to me, and I stepped back for her to wash her hands.

"Sure, but I've gotta go." I spun for the door, and she grabbed me, pulled me back, threw her arms around my neck, and kissed me.

I let myself sink into the moment for a second or two but then untangled myself from her arms. "I really have to go."

And I ran from my house—straight out into the dark morning, the pouring rain, and a puddle a few inches deep.

My socks were still soaking wet as I stood under the hangar looking out at the government jet on the tarmac. Its door was open. That was the good news. The bad news was that I was late, and Jack had very little tolerance for tardiness.

Fat drops of water bounced off the pavement a good four to six inches and pounded the metal roof overhead as if we were under fire. Given the whole "April showers bring May flowers" adage, the city should be blooming beautifully by next month. Not that that helped me right now.

It was a good fifty yards to the plane, and looking up at the black sky, I didn't see a break coming soon. But the longer I took, the later I'd be, and the more furious Jack would become.

I took a deep breath. *Here goes nothing...*

I put my go bag over my head and ran out from the hangar. Pellets of rain hit my skin like shards of ice, but I kept pushing forward, comforted by thoughts of the dark roast coffee they'd have on the plane. I ran up the stairs and boarded the plane, mentally savoring the robust flavor while bracing for a verbal lashing.

Jack was standing next to the coffee maker, which was near the doorway, and my colleague—and ex—Paige Dawson was seated at one of the tables, sipping from a cup.

Paige was just another example of the universe's warped sense of humor. Of all the beds I could have fallen into, it had to be hers. And then I found myself on her team with the BAU a couple of years later. Nothing like being in a pressurized cabin with an ex-lover. At least we were amicable—for the most part. We'd be far more than that, truth be told, but the Bureau wasn't a fan of mixing business with pleasure, and Jack would have no problem enforcing the policy. He wasn't a fan of emotions in the first place, and his people needed to walk a fine line between intuition and emotionally charged observations.

I understood where the man was coming from, though I constantly struggled to meet his standards. He'd served in the military before the BAU, and then a divorce saw his ex getting custody of their son. His tough-guy persona wasn't for show; it was him. And his salt-and-pepper hair distinguished him as a man of the world.

"You're late." Jack looked right through me.

"There was traffic and—"

"*Both of you* are late." Jack's gaze went past me, and I turned to see Zach Miles, the fourth member of our team.

I beat *him* here? Maybe this day had a silver lining after all.

"I'm sorry, Jack." Zach brushed past me, and I took that as my cue to get that first cup of coffee.

I dropped my bag on the floor and rummaged in the drawer for a pod of dark roast. There was only light. I picked one anyhow.

So much for my day looking up.

I held the pod, staring at it, as if by doing so, it would change the flavor. But there would be no point in complaining. As the machine gurgled to life and sputtered out the brew, I expected to hear Jack's voice over it all, laying into me and Zach for being late. But no one was speaking. If it had just been me who was late, I'd still be getting an earful from Jack and being teased by Zach. I know that for a fact because I'd been in that situation more than once.

I grabbed my coffee and joined the rest of the team at a table. Jack gestured a go-ahead to one of the crewmembers, and they closed the cabin door.

Jack tossed three folders onto the table, one in front of each of us, and held on to a fourth for himself. "We've been called by Miami PD to look into the case of a missing woman."

My mind froze on *Miami*. I grew up in Sarasota, about 230 miles from Miami, but I considered the whole of Florida my old stomping ground.

"Miami?" It felt like my collar was tightening around my neck.

Jack narrowed his gaze on me. "Yes. Is there a problem?"

"No." *Only that if my parents find out how close I am to them, they'll want a visit.*

It wasn't that I had a bad relationship with them, but my pops and I never quite saw eye to eye. No matter what I accomplished in my life, he wasn't impressed.

The plane started moving, and I looked out the window beside me to the hangar, longing to return there. I'd at least still be in Virginia, a suitable distance from Pops, a long way from Florida, and—

"Wait, you said Miami?" I asked, an idea sparking in my mind.

Jack pursed his lips. "I think that's clear by now."

"There's an FBI field office right there," I said, sitting up and stretching out my neck. "Why aren't they—"

"We've been specifically asked for," Jack cut in. "Now is there anything else or can I continue?"

"There's nothing else," I said, apologetic and remorseful, not sure why I was provoking the man.

"There's reason to believe that a serial killer has abducted the woman." Jack tilted his head to the case files in front of us as the plane rocked violently, speeding down the runway. "Look it over and we'll discuss. We've got a meeting with the locals when we land."

I opened the file and immediately wished I hadn't. The pictures on top were of two decapitated heads. Today was about to get a whole lot worse.

Two

Zach lingered over the case file, stretching out the time it would normally take him and defying his genius IQ and speed-reading abilities. Today his emotions, rather than his brain, were taking the lead. His mind was on his fiancée, Sheri, and a vow he'd made regarding his future family, the one he'd almost lost hope of realizing. He'd told himself that if the day ever came that he had a wife and children, he'd leave the BAU. Now the promise—spoken many years ago and only to himself—sank in his chest like a heavy weight, sucking air from his lungs, haunting him. He had a feeling the day of reckoning was finally here.

But these people—Jack, Paige, and Brandon— were also family. It hurt to think of leaving them. Brandon's lips were moving slightly as he read. Paige was leaned back in her seat, her legs up, knees to chest as she studied the file. Jack was looking back at him.

"Did you want to give everyone an overview?"

he asked.

Paige and Brandon set their files on the table. Paige put her legs down.

"The missing woman is Jenna Kelter, niece of Miami's mayor, Walter Conklin," Zach began, willing his mind to focus on the case. "Apparently, he's Kelter's only living blood relative, but she was reported missing at two o'clock this morning by her husband, Gordon Kelter. It's believed that her disappearance is connected with two prior murder cases given the similarities in victimology."

"They must be quite apparent to jump on this so quickly," Brandon said and looked at Jack.

Jack nodded his head toward Zach.

Zach went on. "Now Jenna Kelter was charged with DUI vehicular homicide four years ago. The other two murder victims— Kent West and Marie Sullivan—shared the same charge. Eighteen years ago, West drove off the road and into a building, killing three of his college friends who were in the car with him. Within that year he was charged for three counts and sentenced to twelve years, which he served. Sullivan's accident was seven years ago. She killed a husband and father and served four years."

"And Kelter?" Paige asked.

Zach heard her question, but his mind drifted to Sheri again and the surprise she'd had for him the night he'd proposed. It was a secret he'd been keeping from his colleagues these last couple of months, a secret that would change his and Sheri's lives.

"Zach?" Paige pressed and glanced at the others.

"Uh, yeah." He snapped out of it and refocused. "Her accident was five years ago, took about a year to go to trial. She was given and served four years in prison. She was just released this past Thursday. West and Sullivan were abducted three days after release from prison, and their heads showed up three days later." He listened to himself recap the case so robotically, so matter-of-factly. Since when did macabre crimes become so mundane, spoken about as if reciting something of no importance? These were people's lives he was talking about, and yet, he'd become calloused to that fact over the years. What would another eight years with the BAU do to him? Do to his future family?

Brandon cleared his throat, and Zach turned to him. "You said they were abducted three days after release? Kelter was reported missing on Monday morning, but her husband last saw her on Sunday," Brandon said, pulling from the file. "Exactly three days after her release."

"That's right," Zach confirmed.

"Is there any indication where West, Sullivan, and now possibly Kelter were abducted?" Paige asked.

"Unfortunately, not," Zach started. "I would

say that it seems our unsub may have an interest in the number three. It's present in the timing of the abductions, when the heads are found, and the occurrence of the murders. West was killed six years ago, Sullivan three years ago, and now, there's Kelter."

"I agree," Jack said.

Zach swallowed roughly, knowing already that this unidentified subject would be one for the books. The case would likely only get darker from here, and far uglier. It was the ugly that Zach had become stained with while working for the BAU, and he feared it might never wash off. But he'd have to learn to bury it if he was going to make a fresh start.

"It's believed the decapitations were the cause of death," Zach continued, "and the rest of the victims' bodies were never found. The medical examiners working the West and Sullivan cases both described the cuts to their necks as being smooth and clean. Neither wagered a hypothesis on what was used to sever the heads." He found himself falling into a rhythm. "Their heads showed very few signs of decomp, but there was some insect activity. The presence of blowfly eggs indicated that West's head was decapitated within twenty-four hours of discovery. Same for Sullivan. But neither's time of death could be pinpointed further than that."

"That's discouraging," Paige lamented.

"That's what we're dealing with," Zach said,

sounding cooler than he'd intended. He was still battling with the reality of his personal life. It had all happened so quickly; he'd gone from being single, to engaged, to an expectant father. He'd known for a couple months, but it still struck him as surreal most of the time.

But he was at work now. He had to get a grip and focus on this case. Kelter's life depended on it. He took the photos of West's and Sullivan's heads from the file. "As you can see from the pictures, both were wrapped in plastic bags, surrounded by tissue paper, and placed in boxes."

Paige pointed out a paragraph from one of the case documents. "West's head was left on the steps of Miami-Dade County Courthouse?" Her gaze met Zach's. "Rather brazen."

"Well, if you keep reading, you'll see that video captured the box being dropped off at three thirty in the morning. It wasn't discovered until start of business by a young defense attorney named Brianna King."

"We've got this picture." Jack held up a black-and-white photo of a person in a hoodie, but the quality made it hard to make out if it was a man or a woman. "It was taken from the video that Zach just mentioned."

"But obviously it hasn't gotten the locals anywhere," Brandon said.

"Obviously," Jack said drily, and Brandon's cheeks flushed red.

Brandon jutted out his chin. "And the other head was dropped off…" He consulted the file, seeming eager to discover the answer himself.

What he was looking for was buried much deeper than where he was looking. "Sullivan's head was delivered to her attorney's office— Hanover & Smith, LLP," Zach said. "It was signed for by the woman at the front desk."

"Brazen again," Brandon said, and he and Paige nodded to each other. "No lead there, either, I take it."

Jack shook his head. "No video either. Now, Sullivan's head was delivered by Miami Messenger, a local delivery service, but Miami PD found nothing there. The law office often used the service, but they didn't have any record of a delivery scheduled for the time and date in question. The delivery people were interviewed at length; their backgrounds checked out, and they were cleared. All we have is the description of a nice-looking man with brown hair."

Brandon drank some of his coffee. "Do we think that the killer is delivering the heads themselves? Then again, it could be someone they are working with or someone they pay to drop them off."

"Far too early to answer that question," Zach started. "But it's possible that our unsub could like to see the reactions to their work firsthand."

Brandon winced. "Very risky."

"Did anything stand out about the delivery

boxes?" Paige asked.

Zach shook his head. "No. They were just standard white boxes with lids. Similar to the kind used in bakeries for cakes. They could have been purchased from any office supply store or postal outlet." He paused a moment. "You also might have noticed from the photographs that the victims' eyes were shut. They were glued—standard adhesive, nothing traceable. Again, no lead there."

"The unsub could've felt remorse or judged with their eyes on him," Paige wagered.

"Or the unsub wanted to be the last thing their victims saw," Brandon offered.

Zach's mind wandered again, his thoughts going to all the death encased within one investigation. Beyond the murders, there was the loss of life caused by the various car accidents. The world of the BAU was drenched in bloodshed. How could he possibly turn off the job as he played with his pure, innocent child? The images, the massacre, would always be there, burned into his brain. But if he was being honest, that was the least of his concerns. One day the job could claim far more than his sanity.

Also available from
International Bestselling Author
Carolyn Arnold

ON THE COUNT OF THREE

Book 7 in the Brandon Fisher FBI series

Drinking and driving may be deadly in more ways than one…

FBI Special Agent Brandon Fisher and his team join forces with Miami PD Detective Kelly Marsh to find a missing woman Kelly believes was taken by a serial killer.

From their first meeting, Brandon sees the detective as competition, and this isn't helped by the personal history she shares with his boss. Brandon sees the similarities between Detective Marsh's missing person case and the two cold cases: all three victims served time for vehicular homicide while driving under the influence and disappeared three days after being released from prison—but is that enough to assume the woman has been abducted by a serial killer? Brandon's not so sure and fears his boss may have let his personal connection to Marsh cloud his judgment. Surely there isn't any other explanation for why they jumped into an investigation less than twenty-four hours after the missing persons report was filed. Then again, maybe Brandon is letting his own differences with the detective affect his perspective. If he can't pull himself together, the missing woman may pay with her life—and one of the team may not make it out of Miami alive.

Available from popular book retailers or at CarolynArnold.net

CAROLYN ARNOLD is an international bestselling and award-winning author, as well as a speaker, teacher, and inspirational mentor. She has four continuing fiction series—Detective Madison Knight, Brandon Fisher FBI, McKinley Mysteries, and Matthew Connor Adventures—and has written nearly thirty books. Her genre diversity offers her readers everything from cozy to hard-boiled mysteries, and thrillers to action adventures.

Both her female detective and FBI profiler series have been praised by those in law enforcement as being accurate and entertaining, leading her to adopt the trademark: POLICE PROCEDURALS RESPECTED BY LAW ENFORCEMENT™.

Carolyn was born in a small town and enjoys spending time outdoors, but she also loves the lights of a big city. Grounded by her roots and lifted by her dreams, her overactive imagination insists that she tell her stories. Her intention is to touch the hearts of millions with her books, to entertain, inspire, and empower.

She currently lives just west of Toronto with her husband and beagle and is a member of Crime Writers of Canada and Sisters in Crime.

CONNECT ONLINE
Carolynarnold.net
Facebook.com/AuthorCarolynArnold
Twitter.com/Carolyn_Arnold

And don't forget to sign up for her newsletter for up-to-date information on release and special offers at
CarolynArnold.net/Newsletters.